THERE WAS A TERRIBLE BEAUTY IN HER, WILD, AND UNTAMABLE. . . .

She stood on the shore, dark seaweed wrapped around her ankles. The wind pressed her skirt against her body, flinging it behind her, fanning her hair like flames, then whipping it against her face.

Naisha touched her arm. Lightning struck and the purple sky caught fire. She spun on him, her amber eyes burning.

"Come up to the rocks! We have to find shelter!"

But Deirdre turned her face back to the wild sea. She was a stranger now. Each time he looked at her, she changed, becoming what she had been in generations past . . . a queen, a witch, an eagle, a child filled with awe and wonder, playing in the foam.

"You can't stay here!" he shouted, but the thunder of the gods rolled over his voice. He tried to grab her up in his arms. Her body was on fire. Her tongue tasted of the sea, as a mermaid's would. Then he was seeking her mouth as fiercely as she sought his. The wind screamed. She defied it as if it were an enemy. He felt a tremor rise in her body and heard the whisper of his name on her lips. . . .

THE
CELTS

Elona Malterre

A DELL BOOK

Published by
Dell Publishing
a division of
The Bantam Doubleday Dell Publishing Group, Inc.
1 Dag Hammarskjold Plaza
New York, New York 10017

Dell ® TM 681510, Dell Publishing Co., Inc.

ISBN: 0-440-20059-8

Printed in the United States of America

March 1988

10 9 8 7 6 5 4 3 2 1

KRI

Special thanks to The Colbert Agency for their tireless work, and to Maggie Lichota, who had faith in this novel.

For Alexandra, who believes in the stories her mother writes, and for Mark, who's creating his own myths and who helps create mine. And in the memory of Chuck Steele, who gave so much of himself to so many.

. . . and yet when all is said
It was the dream itself enchanted me.

William Butler Yeats

And dreamers speak
of the time of the black sun.

And of the swan . . . these dreamers tell
of its flight . . .
and how three feathers . . .
descend like snow . . .
While hunters plunge their fingers in its down
deep as a drift, and drive their hands
up to the neck of the wrist
in that warm metamorphosis of snow

P. K. Page

FOREWORD

In 78 B.C., when Julius Caesar was still a young man, Conor, the cowherd's son, took over the throne of Ulster, the northernmost kingship of Erinn. Caesar never visited Erinn, nevertheless while he conquered Gaul, a Celtic culture prevailed in Erinn, the Island of the Kings.

Julius Caesar writes in his *Commentaries on the Gallic Wars*, The Celtic race "is very much given to superstitions and for this reason those who are afflicted with very severe diseases and those who are engaged in war and danger either sacrifice men as victims or vow that they themselves will be immolated, and they use the Druids as performers of these sacrifices because they think that unless the life of a man be rendered . . . the divine will of the immortal gods could not otherwise be appeased and they have sacrifices of the same kind performed publicly. Others have images of vast size the limbs of which, woven with twigs, they fill with living men which having been set on fire, the men are put to death by the surrounding flame. They think that the sacrifices of those who may be taken in theft or in robbery, or in any culpable act, are more acceptable to the immortal gods, but when a supply of this kind is wanting also they descend to the sacrifice of the innocent." Henry d'Arbois de Jubainville, in his *Irish Mythological Cycle*, writes that the Gaels used to sacrifice children to Cromm Cruach when praying for fair weather and fertility: "It was milk and corn they asked from it in exchange for their children—how great was their horror and their mourning."

The Deirdre story is a well-known legend in Ireland, but not as I tell it. I have read several accounts of the story and these have convinced me that every fiction, if it's successful, tells its own truth.

PART I
The Prophecy

CHAPTER
1

The wooden post at the entrance of King Conor's round-house was called the man-root of Aengus. Aengus was the god of love, and as was fitting for the god of love, his root reached higher than the roof of King Conor's house, and was so big around that even the tallest of Conor's men could not encircle the pillars with their arms.

The sun, midway between the top of the house and the curved top of the man-root, threw a long shadow directly in front of where Lewara and Branwen walked. Both sides of the walkway were lined with King Conor's soldiers holding their spears and swords.

Except for the leggings of cow leather that were bound to their calves and feet with tongs, the soldiers were naked. The soldiers of Conor stood naked in battle so that Bael, god of the sun, could strengthen their bodies, and they stood naked at the first forcing so that both Aengus and Bael would bless their bodies, so that the gods would put strong warrior sons into the bodies of the women.

When they saw Lewara and Branwen, the soldiers began to cheer and shout and lift their spears to Bael and to the Aengus root. Many of the men wore bracelets of gold or crescent-shaped neck plates of gold, and these adornments caught the sun, flashing its brilliance into Branwen's eyes, blinding her momentarily.

Lewara put her hand on Branwen's shoulder and stopped her from advancing any farther toward the king's house. Lewara took Branwen's dress and, with a quick movement of

her wrist, undid the belt, letting the dress fall open in front.
Branwen's heart pounded like a battle drum, and the noise in
her chest and the cheering voices of the men nearly deafened
her. Another movement of Lewara's arm, and Branwen stood
naked before the root of Aengus and King Conor's soldiers. A
roar went up.

"Get down on your knees," the wisewoman told Branwen.
"Then crawl backward along the shadow of the Aengus root
until you get to the foot of the stairs. Don't crawl off the line
of the shadow. The root must bless your cave and womb. At
the stairs stand, walk up to King Conor and get on the forcing
table. He'll do the rest."

Branwen looked at the soldiers, all of them cheering and
waving their spears. She looked at the long shadow of the
Aengus root and up at the stairs where King Conor stood.

He was a tall man with corn-colored hair that curled tightly
and fell to his shoulders. He, too, was naked except for gold
breastplates, bracelets, and leggings. He stroked his beard,
then, with an impatient turn of his hand that seemed to say,
Come on, come on, ordered her down. Lewara's hand on
Branwen's shoulder was gentle but determined.

Branwen wanted to go back the way she had come, to run
away, to return to a moon's change ago, to run where she had
run only a few short nights ago. To run through the grasses
that bit like little spiders at her legs. To run to the river where
the dark stones under the water made it look black. She had
run free as the lambs she tended for her foster parents, and
then the blood had come. Blood red as the yewberry on the
inside of her thigh, and she had been taken to the house of the
wisewoman to be prepared.

Branwen had been put into a wicker cage of hazelwood,
carried to an oak tree, and suspended in her cage from its
branches. Lewara told Branwen that she had to hold her water
all day so her bladder would stretch. A large bladder capacity

THE CELTS

5

was a sign of sexual ability. Holding back the waters strength-
ened the love muscle which was the same muscle that pleasured men. No man wanted a wife who could not pleasure
him. No man wanted a wife whose muscles were slack and
flopping, loose like that of an old cow. The wisewoman told
her it was forbidden for a girl of first bleeding to walk the
earth, for the corn would not grow where she walked, and the
cows and sheep would miscarry if she looked on them.
Cathbad, the Druid, came and entwined her cage with oak
leaves and the "all-healing" mistletoe. Only when the blood
stopped was the cage cut down. Branwen was bathed and
brought to the king. The cage was burned.

Branwen looked behind her, at the walls of the fort of King
Conor, and in front of her, at the long shadow of the Aengus
root, and the naked men lining either side of it. Lewara's hand
prodded.

Branwen got down on her hands and knees, but she put her
knee on a small, sharp stone, and the pain made her cry out.
"Keep your legs far apart when you crawl up, so Aengus can
bless all of you," Lewara said. Lewara said something else, too,
but Branwen couldn't hear anymore, except for the shouting
of the soldiers.

The stones gouged at her knees and at her palms as she
crawled. She couldn't see behind her, and the jagged edges of
stones grew sharper. The shouting of the soldiers grew distant,
the pain in her knees and legs sending it far away, as in a
dream. In her ears her heart sounded like the breaking of the
sea against the shore, and for a moment she was a small girl
running along the sea, the white edges of the foam like lace
between her toes. Her foster mother and father had taken her
there. She couldn't remember the season of the year, only that
there had been fires, great bonfires, and people were hung
above the fires in wicker baskets, and there was great screaming. And afterward the people went to wash the bones in the

sea. Now the roar of the soldiers and the beating of her heart sounded like the sea.

Behind her was the shadow of the Aengus root. On either side of her were the leathery legs of the soldiers; above the leathery cow leggings were the soldiers' own hairy legs, their knees knobby and rough as the bark of the forest trees. As she crawled backward, she noticed the deep scars in the thighs of many of the men, scars from wounds in battle. Some clean, like knife cuts, others jagged. Were they spear thrusts, or tusk wounds from wild boars? And above the thighs was more hair, and the roots of the men, the balls, some of them large as apples, some shriveled, some slightly covered with hair. The flesh was various sizes, some small, gray colored like bald mice, some long, blue, bruised looking like hunks of raw meat.

Branwen's hair was long and fell on either side of her face and dragged in the dust and across the stones as she crawled. As she crawled backward her hand landed on her hair, and when she pulled her head back, her hand held her hair to the stones, pulling at her scalp. She lifted her hand too quickly. Her knee struck another stone and began to bleed. Branwen began to cry.

A fly buzzed around her face and she shook her head at it. Her hair whipped at her shoulders and then fell down, hanging on either side of her face again. Another fly crawled on her leg. She slapped at it. It flew up over her shoulders and haunches. She couldn't hear the shouting of the men anymore, only the buzzing of the fly, a black fly the size of her fingernail. When flies laid eggs on the backs of the cattle, lumps the size of a child's fist swelled under their skins. The lumps grew fat and swollen, eruptions of flesh and skin, and the cowherd would squeeze them out. The fat fly worm would be pushed out amid a stream of pus and blood. Now a fly was hovering around her. She swept at it with her hand, back over her hips. She was afraid of the fly burying itself in her private parts. The men shouted louder. As she crawled past them, she could see some of their roots straighten, like short swords aimed at her. And the fly kept buzzing. And the stones made her knees bleed.

At the steps of the king's house Branwen stood up. She glanced behind her, at the soldiers standing in two straight lines. The men were grinning. She looked at Lewara, who stood unsmiling, rubbing the fingers of one hand with the other.

The men began to chant: "Force her. Force her." Lewara nodded her head, an almost invisible gesture, and kept rubbing one hand with the other. The men raised and lowered their spears in time to their chanting: "Force her. Force her."

Branwen looked up at the king. His root branched out from between his legs. Even from where she stood, she could tell it was huge, almost like the root of a horse. Her legs felt weak, soft, like boiled corn gruel. There were seven steps up the floor where the king stood waiting for her. She was afraid to walk up, and turned again toward Lewara.

The king made a quick motion with his head, and two soldiers came down the steps. Each took her under one arm and half lifted, half pushed her up the stairs. Their hands were coarse like sand, and one pinched the skin under her arm as he took her up the stairs and laid her down on the forcing stone.

The soldiers were suddenly quiet. Only the rough, ragged cry of a raven tore the silence. A fly settled on the blood on her knees. The table was a large, flat stone placed on three squat, vertical stones. A sheepskin covered the table. Conor grabbed her by the waist and pulled her toward him. His fingers felt hard as flint. The sheepskin scratched her back.

Cathbad, the Druid, pulled a piece of dried flesh from a pouch at his belt. The flesh was a chunk of the root of a stallion. The Druid put the dried flesh into the king's mouth. "Make the sinew grow that shrinks against the hollow of the thigh. Make the seed of the king as plentiful as the fishes of the sea." The Druid sprinkled Branwen with oak leaves and scented water. "The king of the ground shall have the maidenhead of all virgins dwelling on the same."

"Force her! Force her!"

The voices of his men fell on King Conor. A man who could not perform his duties could not be king. The land had prospered under his rule. He had shown himself to be a fierce and wise king. The stores of food, cattle, and slaves had increased under his rule, and twice times ten *tuatha*, twenty clans, paid homage to him. His warriors came from all over Ulster, but a man who could not perform his duties could not be king.

This was a pretty bird, he thought, her thighs, white as the belly of a dove, her cave pink, like the roses that grew close to the river. The scent of her was pleasant, like thyme, and apples and young flesh. No girl could come to the king without first being bathed. Apples and thyme and morning glory were dumped into the water to fragrance it, but just as the men sweated before battle, the girls sweated at forcing. Beads of moisture were on the girl's breasts and on her belly, like dew on the morning earth. He wanted to put his tongue to the pearls of sweat, to lift them off her one by one. He wanted to start in the hollow of her throat, then tongue away the beads between her breasts, and the liquid pearls on the inside of her thighs, but it was not fitting for a king to lower his head to a woman.

He remembered as a boy seeing the bulls grazing the pastures with the cows; how, before breeding, the bulls smelled the caves of the cows. Then the bulls lifted their noses in the air, their pink lips pulled back over their teeth so they looked as if they were grinning. Pieces of green grass showed between the white teeth. Mucus ran in streams from the nostrils of the bulls. He wondered, when he was a boy, if smelling a woman would make him grin.

"I have a plan," his mother had said, "whereby you can become king of Ulster."

"Mother," he had said to her, "only a man who has a noble father as well as a noble grandfather can be king. The son of a man who is the overseer of the royal cattle herd cannot be king."

"I have a plan," his mother had answered.

The king grinned at Branwen and rubbed his belly. He had large, square teeth between the yellow moustache and yellow beard. He had curly belly hair. Under his belly there was more hair. His root reached out to the top of the forcing table. He grabbed her hips and pulled her right to the edge of the table. He pinched one nipple. "Well, it's a pretty sparrow we have today. Fine dugs for suckling the warriors of the king." He pinched the other nipple. "Tender nipples. A child's nipples. They'll be woman's nipples before long." He pinched harder. With a flip of his wrist he knocked her hand away. "It's forbidden to touch the hand of the king without his permission. I could have a sword put to your throat for that." He motioned with his head and the two men who had brought her up the stairs moved to either side of the forcing stone and pinned her wrists with their hands. "It's the young breasts I love best. Young breasts in the first swelling of womanhood." He traced a line from her breasts down her belly, and jabbed between her legs. "A nice tight, tender cave. Soon to be stretched by the greatness of the king." He laughed, and the men cheered.

"Force her! Force her!"

The smell of men burned in Branwen's throat. The sheepskin itched under her back, scratched as though it were made of gravel. The king's hands jabbed her and hurt. She tried to pull back, but his hands wouldn't let her. She wanted to kick at his face. She tried to look at him but the sun blinded her.

When she closed her eyes the sunlight penetrated even behind her eyelids. She wanted to cover her eyes with her hands, but the soldiers held her hands. The yellow behind her eyes grew so bright that it turned black, black dots like small flies swirling in circles behind her eyes. The sound of the men rolled like thunder in a rain storm. "Force her! Force her!"

The rough fingers of the king no longer jabbed; instead a smooth hardness, like the handle of a sword polished with use, prodded her. She felt herself separated by a strange coolness, and then a pain of stretching!

The girl tightened against him. He could feel her close like an oyster against the knife, the inner pink of her flesh hidden from him. She pulled back. He felt her hips twist and he slipped out, only the tip of his root left shiny from her wetness. He dug the fingers of his left hand deep into her buttocks, and with the fingers of his right hand positioned himself again. It was ill luck for a king to hold his root at a forcing with his left hand for it was the weaker hand. It was ill luck for a king to hold a sword with his left hand unless he could hold a sword in his right hand at the same time. A man who was left handed could not become king. But he wanted to hold the girl with his right hand, which was stronger, so she couldn't pull away from him again. A man who could not perform his duties could not be king. He pinched tighter with his left hand and she cried out, shifted once more. He slapped her. Twice! Once on each side of the face. His hand left a mark, like a large red leaf, on each side of her face. The men were suddenly quiet again. The girl started to weep, her belly muscles heaving like the belly of a dog after a hunt. He grabbed her roughly with both hands, pulled her up to him, and pushed.

The pain put out all her senses, the stretching like burning, like cutting, entered her farther and farther. She tightened her hands, felt her fingernails dig into her palms. If she could make the pain in her palms great enough she wouldn't feel between her legs. Lewara had told her to relax, to breathe deeply, to pretend she was a leaf floating down the river. "Only the first forcing hurts," Lewara had said. "After that you'll have pleasure. More pleasure than any child can imagine. You'll know the pleasure of a woman." But it hurt. Why didn't the pain stop? But he kept forcing in, like a sword slowly pressed, as if he were seeking out her heart, searching for it from the bottom. She felt he was going to come right up and out again through her mouth, and she opened her mouth to let him out there, but only a cry came out of her, like the cry of a calf when its throat is cut. "You will have pleasure," Lewara had said, "more pleasure than a child can know," but she had felt only pain.

The king stopped. There was more movement between her legs and then a sudden coolness where the king had been. There had been burning, but now there was a coolness, a wet coolness, like a stream running down from her.

She heard Cathbad's voice. "May the Gods bless the first forcing," and he put a plug in where the king had been. Branwen tried to open her eyes, but the sun closed them. She wanted to reach down and feel what the Druid had put into her, but the two soldiers who still held her wrists suddenly pulled her up and she stood in front of the forcing stone. Cathbad put a wreath of oak leaves on her head. "The seed of King Conor and the blood of a virgin make warriors of the strongest heart."

One of the soldiers lifted the sheepskin from the forcing stone and showed the bloodied side to the lines of men. "The seed of King Conor and the blood of a virgin," Cathbad shouted. The men raised their swords and lances and cheered.

"She has been forced by the king," Conor said, swinging an arm out over his men. "Let a husband come and claim her." He turned his back and walked into his house.

CHAPTER 2

It was the Time of the Fires of Bael. Cathbad, Druid of Ulster, Kingdom of Conor, waited for the signal fire. His apprentices had piled the wicker high in preparation.

For three nights, not since the night of no moon, had fires been permitted anywhere on Erinn, the Island of Kings. That night, Cathbad had given the order to extinguish all flame. Every ember had to be put out. For three nights and three days no roasted flesh, no boiled water, had touched the lips of any Celt. All light came from darkness. All life came from death. This was the law of the ancients.

Cathbad stood alone in the oak circle on a hill outside the fort of King Conor. For three nights he had not slept. He had drunk tea from the magic herbs and leaves of the mountains, and stared upon the stars.

He pulled his cloak close and shivered. It was midnight, the night of midsummer, but the wind, wet with the sea, was salty and bitter, penetrating through the white wool cloak. Aside from dried mushrooms, Cathbad had not eaten any solid food for three days and his stomach grumbled loudly. He was glad that he was alone. It was unfitting for a man of the gods to be subject to growlings.

He licked his lips in anticipation of the feast fire. Two white bulls, their horns wrapped with sacred oak leaves, stood outside the circle, and he could occasionally hear the shifting of their feet on the stones. The night was quiet, except for the slow howl of a wolf, and the hooting of an owl somewhere in the distance.

The preceding days had been full of ill signs. The night before No Moon, a hen had crowed in the fort. "Feed the cock but sacrifice him not," the ancients said. The cock was sacred to Cromm Cruach and to his son Bael. But a hen that crowed was to be detested.

Cathbad had sought out the hen and tossed it in the fire, for a hen that crowed had to be killed in accordance with the rituals of the ancients.

But still the sound of the hen's final, frantic crow had stayed with Cathbad long after he had cried out the order for all fires to be extinguished.

For three nights, time past, time present, and time future, Cathbad had gazed upon the stars. A swan had flown across the sky, blocking his view of the evening star, Caillech, goddess of women. That meant a birth would take place. But a hen had crowed, and it did not bode well.

There! In the distance Cathbad saw the signal fire. At Beal-Tinne the high Druid Midhe lit the first fire at Tara Hill. From that, other signal fires on other hills were lit until Bael fires were blazing all over Erinn. His own fire would be a signal for the other Druids farther north at Sliabh and Ailech.

Spittle was a substance of life and soul, and no ceremony to the sun was undertaken without it. Every morning when he greeted the sun, the Druid would spit on his hands and lift his palms to the sunrise. Now he spit on his hands and lifted them in the direction of the signal fire before picking up the flint.

Cathbad struck the flint stone, throwing sparks into the pile of leaves he had gathered for kindling the Bael fire. He had plucked the leaves from the sacred grove of twelve oaks. Twelve oaks signified the twelve offspring of Bael.

He had picked one leaf from each oak and dried them for a moon change.

Cathbad struck the stone once more, and sparks like miniature stars fell into the dry leaves. The fire sputtered, looked as though it would die, but then flared.

From the leaves the fire sprang into the twigs. They crackled like a happy man's laughter. A fire that sang was a good sign, but a hen had crowed. The flames leapt higher into the large pyramid of wicker that had been piled inside the circle of Cromm Cruach, and began to burn, big as a lion's head, then bigger and bigger until the bonfire blazed like a sun.

The ancients told how earth and sky had once been joined, two lovers in a tender, perpetual embrace. For ten times ten thousand years they were joined together, unceasingly making love, together their bodies encompassing all things, male, female, light, dark, earth, wind, water, fire, man, beast, grass, and trees.

But their offspring tired of perpetually living in their parents. They came together in a council, and Fearha, father of men, wanted to kill both parents outright, but the others refused. The father of the forests, Tacranne, had a suggestion to separate his parents.

He pushed a rooted foot against the navel of his mother and strained with his powerful oak legs and lifted his father up. Immediately light and dark were separated, and water from earth, and fire from wind, but there was also bitterness. Cromm Cruach, god of all things, railed against his children for separating him from his beloved earth, and took revenge by heaping pain and destruction on all things.

Bael, god of light, succeeded in persuading his mother to intervene for her children. Earth reached up with her breasts and began to stroke them against the sky. She pulled Cromm Cruach into the deep canyons between her legs and held him in love. And the god of all things temporarily forgot his anger. But he was no longer as virile as he had been.

After once dropping his seed into the earth, the magnificent shaft, which had been longer than the distance a man could see standing on the highest hill, grew puny, smaller than a gray mouse. Cromm Cruach raged once more against his impotency.

The sun pleaded again, promised that the offspring would give back a portion of themselves so that the father's vigor could return. The oak would give of itself, and man, and the beasts.

All through the year the gifts had to be made to Bael so he could offer them up to his father. Bael-Tinne called for the sacrifices of fire.

CHAPTER
3

The wisewoman's hands held the child's head as it emerged from between Branwen's legs.

"Push, Branwen," said Lewara. "One more push and he'll be out. It's a fire-haired babe you'll be putting at the breast. Push. Come on out, you little squirrel," and she cradled the child, one hand under its head, one hand under its slippery back, and gently pulled it from its mother. "What mischief are the gods planning now? A red-haired boy is fierce in battle, but a red-haired girl and a mole on the left breast will bring nothing but bad luck. I shouldn't wrap it at all. Your husband will want to feed it to the wolves or the bears when he finds it redheaded."

"No," cried Branwen. Her face was blotched, red and sweating from her labor, her reply fierce. "Give her to me. She's mine."

"You'll be wishing she weren't—"

"Give her to me!"

"Mark my words. She'll be causing you nothing but heartache. When Cathbad finds out, he'll be demanding to drink its blood for the altar of the gods."

"I won't let him!" Branwen sat up in bed and reached out her arms for her child.

"Not much you'll be able to do about it when the time comes." But she wiped the child with lamb's fleece, then rubbed the child down with goose grease, turned it over, and spit on it three times for good luck. Then she swaddled the child in a fresh lambskin and handed it to the mother.

Branwen looked at her child. The eyes were not the stone-gray blue of other newborns she had seen, but amber. Amber like the mountain rocks or like the flower petals along the Blackwater River. The child held her mother's eyes in a stare. *I'm here,* it seemed to say. *Now what are you going to do with me?* "Deirdre," Branwen said. "I'll call you Deirdre." She untied her tunic; put the baby's mouth to her breast. The child's mouth fastened to her nipple and began to suck. Branwen felt a tug, like a fierce hook of pleasure catching in the center of her body. Each time the child sucked, the hook pulled tighter in her womb. It was a loosening and tightening in the center of her body. The child made small gurgling sounds, and Branwen, fatigued from labor, closed her eyes. Her mind saw images of a sunset, the red giving way to dark blue. She felt that her center was a flower that closed at sunset and opened at sunrise. Sunset, sunrise. Red to blue to black, opening and closing, and she fell asleep.

Lewara shook her head. The father had to be told. "Slave," she called out, but before she had the word out, there was a rustling from the doorway and another woman appeared. "You've been watching again," Lewara said, "watching and listening, haven't you, you old—"

"Just a wee thing, now, ain't it? No bigger than a fart," said Aya.

"If you tell anyone it has a mole," said Lewara, "I'll cut your skin from your back and feed it to the ravens. I want you to go—"

Aya stooped suddenly and put her hand to the small of her back. "Why is it always me you'll be sending? You got other slaves. Younger ones what ain't got the achings in me back like I do. And me being nearly sixty harvests, if I was a day old."

"You complaining crow. You're not a moon past thirty harvests. You're the laziest—"

"It ain't at all me being lazy. It's that I got me"—Aya

stooped lower, and touched her back gently again—"me achings. You'll be medicining up all the others in this here place. But your own proper slave, you'll be leaving untended like I was a dog in the hen yard."

"I'll give you a whipping if you don't move out of here. You've never had an aching or a fever in all the time I've known you. Except when I send you someplace!"

"Can I help it if the harvests been telling on me back? Can I help it if I'm old, seventy harvests, if I'm a moon's change? And you always sending me off to look for herbs and mushrooms and medicinings. Hoofing me up the mountains and cliffs like I was a billy goat. Can I help it if King Conor's is the biggest fort in all of Erinn? Can I help it if it's a half day's walking for me just to get to his house? And his roundhouse itself longer than three hundred cows standing arse to nose. And him always at the furthest part. I say a curse on King Conor, I say. May he turn into a frog's arse for building this here dun so big—"

"See this knife?" Lewara had pulled a dagger from her skirt pocket. It was the same dagger she had used to cut the child's birth cord. "It isn't as sharp as King Conor's. He'll cut your tongue out and have you drawn and quartered and fed to his hounds. And I'll be the one asking him to do it if you don't—"

"And him always galloping by in his fine chariots. Like he was god of heaven hisself. Fine for him. He ain't having to walk nowhere. Walk, walk. Aya, walk here. Aya, walk there. Like I was a regular walking thing not fit for nothing but walking—" The slave's tirade stopped momentarily when she ducked to avoid a clay pot Lewara had thrown at her. "And it's a fine thing you're doing! You come into a man's house to deliver his child and you break up his cooking pots!"

"I'll break every cooking pot in the house if you don't get to King Conor's house right now."

Aya thought for a moment. King Conor's house meant soldiers! She straightened up immediately and touched her hair. Then she remembered the wisewoman and slumped again, touching her back once more. "Well, I suppose I could be making it to King Conor's house. It ain't being so far. I thought you was gonna be sending me off into the hills again getting medicinings for . . ." She looked at the woman on the floor. "King Conor's house, eh?" She cleared her throat.

"Tell Falim he has a daughter. And if you tell anybody it has a mole, I'll cut your tongue out."

The slave looked at the woman wrapped in the sheepskins on the floor. "What will I be telling him the babe's name is? He'll be wanting to know, he will. Fine thing to have a child. But it's a better thing to have a child with a name so as if you're calling him in a crowd, he'll know that it's him and not another you'll be hollering for."

Lewara looked at Branwen. "Tell him the child's name is . . . Deirdre."

The slave turned and left.

Lewara bent down to where the baby slept beside its mother in a bed of sheepskins on the floor. Both the mother's and child's eyes were closed. The mother's face, mottled and red, bruised almost, the color of raspberries that had been left too long on the cane, showed the strain of her labor. The constant pushing brought the blood to the face and made it look like the faces of some of the old men who drank too much.

Bearing children bruised women. In a couple of days the redness would go from her face, but Branwen would never be the same as she'd been before. Lewara touched the young woman's face and remembered how it had been translucent, polished and smooth like the inside of a shell while she carried the child in her body.

She touched the face of the sleeping child. Nothing was

smoother than the face of a newborn. Nothing. Not the finest
cloth, not any part of an adult's body. Nothing. She touched
the hands, the fingers folded like ferns. She remembered her
own baby's hands. They had not been like these, small delicate
fingers, the fingers of a girl. His had been big hands. Big. How
big had they been? She tried to remember. Looked at her own
hands in comparison. Time took away the memory of things.
How big had they been? How many women could remember
the size of their newborns' hands? When the wisewoman had
come and helped her deliver him, she had joked about the size
of his hands, and his feet.

"Will you be looking at the paws on this pup. And he's got
himself a regular man-sized root already, he has. Be tickling a
few bellies, he will, when he gets growed up."

But her son never grew up. Some of the women were
springing babes from their bellies within a few moons of their
joinings. Lewara and her husband went for three harvests and
still there had been no child. She and her husband had gone
with the wisewoman to the great stone bed near the fort
where Dermot and Grania had lain in love in ancient times.

Dermot and Grania were born of the first race of men in
Erinn, a giant race, but the night that Grania was to marry the
old king, white-bearded Finn of Erinn, she persuaded the
young Dermot to take her away. To flee from the jealous rage
of the king, the couple were forced to sleep in a different place
every night. They took huge stones, some of them as big as the
floor of a house, and made them into their beds wherever they
went. When the couple made love the stars twinkled, for they
had never seen two people who loved so well.

The old Finn prayed to Cromm Cruach, god of all, father
of Bael, and demanded that Dermot and Grania be rightfully
punished. Cromm Cruach sent a lightning bolt as the couple
made love, so they would be seared together, charcoaled like a
piece of roasting mutton forgotten in the fire.

But Aengus, god of love, who was the father of Dermot, intervened and, before the lightning hit the two lovers, turned them into doves and they flew away. And the love of Dermot and Grania grew, and they had many offspring, and if you walked in the Seven Woods, you could still hear the tender voices of the doves, their murmurings, like faint thunder in the forest, talking of the love of Dermot and Grania.

The great dolmens, the stones all over Erinn, where Dermot and Grania had lain, had magic powers. If a couple who did not have children slept there under the full light of the heavenly mother, Mam Caellach, then Aengus would make the coupling fruitful.

On the night of the full moon Lewara and her husband had gone to the bed of Dermot and Grania. They had been led there by the bard and by the wisewoman, the same woman who had been Lewara's teacher.

The bed consisted of four huge stones. Three stones lay vertically, and a fourth one lay on top of them, at an angle so that at its lowest point it reached to Lewara's knees, but at its tallest point the stone reached above her head. As the wisewoman lifted her hands to the moon and began to chant, Lewara and her husband disrobed, laid sheepskins on the horizontal rock, and lay down on it.

Lewara took her husband's root in her hands, and when it was thick and standing, the wisewoman rubbed it with the two fruits of a ram killed after one season's breeding. Then Lewara's cave was smeared with the blood of a hare killed with young in her belly. The blood was thick, congealed and cold, but her husband's body on top of her warmed her. Three times Lewara and her husband had gone to the love bed of Dermot and Grania.

Finally the coupling was successful, and nine moons later Lewara had given birth to a son. He suckled heartily. He was a fitting son for her husband, and they named him Laeg

MacDatho, Laeg son of Datho. He had strong hands and big feet, and a root, small as the baby was, fitting the son of Datho, chieftain of the king. With hands like that, Laeg MacDatho would handle the biggest of broadswords. His father was a chieftain, and his father's father. Perhaps Laeg himself might someday be chosen king of Ulster in the council of chieftains, and live in the king's roundhouse. And she would be mother of the king, and the women in the fort would bow their heads when she passed by and say, "There walks Lewara, mother of the king."

Lewara refused to give the child to a wet nurse. It was unfitting for a babe who was to be king to be suckled by a slave. She had given her own breasts to the child. "My little king," she cooed to him as he suckled. For four nights the child had been beside her in her bed, the body wriggling and warm under her arm. But the fifth morning, the child lay still beneath her. She had smothered him during the night.

She shook the child, trying to shake life back into him. His head rolled on his body, back and forth, like a knot of straw, but he didn't breathe. She began to breathe into him, laid him on the ground and pressed her lips to his lips, and filled his mouth with her breath. "Breathe, Breathe! Mam Caellach, great goddess of women. Tethra, goddess of death. Aengus, god of love. For love and for life, make him breathe!" But her final words no longer pleaded; they commanded. "Breathe!" And when the chest refused to move, she slapped it. She would make him breathe again. She would not let him die, not after waiting so long. She pounded harder. "Breathe! Breathe!" She pounded with her fist. Under it she felt the small bones cracking, with a sound like chicken bones when she separated them with a knife. And still he refused to breathe. She threw him against the stone wall of her house. On her hands and knees she crawled to where he had fallen, his bare body face down on the straw floor, his hands and feet, hands and feet fitting of a king, splayed and still.

She began to wail, a half-bleating sound, like that of a ewe that's looking for its lamb, and a half squeal, like that of a pig when a knife is drawn across its throat. The sound carried through the stones and the thatched roof, and when the wise-woman entered, she found Lewara beating the dead body of her child with a stone.

The wisewoman yelled for her slaves, and together they bound Lewara. They dragged her from the body of her child to the well. They drew up water, and plunged Lewara into a tub of cold water to take away the madness. But Lewara didn't want to live, and she stayed under the water. The wisewoman grabbed Lewara by the hair and yanked her head. Cathbad, the Druid, was called, and he ordered her body to be covered with reeds and piled with stones.

Lewara willed her breath to stop. She prayed to Tethra to make the stones press life out of her, but still she kept breath-ing. She screamed at them to give her a knife so she could die like her son.

The wisewoman wrapped Lewara's head with a poultice of fresh cow dung and mistletoe, a length of linen smeared with the warm stuff to draw out the madness. Bits of dung fell into Lewara's eye, and stung, but she couldn't lift her hands to remove it. She began to weep again. She railed at the gods and at the slaves and the Druid to let her die. She railed until she spit blood, and when she couldn't rail anymore she cried. The bard was called and he played music to quiet her, and in exhaustion she fell asleep. Finally the madness had been stilled by stones.

When Lewara awoke, the wisewoman ordered the stones lifted. The wisewoman bathed Lewara in warm water and gave her warm milk with honey to drink.

After birth a man had to stay separate from his wife until

the birth blood stopped, for if a man was touched by it, he would become as weak and full of fear as a newborn. When Lewara's husband returned, he sent her from his house, for no man wanted to sleep with a woman who had lain on her own son.

The wisewoman called to Lewara. "Come," she said. "The birth madness makes a woman see. I am old. Only a woman without husband or children can replace me. A husband always wants his pleasure. Children always need roasted meat and boiled corn put in their bellies. A wisewoman must have time to learn."

Now Lewara looked at the child that lay sleeping on Branwen's breast. The child's hair was the color of flame. If Cathbad learned of the mole he would demand the child for sacrifice. A red-haired boy meant a brave, hot-blooded warrior. But a red-haired girl . . .

Lewara lifted the child from its mother. The child slept but continued to make sucking sounds with its lips. The same sounds her own son had made. A wisewoman must have time to learn.

CHAPTER
4

Aya didn't walk in the direction of the king's roundhouse, but turned the other way and headed back toward Lewara's house. She couldn't go to the king's house without combing her hair and reddening her cheeks. She hadn't even had time to comb her hair because the wisewoman had been chasing her around all morning. "Slave, get this. Slave, get that. Slave. Slave. Slave." Wasn't fair, it weren't.

The old man, Lewara's father. He had known how to treat a slave. Him patting her crackers if she walked by him, and taking her to bed with him at night. Him snorting beside her comfortable like. His stomach keeping her back warm all through the whole night long. And Lewara herself not doing nothing but screaming. Screaming and yelling at her and threatening to bury her bones in the hen yard or both. And Lewara not even having a man for Aya to sleep with.

People wasn't meant to sleep alone, least of all Aya. If the gods had meant men and women to sleep alone they wouldna have given men roots that fitted perfectly into the caves of women. Wouldna have given men hands what cupped a woman's titties warm when the rain was coming down outside all night long.

Aya hadn't slept with a man for a full night, not since the old man had died. That's when she, and the other slaves and the old man's cows, had been divided between his children, Lewara and Lewara's two brothers. Property divided equal among the children is what the laws said. Except that

Lewara's brother got Geena the man slave, and now she had to sneak out at night like a common dog to meet him.

Honk! Honk!

Aya stopped walking.

In front of her stood Lewara's house. A circular house of larch poles and a thatched roof of wattles, wooden rods and stakes interwoven with twigs and tree branches and covered with clay. A sheepskin hung over the door to keep out the cold, and in front of the door stood two geese.

The geese were looking at her suspiciously, blocking her way. It just weren't fair that a body what couldn't get into her own proper house to put a little color on her own proper cheeks and some scent on her neck so as the soldiers would get to noticing her. Aya searched for her stick and complained. "And her not even keeping a dog like normal people keep dogs. Her using geese to guard her potions and mixings."

When she found her stick, she shook it at the goose. "All right you mangy, honking thing. Come."

But the goose held his ground and just looked at the stick.

"You're afraid of the stick, ain't you? You noisy, bothersome thing."

The goose hiss-honked, but he didn't come any closer.

Without turning her back on the goose, she reached behind her and pulled the door of the house open.

Lewara's house was similar to all the other houses in Emain. Except for King Conor's roundhouse, which was built of oak timbers, all the houses in the fort were built of poles with thatched roofs. The houses in Emain were all round with only one door, which faced the direction of the sun. The houses contained no windows, but a gap in the top of the thatching allowed the smoke to go out. The center of the floor of Lewara's house contained a circle of stone, the fire circle.

The floor of the house was clay, spread with straw and rushes. A couple of cowskins served as rugs. Close to the fire were two beds made of sheepskins. Assorted clay pots and wicker baskets stood on low wicker shelves lining the walls. To one side of the fire stood a loom. Aya bent down and put a couple of chunks of peat into the embers that glowed in the fire circle.

Then she searched through the wisewoman's pots and found a jar of berry red, called *ruam,* and raddled each cheek. Then she took a horn comb from under her pillow, unbraided her hair, and retied it with a leather thong. She found a pot of tallow scented with rose petals and lily of the valley and rubbed some on her shoulder. She smiled to herself.

Maybe Bov would be on guard duty. Bov with his shaft hardening quick as you please. Last time he had pushed her up against the wall. When Aya thought about it, she felt tinglings all over her, from the bottoms of her toes to the roots of her hair. It made her happy just thinking about it.

She went to the door of the house and looked for the goose. But he wasn't by the front. Aya hoisted her skirt above her knees so she could run faster and scooted off in the direction of the king's house.

It was Cathbad and Lewara who mixed the magic and curing potions. Lewara was only allowed to grind herbs to make sick people better. She was not allowed to mix the magic potions for love, or to bring adulthood to girls, or the courage potion for men, or the blessing potions. It was Cathbad who did these, and kept the recipes secret.

But Aya was a sort of magician herself, and could transform herself with a single movement of her body. She was a solidly built woman, tough from constant movement. She had strands of gray in her dark hair, but her eyebrows were black as a crow's beak. Her face was weathered by the sea wind and forty corn harvests, and when she was around Lewara she let her belly sag and her lower lip droop halfway to her chin. She stumbled instead of walked, so that she would resemble a crippled crone. And if Lewara yelled at her too much, then Aya could make her eyeballs roll in their sockets like someone who was having a fit. But when Lewara was nowhere to be seen, Aya stood straight, sucked in her belly, and held her head high. When she smiled at men, they didn't notice the gray in her hair. When she wanted to, Aya could outrun women half her age, and to make up for lost time, she ran as fast as she could to the king's house.

Emain, the fort of King Conor, was a circular fort, the largest in Ulster. It was surrounded by a wide raised bank of rocks, earth, and sod, which was topped with birch poles sharpened to a point to keep out raiders from Connacht and Leinster. Inside the circular walls of the fort were dozens of small houses almost exactly the same as Lewara's house. There were bathhouses and wells, and corrals for the animals. At night the cowherds and shepherds brought the king's cows, horses, and sheep into the corrals so raiders could not steal them away. In the center of the fort stood the king's house.

The king's house was itself a miniature fortress. It stood on a circular mound of earth twice as tall as a man and with a diameter measuring a hundred cows standing head to tail. There was only one entrance to the mound, a stone-and-earth ramp guarded at the top by a heavy wooden gate. Topping the outer edge of the mound was a palisade of sharpened birch pillars. Inside the pillars was a maze of more sharpened poles. Only after someone had navigated the maze did they enter the king's walkway, which opened to the man-root of Aengus and the front doors of the king's house.

Aya arrived breathless at the top of the ramp and noticed dozens of heads hanging on the poles of the king's mound. Heads from Leinster. She'd heard the noise the day before when King Conor came tearing through the fort, and his men behind him in chariots. All of them shouting and yelling. The heads had been tied to the horses' manes and to the chariots yesterday, the horses jumping and whinnying from the smell of blood. The king had been out hunting for wild boar, when he came across a raiding party from Leinster. The king and his men had made short shrift of the Leinstermen. They'd killed over fifty and captured seven more. They were being kept for sacrifice. Geena said he'd seen them being led away in chains.

"Leinstermen! Hummph!" Aya snorted. Nothing but pudding in their bellies. "Connachtmen! Them's real men. Conor and his troop wouldn'a had such an easy time with Connachtmen." Aya knew all about Connachtmen. That was where she came from. Connacht, before she'd been taken as a slave.

She spit at one of the heads hanging on the palisade, and then she smiled to herself. Men who fought and took heads were always in a mood for taking something else. But in a moment she felt a twinge of disappointment. Although both guards had their backs turned, she didn't recognize either of them as Bov. Bov had a back wider than the spread of bull's horns.

The gate guards were passing a large cup back and forth. Someone had brought them something to drink and they were talking loudly.

There had been no feasting last night because of the Fast of No Moon. Cathbad had given the order. Only this morning had the great fire in the sacred oak grove been kindled. Lewara had gone there in the procession and brought the embers back to rekindle their own fire. Lewara in a robe of white wool. Aya, because she was only a slave, was not allowed to go to the fire-bringing. At dawn she had watched the king at the head of the procession walk through Emain, holding the new fire for his hearth in a protected dish. Now in the king's house, the king, his noblemen, his charioteers, shield makers, and his 365 foot soldiers, the same as the days in a year, as well as pipers, herdsmen, all would be feasting. Six bulls and a dozen boars had been slaughtered for the feast. Aya's stomach grumbled. Nothing but bread she'd eaten for the last three days. Not even a boiled onion.

Now she could smell the cooked meat. In the great banquet hall, all of Conor's men would be seated according to rank, and eating either a pig's shoulder, or leg bone, according to rank. The king and the Druid got the rib portions 'cause that's where the meat was juiciest and tenderest. And the king had to eat the boar's heart, so he would have the ferocity of the boar. And he had to eat a bull's balls so he could make strong sons. The charioteers, stewards, and horsemen were given boar's heads to eat; harpers, drummers, hunters, and craftsmen were given pigs' shoulders, the king's doorkeepers got chin pieces, foot soldiers were given leg pieces, and buffoons were given pigs' feet.

Aya would only get to eat something after all the others. Kings, noblemen, soldiers, freemen, slaves, and dogs was the order the bones got chewed on. Still, it was the bits about the bone what tasted best.

One of the gate guards finally noticed Aya. She smiled at him. He didn't smile back. Because of her clothes, Aya was immediately recognizable. Only certain ranks were entitled to wear certain stripes of color in their clothing. Domestic slaves were allowed no color, only plain gray cloth. Ploughmen and tillers of the soil could only wear brown. Craftsmen and free farmers could stripe their brown or gray garments with blue. Foot soldiers could wear plaids that were striped with green, provided that the green was no wider than the width of a man's smallest fingernail; charioteers could wear wider green plaids. Yellow and white was reserved for the chieftains and clan heads; and only the king, princes, and the high Druid could wear red. All classes of men could wear gold jewelry, except for slaves.

These soldiers wore green tunics, which reached just above

the knee. Each wore a robe of sheepskin, fastened with gold brooches. They wore leather leggings. Each man held a spear in one hand, and had a sword and knife fastened to his girdle.

"What do you want, slave?" one soldier asked. He had a large face and a nose that looked as if it had been broken.

Aya could hear the meanness in his voice. Too much beer or mead did that to some men. No matter what a woman did, the men still pinched or hit them.

The second guard turned around. Aya recognized him. He'd been on guard duty with Bov one day. "I remember you," he said. "You're the wisewoman's slave."

"I'm remembering you too," said Aya. "Not your name, but . . . other things." She smiled broadly, planted both her hands on her hips, and lifted her skirt slightly.

The second guard smiled.

The first guard asked, "If you're the wisewoman's slave, be off with you. Ain't nobody sick here. You ain't got no business here." He lifted his spear.

"I got a message for the king and for Falim, his charioteer. There's been a birthing. I been sent by the wisewoman. And if'n you don't let me pass, I'll be telling her to mix you a double batch of tar-water the next time youze got an aching in your bowels."

"Mind how you talk, slave, or I'll—"

"I'll take you in," said the second guard.

The first guard looked at him and frowned, turned his back, and walked away.

Aya smiled at the second guard. She followed him into the maze. They made a right turn, then another and a left. Then the guard stopped. He had a cork-colored beard, and there were bits of roasted meat clinging to it. Someone had sneaked food out for the guards. He leaned his spear against the wall of the maze. He put one hand on Aya's shoulder. The other, he put on her breast. He was much taller than Aya: she only came up to his chest. Aya leaned back against the wall of the maze. The guard slid his hand from her breast to her belly, and under her skirt. He made a smacking sound with his mouth. Aya reached under his tunic. Took his man root in her hand. It was soft and smooth like a cow's teat during milking, and she began to massage her hand back and forth along it. He pushed her harder against the wall. There was a knothole or something rough on the pole that bruised her backside, and she shifted her weight to the other leg. The guard, because he was so tall, had to bend his knees, and he grunted as he tried to get into her. Aya stood on her tiptoes. She put her hands on his shoulder, tried to lift herself higher. The guard tried to get lower, but the wall got in his way. Finally he grabbed Aya by the backside and lifted her up to his hips. Aya felt him go in, and sucked in her breath. She liked men who went deep. In a moment it was over, and she slid back to the ground, feeling dizzy and weak. She leaned against the wall for a moment. The guard smiled at her, wiped his member in his tunic, then let the tunic down. He picked up his spear. Took Aya by the shoulder, turned her around, and slapped her lightly on the backside. "You'd better be off and tell them what you got to tell them." And he smacked his lips.

Aya continued through the maze and found the king's walkway. "Aie," she said appreciatively, when she saw the manroot of Aengus, "what a woman couldn't be doing with that!" Then she looked up at the stone steps to the king's house. "Well, won't the gods be blessing Aya today! If it ain't Bov be guarding the king's proper doors."

Bov looked at her and grinned, large broad teeth like a cow's, showing out yellow from between his red beard and moustache. Nonetheless he had the finest marrow bone of any man in Emain. And Aya had felt plenty of 'em, she had. Bov had a wart on the end of his, and there weren't nothing like a wart on the root of a man to tickle a woman's belly.

"You got your spear ready, for the warrior what's coming?"
she asked him.

"Tested it out this morning. T''is in fine shape, me spear."

She made a motion to pinch his cheek, but just then the
other guard came around from the side of the house.

Dressed like Bov, the other guard wore a green plaid tunic
with a sheep's robe, leather leggings and gold bracelets. Bov
winked at Aya. "Falim's wife birthed a youngun?" he asked
her. "That why you come?"

"Aie. Nothing but a wee thing, she ain't. Pretty as a sparrow."

Bov looked at his guard partner, then said to Aya, "Come,
I'll take you to Falim."

He leaned his spear against the doorjamb. The doors were
polished oak, twice as tall as Bov, and as wide as a dozen men
standing shoulder to shoulder. The handles were brass, and
engraved with circular patterns like intertwining bird's claws.
The door creaked heavily, like an old man coughing.

Drum music, harps, and loud men's voices bolted through
the doors when Bov opened them. Inside the doors stood two
more guards, and they nodded Bov and Aya past them. The
house smelled of feasting, of boiled beef, roasted goose and
pork, and warm mead wine. Pipes, harps, the clanging of
swords, and drunken men's voices echoed through the halls.

The king's house was made of nine compartments. Each of
the partitions dividing the compartments was forged from
bronze, over thirty feet tall, and edged with gold. The circular
pattern of intertwining birds' claws, beaks, and the antlers of
deer adorned each partition. The walls of each compartment
were polished red yew slabs, and the wooden ceilings were
painted with pictures of silver-antlered deer, gold-toothed
hounds, and silver-hoofed horses.

Off from the first compartment was a shallow alcove. Bov
motioned Aya in. He pushed her down on her hands and

knees and got down behind her, his sword clanging against the wood floor. She lifted her skirt for him.

"Feels like I'm the last man in your larder," said Bov.

"All the better to ease you in. Anyway, last man in weren't but a boy. I needs a man to be pleasing me."

Bov grunted. Twice Aya hit her head on the far wall of the alcove. She vaguely felt the second bump but wasn't sure.

Then Bov stood and helped Aya to her feet. "It's a fine place you got, woman. A fine place for a man. The tightest muscle cave I ever felt. Like putting me root into the mouth of a snapping turtle. Come on, old girl. The other guard will be wondering where I took you."

"Don't you be snapping it off nowhere. You keep good care of it for Aya." And she patted his groin.

"All right, then. Let's find Falim for you. The king'll be pleased to hear of the birth of another youngun. He's in a fine mood after yesterday's squirmish. Pardoned two thieves, he did, what got caught stealing some eagle's liver from his table. Was going to have them thrown into the Bael fires. But instead he just ordered their hands cut off."

Aya smoothed her hair with her hands, and followed Bov. The banquet hall was filled with the warriors of Ulster, playing sparring games with fists and swords, singing, trying to outdrink each other, outboast each other, and outdance each other, and the noise was deafening. The air was a close smell of feasting and the sweat of men.

The ceiling of the hall was held up by rows of bronze pillars, the headpieces of which glittered with silver and gold. Six fires blazed in pits placed lengthwise along the center of the hall, and the six fires reflected a thousand times from every scallop in every edge of the bronze pillars, and a thousand more times from the silver and gold ceiling so that the hall was equally light in day or night.

The king sat near the middle of the hall, on a gold throne,

encrusted with red enamel, rubies, and pearls. On either side of the throne stood two spears with a mutilated head impaled on the point. To his left hand hung a silver gong, wide as a chariot wheel, suspended from the roof tree of the house, and when King Conor struck the gong with his silver rod, all of the men of Ulster were silent.

Bov and Aya pushed their way through the crowd of men. Celtic warriors scorned death by fighting naked, in a sacred frenzy in which life and death were one. Feasting was the same sort of frenzy. About three quarters of the soldiers in the hall were naked, and Aya looked at each of them.

There was Fergus of the red eyebrows. Once king of Ulster, now drunk on the floor and asleep in his own vomit. Some king he had been. Giving away his kingdom for ale and for a woman.

Aya, keeping a fixed, appreciative eye on a hairy-chested warrior who was dancing over two swords laid on the floor, pushed forward into the banquet hall, when suddenly she screamed out in pain. Another dancer, naked, exuberantly drunk, and showing off his ability to leap through the air, collided with her, landing with his foot on her right foot.

She exploded from the shock, upbraiding the soldier with more vehemence than a slave should use. "Ouch! Curses on you. May the sky fall on your head! May you turn into a frog's arse, if you don't watch where you'll be planting your pegs. Drunk as a boiled owl, you frog's arse, and walking all over an old woman's feet like they was made of the earth itself."

The dancer grabbed her hair, pulled her head back. The only things he wore were leggings and a leather belt. A knife hung at his belt and he pulled it from its sheath, drawing the blade across Aya's throat. "Shut up, slave. You bastard's bitch, I'll show you—"

"All right. All right. Leave her alone! She has a message from the wisewoman," Bov intervened on her part.

"Ain't no slave gonna talk to me like that! I'll feed her tongue to the crows!"

"Go back to your jigging! You'll not be dulling your blade on the skin of a woman, surely!"

The leaping soldier looked at Aya and let her go. Aya swallowed hard, straightened her shoulders, and followed Bov.

Ropes were stretched from poles stuck into the floor on either side of the six fires, and on the ropes above the fires, Conor's charioteers were performing acrobatic stunts. Falim performed on the fire immediately in front of the king. The first thing Aya noticed about him was his nakedness. No wonder the child was such a beauty. Above the fire Falim's body glistened as though it were a bronze statue of a god. Aya swallowed hard and began to rage inside.

She hadn't always been a slave. She had been a daughter of one of the infantry men of Queen Maeve of Connacht. Had she not been stolen away by King Conor's men, she, too, could have had a man of such beauty.

Falim ran along the rope. Over the fire he stopped to do a handstand. If he lost his balance, he would fall directly into the fire below. His beard and hair hung down below the rope as he kicked his heels high in the air. His body was straight as a spear. He reached one hand beside his head. He held himself with only one hand.

Aya held her breath.

Falim jerked the rope from side to side with one hand. Aya covered her eyes with her hands, but spread her fingers so she could peek through the spaces, as if she were a child who was frightened but curious at the same time. And just as Aya thought he was going to fall into the fire, he grasped the rope with both hands. He swung down, his bare feet actually going through the upper flames of the fire; then, with a somersault, he stood on top of the rope again. All the men around him cheered, shouted his name. "A toast! A toast! A toast to Falim MacBrian. To Falim son of Brian!"

Falim danced along the rope to the end, and leapt to the ground. Bov, with a motion of his hand, caught Falim's eye and pointed to the wisewoman's slave, just as the king sounded his gong.

Immediately the hall quieted. "Falim," cried out the king, "Falim MacBrian. My finest charioteer, son of Brian, finest charioteer of my father, King Fergus before me . . ." It was then that the king noticed Aya. "What is it that sends the wisewoman's slave to you in this time of our feast?"

"My wife, Sire," said Falim.

"What about your wife?" The king glanced around the hall. "Is she here that I might show my pleasure to both of you for entertaining me, and for driving my horses with the speed of the wind?"

Falim bowed low. "No, Sire. She's in childbed."

Aya noticed a dark birthmark about the size and shape of a peach stone on his left buttock.

". . . and will she bless the best charioteer of the king with a son to follow in his father's footsteps, like his father before him, and his father's father before him?"

It was then that Aya noticed Cathbad standing behind the king. Hoity-toity Cathbad. With his nose in the air like a duck's arse. Looked just like a goose, he did. White robe and all. He had a long white beard that reached down to his belly. He didn't have any hair on the front of his head, but the hair in the back was white and reached nearly to the backs of his knees. He had fingernails that grew long and curved like an eagle's talons. And if she looked close, Aya was certain she would see the caked blood under them. He had eyes like a cat's. His pupils weren't round but long black slits, and the colored part surrounding them was yellow.

"I hope it is so," said Falim. "The slave was just about to tell me."

"Well, slave? Another charioteer for the army of the king?"

Never in her life had Aya spoken to the king. She had seen him go by hundreds of times in his chariot pulled by his white horses. She had often thought about throwing a stone and hitting him right in his royal arse so his head would come down more ordinary like. But she had never dared, and the king never paid any more attention to her than to a pebble on the road. And now he was talking to her. And her foot ached. And the juice of two men was creeping down the inside of her thigh. And she hadn't even heard what the king said.

She looked at Falim. Looked at Bov. But neither man gave any hint.

"Well, slave," bellowed the king, "has the wisewoman finally cut out your tongue? Used it in a potion to give back the voice to someone else?"

The warriors in the banquet hall laughed. Aya wrung her hands, bowed low, let her shoulders slump and her belly hang. The king might have compassion for an old woman. "No," she barely whispered.

"What?" shouted the king.

"No, Sire." She could barely hear her own voice.

"Guard. What is this you've brought me?" The king was feeling convivial. "The wisewoman's slave, or her pet dormouse? Someone find me my cats! Squeak! Squeak! Squeak!" The king laughed out loud. The soldiers laughed too. The king looked around him. It pleased him when he could make his men laugh. A king who could make his men laugh could make his men bring home many heads from battle. He continued, "A nice fat mouse for my cats. I'll wager she's a tough old mouse, though. Would give the cats a case of royal stomach burnings." There was more laughter. The king, waiting for it to subside, stroked his beard. Then he struck his gong. Immediately the soldiers quieted down. "Enough amusement from the slave. Answer us! Has Falim's wife blessed him with a valiant charioteer to follow in his father's skill?"

That was what Aya had been waiting for. That frog's arse of a king could have asked her that in the first place. "No, Your Highness," she almost shouted.

"Stand back! Stand back," shouted the king. "The mouse has farted." Everybody laughed.

Aya saw Falim's face droop with disappointment.

"So the mouse *can* speak. Speak again, mouse, so that we know the noise just wasn't rear belching."

Aya looked at the king. There was only one rear belch in the banquet hall. And that one was sitting up on that there throne. Furthermore, that frog's arse had no right to be there. He was nothing but a cowherd's son come to royalty by conspirings and devisings. Still, he was king. "No, Sire. Falim's wife has given birth to a girl. She has . . ." And then she remembered the wisewoman's words. "She has been named Deirdre."

"Deirdre, the raging one." The king frowned. "Pity she's a girl. Cathbad, because I'm in a jovial temper, cast her horoscope. Tell us what will become of Deirdre."

The Druid rubbed his hands, and from nowhere there materialized a set of runes, flat stones with magical carvings on one side. He threw these to the floor, then got down on his knees and looked on them.

A low murmur from the soldiers rose through the hall.

The Druid raised his hands toward the ceiling.

The king hit his gong, and suddenly all was silent except for the cracking of the fire, and the voice, like a reed pipe, of the Druid.

"Beauty she will have. Much beauty. Beauty to take away a man's breath. More than any other woman in Erinn." He waved his arm so the white fabric of the bell sleeves glided over the stones. "A chieftain. A young chieftain, with hair black as a raven's wing. With lips red as the blood of a freshly killed bull. A chieftain with the beauty of a stallion. Such she will woo, and win. And there will be many clashings of swords, and the crunchings of leg bones of men under the heels of other men. And there will be the shrill, terrible cry of wounded horses in battle. And their bleeding will redden the earth. And I hear the cries of mothers who give up their firstborn to the fires because the corn will not take seed in the earth. Death and Destruction and Ruin shall come to all of Ulster because of her beauty."

Immediately a cry went up among the warriors. "Death! Death! Put the child to death. The lives of many for the life of one. Death to the child."

Conor thought of his own wife, Lieve. He thought of the way her breath rasped at night, and the way her cave scraped at his root when he lay on her. He had to smear animal tallow on his root. A woman grew dry with age. A man needed. A king . . . especially a king, needed a young woman to keep him young. If a king had a beautiful wife . . .

He slammed the gong with his rod. "Quiet!" he shouted, but even the gong was not enough to silence his men. "Death!" they shouted. "Death!" And their voices rose out through the chimney holes, out like smoke to the clouds, out to the ravens and beyond.

PART II
Deirdre

CHAPTER
5

The seasons of the moon passed. Snow fell and the Druids supervised the sacrifice of the bulls at Nuadhullig, when the all-healing mistletoe was cut with a golden sickle from the crotch of the oak trees. Abran followed, with the budding of trees, and the oxen's pulling the plough in the direction that the sun turned, and Bael-Tinne once again announced the rising of Bael to his point in the summer sky, and it was time to put out the fires and rekindle them according to the ritual from the high hill at Tara. La Lughnasa followed, the anniversary of the moon at the end of summer, and the feast of women when female dancers wearing the red cloth, which was forbidden to them at other times of the year, alternated in the circle with men dancers wearing the white cloth. And together they danced. They danced in the direction of the moon, from right to left in the fairy rings in the grass outside Emain. They danced till the men and women fell together in a frenzy, and the red dancers wearing the cloth of the moon blood were impregnated by the white dancers. Samhain followed, the anniversary of the sun, when the corn was harvested and the straw men who had stood guard over the corn, with dead crows hung at their belts to scare away others, were burned along with the corn husks. And the smoke of burned men rising across the fields came and went twenty times.

CHAPTER 6

In a secluded area around Loughadalla, the lake of two swans, a few hours' ride in the direction of the North Star from Emain, a young man rode through the forest. As was fitting to a man who had sat on horseback before he had learned to walk, he rode with an easy form, as though he were part of the stallion itself, an extension of the great shoulders, withers, and neck, rather than something apart from it.

His name was Naisha, and he had the powerful hands and arms and legs of a man who had been raised to be a warrior. His black hair, which was as thick as the horse's mane, flew back from his face as he rode. The horse's name was Sdoirm, which meant storm.

Naisha was the only son of Usna, one of the chieftains of King Conor. The family of Usna had for generations bred the finest horses in all of Ulster. At the end of each summer, at Lughnasa, the anniversary of the moon, just before harvests were taken in, horse races were held at Emain. The winner of the races could choose a mare and a stallion from among each of the competitors' horses, including the king's. Sdoirm had never been beaten.

The races had begun before Erinn was divided into four kingships of Munster, Leinster, Connacht, and Ulster, when Lugh the Good, descendant of the giant Finn and of Bael, the sun god, was king of all Erinn. Bards strummed their harps and sang of the tales of ancestors. They told of how Lugh had fought four battles, one in Ulster, one each in Connacht, in Leinster, and in Munster. They sang of how Lugh had fought and overcome the Firbolg kings, Gend, Sengand, Morc, and Conann, who had invaded Erinn from the North Seas. But the Firbolgs had an evil magician, Miled, and he sent a plague that killed all the descendants of Lugh except for Dalny, a girl child. Deprived of their king, the clan of Lugh again fell under the power of the Firbolg.

Dalny came under the protection of Aengus, god of love, who sent her to secret fosterage as a slave girl in Dun Severick, the farthest, most northern point of Erinn. Here Dalny gave birth to Etain, a girl of such beauty, with hair black as cat's fur and eyes blue as pools, that Miled learned of her parentage.

Miled disguised himself as a milkmaid and poisoned the milk that Etain drank and she died. Aengus, God of Love, unable to release Etain completely from the spell of Miled, turned Etain into a butterfly. He made a sunny bower for her, planted honey-laden flowers around it, and for seven years she lived thus.

Her mother, unaware of her daughter living close to her as a butterfly, died of a broken heart, and Etain's father remarried with a woman named Aeda. Aengus sent a wind and blew Etain through a window back into Aeda's cup of wine just as Aeda was about to drink from it, and Etain regrew in Aeda's womb. Etain had been the ancestral grandmother of the ancestors of the great-grandmother of Naisha's family at a time before time was kept.

Naisha passed in front of a low hill where a stream ran down. He had never been in this place before. The trees rose high above, making a ceiling with their branches. In this place the moss covered the rocks so they looked like green pillows. Sporadically in the green moss stood small red flowers, so that it looked as though the moss had been pricked with a pin and was bleeding. The sun didn't shine brightly here, but flitted from place to place in dreamy, muted streams as the breeze

rustled the oak leaves. Where the thin shafts of sun touched
the moss, a red flower stood.

The woods were hushed except for the soft sound of the
stallion's hooves on the forest floor, and the metal of his bridle
as he tossed his head. In front, Naisha saw a moss-covered
stump. Something stuck out of the stump, and he dismounted
to look at it. It was a split hoof and a leg, the lower leg of a
deer. The deer, running from a predator, must have caught its
leg in the stump. Foxes and wolves had taken the rest, and the
moss and new tree growth had absorbed the bones, all except
this leg. He pushed at it with his hand, but it was solid as a
tree itself.

Then Naisha heard something . . . a whistling, a slender,
wavering whistle, like a fine thread of light coming through
the trees—a human whistle. Naisha moved in the direction of
the sound, following the stream. Up ahead he saw a flash of
silver. The whistling stopped, then started again. Naisha
crouched and quietly moved forward.

A young woman stood at the stream's edge. Was it she who
had whistled? He remembered a saying he had heard when he
was just a boy: *A woman who whistles and a hen that crows are
the unluckiest things under the sun.*

The woman held a clear comb of silver in her hand; the
comb was adorned with gold. She bent over and set a silver
washbasin on the ground. Molded around the edge of the
basin were four golden swans. The rest of the rim was adorned
with jewels, emeralds, rubies, and stones he had never seen. A
bright mantle waved around her, and beneath was another
robe ornamented with silver fringes. Her face was turned from
him in the direction of the stream, but as she stood he saw
that her outer mantle was clasped over her left breast with a
golden brooch. She wore an overtunic with a long hood that
covered her head. The tunic was glossy with green silk and

embroidered with the red gold of Erinn, and the gold and green flashed against the sun.

Then a hawk or owl dropped from the sky somewhere and struck a rabbit, which screamed out like a child along the riverbank, and the woman stopped whistling and turned her head.

Naisha had never seen anything so splendid. It wasn't that she was beautiful. The kingdoms of Erinn were filled with beautiful women, and he'd had his share of them. But he'd never seen anything so exquisite. Her face was fierce, her head thrown back in a proud, arrogant pose, and her back was erect. Peeking from beneath her hood were two tresses of fiery hair. Each tress had been plaited into four strands, and at the end of each strand was a little ball of gold. She tossed her head, lifted off her hood and reached her fingers to her hair, untied the little balls, and began unbraiding the plaits. Her hair tumbled down her shoulders like a burning bush rolling down a hillside.

Her eyes were amber, like two small suns in her face, her lips crimson as the yewberry, and each of her cheeks was bright as the foxglove. Very high and white were her shoulders. White as the foam of a wave was her long, slender neck, but her wrists, hands, and forearms were tanned and strong like polished oak.

She wore a sword girdled round her cloak, an old, beaten gray saber like one a lame warrior would wear. She ungirdled it and laid it down beside the silver. She bent and unlaced her sandals, so the curve of her thigh showed under her cloak. White as a dove's wing were her feet. Then she pulled off first one robe, then another, so she was naked in front of him, her breasts hidden only by the fire of her hair.

Then a small breeze came and lifted the strands from her right breast, exposing a nipple that looked like a pale raspberry. Naisha could taste the fruit of her, like sunlight on his tongue. Then the breeze calmed and the nipple lay covered again.

Oh, but she was stunning. She was fierce and soft. She was the eagle's fire and the dove's milk and he sent a silent command to the breeze to blow again. "Blow," he whispered, "blow," and his lips came together and he blew gently, but then sucked in his breath as she lifted her splendid arms to her neck and threw the fiery red hair off her shoulders. There was something on her left breast . . . a—

"Rawwwkk. Raaawwwk! Frog's arse. Boneyard. Boneyard!"
Naisha's hand reached instantly for his sword.

"Rawwwkk. Frog's arse. Cut your tongue out. Tongue out!"
Naisha looked for the rough-throated speaker but all he could see was a raven sitting on a branch. And then the woman started to whistle again and all Naisha's attention went to her. *A hen that crows and a woman that whistles* . . . but the melody lifted his mind from all except the sound and the look of her. She turned her back to him. Her buttocks were taut as a bow and as she moved he could see the tightening of the muscles under the pearl-white skin.

She stepped into the water and stopped whistling. He saw her back quiver from the shock of the cold water. She went in slowly, first to her knees, then her thighs were absorbed in the sparkling water. She reached out her hands and plunged in to her neck, her hair streaming out like red lily pads on the water behind her.

"Raaawwk. Bury your bones! Hen yard. Hen yard!"
Naisha had heard of parrots from far-off places, of brightly colored birds who could speak the words of men. But he had never heard of a crow talking. Was this a magic woman who now swam in the stream, bobbing her head as though she were a mermaid? A Druidess who could teach speech to animals? Yet she had not worn the white cloak of a Druid, but rather the satins and blue silks of a royal personage.

The woman dived, disappearing under the river's surface. The sun shone on the water so it glistened, sometimes silver, sometimes emerald, sometimes gold, sometimes white as the woman's skin itself. The water spread in crested circles from where she had dived, large, easy circles, as though someone had cast in a stone. She surfaced. Then dived in again.

Naisha walked out to where her clothes lay. The raven eyed him with black eyes, shiny like apple seeds.

"*Rawwwk. Rawwwk. Bury your bones. Frog's arse.*" And he returned to grooming his black wing with an even blacker beak.

Just as Naisha reached out to touch her clothes on the ground, the woman's head surfaced.

"Get away!" she shouted. The wetness had darkened her hair, and it lay flat against her skull now. Drops of water glistened on her forehead and her nose and on her shoulders and then on her breasts and waist. She emerged quickly, her anger pushing the water so it rose ahead of her in waves, as when a boat moved through the water. She had been splendid as she stepped out of her clothes earlier. Now as she stepped out of the water, she was resplendent as a sea goddess. The beads of water on her skin glistened under the sun, breaking its rays like a thousand prisms. On her shoulder hung a rainbow and another between her thighs.

"Give me those," she said, grabbing at her clothes in his hand.

"Who are you?"

"Give me my clothes!" A drop of water fell from a strand of her hair, traveled down her right breast to her nipple, where it hung like a pearl.

She reached for her sword, but Naisha put his foot on it.

"Tell me your name. I'll even dry your back with your cloak."

She reached to the ground, picked up a handful of pebbles,

and threw them at him, temporarily blinding him. Then she grabbed a large flat stone and hurled it so that he had to step sideways. She rushed to her things, picking up her sword and dagger.

He laughed at her. "All I asked was who you are." He sidestepped her jab, but she was quick and caught his upper arm, drawing blood.

In one hand he held her cloak. With the other he reached for his sword. "So you want to fight! I'll find out who you are soon enough. If you won't tell me your name peacefully, then you'll do it at the point of my sword."

She deflected his blow and thrust at his belly. He had no shield and was obliged to leap back. She lunged up with a head cut and when he parried, she lunged again at his belly. Whoever she was, she had been well taught. She didn't waste a movement. He tried to knock the saber from her hand with hard blows, but she had a powerful, quick arm. The swords struck at each other, metal haranguing metal, again and again, clangings sounding above the stream and the forest, and the commentaries of the raven. *"Rawwk. Cut your tongue out. Cut your tongue out. Frog's arse in fly time."*

Then he sidestepped a lunge and slammed his sword against hers with both hands as she followed through. He felt the jarring of metal on metal right up through his shoulder. The impact knocked her to one knee, and spinning around, he pushed her shoulder with his foot, so she tumbled. He threw himself on top of her. She bucked like a horse, managed to get a bare foot under his chin and kick him off.

Now she leapt on top of him, and he saw the dangerous flash of sun in her dagger blade. She jabbed for his throat. He jerked his neck out of the way, grabbed for her wrist. Missed. Grabbed a second time. Caught it. Once he had grabbed the rear foot of a yearling colt. The fetlock had been thin, no bigger around than a child's arm, but he had felt the force of the kick throughout his body. The lean forcefulness of this woman was like that. She jerked back the knife, accidentally cutting her own shoulder, and when she ripped it back the dagger tip caught his chin. He grabbed her knife-wielding arm with both hands and roughly jerked it down, making her somersault over him. Now she was under him and, straddling her, he pressed his knees onto her shoulders. Her left hand still held the dagger. He tried to wrench it from her but both sides were sharpened and he cut his thumb. He lifted her arm and hit it down on the ground so the knife flew from her hand. She threw her body up against his, but now he had her.

Her breasts and face glistened with wetness, but it was no longer the wetness of the river that shimmered on her skin, it was the sweat of struggle. Her body smelled warm, like the forest when the sun came out after a rain.

Her breasts heaved under his buttocks, like the sides of a horse after a race. The shimmering, pale hollow at the base of her throat throbbed.

Once he had caught a butterfly in his hands. He remembered the strange movement, the frenzied wings against his clutching fingers, alternating with moments of tremulous peace in the soft center of his palm. A furious surge, then quiet. In the hollow of her throat the woman's pulse beat under her confining skin in that same way.

"Who are you, woman, that you make Naisha, chieftain of Ulster, breathe as though he'd fought with a man?"

"I'll have no frog's arse ask me what I don't care to answer."

"A woman who looks like a goddess talking like the crow! Did you teach him to talk, or did he teach you?"

"Let me up!" She pushed at him with her chest and tried to bite his wrists.

"There's no use to fight. You're capable enough as a swordsman, but without it . . . See, my hand is twice the size of yours. Forearms too. I'll hold you here till you tell me your name."

"You'll kill me before I tell you anything!"

"It would be a shame to kill someone so lovely simply because she didn't tell me her name."

"Ask the wind! Ask the raven!" Her chest heaved and her amber eyes sparked with green. "They'll tell you before I will."

"A man has ways of making a woman talk."

"Rawwwk." The raven flew over, his wingprint shadowing her face.

"Bugger a frog's arse, if you care to know."

He slapped her. "I'm chieftain of Ulster. No one speaks to me like that!"

But her freed hand flew at his face, slapping and scratching till he pinned it again. The green-brown eyes were almost yellow. For a moment he thought he recognized the anger from somewhere. And there was something familiar about her defiant chin.

"Hit me again." She turned the other cheek. "Hit me. Hit me again. Hit me a thousand times. Hit me until the blood flows from my face . . . from the very bones. I still won't tell you."

A red handprint marked her right cheek. He had spent all his life training horses. During that time he'd learned he could never overcome a horse with brutality.

He brushed his lips against her neck. Strands of hair were wet and cool but her skin was warm and moist. He nuzzled against her ear. "Who are you?" he whispered. "Who are you?" he whispered again, brushing his lips back and forth across her ear.

The feel of his breath so close stunned her. Fight! Fight! She could fight anybody. MacFith had told her she was the best swordsman he'd ever seen. She'd knocked his sword from his hands a thousand times. But this breathing, "Who are you? Who are you?" Aya had a seashell, a large conch shell, and sometimes she held it to her ear. "Listen," she would say, "listen to the sea." "Who are you? Who are you?" The slow sound of his breath rose and fell in her ear like the sound in a seashell, like the sound of the wind in the leaves.

She struggled under him, trying to push away his face with hers, but the gentle whispering, the strange, persistent touch of his lips at her ear and neck, brought tinglings in the small of her back as though a butterfly were captured and fluttering its wings there. His lips brought butterflies to other places, too, places where she'd never felt such things. "Who are you?" he whispered.

His lips traveled from her ear along the line of her chin. Warm lips. She turned her head away, but the butterfly wings were still quivering, and she turned her face toward his. His breath was soft, as though he'd just eaten an apple. He smelled of horses and leather. His grip on her wrists lessened, but she didn't fight him. His lips were near hers, coming nearer and nearer, and her insides fluttered like a netted bird. She opened her mouth, "My name is—"

"Ceantine!" A voice called in the forest. A man's voice. It came again. "Oh, Head of Fire. Ceantine. Where are you?"

The young woman's shoulders stiffened and her eyes opened in panic. Naisha could see the whites above the amber irises. "Let me up!" This time there was no anger in her words, just pleading. "Please!" She struggled.

"Ceantine! This is your king. And he doesn't like games of hide and seek."

"The king!" Naisha looked at the forest in disbelief. Then at the young woman's face. He had heard that the king had—

"Let me up. Please! He'll kill us."

The amber eyes glimmered with a strange quality, like the

last embers in a fire when doused with water. "Please! He'll kill Aya and MacFith."

Naisha lifted himself off her and she leapt to her feet, grabbed her clothes to her breast, dropped a sandal, bent in a flurry to pick it up, and, dragging her robes across the ground, ran toward the forest.

At its edge she spun around and looked at him. "Leave," she said. "Please. He'll kill us." And the last Naisha saw of her was the ivory curve of her buttock, disappearing like a moon in the forest with the raven following.

"Ceantine. Head of Fire!" Naisha heard the thrashing of branches now. "Come to your king!"

Something flashed on the ground as Naisha turned to where the voice came from: the sun reflected in the polished metal of the bowl. And there on the ground was the dagger. Naisha picked them up. There was blood on the blade tip. His blood and her blood mingled on the dagger.

CHAPTER
7

She ran with the speed of a messenger through the forest. Aya had taught her that whenever she ran she should repeat the same words over and over again to give her rhythm and speed. That was the way they trained women in Connacht. "Run fast. Run fast," she would repeat as she took her run each day. "Run fast." Each word in her mind echoed with each footfall. But now as she ran different words echoed, in a different voice. *Who are you? Who are you?* She had not been afraid of the man's sword. He had beaten her only by trickery. MacFith had taught her well. But the weight of the man's body pressing against hers. His breath so near she could taste the apples on it. That had frightened her. And hair so black, and the beard. She had never seen hair like that. MacFith had no hair. The only place he had hair was growing out of his ears. His head was so shiny and polished, like the top of a stone, and when the sun shone and he turned his head in certain directions you could see the shadow of his ear on his head. And the king! The king!

She had to get dressed, but her shoulder was bleeding. She grabbed a fistful of leaves and wiped away the blood, then threw the leaves to the ground. Slowly she slipped into her robes. When he visited, the king brought her these clothes which he said were robes for a queen. He wanted to see her wear them. She looked behind her, but no one was following, at least not that she could see. The king would kill her, and Aya and MacFith, too, if he found out. She trudged slowly in the direction of the crannog.

The crannog was the only home she'd ever known. It was on the shore of Loughadalla, the lake of two swans. The crannog itself was built on a manmade island just at the edge of the lake. The sides of the crannog were edged with sharp willow poles and the island was separated from the mainland by a trench of water, about as wide as she was tall. At night MacFith, when he wasn't off in the forest getting drunk, would herd the dozen sheep, six cows, and five goats across the footbridge to the crannog, where they would be locked in for the night. The crannog wasn't large. There was a hut on it, and a bathhouse where the stones were heated, and a stable. But it was safe. It had kept out the wolves and the bears and the fairies and leprechauns that Aya said were always up to mischief.

There were the king's chariot and his two white horses tied to a pole. Deirdre carried the soft leather sandals called pampooties, as though they were a burden. Her bare feet made a hollow slapping sound on the wooden poles that led across the trench to the crannog. She felt the roughness under her feet, and for a moment thought she should have put her pampooties on. The last time she had crossed the walkway in bare feet, she had gotten slivers, and Aya, complaining all the while, had to dig them out with a bone needle and a dagger. "I should be leaving them in your feet, I should. Any woman what doesn't know better than to be hoofing it bare-toeseyed across them poles don't deserve nothing but to have *slivers* in her feet." But Aya had taken them all out, and afterward had washed Deirdre's feet with cool mint tea, and then rubbed them with lanolin. If she got slivers this time, Deirdre could use it as an excuse not to have to walk with the king.

"In the name of the gods, where have you been?" Lewara said. "And why aren't your shoes on? You're not a slave girl." Lewara wore a green scarf tied under her chin and her forehead furled down so that her gray eyebrows almost covered her eyes.

"I've been . . . I've been wrestling with young men."

Lewara clutched her hands to her heart. *"What?"*

"Washing. Like you told me to."

Lewara, lifting her eyebrows looked at Deirdre. "What's this—your wrestling with young men?"

"I was teasing. You have no sense of laughter."

"There's no laughter in the king killing you and me."

Deirdre sighed. Lewara scowled. "Where is that lazy slave? We have to comb your hair for the king. And put on your jewels. The king brings you gowns and bracelets and brooches and you shun them."

"Do you know how I feel about the king's gifts? Do you know how lovely the sundew plant looks, with its colors? With the white flowers and the red hairs that grow from the green leaves? How when the sun shines, that droplet of fluid that grows on the tips of the hairs looks like silver dew left from the morning? And the red hairs give the droplets a pink sheen, and butterflies settle on the leaves thinking they might have a drink? But the pink-silver dew is fatal. It's sticky, and the more the butterfly struggles to fly, the more it sticks to the plant. The hairs close around the butterfly and suffocate it. I feel like a butterfly when I'm with the king. His gifts are like the leaves of the sundew."

"Nonsense. You're talking silliness now. The king will be angry when he doesn't find you by the river. Aya! Where is she? Good for nothing. I thought you'd gone clear across the mountains to bathe in the sea. I told you to hurry." Lewara pushed Deirdre's shoulder, the sore one.

Deirdre pulled away. "Why must I always hurry when the king comes?"

"Because he's the king."

"I don't like the king."

"Nonsense. You don't know him, is all. And I thought you bathed. Look at your hands. They're filthy. Like a scullion's brat. What is that under your fingernails? Blood! Have you finally—"

"Nothing!" Deirdre pulled back her hands. "Nothing. I was picking flowers. Roses. I pricked my fingers on the thorns."

"Will you never grow up? Picking flowers and rubbing your hands in the dirt like a child! And why is it that the moon blood doesn't flow?" Lewara's voice was getting louder. The way it often went before she started to rock. "Oh, come on! No time to talk now. You can't meet the king looking the way you do. You're going to be queen. Isn't it time you started acting so, instead of running in the hills like a wild thing?"

"I don't want to be queen."

"Nonsense! Think of what it will mean."

"What will it mean—being queen?"

"You'll give birth to the king's son. And everywhere you walk, people will part to let you pass. And behind you they will say, 'There goes Ceantine, mother of the king's son.' "

"I don't want to be mother of the king's son. He touches me, Lewara."

"He has that right. As sovereign he can touch you or me or any woman in Ulster."

"But I don't like the way he touches me."

"He won't touch you for long. After he's slept with you awhile, he'll tire of you and find a concubine."

"When he pulls me onto his knees, he lifts my skirts. And when I press my thighs together, he pinches me."

"That's the way with men. That's the way they show affection."

"I hate him. I want to spit in his face."

"I won't have you saying such things. The king loves you. He's going to talk to Cathbad about a potion for you. As soon as the moon blood comes you'll be his queen."

"I won't be his queen. I don't want any part of his love. I
don't want anybody to love me. I hate him. I can't stand it
when he touches me"—and she twisted up her face— "with
his twisted yellow fingers." As she spoke, Deirdre looked inadvertently at Lewara's hands.

"Yes, child. My fingers are twisted too. You know why
they're gnarled like tree roots? Because of you. I worked them
to the bone for you. Hewing wood and hauling water. I'm
supposed to be a wisewoman." Lewara's voice was changing,
growing higher and thinner, and faster, the way it did before
she started to rock. "I'm supposed to mix herbs and grind
leaves for medicine teas and salves and ointments. I'm supposed to help women with their birthings. And yet what do I
do? I'm sent out here onto this tiny island . . . in the middle
of nowhere with a lazy slave who would copulate with the
goose if she could, and a half-wit, half man who talks of nothing but the men he's driven through with his sword. And I'm
sent out here with a maiden who refuses to become a woman.

"Sent out . . . here . . . because of a prophecy, so that
you'd stay a virgin for the king. *You* dip your fingers in and out
of cold water. *You* lift the heavy branches for the fires. *You* dip
and you lift and weave, for more harvests than I can remember"—she grabbed Deirdre's hand— "and see how twisted
your pretty fingers grow. The least you could do is be thankful
to me. I can't leave this place until you're married to the
king."

"I *am* thankful . . . I . . . It's the king. I can't help it.
Oh, don't you understand?"

"I understand. I'll tell you what I understand. When you
were born, there was a prophecy. I understand that the
soldiers wanted to kill you. Right there and then. 'Throw the
child to the swine troughs to be destroyed. Kill her! Death!
Death!' they shouted again and again. 'One life for the lives of
many!' But the king, in the goodness of his heart, saved your

life. He said that he would marry you when you became of age. I understand that in return for saving your life, you've turned into an ingrate. A spoiled, headstrong, wild girl. You're ungrateful to the king and ungrateful to me."

"I'm not ungrate—"

"I've spent the best years of my life being mother to you. Me, Lewara, who could have been the mother of a king. And when I couldn't be mother of a king, I studied to be a wise-woman. Then that was taken away from me. And now I could be the mother of a queen, but you refuse to give me that.

"I should have known you were going to be trouble. I should have known when I saw your red hair. I should have killed you then. I held your birth dagger in my hand. You should've died with your mother. But I felt sorry for you. Just like the king felt sorry for you. Now I'm tired of feeling sorry for you.

"It's ill luck to have a maiden past eighteen harvests. Too much snow will fall from the sky. And the cows begin to drop their calves before they come to term in their bellies. A woman has to be forced, or else the gods grow angry.

"I'm tired of caring for one so ungrateful as you. Either the king forces you and marries you and you have children, or he has you killed. I'm tired and old. I'm tired of living on this crannog with a girl who does only what she wants without regard for reason. I'm tired of being mother to a child that isn't mine. I want to go back to Emain. It's about time you gave me back some of what I've given to you after the years here on this . . . this *crannog.* You owe me that much!"

"I won't marry the king. I hate him. I hate it when he's near me."

"It is treason to speak so."

"I don't care! I'd rather die than marry the king."

"You're not to say those things!"

"When I'm near him I want to throw up! I won't marry the king."

"You will!"

"I will not!"

"You will learn to do what is expected of you. The king will force you, and I will leave this place."

"I'll die first!"

"I won't have you talking like that!"

"I'll talk any way I wish. I hate him. I hate it when he touches me. He touches me. Do you hear? I hate him."

"He'll hear you and have us all put to death!"

"I don't care! I hate—"

"Stop!"

"I hate him and I hate you—"

Lewara slapped her. Deirdre's face stung from it, but it was Lewara who was crying. "I have spent twenty years looking after you. You were two days old when he sent us here. You, me, MacFith, and that slave. All of us loaded into a cart. I want to go home. I want to go back to Emain."

Deirdre spun on her heel and ran into the hut.

CHAPTER
8

Naisha, carrying the washbowl and dagger into the forest, looked for the young woman. But she had disappeared. Through the woods he heard the king's voice. "Ceantine. Enough of your silly games. I order you to come." Three hills stood in the distance, the hills of the Three Sisters. The sun was now over the head of the second sister, and Naisha thought of Branwen. It was time for him to meet her, but instead he continued to look for the young woman, to track her, looking for footsteps on the moss, or bent grass.

He searched as though looking for a lost child, looking behind logs and under ferns, and even up in the trees—and he saw a flash of green cloak! His heart leapt. There she was, he thought; but it was only the breeze. And he continued walking. He wanted to call out her name . . . Ceantine. Head of Fire. But he didn't dare. Then he saw a pile of fresh leaves thrown to the ground, and on the leaves, he saw blood.

The river bent backward into an elbow. He could hear the splashing sound as it ran, and he approached carefully. In the river bend he saw the thatched roof-tip of a house built on a crannog.

Often farmers whose lands bordered lakes or rivers built crannogs, since crannogs afforded better protection than simple stone-walled farms. Crannogs were made by digging a large canal or trench beside a river or lake. A circular mound would be left in the middle which then would be surrounded with pointed poles. The poles would be interwoven with willow branches, making a small fortress.

This crannog had a walkway, and standing at the end of the walkway, Naisha saw the king's white stallions and his red-gold-and-purple chariot, emblazoned with a gold lion which was his coat of arms.

Naisha returned to where his horse was tied and the stallion greeted his master with a low, murmuring neigh. Naisha stroked the animal's proud high neck. "Oh, Sdoirm. If only you'd seen her." The horse stamped a hoof against the ground, his shoe striking a spark from a stone. Everything about the animal told of his breeding: The hard muscles that stretched and relaxed beneath the fine black skin, which looked as smooth as satin; the hot-blooded veins that carried the finest blood in Erinn; the sculpted, proud head of the horse; the sparkling, courageous eyes; and the crimson nostrils. *Her head, so arrogant when she demanded her clothes back, and the fine skin of her nostrils and her breasts heaving under him.*

The stallion smelled the silver bowl, snorted loudly, then bit the head of a golden swan. Naisha pulled the bowl away and the stallion pushed his master's chest with his powerful, strong head, nearly knocking him over. He pawed the ground again.

"Watch my feet," Naisha scolded, and the stallion nipped at his master's sleeve.

Who was she? Naisha wondered. He pulled the dagger from his tunic. Obviously she was of high parentage, for her dagger was silver with gold lacy filigree on the handle, ornamented with red and green gem stones. The horse snorted again. Ceantine, the king had called her. He had felt her heart throbbing under him. And now his armpits were wet with wanting her. She was the king's woman. Branwen was the king's woman. He, Naisha, was chieftain of Ulster. Fergus, his uncle, had been king of Ulster. Conor had no blood tie to Fergus. Conor had no blood tie to the kingship.

Naisha wiped the dagger blade on his leather leggings and

tucked it into his own belt. Already the sun had crossed to the
middle of the three hills in the distance. The Three Sisters,
they were called. The three daughters of King Nemed, turned
to earth by their jealous stepmother. Naisha was supposed to
have met Branwen when the sun was on the second head. He
put the silver bowl in the saddlebag, loosened the stallion's
reins, and, with a leap, was on its back.

The stallion bolted the moment he felt his master's weight.
Naisha gave the animal its head, pressing his thighs against
the animal's withers. The stallion's stride quickened and
lengthened. The head no longer rose high, but low so that as it
ran, its front hooves nearly struck the nostrils. The forest
cleared and the stallion raced faster. The wind struck Naisha's
eyes so that he saw the green countryside as a blur. He remembered the yellow fire of her eyes.

CHAPTER
9

"Child, child! What is it, lamb?" Aya reached out her arms to Deirdre, who buried her face in the slave's pillowy chest. Aya kissed the top of her head.

"Nothing."

"You ain't telling Aya the truth. Aya might just be a slave about this wet, slimy place what ain't fitting for nothing but frogs, but Aya knows when something's the matter. Tell me, child."

"Why aren't you my foster mother? I don't . . ." Deirdre shrugged.

"Why I ain't indeed. I ain't got no say over that. She has." Aya gave a nod in the direction of the outside.

"I hate the king. I hate Lewara too."

"What I been telling you all along. The king, he ain't nothing but a frog's arse, is what he is. And Lewara—sour old woman. Fine thing we is. You, me, Lewara, and MacFith. The blind leading the cripple. With the king for company."

"She said that it's because of me that her hands are gnarled."

"Ain't you seen the king? Or ain't he seen you?"

Deirdre shook her head.

"He'll be in a blue stew when he can't find you."

"I hate him!" Deirdre looked at her hands. "Lewara says I made her hands twisted and wrinkled. That it was because of me." Deirdre started to cry.

"Child! Stop being silly. It's old age what cripples fingers. Look! Me hands. Lewara's and MacFifth's, what he's got left of 'em. All our hands. Look at them. Brown with spots the likes of chicken livers. All of them, and twisty like a pig's tail. You the cause of nothing but joy in this here slime pit. Oh, someday. Someday, Aya's going to . . ." She clenched her fists together, then sighed and looked at Deirdre. "Aie. I'm an old woman. She can't do me no more harm than what's been done. But you. You're the likes of a rose at first blooming. And she wants you to be courting the king. Like giving a flower to a frog to stick his arse to." Aya sighed. "Aie, child, once me skin was loverly. The likes of yours. Once I was running singing through the hills. Whistling, the same as you do." Aya clapped her hands together. "But every moon we gets older. See here how me veins rise. Blue the likes of worms under me skin. Death starts the day we's born. Same happens with all of us. Men, women, kings, and dogs. Time takes us all." Aya tilted up Deirdre's chin. "Even you, my pretty."

"Lewara says it's ill luck for me not to have the moon blood. She says that the cows—"

"Lewara!" Aya spit. "You listen to Aya. Listen to Aya who loves you." Aya brushed the hair back from Deirdre's face. "Not to Lewara, who ain't got a speck of love nowhere in her whole sour, shriveled body.

"In Connacht where I was birthed, ain't no king what's king, but a queen. I seen her once. Aie! She's . . . loverly. She's the most beautiful woman I ever seen, excepting for the likes of you who's loverlier than all the flowers in Erinn. Child, sometimes when I looks on your face, you make the tears come to me eyes. No, don't look away, child. Don't ever be timid about loverliness. Loverliness is a gift of the gods. Ain't you ever be shy about it. Well, excepting for you, Maeve's the most beautifullest woman what I saw. Tall she is. Almost as tall as a mountain. Almost as tall as you. As strong as most any man. I seen her in a chariot once. Holding four horses—the color of the sun—what most men couldn't hold. A dazzling

cloth of gold on her, but one breast bared. And a bow at her
ear. A warrior queen, who won't be taking a man to her bed
less'n he can be beating her at swords. And I heard she kills
plenty in each fight. Each year her consort, is what he's called,
has to fight other men. And the winner of that contest is to be
her mate for the year, providing that he is strong enough to
pin her arms above her head, and love her.

"Her armies! Ain't no army can beat them. King Conor's!"
Aya spit out the words like bitters. "That frog's arse that calls
hisself a king. Queen Maeve's army is men *and* women. When
the girls takes nine harvests, they's taken along with the boys
into the camps. There the girls is showed running, and dancing, and gymnastics and swords, and bowing, and javelins. The
muscles of the girls gets hard like that of the men. Not big and
round, but strong. The girls with all that running and jumping
and hurling don't get the moon blood. And I'll tell you, we
ain't hearing none of this nonsense about cows losing their
calves, and the corn freezing on the stalks. That's Cathbad's
and King Conor's mumbo-jumbo."

"Lewara says if the moon blood doesn't start, the king will
have me killed. You and MacFith too!"

"Know why she always talks about killing and death? 'Cause
she's dead. She's a living dead. Dead from the time I knowed
her, which is almost as long as I knowed you. There's the dead
that's dead. And the dead that's dead will be living in the land
of Tir-na-n'Og, the place of everlasting youth. And the dead
that's dead knows how to be having a good time, because in
Tir-na-n'Og, there ain't nothing allowed excepting for loving
and singing and dancing. And then there's the dead that's
living. And Lewara. She'll be part of the dead that's living.
Ain't got no love in her. Love for nothing. Not for the shining
stars. Not for the flowers growing in the meadows. Not for the
lambs jumping across the meadows. And none for you.

"And if'n she was to be eaten like that scoundrel MacFith

tells me some peoples is wont to do across the sea, why she would taste sour inside. The likes of apple vinegar. You come now and you be ordering yourself for the king. No king's going to be killing someone what's as pretty as you. We'll keep our secret a while longer. Lewara is rocking more and more these days. She doesn't know and thinks that Aya's too stupid to know nothing. You keep running and leaping and swording with MacFith. The king is dead afeared of forcing a girl who ain't had the moon blood. Girls is the likes of bees. They'll be needing young flowers to make honey. Not shriveled old prunes, even them prunes what goes about calling hisself a king. Let him find a slave girl, the likes of what's in Emain."

CHAPTER
10

"Ouch! Do you have to pull so hard?" Deirdre rubbed at her scalp.

"Do you have to be complaining, always like a complaining thing? How can I be braiding your hair, if I don't pull it? If you'd be hurrying sometimes instead of whistling away like you always does, I wouldna had to braid it wet like it is. Takes time it does, to uglify you. Same as what it does to beautify others." She finished braiding the strands of long red hair and tied them with a leather thong. The braids were thick as Aya's wrist, heavy splendid braids. "Aie, child! What I woulda done with hair lovely such as this!" Aya sighed, twisted the braids around Deirdre's head like a tiara, and fastened them with two bone combs edged with gold. She looked at her handiwork, crossed one arm in front of her waist, and rested her chin on the fist of the other hand. "Hummm. No. You're too pretty, you is." She unbraided the hair so that strands hung down around Deirdre's face.

As Aya talked, Deirdre's mind flitted with a strange unrest. A fever crept into her body, a warmth like the warmth of the man who had covered her nakedness. She remembered the brilliant flash of his teeth as he smiled at her. *Tell me your name. I'll even dry your back.* The tinglings returned like small silent bells being rung in her body.

". . . Can't be leaving too many what's straggly or the sour one'll be beating Aya with a stick, she will. Leaving you pretty enough so as Lewara don't think we fudged you. Yet trying to ugly you so as that frog's arse won't be thinking about . . .

We'll darken here just under the eyes with walnut juice, and I'll give you a rub here with some ivy so as you looks like you got the beginnings of some pimplies what's coming on your face."

"Ouch! That hurts!"

"Won't hurt near as much as what'll happen if'n you marry the—what's this! Here on your shoulder?"

Deirdre pulled away. Lifted her cloak up higher to her neck. "Nothing. It's nothing."

"Don't be telling Aya it's nothing." She pulled Deirdre's robes off her shoulder. "I can see with me own two eyes it's something. What you been doing to yourself, girl? Where you been?"

"I scratched it on a branch as I came home."

"This! You be telling Aya the truth. This ain't no branch cut. And will you be looking at your hands, blood on them. And dirt! Like as you been playing in the dirt the same as you did when you was a wee thing. Making mud cakes you wanted us all to eat. You're worse than MacFith, you is. Tell you to do something, and you comes back with it only half done.

"Give me your bowl so as I can clean you proper. The sour one'll be skinning me living if'n you goes to the king dirty fisted."

"My bowl . . . ?"

"Yes'n your bowl, child. The one the king gave you."

"It's . . . I forgot it . . . Down by the stream. When I heard the king, I came running back here and I left . . ." She looked at the floor. "And I forgot my birth dagger too."

When a woman became pregnant the father of the child went to the metalsmith and asked that a birth dagger be fashioned. Depending on the rank of the mother to whom the child was born, the dagger was fashioned from silver or from iron. The wisewoman would use the birth dagger to sever the newborn from its mother. When the child went into fosterage, the birth dagger went with the child. It was the foster parents who taught the child how to use the dagger. The boys were taught to skin rabbits and deer, and to throw the daggers at targets and to cut an enemy's throat. The girls were taught to use the daggers for cutting wool for weaving, and for chopping parsley for soups, and for digging roots for stews. If the foster parents of the child were of high rank, they often encrusted the dagger handle with precious stones. Deirdre's birth dagger was made of silver, and Conor had brought with him to Loughadalla a pocketful of garnets which he had ordered MacFith to inlay in the handle. To lose a birth dagger was considered ill luck.

Aya grabbed Deirdre's shoulder. "That's what you got cut from, ain't it? A dagger. Telling Aya you . . . this ain't no bramble cut. Who you been fighting with?"

"What are you two doing in here?"

Aya quickly covered Deirdre's shoulder as Lewara walked in.

"What have you done to your shoulder?" Lewara asked.

"I know'd this is the clumsiest child that ever put two feet in front of each other on this here earth. Her falling into the bramble bushes, just like a regular falling thing. Stubbing her toesies on rocks and falling all the time. Ain't old Aya got better things to do than to be fixing up scratches and cuts? You shouldn't be running like a wild thing. Should be thinking about marrying. Like I keeps telling you—"

"Look at her! What have you been doing again? I told you to comb her hair and look at her! She doesn't look like a queen. She looks like a ruffian's woman. Something you'd give birth to."

"That's just what I been saying, I has. Telling her I had to comb her hair. Fix it so she'd be pretty—"

"Stop talking all the time and just do it. Just do it for a change. I want to leave this place. I'm going mad here." She rubbed her hands up either side of her face and pressed the top of her head into her palms.

"Just what I been saying. The king'll marry her and take us away from this slimy place that ain't fit for nothing but snakes and crawly things. That's exactly what I been telling this child. That she's got to quit being a children and marry the king, and wearing them clothes made of silver and gold . . ."

Lewara sat down on the floor of the house and started picking at some of the straw. "Twenty harvests. Me a wisewoman. Nothing but a nursemaid. Like a common slave. Wasted . . . my life. No children. No husband. My learning gone . . ."

". . . dresses what's the color of the sun during the day," said Aya, "and the color of the moon at night. Silks what's the color of the sunrise and the sunset and the evening sky. And you'll have necklaces and broochies of gold and brilliant emeralds what's red, and rubies what's bluer than the sky. I seen Queen Maeve wear them long ago . . ."

"My life . . . My life . . . My son . . ." Lewara held her face in her palms. "My son . . ."

". . . and enamels more colored than robin redbreast what goes tweet-tweeting in the treetops. And a diadem like the sun in her hair. All these things I been telling her. Like how good it'll be when she's queen, and that she's got to hurry and stop being a girl and start being a woman so she can wear dresses the color—"

"Shut up!" Lewara stood up. "Shut up! I'm tired of your talking all the time. Tired!" She grabbed a pot and threw it at Aya. "Voices." Lewara covered her head with her arms. "Voices. All of them talking! Talking! My head! It hurts! My own medicines. I can't even cure my own head. Get out of here! Both of you. Go and find the king! Get out of my sight!"

Aya stood behind Lewara, hunched her shoulders, grew small and shriveled looking like a walnut, and grimaced a sour expression behind Lewara's back as though she'd just bitten into a green apple.

Deirdre had to turn away.

"Get out of here!" screamed Lewara, and she took up a stick and started chasing Aya. "A gamy king. A woman child. A lazy slave. A half man. And my son!" She dropped the stick. "And the voice of my son!" She fell to her knees, covered her head with her arms, and began rocking back and forth. "My son . . . my son."

CHAPTER 11

Deirdre went reluctantly to look for the king. Had it been her own life, she wouldn't have gone at all. But the others . . . they depended on her too. MacFith had told her how the king had put half his kitchen servants to death once, just because the mutton they served him was gristly. Another time he'd ordered his stableboy's hands chopped off because the boy hadn't curried his horse; instead, he'd been smugging with a scullery maid in the straw. Aya, too, had told stories about the frog's arse.

"Rawwwk! Frog's arse. Frog's arse."

"SSSShhhh. Don't you be going saying those things when the king's around." *Did you teach the crow to talk, or did he teach you?*

The raven came close and perched on Deirdre's shoulder. It began to tug at one of the leather thongs that held Deirdre's hair.

"Ouch! Now! If it isn't Aya who's pulling my hair, it's a crow."

"Rawwk."

"Aya was right. I should have left you where I found you. Left you for the foxes to eat. Small thing that you were."

His hair had been the same color as the raven's wing. She had noticed that. When first she lifted her eyes from the water, she thought it was the raven who was flying about, but in a moment she realized he was a man. What right did he have to try and steal her clothes? Chieftain of Ulster, he said he was. Chieftain of Ulster. He knew the king. Would the king know of him? She secretly touched her left wrist with her right fingers, and squeezed it. His touch had been firmer than that. Then lighter. His fingertips hard. Then lighter. She touched herself under her right ear and on her neck, where he had touched her.

"*Rawwk!*"

She lifted the bird from her shoulder, held it in her hand, stroking the ebony feathers. The bird's clawed feet dug sharply into her palms. She and Aya had found the small bird beneath a tree. "Felled clean out of its nest," Aya had said. Aya had wanted to cook him. "Makes a regular tasty stew, it does. Young crow. Put him in a pot—"

"I won't have you putting my pet raven in a stewpot."

" 'Tis the strangest, stupidest thing what I ever hearded in my life long. Pet crow. Dogs is for pets. And cats. And thrushes sometimes. Not crows. Crows, especially when they're young, as this one is, is for eating. With turnpips and onions and a cabbagee. Mmmm, good! And for target practice for boys what's got themselves their first slingshots so as when they get bigger they can shoot straight at Leinstermen. That's what crows is for."

"He isn't a crow. He's a raven." And Deirdre had dug worms and caught flies for him and held them in her fingertips to the beak of the small bird. The raven would fly to Deirdre's hand when she held it out. She named it Duff, which meant black. Then Lewara had taken the raven and forced open its beak and slit its tongue, so the bird would learn to talk. That was many springs ago. Lewara was nicer then. She would walk with Deirdre, put her arms around her shoulders, and touch Deirdre's cheek, and call her my beauty. My young queen. But Lewara had changed.

Aya had said, "You'll not be teaching no crow to talk. As if'n I ain't got enough to do, hoofing around this here slime pit what ain't fit for nothing but rats and crawly things. Now I got to look after a crow what's supposed to be learning to talk. And me with so much to do, soon you'll be burying me bones in the henyard. Then you'll all be sorry. No Aya what's cleaning and cooking and weaving and cleaning. I'll be turned into a frog's arse if'n that crow utters one single solitary word."

The first words the raven learned were *frog's arse*, then *hen yard*. Aya threatened to cut his tongue out, and he repeated that phrase, too, and these three phrases had remained his favorites despite Lewara's attempts with honey-coated apple chunks to dissuade him from saying "frog's arse." Aya threw stones and curses at him. Deirdre fed him chunks of roast chestnut, and boiled apples, acorns, and roasted mutton, and petted him. Lewara had been pleased that she hadn't forgotten all the things that the wisewoman had taught her.

"May the gods save you, Ceantine." The king startled her.

"The gods save you, Sire." She knelt in front of him and kissed his hand. He put his hand on her shoulder, indicating she should stand.

He was a big robust man, with thick gray hair and beard, but plenty of color high in his cheeks. "Why are you never about when I come looking for you?" The king stood with his legs wide apart and his hands on either hip. Behind him Deirdre could see the forest. He would take her in there, he would sit on the fallen tree trunk which stretched across the path. He would sit on the trunk and . . . "I wasn't aware that we would be blessed with your presence, Sire." He would reach for her hand . . .

"I sent you a message with MacFith. . . ."

The king'll be sending you his greetings, luv. The day after four nights, he'll be here hisself to see your prettiness. "MacFith grows . . . forgetful at times. Sometimes he returns from Emain without messages," she lied.

"Next time, I'll send him back without his head."

Deirdre turned away from the king.

"He means no harm, a man who has lived as long as he. His sword arm grows weak. His brain is subject to the same weakness. No one is immune to age, Sire, not—she looked at him a moment—"not even you."

"That's the reason I've come." He took her hand and tucked it under his arm. "Let's walk." Her feet refused to move. She felt the pressure on her hand. "Ceantine! Your king wishes to walk!"

Deirdre hated him. She hated what he was going to do. In her mind she saw herself draw his sword. She saw the sword enter at the point below his throat. She saw the sword tear down his belly and she saw his entrails spill like chicken parts onto the ground.

He led her to the log in the forest, but didn't sit down.

"I bring you gifts from Emain. Bracelets and a torque of gold to go around your splendid neck. Stand here, child, that I may put it on you." He held up a brilliant collar-plate of sculpted gold. It was nearly as large as a plate, decorated with ornate curves, and spirals like bird's claws and circles of snakes eating their own tails.

"I have no need of splendid things. Look around you." Deirdre lifted her hand toward the forest. "Who is to see me in them? The trees? The jackdaws? The ravens? The snails, or the hares?"

"Nonsense. I've come to tell you you will be my queen. Turn around that I may put it on you. It was made for you, Ceantine, by my own goldsmith. See this." He showed her the back of the torque. A horizontal line was drawn with a series of bars.

"This is your name. Ceantine. You have not been taught to read the ogham. And so it is. Only the wisewomen and the Druids are learned with writing. But Cathbad under my or-

ders gave the instructions to the goldsmith. You are the first
queen to have her name thus engraved in the sacred ogham
writing. I am king and this is my wish. Now, turn around."

"It is lovely, Sire. But my name is not Ceantine. My name
is Deirdre."

"Do you forget to whom you speak? I am your king. I will
call you whatever I wish. I do not like the name Deirdre. The
raging one. It was a fine name for the daughter of a charioteer.
But it is an unsuitable name for my queen."

"Deirdre has no wish to be queen. She wasn't raised in a
great hall with dining tables and polished oak and silver gongs
such as Lewara says you have at your hall."

"You will soon grow accustomed to them, just as you will
soon grow accustomed to the feel of a man inside you. In the
last two score years I've slept with two queens and dozens of
concubines and the wives of all my chieftains as I paid them
visits all through Ulster. And during that time my desire has
grown greater with every moon change. I will not be put off
any longer. Now, turn around so that I may give you my
bridegroom's gift."

"But I am not a woman yet! The moon blood has not—"

"I will not be put off any longer. I have spoken with
Cathbad. He knows the ways of women's magic. He says
Lewara grows addle brained. He says it is not normal for a girl
of so many harvests to be so delayed. He returns from the sea
this night. I will send him to you. Enough of women's medicines. He will give you a potion. He will begin the moon blood
so that the first forcing can take place. I will have my bride."

"But, Sire . . ."

"No but Sire! Enough of waiting! Each night I grow older.
Each night my desire grows riper. As with a fruit, too much
ripeness leads to decay. I will not be put off any longer. Now,
come, that I may place this torque on you."

"But . . . just one more harvest."

"And next harvest, you'll say one more harvest again. And the one after that. Just one more again. No. I've had enough of your putting me off. Cathbad is coming!"

"But, Sire!"

"Enough, I say! I grow impatient. I grow impatient with all of you here. Which of the half-wits out here have turned you against me? I'll have them drawn and quartered and their limbs hung in the trees for the birds to pick at. And still I'll have you for my queen. Now, I order you, turn around so that I may place my gift around your neck."

Deirdre turned her back to him. She felt his hands on her shoulders.

"Ah! Nothing like a young queen to rejuvenate a man. Just looking at you, I feel like a young buck again. As if I could leap through the air."

She closed her eyes tightly. She couldn't stand when he touched her. She felt his hands at the back of her neck.

"You'll have to have your hair cut. The belief among my soldiers and their wives is that a redheaded woman spoils the butter making. I want no ill beliefs about my queen. Cathbad will cut your hair and you'll wear a turban as do the dark-skins who live in the direction of the sunrise. Now turn around so that I can see you.

"What a splendid wife I have chosen, and what a splendid gift I have chosen for her. Kneel down in front of me." He touched the gold torque that covered her collarbone, and ran his fingers along the edge. Then his hands began to follow the curve of her breast. He lifted one breast gently with his fingers, then began rubbing her nipple through her clothes. Deirdre's body stiffened. She felt as though the king's fingers were lizards crawling on her body. "Ah, Ceantine, your skin is softer than any I have ever felt."

Deirdre's mind forced the fingers away. She tightened her arms against her sides and dug her nails into her palms. If she could only dig her nails deep enough into the flesh, so that she could feel nothing, nothing but the nails in the flesh. If she pressed the nails into the flesh hard enough sometimes, something happened. Sometimes the shell of her body stood there and she could step out of it, and she could turn her face away from it as the king stroked her. If she pressed the nails hard enough she didn't feel the king's hands travel down her belly, and reach between her legs, his fingers hard and pinching.

His voice softened. "It is always the same with young girls. They have no desire until they have been with the king. First they must be penetrated. Desire comes after. See how my desire grows with just the talking of it? Give me your hand." He pulled her hand around the stiff, hard stump that jutted out. "Feel the stiffening. Youths half my age don't have stiffenings like this. Feel how it weeps for you, wets with anticipation. The laws of the ancients forbid my pleasuring you until the moon blood has come. But I'll send Cathbad to you. Soon you'll feel its strength in you."

If only she could dig her nails into her palms hard enough. She thought of the story Aya had told her. Of how Loughadalla, the lake of two swans, had got its name. Two lovers were pursued by an old king who claimed the young woman as his wife. The young man had hair black as a raven's wing and the woman hair like fire. Two lovers who, at the moment of capture, were turned into swans by Aengus, god of love. They flew up, up, joined by a chain of gold.

The king began rocking. "Yes, yes, yes," again, over and over again he said it, rocking and speaking.

The harder she pressed her nails against her palms . . . she saw herself turning, the feathers white, she saw herself rising, while a feather fell like a single snowflake to the ground.

CHAPTER 12

At the foot of Slieve-nishfinne, the hill of the white fawn, a woman smiled when Naisha rode up. She sat on the ground, her legs pulled up in front of her, as she picked at the grass. Naisha sat on his horse and looked down at her.

She picked up a clover, held it carefully in her fingers, and looked at it. "Four leaves it has, this shamrock. It'll be meaning good luck to me. It has brought you to me. Two moons it is since I've laid eyes on you." She looked at Naisha.

"There was a time when you would leap off your horse before it came to a standstill, and run to my arms."

He dismounted slowly. "Branwen, I saw the stag," he said.

She looked at him askance. "I have not seen you for over two moons, and you'll be talking of stags, as though it was a hunting companion that I was, instead of coming and kissing me."

"It was you who told me of him."

"And where was it you saw him?"

"Down by the river, like you told me. A white stag . . . white, the color of the moon. Dipping his head for water. The antlers . . . you were right. They must be as wide across . . ." He spread his arms, trying to gauge the distance. "They were wide. Do you know why the king comes here?"

"Did you see the king?"

"Only his horse."

"And it's best that that's all you'll be seeing of him. He'll be having your belly opened if he knows that you've been riding about the Valley of the Swans."

Naisha's lands bordered those of the kingship. The lands of the kingship were common land, and belonged to all the chieftains as well as the king. But the area about the Valley of the Swans was private to Conor MacNessa, and trespassing there was punished with torture and death.

Naisha was the only child of Usna, and when his father died, Naisha had little use for the politics of chieftainship. The chieftains were constantly being called to Emain to prove their loyalty to the king. There they tried to outdo each other with flattery and bootlicking. Contests were constantly being held to see who was the best swordsman, and who was the best charioteer and the best acrobat. Naisha knew his strengths. He was the best swordsman in Ulster, and to prove himself over and over again became tedious. The life at Emain was narrow. King Conor and the other chieftains acted as though Emain were the center of the world. He, Naisha, had traveled across the great channel, had traveled to what he thought would be the ends of the world, and still he had not run out of lands to see. When he came back to Emain and told of places where men rode horseback instead of being pulled behind them in chariots, King Conor had ridiculed him, and since Conor had ridiculed him, so did the other chieftains. The fort of Emain was inward looking, so Naisha had left the fort. But not before he had met Branwen. This was their secret meeting place, for when the king came here, he came without soldiers or guards. He left Branwen at the foot of the mountain, and then traveled on alone.

"Why does he come here?"

"To be seeing a sorcerer. Sometimes Cathbad's magic won't be being strong enough."

"Have you ever seen this sorcerer?"

"I'm a concubine. It's not allowed. What is it you've been doing to your shoulder?"

He rubbed it. "It's nothing. Just a branch as I was riding here. I was in a hurry."

"Am I still being able to make you hurry for me?" She reached out her hands to him and he kissed one, then the other, and knelt down in front of her. She was no longer a woman of first youth, but she had vibrant skin, like apples in spring when they first began to turn with the hint of red. She had high, angular cheekbones, and her thick hair held much of its nut color from youth. Her back was rigid as a carpenter's rule.

"You should be going back to the river," she said. "You should be finding the white stag. A man should be taking the top prong of the antler from each side of the head and grinding it to powder, then mixing the powder with eagle's blood and drinking it. And he'll be being blessed with the courage and farsightedness of the eagle, he will, and the stamina and speed of the stag. And he'll be rising above other men same as the eagle'll be rising above the other birds and he'll be rising to be king of men the likes of the eagle, as king of birds and the stag king of the forest."

"I have no desire for the kingship."

"But 'tis you who'll be having the blood of kingship in your veins, and Fergus being your uncle and not Conor's father. He'll be having no right."

"Fergus made Conor his son—"

"With treachery and dishonesty, surely. I was a wee snip of a girl when it was happening. I'll be remembering the women talking. Conor's mother, corn haired she was. Nessa, she called herself. Of the golden hairs, and her making Fergus unfit for kingship, and then asking Fergus to name her son king for just a year. I'll be remembering when Fergus was standing on the platform in front of his long house with the root of Aengus beside him. He lifted his crown from his head with his one good hand and placed it on Conor's head. His

other hand was wrapped with the blood seeping through the
dressing, and I was asking my mother what was happening,
and she was putting her fingers to her lips, saying 'Sssshhh.'
Telling me I should listen. And so I listened. I'll be remembering Fergus's words. 'King for one harvest.' "

"Conor has been a good king even if he knows nothing of
the world beyond. You know the prophecy. Conor has the
respect of the chieftains."

The prophecy said that there would never be peace in
Ulster because of the curse of Macha. The legend came from
ancient times when Ulster was called Uladh, and the people
who lived there were called Ultonians. The legend said that a
very poor farmer named Crundchu, son of Agnoman, dwelling
in a solitary place among the hills, found one day in his *dun*,
his fort, a young woman of great beauty and in splendid array,
whom he had never seen before. Crundchu was a widower, his
wife having died after bearing him four sons. Without a word
the strange woman set herself to do the household tasks, prepared dinner, milked the cow, and took on herself all the
duties of the mistress of the household. At night she lay down
by Crundchu's side and he had his desire with her. Her name
was Macha, and together she and Crundchu prospered.

One day Crundchu prepared himself to go to a great assembly of the Ultonians where there would be feasting, chariot
racing, tournaments and music, and merrymaking of all kinds.
Macha begged her husband not to go, but he persisted.
"Then," she said, "at least do not speak of me in the assembly, for I may dwell with you only so long as I am not spoken
of."

Crundchu promised to obey the injunction, and went to the
festival. Here the two chariot horses of the king carried off
prize after prize of gold in the racing, and the people cried:
"There is not in Erinn a swifter pair of horses than the
king's."

Crundchu looked upon the prizes of gold with greed and said, "I have a wife at home who can run quicker than these horses."

"Seize that man," said the angry king, "and hold him till his wife be brought to the contest."

So the messengers went for Macha, and she was brought before the assembly, and she was with child. The king bade her prepare for the race. She pleaded her condition. "I am close upon my hour," she said. "Then hew her man in pieces," said the king to his guards. Macha turned to the bystanders. "Help me," she cried, "for a mother hath borne each of you! Give me but a short delay till I am delivered." But the king and all the crowd in their savage lust for sport would hear of no delay. "Then bring up the horses," said Macha, "and because you have no pity, a heavier infamy shall fall upon you." So she raced against the horses, and outran them, but as she came to the goal, she gave a great cry, and her travail seized her, and she gave birth to twin children. As she uttered that cry, however, all the spectators felt themselves seized with pangs like her own and had no more strength than a woman in her travail. And Macha prophesied: "From this hour the shame you have wrought on me will fall upon each man of Ulster. In the hours of your greatest need ye shall be weak and helpless as women in childbirth, and this shall endure for five days and four nights—till the ninth generation, the curse shall be upon you." And so it was that the Ultonians were constantly defeated, until Conor MacNessa, who was named for his mother, Conor son of Nessa, came to the kingship.

When Conor was a youth, he could run faster than any man alive. His mother had been a cowherd's daughter, who, some said, was the spirit of Macha come back to Erinn, for she could run faster than any man or woman in the kingdom.

"But Conor's speed will be failing him," Branwen said to Naisha. "And as his belly'll be growing bigger, his reason'll be dwindling. His warriors are in terror of him. He sees treason everywhere. He ordered Rury of the strong thighs and Neil of the curly hair tortured. Mercifully someone killed them both."

"Neil has been a troublemaker as long as I can remember. Even when we were in the boy troops together. If he was tortured he deserved to be. He was a torturer of cats, of birds, and a thief. Stealing swords and putting them under people's blankets so that there would be a fight. I threatened to kill him myself a score of times."

"What is it you'll be knowing of Emain? You're always gone. Naisha the wanderer. Soldier of fortune. Wanderer across the stormy channel. Prefers the company of horses to the company of men. What do you know about men?"

"See this sword? Conor girded it to me when I finished my training in the boy troops. With his own hands. I cannot rise up against him."

"See this girdle? Tonight, after I've been with you, Conor will be putting his hands on this girdle. But he will be not tightening it. Loosening it is what he'll be doing. And he will be putting his hand here, and here. And *here*. It is his right. I am his concubine."

Naisha looked down.

"And when you'll be choosing your wife, and when you'll be growing hard because you desire her, Conor will have her first. He'll be lining his soldiers up and he'll be spreading her legs far apart, and if she is frightened or ill at ease as young girls are wont to be, he'll be slapping her, and pinching her and making her cry out. Then she will be yours. After her cave is filled with his wetness. But anytime Conor wants her, he will call her to his bed. Or if he comes to your rath to visit. He will call her to his bed. Only your horse you can call your own, your wife you cannot. You've been gone from Emain for nearly two moons. Come to Emain. Come see what your king does."

But he grabbed her roughly and kissed her silent. Her mouth tasted slightly of mint leaves. His fingers pulled deftly at the ties of her tunic, and in moments her clothes lay strewn about her on the grass, so that all she wore was a single gold bracelet around her left wrist. He traced his tongue down the line of her neck, lifting first one drop of the river from her skin, then another. Her body was fragrant as the forest into which she had disappeared. She moaned beneath him, eager to accept him, and he lifted her splendid buttocks into position, then thrust so he lost himself in the first plunge, like a swimmer, like a diver jumping from the Pig Head Cliff and going down, down into the black waters of the Abhain Mhor. The dark, velvet petals of her cave tugged and released and tugged against him again, soft and persistent and firm as a tongue. He forced himself deeper and, with a shudder, collapsed on her breast.

CHAPTER
13

If Naisha had known what was to happen at the Fort of Emain that night, he never would have returned there at all. Tonight was to be the final feast before Beal-Tinne. There would be laughter and drinking. In the midpoint of night Cathbad would shout and all the fires in Emain would be put out. They would remain extinguished for three nights, and at sunrise on the third morning would come the signal fire. Cathbad would rekindle the fire on Ardna-Bo-Tarf, the hill of the white bulls. The two white bulls would be hoisted and shoved and pulled with ropes onto the altar stone. The bulls' legs would be opened and turned so the bulls' roots pointed in the direction of the sunrise. As soon as the great Beal-Tinne, the fresh fire, was lit, and the flames leapt skyward, Cathbad would take his golden knife and cut away the bulls' root and plumbs. The first taste would be given to the king. "Make the sinews of our men that shrink against the hollow of their thighs grow. Make their bodies strong like those of these bulls. Make their seed plenty as the fishes of the sea. Make warriors grow in the wombs of their women."

And when all the men had tasted, Cathbad would cut the bulls' throats, and the blood would collect in a depression in the stone, and starting with the king, each man would lower his head and drink the bulls' blood, and turn his face and lift his arms and his sword to the risen sun. Then the two white bulls would be hewed apart with a golden axe and their flesh would be thrown on the ritual fire. After the fire had died, and only ashes were left, the bones of the bulls were ground and mixed with the ashes and spread over the fields to ensure the fecundity of harvest.

Naisha had lingered at the hill of the white fawn, and then crossed back to the crannog on the lake of two swans, hoping to catch sight of the woman, but she didn't reappear. It was evening before he left. The stallion, after standing and standing, was eager to run, and the green hills were turning purple in the failing light. The stallion's hooves beat out their quick regular rhythm past landmark after landmark: Tullabovis, sheep's hill, Glennamaddy, valley of the dogs, and Glenaulden, the valley of the swans. And because it was the night of no moon by the time the horse's hooves touched on Maghera, the plain of the fort, the countryside was as dark as the sleek skin of the stallion.

In the distance he could see the red sparks from the fires of Emain rise skyward and disappear. Sdoirm sensed the closeness of the place where he would have rest and grain, and the powerful withers moved through the darkness more quickly. Naisha bent low on the horse, so that the coarse mane whipped against his face. He closed his eyes, leaving direction to the horse.

At the gate of the fort Naisha reined in the stallion to a slow lope. Because the soldiers of Erinn didn't ride horseback, but in chariots pulled by two horses, the guards immediately recognized the son of Usna, and lowered their lances, allowing horse and rider to pass. After Naisha passed, the guards pointed to their temples, signifying that he was crazy to ride horseback. A man fighting on horseback had none of the protection that a chariot offered.

At the ramp in front of the king's inner fortress Naisha reined the horse to a stop. A slave from the stable came running up. Naisha handed over the reins. "An extra ration of oats for him tonight. But not before you walk him." Naisha patted the horse's neck, then walked up the ramp. He nodded to the two guards at the gate and maneuvered his way through the maze of birch poles, heading toward the man-root of Aengus. Branwen's words came back to him briefly: *And when you choose your wife, Conor will have her first.* Naisha took the steps of the king's roundhouse three at a time.

"Greetings to Naisha, son of Usna," said one of the guards.

"The gods protect you," replied Naisha. "Has the council begun?"

"Cathbad just now arrived. The gong has not yet sounded." The guard pushed open the great oak door, which creaked on its hinges.

Naisha made his way through the nine compartments of the roundhouse into the feast hall. Since it was the Night of No Moon, the eating and drinking was subdued. There would be feasting in three days' time after the fresh fires of Bael had been rekindled. Only two fires burned in the feast hall. The king stood naked on his throne platform, and a group of youths, also naked, stood in front of him. Cathbad stood on the platform near the king's throne. Naisha looked briefly at the throne, the gold encrusted with red enamel, and with rubies and pearls. Branwen's words kept coming at Naisha like small black flies in the air. *You could be king. You are the rightful king. Fergus is your uncle.*

Fergus sat on a corner of the platform, his head resting against one of the bronze pillars, his old, toothless mouth open, saliva dripping down his chin.

Naisha remembered when Fergus, the brother of his father, had sat on that throne. Fergus had picked him up and sat him on his knee. If he, Naisha, closed his eyes he could remember. It was the first memory that Naisha had, Fergus mussing his hair and rubbing it backward, then picking him up under the arms and hoisting him up onto his knees. "My brother Usna is a lucky man," his uncle had said. "I sit on this throne, but what good is a throne to a man who has no sons? I would give up my kingdom for a son like you." Naisha remembered touching the red jewels in the arms of the throne. Now his uncle Fergus looked on Naisha with unfocused, expressionless eyes, eyes always bloodshot with too much ale. The old man stumbled and fell asleep wherever he collapsed, lying in his own urine like an animal with a broken leg.

Naisha had been sent into fosterage to Tara in Leinster until he was old enough to enter the boy troops of King Fergus. But when Naisha came back to Ulster as a youth, Fergus was no longer king. Conor was. When Naisha arrived back at Emain from Tara, Fergus had reached out his hand to muss Naisha's hair and had toppled over in his drunken stupor.

It was Conor who had welcomed Naisha's entrance into the boy troops, in the year of his tenth harvest. For five years all the young boys of Ulster were trained with swords, with lances, with bows and arrows. They were taught to fight and to track deer, and how to sleep in the forests without shelter, and to race chariots.

Finally, in the year of his fifteenth harvest, the fifth year of his training in the boy troops, Naisha became a man, and took the oath of allegiance to Conor. All the boys had stood naked in this very room. The king, too, was naked, except for the sword tied at his waist. Each boy, in turn, stood in front of the king. Naisha, because he had won all the spear and swording competitions, as well as the lance throwing and running, stood first in line to take the oath. The king had stood in front of his throne, and Naisha stood facing him. Naisha remembered that there had been harp music, but that had stopped when the king raised his arms. Then there was only the snoring of Fergus, and the occasional cough from the soldiers. The king had taken a sword from Naisha's father's hand. It was a special sword that had belonged to Naisha's grandfather. Naisha's hands were sweating profusely and he could feel the sweat running in his armpits and he hoped that the king wouldn't notice. King Conor had unwrapped the belt of the sheath, and then tied it around Naisha's waist. Naisha's heart was pounding. He was afraid that the king would see the vibration of it under the bones of his chest, and shout in his huge voice for Naisha to leave the allegiance ceremony at once, that he had no room in his troops for a mere boy whose heart pounded like that of a maiden. Naisha felt the belt go around his waist. He himself had girded a sword to his waist a thousand times, but never had the leather belt seemed so large, so heavy, and cold and hot at the same time. It was as though the belt were made of ice and the next moment of fire. Naisha shivered and was hot at the same time.

"I Conor, king and sovereign of all Ulster, tie on this sword. Before you wore the sword of a boy. Now wear the sword of a man. Do you, Naisha, testify on the seed of your forefathers and the seed of your father to bring yourself and your sword to the defense of your king, to the defense of his children, his cattle, his lands, regardless of season, regardless of age, regardless of cause?"

Naisha was terrified that he could not mouth the required words. His heart was in his throat. He opened his mouth to speak. He had dreamed of this. Over and over again during the last nights. He had dreamed that he would open his mouth to speak and no words would come out. Try as he might, nothing would come out, until at last a soft whimper like that of a girl child would come from his lips, and the king would laugh at him, as would all the soldiers. He was afraid it would be as it had been in his dream. He was afraid to open his mouth, but the king was waiting. "I, Naisha," he said, feeling relieved, as his heart seemed to descend from his throat to his chest where it belonged, "son of Usna, give testament of my allegiance to Conor, high lord and sovereign of Ulster."

Then the king had reached down between Naisha's legs,

and Naisha had recoiled instinctively, even though he had received instruction about the testament ceremony. The king had taken Naisha's testicles in his hand, and Naisha could feel them shrivel as though he'd leapt into a frigid mountain stream. He was afraid the king would squeeze with his great fingers. Naisha's plumbs had still been relatively small then, and still smooth skinned, almost like a girl's face. The king's fingers had been cool, and almost moist with perspiration. The king had not squeezed but merely lifted Naisha's testicles lightly, as though weighing them. The air was thick with the smell of manhood, the way the sweathouse smelled after an afternoon of the hurling game.

Naisha had been instructed what to do. He looked at the thing that grew in the king's groin. It was long, one of the longest that Naisha had ever seen, and thick. Behind it were the testicles, a kind of horse-lip heaviness and thick blond crotch hair. Naisha, with his right hand, touched the hilt of his sword, and then took the king's heavy testicles in his hand. He was surprised at the wiry coarseness of the curly hair that covered them, and of the weight, like two apples, but more solid and small, and heavier. And there were places underneath where the hair didn't grow, and there the skin was soft, softer than anything Naisha had felt, except for the skin of his own plumbs. He repeated the oath. "I, Naisha, swear by the seed of my forefathers and by the seed of Usna my father and give testament of my allegiance to Conor, high lord and sovereign of Ulster. I swear by the seed in my loins, regardless of season, regardless of age, regardless of cause, to give my arms, to give my life, to the protection of King Conor, to the protection of his wives, his children, his cattle, his horses, his country, regardless of age, regardless of season, regardless of cause."

"Welcome, Naisha, prince of Ulster, to manhood and to the council of Ulster." And the king kissed Naisha on each cheek, and Naisha knelt and kissed the hand of the king.

Then the boy, who was no longer a boy but a warrior, had to speak out his *geisa,* his family tabu, a debt owed to ancestors. Some of the new warriors were never allowed to eat deer meat because their forefathers long, long ago had lived on the earth as deer. Some of the *geisas* were that the warriors could not kill a certain bird, sometimes an eagle or a hawk, because their forefathers had been eagles or hawks. Some of the *geisas* were that the warriors could not be in bed after the sun had risen, or some said that they were not allowed to hunt with bows and arrows, and some had to stay inside on the fifth night of the half moon. This was the first public utterance of each of the young warrior's *geisa.* Naisha's *geisa* was that he could not travel when the moon was full. Then for three days he and the other members of the young warrior troop had to keep silent and walk naked and alone in the forest and meditate upon the responsibilities of manhood, and on the third day they had returned to the hill of the white bulls, had broken silence at sunrise and participated at the sacrifice of the bulls at Bael-Tinne, and had tasted of the bull root that would make them strong like the other men.

Naisha looked at the shoulders of the boy troops. Once they had gone through the ritual of testament, they no longer carried themselves with the gangly, timid self-consciousness of boys, but with the straight, erect backs of men. You could see just by looking on them who had given testament and who had not.

Fergus's shoulders had slipped from the pillar, and now the ex-king lay supine on the platform. The *geisa* of Fergus was that he could not turn down a request from a corn-haired woman. Conor's mother, Nessa, who had worked as the herdess of Fergus's cows had been a corn-haired widow, and when Fergus's wife died, she had arranged an encounter with him and then asked Fergus to marry her. He had to comply, and Ulster had the first queen who was not a virgin. Fergus took to drink. There were some who said that Nessa drugged his ale with stuporing potions of which he needed an ever-increasing amount. The handsome young Conor, Nessa's son, began to make judgments of state. Nessa asked Fergus to adopt Conor as his son, and Fergus, because of his *geisa*, had to comply. Conor's ability won him much admiration. Feuds that seemed to be endless were settled by him. Thieves and scoundrels were routed from the kingdom, and when Maeve rallied her troops against Ulster, Conor defeated them and sent them home like whipped dogs. His fame spread.

Then one night King Fergus, in a drunken stupor, had fallen asleep near a wall where some swords hung. During the night, in the restless sleep of the drunk, he had knocked one off the wall, and it had fallen with such force that it severed his left hand at his wrist. In the laws that the ancients had given, it was stated that no man who had any physical imperfection could be king in Erinn, so Fergus was obliged to give up the kingship. The accident had happened just after La Lughnasa, the festivities celebrating the anniversary of the moon, which fell just before the harvest was gathered. All the chieftains had returned to their forts to supervise the gathering of harvest. Messengers were sent out to all of them. To return to Emain would mean lost time. Farmers and slaves would steal mercilessly from grain and cattle and wool, if the chieftains themselves were not there to supervise the levies made to them. Conor would act as king for one year. Fergus had already adopted him as his son, and Conor had proven himself to be skilled in the techniques of kingship. Then in a year's time at the festivities of La Lughnasa, the chieftains could, among themselves, choose another king.

During the following year Conor continued to excel in matters of statesmanship. Ulster again prospered as it had in the times of the ancients. The chieftains cast stones into a circle. Black stones for those who were in favor of choosing a new king for Ulster, and white stones for those who were in favor of keeping Conor as king. The white stones outnumbered the black.

Naisha looked at King Conor. He was no longer young, but despite a thickening about the waist, the king still had the force of a bull. When the king reached his arms out to either side so that his robe could be slipped back on him, Naisha noticed the skin under Conor's arms was beginning to hang. Not a great deal; it was barely noticeable, but that was where a man turned old first. Had Branwen been right? Was the king losing his strength?

The king slipped on the robe of purple and gold and sat down again on his throne. Cathbad hovered close and began to make quick hand movements about the king's face and above his head. It was the hair-cutting ceremony. In the laws of the ancients it was stated that hair, fingernails, and toenails could only be cut on the Nights of No Moon. Each man, woman, and child was careful with the trimmings and secretly hid them, because if a person found the trimmings, that person could have control over the body from which the trimmings came. Naisha glanced at his own fingernails quickly. His thumbnail was too long, and using the dagger he had taken from the young woman he had seen, he cut it off. He threw the piece of fingernail into the fire, disdainfully. How many times, when he was hunting in the forest, had he ripped fingernails, or left strands of his hair when it got caught in branches. No one exercised any control over Naisha, chieftain of Ulster, except when Naisha, chieftain of Ulster, allowed it.

Naisha was thirsty and went toward the huge oak barrels to where the ale was kept. A man stepped out in front of him. He was the same age as Naisha, but blond, with ugly eyes. The man held a dagger, the blade of which he kept slapping against the palm of the other hand.

"Well, well. Naisha, son of Usna, has finally deigned to

come to the king's council." It was Owen Campbell who spoke, Campbell meaning crooked mouth.

"I come to Emain whenever I feel the need. It gives me no pleasure to stay here season after season, as you do."

"There is much to be learned by staying close to the king. A new campaign is being mounted into Connacht to recover the black bull of Fergus stolen by Queen Maeve."

"I will go to Connacht if I am called to do so, but until then I have my horses to keep me busy at Ballynagree."

"*Ballynagree!* The homestead of the stallion! Naisha, do you know how ridiculous you look—riding on top of your horse? Like a monkey on a dog's back!"

"The only thing ridiculous is you, Owen. Why do you always stay here at Emain, licking the salt from between the king's toes, like a dog?"

Owen put his hand to his sword.

"Stay your hand, unless you wish to die. It was I who always beat you in the games when we were in the boy troops."

"Wait, Naisha. You killed my father. At night I see his face in my dreams. I hear his voice in the wind at night. I will kill you one day."

"I didn't mean to kill your father. It was he who forced my hand."

"It was you who struck him first."

"I will not stand to see any man mistreat a horse the way he did. It was one of his finest mares that he was—"

"It was his horse. He can do with his property as he sees fit."

"Brutality is no way."

Owen spit. "Brutality. You're the one who killed, and you speak of brutality."

"I walked away, Owen. He came after me."

"I walk away, too, Naisha. Today, tomorrow, the day after, I'll walk away. But someday I won't. Someday I'll kill you. My sword in your heart." Owen touched Naisha's chest. "Right there. Just as your sword penetrated him."

Naisha thrust Owen's hand aside. "I'm ready whenever you are." And he turned his back on Owen and walked toward the ale barrel.

Owen smiled to himself and touched his waist under the sheath of his sword. A square of fine linen was hidden there— a handkerchief he had found close to the mountain of the white fawn. It belonged to Branwen of the fair shoulders, one of the concubines of the king. And Owen had seen the black stallion of Naisha speeding away from the place. The king would be furious. Branwen was his favored concubine. He would order Naisha mutilated and tortured before he was put to death. But Owen would need proof, more proof than just a handkerchief and Naisha riding away from where it was found. A false accuser was punished with the same punish-ment as though he himself had committed the crime. Not only that, but it was forbidden for all men to travel on the king's personal territory. Owen himself would be killed for going there. Owen would wait. The festivities of Bael-Tinne would last ten nights. He would watch. During those ten nights it was inevitable that Naisha would seek out Branwen. Then he, Owen, would have proof. He, Owen Campbell, de-rided because of his crooked mouth, would be rewarded.

CHAPTER
14

King Conor was in a foul temper. He had spoken to the Druid about administering a potion to Ceantine that would make the moon blood flow so she could be forced. Only the Druid could act as intermediary with gods, and no king could perform any rite without the Druid's presence. But the Druid had refused to do anything until after all the celebrations of Beal-Tinne had been completed. That included the sacrifices, the animal fair, the hurling games between the soldiers, the races, the competitions. The entire ten days. After the first blood came, another ten days were needed for the preparation of the maiden. It would be a moon change again before he would have his bride.

He had waited nearly a score of years for her, and was tired of waiting. He got up from his throne and kicked at the wolf-hound that lay at his feet, and when his slave didn't move quickly enough out of his way, Conor cracked him across both sides of his face, knocking him to the ground. Just to be around her made him feel he was twenty years old again. He felt as if he were a young buck, as if he could leap through the air. As if he could run across the fields with the youths in the boy troop.

But the Druid was keeping him from claiming what was rightfully his. What did the Druid know about manly things? He was ancient as the earth itself. Too old to feel the urgency of manhood. The thought of her made his manhood rise and throb. Conor punched his right fist into his left palm repeatedly, making a smacking sound as he paced back and forth

across the platform in front of his throne. There were places
in the world, places across the sea, where the king's word was
law. Where even the priests obeyed the kings.

The Druid had disappeared momentarily from the platform
but was now back with his gold-bladed knife. The king looked
at the knife. "Must we do this now?" he asked Cathbad.

"You know the laws of the ancients, Sire. The king, at each
new moon, must have trimmed his fingernails and hair."

The Druid bowed his head in front of the king, and made a
motion with one hand over the golden knife. The king sat
down nervously on his throne. He could see the blue veins in
the top of Cathbad's head where the hair had fallen out.
Cathbad looked up. "Your will be done, Sire." It was the
Druid's duty to trim the king's beard and nails, but if the
Druid chose no longer to serve the king, then the Druid could
cast a spell on the king's cut hair or his nail clippings and
bring about the monarch's defeat in battle or through illness.

Was the Druid on his side? Conor felt treachery among the
chieftains. He was sure of it. It was the way their eyes moved.
You could tell. The way they looked at each other. And at
night he had dreams. That they stabbed him over and over
again, while he slept. And he woke up screaming and then was
afraid to go back to sleep. He slept with knives under his
pillows, and in the morning his right hand was stiff from
clutching the handle. He started at the slightest noise, and
saw figures in the shadows. He was just a cowherd's son. They
were talking about him. They wanted a true son of a nobleman to be king. He needed a new wife. A new queen in the
roundhouse would stir the loyalty of his men. He would perform the first forcing in front of all of them, and once again
they would see that he was as fit for kingship as any of them.

The Druid looked at the king, then smiled briefly and
bowed again. The king didn't like to look at his eyes. They
were blue, blue as the waves of a calm sea, but the center part,

the black part, was uncanny. The Druid didn't have round, dark pupils like other men; he had pupils like those of a cat, long and elliptical. The Druid served the king, but a king could only be king so long as the Druid willed it.

The Druid took a small golden bowl filled with water from the sacred well and in which rose petals had been scattered, and dipped his fingers into it and sprinkled the king's head. The king shivered from the water dripping down his neck. Then the Druid took the golden knife and began to saw through the ends of the hair. The hair had once been the color of corn, but now most of it was a yellow-gray, like straw faded after many seasons of rain, snow, and sun.

The king breathed loudly, and nervously scratched at his neck.

"Sire, I beg you to sit still. My knife is just today newly sharpened."

The king drew back.

"Sire, please, I beg you. Be still. You know the laws of the ancients. I must do this." When the king didn't speak, the Druid continued. "I must leave tonight for the circle of the stones. You are aware, Sire, that the embers of the fires must be allowed to die tonight, and that no one but myself is allowed to rekindle them."

"Yes, Cathbad, I am aware of what I have to do, and what you have to do. I do not have to be reminded."

"Yes, Sire." The Druid bowed low again. The king looked away from the long, elliptical pupils.

"Have no fear, Sire," the Druid continued. "I have a magic place for the royal clippings. No physical harm can come to you as long as"—there was a pause—"I guard the clippings."

Was the Druid on his side? One night Conor had not been able to sleep, and got up, and putting on his fleecy slippers, left the roundhouse and walked about outside. Over the maze of birch poles that surrounded his roundhouse, he overheard two of his guards talking.

"The bleeding stupidity of it. Mounting a whole expedition to Connacht for one black bull. He must be going mad. Thinks his bull is the Great Dun Barruch, the giant bull of Aengus who could carry fifteen men on his back. Think of it. Hundreds of men for one bull. He has dozens of bulls."

"Mad or not, he's the king."

"Some of the others feel the same way. They think it's time the kingship was turned over to someone else."

"Ssssh! Such talk is treason, and even the walls have ears. You know as well as me a king can't be forced out unless he has a physical imperfection, and Conor has none. The gods won't allow it. Be patient. He gets older and older. He'll be feeble before long. My wife tells me one of his concubines has already confided in her that he can't pleasure her."

"Well, then. That's a sign in itself surely that he must be removed."

"Arrracch. You're being a fool. Imagine if a man was removed from his position each time he failed to pleasure a woman. There wouldn't be a chieftain, a warrior or a soldier, or even a gatekeeper anywhere in Erinn."

"But a king isn't like other men. He must be more than other men."

"And Conor has been more than other men. Time takes us all. One day he'll be walking, and he'll walk more slowly, or his hands'll start to shake when he reaches for his scepter. That's when a king is replaced. Not because he orders a cattle raid."

"The troops are tired. This will be the second raid into Connacht since last summer's harvest. The chieftains want to return to their forts. They don't want to slosh through the bogs to get to Connacht, for one bull."

"The chieftains will do what Conor says."

"There's talk. I've heard it. There's talk that Conor maintains his physical qualities but that his brain is going addled. He forgets things and imagines things that aren't so. Just because you can't see physical imperfections doesn't mean they don't exist. I've heard whisperings that even some of the chieftains have enlisted the aid of Cathbad, so that some infirmity will befall Conor."

"Arrachh. Cathbad. He serves no man but himself. He cares not a pig's grunt who's king. The only thing he cares about is getting enough sacrifices so the gods won't be bringing pestilence and famine."

"He's got the easy end of it, the Druid, doesn't he? No night watches. No marching. No fighting. No nothing but himself. It's a bit of all right, it is, being a Druid."

"I wouldn't want to do what he does. Out in the middle of the forest somewhere. Living in caves, same as what the bears and wolves does. Up to my elbows in blood all the time. He can have it. Living abstemiously. Skinny as a crow's leg, he is. I ain't never seen him pack a morsel of food near his beak."

"And what do you think you do? Up to your knees in blood sometimes on the battlefield. Blood is blood, and I'd rather see someone else's spilled rather than be looking out for me own all the time."

"A bloody poor Celt you are. Don't like fighting. Don't like cattle raiding. Talking about dethroning your king."

"Well, I'm as good a Celt as you in other things. Did you see some of them girl slaves we brought back from Connacht? Legs what goes all the way up. The king must've had hisself a real good time with those. That is if he could've got it up."

"Course he got it up. A strange woman's different from an old wife or a concubine what's been with you nearly as long as a wife. New flesh makes the blood run fast enough."

"Now I know why you're talking about dethroning Conor. You're just jealous. You want first cracks at all the women, eh?

Not me, by the gods. Give me used ones that's opened and greasy. So as I can just slide right in."

Conor had ordered the men tortured to find out who was behind the treachery, but someone had sneaked in and stabbed the two guards before they talked. One guard was named Rury of the strong thighs; the other Neil of the curly hair. Rury was married with five children, and Conor had been furious that Rury had so easily escaped torment. Conor gave orders that Rury's wife and children be tortured, but as he paced back and forth in his chambers, reason rather than pity overcame him. Treason was one thing. Torturing children was another. His chieftains would accept the death of traitors, but if there was a spark of treason, the murder of innocents would only ignite the flame. Conor suspected from where the first sparks had come. He had sent Owen hunting boar with the two chieftains. Owen, because of his crooked mouth, could never have aspirations to the kingship. He at least was free from thoughts of treachery, and Owen had shown himself eager to please and reliable. Conor would have future use for Owen.

The Druid crossed his arms on his chest so that the leather pouch containing the king's trimmings disappeared between the great wide sleeves of his white garment. The Druid blinked his eyes so that the long, elliptical pupils were covered and then bowed low. "I leave you now, Sire." He smiled, the strange eyes almost closed. "May the gods smile favorably on you at Bael-Tinne."

The Druid had treachery in his eyes, the king was certain of it. He could feel the treachery. "I'll take the clippings, Cathbad."

"Sire? A king does not dispose of his own clippings."

"I said I'll take the clippings. I am king. Do as I say."

"A king does not dispose of his own clippings," the Druid repeated.

"Am I or am I not king?"

"Yes, Sire."

"I will dispose of them myself."

"I cannot allow the sacred clippings of the kingship to be disposed anywhere but on secret ground. It is forbidden by the ancients." The elliptical eyes were adamant.

Conor took a deep breath. If he insisted too much, the Druid would know he suspected him and would be all the more dangerous. Conor would take an extra dog into his bedchamber tonight. But the Druid could mix a sleeping potion. Would he never be rid of this Druid? He couldn't even ask Owen to kill the Druid, as he had Diuran, chieftain of Magh Tuiredh, and Ailell, chieftain of Sliabh Callainn. A man who was ugly, with the promise of enough gold and land, could be bribed to kill a nobleman and make it look like a hunting accident, but no one would ever dare kill a Druid, not even Owen. To kill a Druid was to bring down the most terrible vengeance of all the gods.

"Go, then!" And then more softly, because he could not afford to antagonize the Druid, "May the gods go with you."

The Druid bowed and smiled.

Conor wanted to kick him off the platform, but he looked away. He had devised his own way of deciding who was loyal to him, and who was not. Now he would find out. The king stood up briskly and threw another kick at the gray wolfhound. Conor grabbed the gong handle from the slave and, knocking him to the side, struck the gong five or six times in fierce, hard repetition. Instantly, the feast hall was quiet except for the echo of the gong's silver sound, and the crackle of the dying fires.

"Bring in the cart," he boomed.

The double doors to the banquet hall were opened and two slaves pulled in a large, closed wooden cart on wheels. From the cart came the terrible squealing of rats.

CHAPTER
15

"**I** order every man in this room, every chieftain and every soldier, to eat a live rat. Silence! I am your king." He slammed the gong again. "Silence! I am your chosen king," he shouted. "You have sworn allegiance to my orders. All of them. Now do as I order or suffer the penalty!"

The hall was absolutely still except for the crackle of fire and the squealing of rats.

There was a movement from the side of the hall and a man came toward the cart. It was Owen. Owen reached into the cart and grabbed a gray-black rat. It squealed loudly as he picked it up, but it was silenced immediately when he laid it on the table and severed its head with one quick stroke of his sword. There was the sound of retching and vomiting in the back of the hall, as Owen put the black, furry head, dripping with blood, into his mouth and began to chew. A trickle of blood dripped onto Owen's chin, but he ignored it and continued to chew. The decapitated body of the rat lay on the table, bleeding silently. The rats in the cart smelled the blood and screamed louder. They sounded like crying children. Owen smiled a bloody, toothy smile. Chunks of rat were stuck between his teeth.

"We are chieftains of Ulster. You cannot make chieftains eat rats," boomed a voice from the side of the hall.

"Who dares to question the orders of the king? Seize him! Take him to the compound with the prisoners," shouted the king.

"Sire!"

"Seize him!"

"Sire," said one of the soldiers. "It's Naisha, son of Usna, who speaks."

"Seize him."

"It's Naisha. Nephew of Fergus."

"Seize him, in the name of the gods who will bring the sky on your heads and on the heads of your children if you disobey your king. I'll have you all skinned alive."

"Any man who approaches is dead." Naisha had his sword drawn. A dozen men surrounded and faced him, spears and swords in hand. Naisha's back was to the wall. On the other side of the circle of men stood a door.

"Sire, you have been wise in your campaigns and in the dealings with the kings of Erinn. Don't bring blemish to your rule by humiliating your chieftains. We are men, not dogs."

"Seize him. I order it."

"Sire, it is I, Naisha, son of Usna. You girded my sword when I graduated from the boy troops."

"And you swore allegiance to your king. I am your king. I will not allow disobedience. The gods do not allow disobedience."

"Sire, it is Naisha, nephew of Fergus," said one of the soldiers.

"Seize that man. And seize the son of Usna and take them to the prisoners' compound. And any man who attempts to leave. I am king." He grabbed the gong and struck it. "I am KING," he shouted. "I am KING. . . ." He kicked the dog off the platform and struck the gong again. "I will not be disobeyed."

The noise of the gong was deafening, and the men were adding to the confusion.

Naisha had drawn his sword, and about a dozen men stood in front of him with spears and swords in hand. "Sean, Daol,

Eric. Don't draw your swords on me. We are kin. We came through the boy troops together."

"Naisha," said the one called Sean, "we can't disobey the king. The gods forbid it."

"It is the chieftains of Ulster who choose the kings. It was my father who cast a white stone favoring Conor as king. I will not stand by while he makes a mockery of us."

"Mockery! Do I hear the word *mockery* used against the king? Seize that man! This is your king speaking."

"Naisha, eat the rat. You have eaten worse things than rats in your life. When we were in the boy troops. Remember how we dared each other to eat raw frogs?"

"That was different. That was boy games. Those were our choices. This is a king. A king is like a husband to the land and the chieftains. It is a rule of trust and justice. Where there is no justice, there is no kingship, just tyranny."

"Naisha, don't allow your hot blood to stand in the way of reason. All that you have will be seized."

"And your honor has already been seized. It is just a matter of time before he takes your lands too."

"The laws forbid the taking of land except those of traitors."

"And the laws forbid a king treating his chieftains like slaves."

"We must obey his laws."

"We must obey the laws of a wise king, of a just king, not of a madman. You will not allow a man with one hand to rule you, yet you allow a man with addled brains to remain king."

"The gods have not permitted men to see inside of other men's heads."

"The chieftains choose the kings. It is for the chieftains to decide when there must be a new king."

"The gods are present in the spirits of men at the ceremony of the kingship. The spirit then passes onto the chosen one."

"The spirit of kingship has left Conor. Any fool can give judgment, but only a great man can give justice. Conor no longer gives justice, only judgment."

"Have you killed him?" shouted the king. "Bring his body to me. Now, I order it!"

"Reconsider, Naisha. You know the colloquy of the ancients:

> 'Whoever transgresses the law of the kings
> should not thrive in his tribe
> but live as an outcast forever.
> That he will dishonor his kin
> And die for his mortal sin.' "

"Let me go. Rather a wanderer of the landscape than a traitor to my own heart. I will not obey a king who has broken his promise to honor his chieftains."

"I order it now! Kill him or be killed yourselves!"

"You leave me no choice, Naisha. His word is law."

"Put down your sword. You were like my brother. I don't want to kill you."

"I beg you as your kin, eat the rat, Naisha."

"I am chieftain. I will not be humiliated."

"KILL HIM! I WILL NOT BE DISOBEYED!"

Another sword broke into the circle. It was Owen. "The time for revenge on the son of Usna has come."

"I wouldn't waste a breath on an eater of rats."

"Seize him. It is the king's orders."

"Seize me yourself, Owen. If you can." A stool stood close to Owen and he kicked it at Naisha and went for Naisha with his sword. But Naisha was quick as a cat and knocked Owen's sword from his hand. "The only reason I don't kill you, is because any man who eats rats with such relish doesn't deserve the honor of dying by sword." Naisha reached the door and flung it open. A tapestry hung on a wall, and he pulled it down. He grabbed a torch from the wall and set fire to the tapestry, so that he couldn't be followed through that door.

The gong sounded again. "Seize him! Kill him! I will not be disobeyed."

Owen rushed to another door. He knew where Naisha was headed. He, Owen of the crooked mouth, would get there first and wait for him.

CHAPTER 16

In the distance on a low mound by a riverbank, Deirdre saw a standing group. At first she thought they were people and thought she saw movement, but as she approached she realized that they were stones set in a circle, some tall as she was, some of them no taller than a dog.

She had never before seen a stone circle, but Aya had told her about them. "Aie, child. It's where the fairies lives. Descendants of the evil Fomorians. Once huge as mountains now shrunk to size. It's where they keep changelings what they puts in the cradles of decent folks. Steals aways the real babes, and leaves changelings. They're the children what you sees what's dumb as oxes, and deaf. Or deformed with club feet same as what a horse has. Or big swooled-up heads, and tiny slanty eyes. But sometimes changelings looks normal. Same as what you and me looks. But at night when the moon ain't shining. When it be hidden by the mist and fog. Them changelings' ears grows pointed and they'll be making mischief and doing bad things in people's houses. Only one way of telling if a child's a changeling. I seen it done. Take the child and put it on a shovel and hold it over the fire, saying, 'Burn, burn, burn if you be of the demons. But if of the gods, then safe from harm.'

"Aie, child. Fairy rings. And don't you be staying near them when the sun's gone down. A pretty child like you. May the gods bless you so as the evil eye don't come looking for you." Aya spun around twice so that the evil eye wouldn't be able to tell what it was that she had looked at. "Aie, a woman like

you. A fairy king. A *sidhe** king is the ugliest. With pig's
snouts and wolf ears he'll come. He'll take you down under the
stone circles and use you for his own in spite of yourself. And
Aya won't always be around to look after you, so you has got to
be learning to look after yourself, you has. And I wouldn't be
going near a fairy ring after the sun goes down.

"Me own sweet girlhood in Connacht. Me mother told me.
She and her sister and a kin-girl had been playing. And they'd
been warned, same as what I'm always warning you. But
what's the child what'll be listening to his elders? And there
they was a playing. Cat's cradle with the flax twine. And blowing dandelion fluff. And suddenly they heard a cry, and an
ugly little man no bigger than me thumb jumped up from
under a stone. And a great cloud from heaven just floated to
the earth. And the gods knock me dead, and may the sky fall
on me head, if me mother never lied. And the little man.
Quick as you please was taller than a horse. And me mother
ran away fast as the hares with her sister. But me mother's kin-
girl. She had a foot which pained her. On account of her
falling and busting the bones in it. And me mother never seen
her kin-girl again. Taken away, she was. Under the fairy
stones."

Deirdre gave the circle a wide berth as she walked toward
the river, but kept glancing at the stones, making certain that
no fairy king was there. Again she thought she saw movement
out of the corner of her eye and she started, and spun around,
but it was just movement from Duff's wingtip. She noticed
her shadow. In it she looked like a giant warrioress, her spear
tall as a tree. There was nothing behind her. Besides, she
could fight off anything that attacked her, and she descended
to the river.

From where she stood the river seemed to be running both

* Pronounced *shee.*

ways. The current carried the river along the valley, but the breeze from the other direction tugged the waves into little crests where the sun brindled them with gold before they fell again and were green. Green and gold. Those were the colors of the robes of a queen.

She didn't know how far she had come. When she had left the crannog, darkness hung like a cape over the shores around Loughadalla. She had hidden in the forest, and when morning broke, brilliant as a rooster's comb, she had heard a sound in the distance. It sounded like a ghostly wind. *Whooooeeey . . . Whooooeeey. Whoooeeeeey.* The sound came closer. It was a troop of swans, their splendid necks and great wings beating as though they were racing from the sun. They came closer and closer, and for a breath's time, it looked as though they could beat the sunlight across the sky. Then the rays of the sun caught the white feathers, turning them crimson. Red swans swept in the sun's fire. The sound of their burning wings was deafening.

They were headed the same way she was, in the direction of the sunset. MacFith, when he played his harp at night, often sang of the Great Finn MacCoul, the first giant of Erinn. The giants of Erinn had waged war with the giants of Alba.* Finn MacCoul, one day, had picked up a clump of dirt and thrown it at Far Rua, a giant who stood on the shores of Alba, and killed him. The rains had come and filled the place from where Finn had torn the earth, and that place was called Lough Neagh. It was to the north, and was the largest lake in all of Erinn. Then the country had been at peace for a thousand times a thousand years.

If you walked to the south, MacFith said, you could see where the giant Finn was buried along the Liffey River. There was a great hill there, and that's where his head was. The giant

* Ancient name for Scotland.

had felt himself growing old and he lay down along the river, and covered himself up with dirt.

Deirdre wasn't interested in going to see the north, nor to the south to see where Finn MacCoul was buried. She was going to the west, and her face was already turned in the direction that the swans had gone. She began to walk. Her shadow cast long and dark in front of her, and she was proud of the way it looked on the furze that bloomed yellow and fragrant on the bog edges. It was a warrior's shadow. She began to run slowly and the spiny furze brushing against her legs seemed to say, *Deirdre, Deirdre, Deirdre,* and that was the pace she set for herself.

As her shadow shortened, the bogs gave way to grasslands and to low green hills called drumlins. She walked up the hills and ran down them. When she walked, Duff sat complacently on her shoulder grooming her hair with his beak or gently nipping at her ear. When she ran, he squawked loudly and, complaining about the bouncing, gave up his perch and flew behind her.

When she saw the stone circle, the sun had moved so that it was in front of her, and she had to shade her eyes with her hand before she could see the circle clearly. She came to the water's edge. The stone circle was behind her now, partially hidden by brush. She glanced at it one more time, then turned her face toward the setting sun. Tomorrow, in the morning, after she was strong from sleep, she would swim to the other side of the river.

She bent to the river and cupped her hands in the water and drank. The water tasted different here than at Loughadalla. Was that the first thing a person noticed about a place, the taste of its water? Did river water taste different than water from a lake? She drank again. At Loughadalla, the water had an . . . almost pine taste. Here the taste was more . . . like . . . The water smelled like stones. She splashed

the coolness onto her face and splashed again, allowing the
water to run down her face and onto her hands. Again she
cupped her hands in the river and lifted the water to the back
of her neck under her hair. But she started. In the bend there
was a flurry of movement, and her hand went to the spear she
had laid on the ground.

But she smiled to herself. A kingfisher had dropped to the
river and seized a fish and now beat the fish against the tree
branch. The bird then tossed the fish into the air and caught
it, head first.

Duff flew up off her shoulder. "Frog's arse, frog's arse," he
said in a disconcerted caw.

"You're just jealous because you can't catch fish," Deirdre
said to him. "I am too. I'm starving." And she reached into
her pouch, looking for a piece of bread and cheese.

She wondered how much farther she had to go. She was
thankful she had been able to run as far as she had. It had
been Aya who had first told her to run, to keep the moon
blood from coming so the king couldn't force her. Then there
had been the thin trickles against the insides of her thighs,
and Aya had whispered to take moss and wrap herself. And
not to tell Lewara. If she ran far enough and often enough,
the moon blood wouldn't come at all, and Lewara would never
know. Every day Deirdre ran the distance from the crannog to
Drumhillagh, the sallow hill, and in the time it took Deirdre
to run to the hill and home again, the sun would move across
the hill. How many times had she run the distance, she
couldn't remember. In the beginning Aya had run with her.
And sometimes they used to race from the *derry*, from the oak
grove, to the edge of the lake.

"I won," Deirdre would shout between pants of breath.

"Aie, child. Win you did. Sure as the wind what's blowing
across Ulster."

It took Deirdre a long time to realize that Aya was letting her win. "Why do you always let me win, Aya?"

Aya had bit at her fingernail. "Me! I wouldn't be letting you win!"

"Yes you do. I saw you the other day, chasing the billy goat after he'd chewed your shoe. You never run that fast with me."

Aya continued to chew on her fingernail. "Well, you'll be seeing. It's this way. If'n I was to have won all the time, you would've thought that you could've never won, and you wouldn'a run no more. You would've stopped."

"Don't let me win anymore, Aya. I want to see if I can beat you."

In the beginning Deirdre couldn't beat Aya. Then the distances between them became shorter and shorter. And one day Deirdre touched the pole at the edge of Loughadalla before Aya. Aya held her hand to her chest and gasped for breath. "I'll be getting too old for this kind of nonsense. You're getting big enough now so as you can run by yourself. And MacFith, he's got to be teaching you the swording. But you can't be letting Lewara find out, 'cause she'll be telling the king. Ach! Ulstermen and Ulster kings. Thinking that women's only good for tending men and tending babies. Queen Maeve. She'll be knowing better."

Yesterday, before the sun set, Deirdre had put some bread and cheese and a flask into a pack and had hidden them at the foot of her bed. Then in the middle of the night, when Aya's snores were comfortable and regular like the purring of a cat, Deirdre had slipped from her bed. MacFith wasn't in the hut. He had managed to sneak away from Aya during the day and was in the woods somewhere with his cask of ale. Lewara lay on the other side of the hut. Sometimes when she got into her gloomies, which happened more and more often now, Lewara would lie in her bed for five or six nights and days without ever getting up, just wailing and rocking her head back and forth on the sheepskins.

Deirdre had knelt down beside Aya's bed. She couldn't take Aya with her; Aya couldn't run fast enough anymore. In the darkness her face looked gray, but if darkness took color from the face, so it took away the imperfections, the deep lines, the brown discolorations that Aya said came with age. In the dark the thin lips were chiseled and lovely, the cheeks and forehead perfect and still as polished stone. Deirdre had never seen that face in repose. During the day the lips were always flaying curses on the geese, the goat, or MacFith. Nowadays, Lewara always said to Deirdre, "I wish you would've died with your mother."

Aya always said, "Why do you always want to be bothering me about your mother, child? I'm your mother." Always the scolding. "Don't you be walking about without your pampooties like a slave girl from Leinster. Don't you be walking about whistling like a common crow. Don't you be sitting on the ground like that. It'll be piles you'll have on your arse end. Don't you be killing butterflies or it's ill luck you'll be having for a whole harvest. Don't you be . . . Don't you be . . . Don't you be . . ." and in the same breath, "Aie, child. But you're a beautiful woman. What would Aya be doing without you out here in this slimy place what's only fit for slimy things and frog's arses."

The old woman had sighed deeply in her sleep, then smacked her lips and said a name. "Bov," she said, "where'd you find that sheep?" Aya smiled in her sleep, and then the face was quiet again. The gnarled fingers of one hand lay uncovered by her side. Deirdre lowered her lips to them. "Good-bye, Aya," she had said softly, "Good-bye, mother." And she had left the crannog.

"*Raawwk!*" said the raven, flying up. Deirdre sensed movement behind her, twisted around, and saw two men standing there.

"Well, now, what has us found here? A tasty little heifer, says I."

"Who are you?" asked Deirdre. Her spear was just out of the reach of her hand. If she reached slowly . . .

"We might be asking you the same thing. And what it is you'll be carrying in your pouch," said the second man. Both men wore filthy ragged clothes, their faces brown as peat, and both carried swords. The first one who had spoken had a long nose and lips that stuck out so he had a face like a dog's snout. The other man had deep, deep wrinkles in his forehead, and only one ear. Were these the fairy kings that Aya had told her about? Her hand edged closer to the spear. Her other hand went to her sword.

But the snout-faced man put a big muddy foot on her spear. "You won't be needing that, now, will you? The gods don't be liking it when a heifer ain't being hospitable to strangers."

The other one asked, "What's a girlie like you doing here all by yourself?"

"I'm not by myself. MacFith, the finest swordsman who ever fought in King Conor's army, is with me. And Bov and . . . and Aya. They're just coming over that hill now. And the king too."

The one-eared man looked up at the hill. There was nothing there.

"They're just a little ways over. They were a little behind me."

The one-eared man licked his lips. He had no teeth. "And where is it that you and the king and them others is heading?"

"To Connacht. To the fort of Queen Maeve. I was told it lay in the direction of the Great Sea. In the direction of the sunset."

"Whomever what told you that told you the right thing. What is it you'll be carrying in your pouch, girlie?"

"This one. This one has *usquabaugh* in it. MacFith makes it. Says that all the campaigns he went on with King Fergus, he didn't do a single one on the thirst-quenching qualities of ordinary water, but rather, on the 'medicining and healthfuling benefits of *usquabaugh.*' Here, you're welcome to it. Taste it. It's good enough if you don't mind the . . . bitterness."

He took it from her, pulled the plug, and swallowed long and hard. Deirdre watched the lump in his throat move up and down like a chicken's gullet as he drank.

"Hey. Leave us a bit, will you? I got a thirst on me."

"Ach." The one-ear wiped his mouth. "Man what makes ale like that has got to be finding favor with the gods."

"Give it over, will you?"

"One more swallow."

"Now." And the dog-snouted one grabbed it from the other and swallowed. As he drank, streams of ale ran out the side of his mouth. When he finished, he belched loudly and threw the pouch to the ground.

The earless one asked again, "What is it you're carrying in the other pouch?"

"Just some bread and cheese. I don't have much left."

The dog-faced man said, "A heifer wearing fine clothes same as what you're wearing must be having fine things under them too."

"Rest easy, Mullin." Then to Deirdre he said, "Why don't you be showing us what you got in your pouch?"

She pulled it closer to her. Along with the food and flint stone, she had packed the gold torque the king had given her as well as some of the bracelets and brooches. "I told you what I have." She reached cautiously into the pouch and took out another piece of cheese wrapped in a cloth. "Here, take it."

The earless one reached for it but his hand stopped—

"*Frog's arse! Frog's arse!*"

Both men spun around. "Who is it you'll be calling a frog's arse?" said the earless one. Deirdre's hand went to her sword, but the dog-faced man was faster.

"Don't touch it," he said, his sword already drawn.

Deirdre tried not to look where Duff was. He was high up, hidden by some branches. "It's MacFith," she said. "MacFith is the best swordsman that ever fought for King Conor. You'd better leave or he'll slice your throats before you can blink."

"*Cut your tongue out!*"

"King Conor can't be far behind. If he sees you with your swords drawn on me, he'll have you drawn and quartered."

The earless one put his sword back into his sheath, but at that moment Duff flew down to the rock. "*Frog's arse. Frog's arse, Raawwwk!*"

"MacFith, is it! The king, is it! Nothing but a bleeding bloody crow it is." The earless one drew his sword again. "Why not just hand us over the pouch, girlie, and we'll see what you got in your bag."

The dog-faced man grabbed her arm roughly. "Redheaded women buck like goats, they say." He pulled the pouch from her.

"Give it over." The earless one reached for it and the other man passed it to him.

"*Cut your tongue out! Raawwwk!*"

"I'll cut your tongue out, all right," the dog-faced man said to the raven, and then to Deirdre, "Mighty clever ruse, that. Teaching a crow to talk. Think you could fool old Mullin, eh? One thing you ain't fooling old Mullin about. Come here!"

She pulled away from him, but his sword went to her throat. "No dugs finer than them what'll be growing on young heifers. Give us a look-see." And he ripped away the front of her shift.

"Well, well, now," said the earless one. "Won't the gods be

smiling on us today," and he pulled out the gold torque from her pouch. "What's this girlie bringing here?"

"Put those back. They're mine."

"Hey! Mind, now. I'd hate to pierce such a pretty throat as this is, specially afore as what I got a taste of the goods."

"Yours, is they, now? These articles such as is in this bag is joolry what is belonging to the king."

"They do belong to the king. They belong to King Conor. And I am to marry him."

"You're to be his wife now, is you? That's why you're heading across this here river to Queen Maeve's fort."

"Yes. I'm Queen Maeve's daughter. I'm going home for a visit."

"I'll wager it's a thief you are, same as what we is. Only you've had better luck with your triflings than we's had up to now, that is." He put the bag inside his pocket.

"They're mine."

"They belongs to him what has them. And now I'm the one what has them. Now, let's have a look-see at your other treasure!" The dog-faced man grabbed her arm roughly and pulled her to him, but she landed a punch on his snout.

"Bitch's bitch!" He pulled back his hand. Deirdre saw everything as though it were happening very slowly. She saw the dark hairs growing between his knuckles, and the dirt in the cracks of his fingers and under his fingernails. She knew the feel of his fist before it hit. She fell. The earth jarred her elbows, her knees, her teeth. A kick to her stomach turned everything black. She wanted to pull up her legs, wanted to fold into herself, but the other one held her legs and the pain from her belly rose through her chest and vomit burned in her throat.

"Frog's arse. Frog's arse."

Now a weight on her chest, heavy as stones. Opening her eyes briefly, she saw the man with the dog face sitting there.

Blood on his face. The sun blinding. The stink of his breath. Rotting clothes. Trying not to breathe his breath. "So you want to hit old Mullin, eh? Excepting that Mullin hits back." The stinging, stinking smacks across her face. The pain, bright and yellow, and red. Smack, Smack. Blackness again. A knife in her belt . . . if only the knife . . . Her legs wrenched apart. "Hurry it up. I got a rut on me what would make a bear snort." She kicked. "Aaaaiiiiee. Can't hold a heifer's hind quarters, eh, Mullin? I'll show you how to bust her bean. Right up to her belly."

"Frog's arse. Frog's arse."

"And after, I'll kill me that crow. Hitting old Mullin, eh?" *Smack. Smack.* The knife. If only the knife . . . She tried to reach. "Hitting old Mullin, eh, and thinking you can get away with it!"

CHAPTER 17

But Mullin didn't do anything. Deirdre felt a shudder go through him; she heard him groan, and in his hesitation she touched her knife, and in that motion she felt something fluid and warm run down her chest, and when she opened her eyes she saw a headless body teetering on her, dripping blood from a severed neck. She screamed and closed her eyes and pushed at the headless torso, and it toppled off her to the side, where its bleeding head already lay face down on the ground. Then she saw the headless body of the other thief, and she saw the huge black shadow of a horse.

She screamed and she screamed, stumbled to her feet, and began to run. These were the Dullahans that Aya had told her about, headless beings that came to take people to Tir-na-n'Og, the land of the dead. And they had come for her, bringing along their nightmare horses, the Phouka, horses that lived on the flesh of human beings, horses who behaved like mad dogs ripping apart men and women.

She heard the terrible hooves of the horse following, getting closer and closer, the shadow of death following her, noisy and rasping in its breathing. She ran and her chest burned as though the inside of her lungs had ignited with a thousand small fires, but she wasn't fast enough. She felt herself grabbed, and she screamed out so she saw nothing but white. But it wasn't the horse's teeth she felt, it was the powerful hand of the man sitting on top of the horse.

Deirdre screamed at the man. She pounded at his chest. "Put me down. Let me go! Let me go!" Her arms were bloody from the thief and as she pounded on this man's chest, she left smeared prints on his chest. He pinned her arms behind her back but they were slippery with blood, and she slipped out of his arms onto the ground.

She regained her footing and began to run again. Now he followed on foot. She heard his sword jangling at his belt. She still had her dagger, and she reached for it and turned on the man.

She was exhausted and crying, and saw him through tear-blurred eyes. "If you want to kill me, kill me! But you won't do it without a fight! Come and get me, but you'll have to take this first." She waved the dagger at him.

"Deirdre," he said, "I don't want to kill you."

She blinked twice and looked at the man. It was the man who had tried to steal her clothes by the river yesterday.

She wiped her wet face with the back of her hand. Her hands were bloody. Her chest was bare and bloody. "So much blood." She sobbed. "So much blood. I'm tired." She let the knife fall from her hands and slid to her knees. "I don't care if you kill me. I'd be willing to die if I knew death was sleep."

CHAPTER 18

When Naisha left the king's banquet hall, he raced out through the maze, leapt down the ramp of the king's inner fort, and ran to the stable. In a moment he was on the stallion's back. He dug his heels sharply into the horse's flanks and galloped through the fort. The stallion was fatigued and he stumbled and Naisha toppled forward across his neck, then regained his balance and whipped the horse forward, out of the gates and onto the plain away from Emain.

Not one of the others had the courage to stand up to the king. Like sheep. Like cattle. All of them. Sean, and Cyril. And Padh. They could stay if they wanted, but he, Naisha, chieftain of Ulster, would not be treated like a dog.

In Erinn it was the custom to send the children of chieftains, kings, and nobles to other provinces for fosterage as soon as the child was weaned. It kept peace in the land. He, Naisha, chieftain of Ulster, had been in fosterage in Leinster with King Mesgedra. Mesgedra would send warriors. If a king's life was sacred, then so was a king's word. Conor, too, had made a testament: to honor his chieftains. If the gods forbade the chieftains from rising against their king, why was it that they allowed the king to betray his pledge to honor his chieftains?

But before Naisha went to King Mesgedra, there was something that he had to do, and he reined his horse in the direction of Loughadalla. Night was like a cat's fur as he galloped, and he whipped his reins across the flanks of Sdoirm. Sweat lathered on the horse's flanks and flew from his neck back onto Naisha's face, and still he whipped the stallion on. A wind had risen from the sea and howled, but there was a sound in the distance that was higher than the howl of wind. And just as morning broke he heard the flight of swans through the wind.

He wasn't far now. The river where he had seen her was just ahead, and over in the darkness against the lake he could see the darker shadow of the crannog.

The gate was closed, and he left the stallion outside. A goose honked at him as he crossed the yard, and he heard a goat or a sheep bleat. There were three huts on the crannog. One would be the stable; the smallest one would be the sweathouse; and the third the living hut. There was only one door and no window. Inside he heard the regular breathing of sleep. It was dark inside, only a faint pink glowed from where the embers of turf had been nested for the night. Here, it seemed, they didn't have to follow the orders of no fire for three nights before Bael-Tinne.

He stirred the turf lightly with a poker. As his eyes grew accustomed to the dark, he saw a woman lying on a bed by the wall. There was only the palest glow from the fire, but he saw her high cheeks, and the perfect straight nose, and the quiet lips. Her hair was not as long as he remembered, and in the shadows it was dark. But he touched her forehead, and then kissed her lips.

"MMMmmm," the sleeper moaned and smacked her lips loudly. "Bov, you liver-lipped toad, best root I never felt!" But then she suddenly sat up, wakened by her own voice. "May the gods be praised. They've finally smiled on Aya. They finally sent her a man."

CHAPTER 19

When Deirdre awoke, the sky was dark. She wasn't sure where she was at first and listened for the familiar sounds from the crannog, the sounds of Aya's breathing and muttering in her sleep, the plash of a water rat or muskrat sliding into the water. The chorus of frogs. There was the sound of a horse snorting, and water lapping against the shore, and the smell of meat roasting, and the crackle of a fire. She was lying on something soft, a sheepskin, and was covered with another one. She turned. The man sat by the fire, roasting a rabbit on a spit.

"You're awake, are you?" he asked when he saw her looking at him.

"Who are you?"

"Naisha, son of Usna. Once chieftain of Ulster. Now wanderer."

Underneath the sheepskin she was naked. She felt stiffness throughout her body: the aching in her shoulders where the thief had pinioned her, and in the small of her back. But the greatest pain was in her stomach. She had barely eaten anything all day, and the smell of the roasting rabbit made the hunger even sharper.

"Are you hungry?" he asked.

"No," she said.

"It's a charming tone of voice you'll be using for someone who saved your life."

"You didn't save my life. I had my knife. It's . . ." But she was completely naked under the sheepskin. "And what did you do with it? *And* the one you took from me yesterday?"

"Here!" He tossed a dagger to her, expecting her to let it fall to the ground; but her hand flew out and she grabbed it by the handle. He tossed her the other one; she caught it as well. "I suppose MacFith taught you that, did he?"

"Yes. And he taught me swording. He said that I was as good with a sword as any man he'd ever trained."

"That's why I found you earlier, defenseless as a doe between two wolves."

"I was just going to use my knife on the one when you came along. Where are they?" She sat up, pulling the sheepskin in front of her.

"Back there! I left them for the crows to eat. And the foxes. Ruffians like that don't deserve burial. And the least you could say is thank you."

"Thank you! Thank you for scaring me half out of my wits."

"I saved your life."

"You don't save a body's life by scaring it to death! Chopping off heads like that. How do you know about MacFith?"

He walked over to her, bringing her a piece of roasted rabbit, which he now put in front of her. The smell of the meat was exquisite.

"Everybody knows about MacFith," he said. "You'd better eat something."

"I'm not hungry. How can everybody know about MacFith? He's been living at the crannog as long as I can remember."

"The world does not begin and end with your memory." He returned to the fire, put more wood on it, and then sat down. She could see the cut on his chin. She vaguely remembered it bleeding yesterday, and she inadvertently touched her own cut shoulder. He began to speak. "When I was still a child,

MacFith lived at the royal fort at Emain. I had just come back from fosterage in Leinster, and was taking the pledge to enter the boy troops. MacFith was our teacher. He was the best swordsman in Conor's army. But then he had a battle accident. He was castrated. It's ill luck to have a man who's not a man in charge of the boy troops. Everyone said he had gone away like an old wolf who's too old to defend his pack. No one knew he was at Loughadalla. I saw him this morning."

"Did you see Aya?"

He smiled and rubbed his black beard with his hand. "Aie. I saw Aya. She was sleeping when I arrived."

"I'm supposed to marry the king."

"I'm supposed to eat rats."

"I'm not joking!" she said angrily.

"Neither am I." He speared her with a look that was as sharp as a sword point.

She covered her shoulder. "Those two didn't believe me. They thought I was a thief."

"Didn't the king give you that jewelry?"

"Yes."

"And aren't you running away with it?"

"I'm going to Queen Maeve's. To Connacht."

"And are you taking the jewelry with you?"

"Lewara always said that gold was valuable. That men—"

"If you take something that doesn't belong to you, then you're a thief."

"I'm not a thief! The king gave me that jewelry."

"He gave you that jewelry because you were to be his wife. But you're not his wife, so you're a thief." He reached inside of his cloak. "Here, thief. You may as well have this." He walked over to her and placed the swan-decorated bowl on the ground beside her.

He stood above her, his hands on his hips. He had very broad shoulders and eyes so dark that she couldn't see where the pupils began or ended. The fire reflected like a needle-point from each of his eyes.

"You stole my bowl and you tried to steal my clothes, and still 'tis I who am called a thief."

He reached down and ripped the sheepskin from her hands. "Aie," he said, and smiled wickedly. " 'Tis a weakness I have. I spend my days riding about the country stealing clothes from bathing maidens and helpless women." He tossed the sheep-skin back to her.

"I'm not helpless!" She covered her breasts with the sheep-skin.

"It's little good that does. If I wanted to see your breasts, it wouldn't be your puny arms that would prevent me from do-ing it."

"My arms aren't puny—"

He grabbed her wrist, yanked it away from her breast. "My wrist is twice as thick as yours. I could crush your bones with one hand." He squeezed. "And that's not all that I could do." He gave her breasts a hard, appraising look.

"Crush my bones!" She slapped at him with her other hand. "Crush this one too. Crush my body. A cow's head is twice as thick as a man's, and it's nothing but a cow's head."

"You're a feisty one, aren't you?" He grinned and let her wrist slip from his hand. He had solid, strong teeth, made whiter by the blackness of his beard. "The king would have had his hands full with you. An old stud with a young filly. You'd finish him by the time harvest's in. Maybe I should take you back to him."

She grabbed the dagger that lay on the ground and pointed it at him.

He looked at the dagger with disdain. "Conor would restore a man's rightful position. You'd do him in, and a new king would have to be chosen."

She sat straighter and moved toward him in an aggressive gesture.

He reached over and wrenched the dagger easily from her and tossed it aside casually. "You think *you* could prevent me from taking you back?" There was something unpredictable and dangerous in his dark face.

"I'll kill you, or I'll die trying."

"You'd better eat something if you're going to try to kill me." He pushed the plate of food closer to her.

"I'm not hungry."

He got up and walked to the fire. "Your clothes were bloody. I washed them." From a branch he removed her garments and threw them to her. "Course your dress isn't worth much now." He reached into his pack and pulled out a leather shirt and threw it to her. "You'd be better off wearing that." He tossed it at her as well.

She looked at the shirt as though it were a squashed lizard. It was the raven that spoke. *"Frog's arse. Frog's arse."*

"Nice language for a queen to be teaching a bird."

"I'm not a queen. I don't want to be queen."

"Queen Deirdre! Shall I pay homage to you, Queen Deirdre?" His voice was dangerous.

"I'm not a queen."

"Deirdre, the runaway queen."

"I'm not a queen."

"You'd better eat something, Queen Deirdre."

"I'm not hungry."

"You eat something, Queen Deirdre, or I'll force the food down your gullet like they do with a goose. I'll not have you fainting on me tomorrow from lack of food."

CHAPTER 20

Faces in her dream merged, so that Conor's gray-yellow eyebrows sprouted on the thief's bald head, and that face kept turning round and round on his neck like a wooden top that MacFith had carved for her when she was little. "Bust her bean, bust her bean," the grinning face kept saying. Each time it spun around, bloodied hands tried to reach out and pinch her, and each place the hands pinched, her skin began to spurt blood. It seemed her skin had been pricked a thousand times, and there were a thousand fountains spurting blood. The blood rose up around her, first a puddle, and then a creek. The waters of Loughadalla had turned to blood. And when the blood ran over the rocks, there was red foam. And she filled the lake with her own blood, and the dog-faced thief came at her with a sword, a golden saber. He was in a boat, standing up, and he kept slicing at her head with a saber. Conor was with him. And they sliced and she ducked. Her own blood rose up through her nostrils, like water in the mouth of a swimmer. The lake was black with blood. She was drowning, drowning in her own blood. Strange arms reached into the blood. A black-haired man with a black horse that ran across the sea of blood, and the man reached into the sea and pulled her up, but she was blood-soaked and slippery and slipped from his arms and went down, down . . . . down. She struggled, and the arms came to her again, warm arms. "Deirdre! Deirdre! You're dreaming."

He knelt beside her, but exhaustion pulled her to sleep, to a deep, black peacefulness. He was close. She could feel him. A keen, warm smell. His breath was on her neck. She was a shell, white and pink. He opened her gently, and the shell turned into a swan's wing, and in the dawn the swan's wings were on fire.

She woke to a gray sky. It wasn't raining yet, but the air was heavy. Rain wasn't far off. The man was not around, but the horse was tied close by. His head was lowered to the ground where he clipped at the grass, his teeth making happy, noisy, tearing sounds. Duff perched on the horse's withers.

"Well, I can see whose side you're on," Deirdre said. Periodically, the horse would raise his head and then dip it delicately to nip at a thistle leaf. The horse curled back his lips so that the thorns wouldn't prick. "Serve you right," Deirdre said, "if they rip your mouth apart." It wasn't that she disliked the horse, it was that she didn't particularly like the man who owned the horse. He was arrogant, rude, conceited, thinking himself a lot more than he was.

The river was gray and chilly-looking, and the last thing she felt like doing was swimming across it. He had laughed when she told him that she thought he was a Phouka, when she had seen the shadow of the black horse following her. Had thrown his head back and laughed as though it were the funniest thing he had ever heard. He had forced her to sleep in his sleeping skin. Said she would be cold otherwise. He had sat down with his back against a tree. "Aren't you going to sleep?" she had asked him.

"I've fought in battles where I've gone three nights without sleep," he said.

She had tried to fight sleep, kept looking around her, didn't want him watching her while she slept, but fatigue carried her away immediately after she'd eaten. She vaguely remembered him holding her during the night. Or was it a dream? "Dreams, a fool's mind at work," Aya always said.

The horse snorted, stamped his feet, swished his tail, and shook his head.

"What's the matter, a thistle get up your nose?"

"Frog's arse. Cut your throat!" The raven didn't like having his perch move under him.

She was warm in the sleeping skin. She had never seen anything like it. It was like a large sack, joined at the bottom and on both sides, the sheepskins sewn together so that the soft fleece was on the inside and the hide on the outside. At the crannog, all they ever slept on was the skins themselves and threw others over them. Sometimes during the night the covers slid off and your side or legs got chilled. Where was he?

The horse snorted again, and she leapt out of the sack. She could make it in half the time to Connacht with a horse. She would take the horse and ride to Connacht. Let Naisha, chieftain of Ulster—he said it as though he were the king himself —let him walk. All full of self-importance, he was. And besides, she could never tell whether he was sneering or smiling.

The horse's halter was tied to a tree. It was rough rope, thick, nearly the size of her wrist and the sharp fibers cut at her hands. Did he have to tie it so tight? That was just like him. What did he think he was tying to the tree—a bear, or a dragon?

Duff settled on her shoulder and began to groom her hair. "Not now, Duff!" She pushed him off.

"*Fly time! Squaaaawk!*" he complained, and settled on a nearby branch.

The stallion snorted and pulled back at the motion of her hand, making the rope even tighter. "Curses on you, horse! May the worms come and eat your bloody eyes out, and those of your master, for tying this rope so tight." She kept looking up. Her heart pounded in her ears. She expected any moment to see Naisha, chieftain of Ulster, come through the trees. She went behind the horse and slapped the sleek black rump. He kicked back, narrowly missing her.

She was stunned. It was the first time she had seen a horse kick. The old gelding that MacFith had, never kicked at anything. Some of the cows did. A couple of them had landed MacFith on the ground when he milked them, but never his old horse. But at least he had moved forward again.

Deirdre had never seen anyone ride horseback. The king always came in a chariot.

MacFith used to have a horse. The horse was called Corr, which meant heron, because he was tall with long, skinny legs and a skinny neck. MacFith used to lift Deirdre into the cart, and as he went about the forest gathering wood for the fire, and acorns to feed to the pigs, he would sing songs and tell her stories. Corr died. MacFith said it was from old age. One morning he had come out to the corral and Corr lay on his side, his legs stuck out straight, stiff as larch poles.

MacFith had brought another horse back from Emain, but Deirdre had never seen MacFith ride it either. Never mind. If Naisha, chieftain of Ulster, could ride horseback, she could too.

She looked up to the trees and, when she didn't see anything, went back to the rope. Her back was turned to the horse, and she felt him nuzzling at her hip, then suddenly he nipped her. She swung around, her fist raised at him. He jumped back and tried to rear, striking at her with his front hoof. He frightened her now, the flared nostrils, the thick, arched neck, and the impatient, quick hooves. Curses on her fright. If the man could ride the stallion, then she could too.

"Get up here!" She slapped the rump, and jumped forward when he kicked. Now the rope was slack again. If Naisha, chieftain of Ulster, came, what would he do? Chieftain of Ulster. Frog's arse. That's what he was. She would tell him she was going to take the horse and give him a drink of water.

The knot finally fell open under her fingers. She took a last look at the sleeping skin on the ground, and her own pack nearby. Leading the horse, she ran to the pack, lifted it to her back, and tied on her sword. If Naisha, chieftain of Ulster, came . . . She had to hurry. Let him keep his sleeping skin. He would need it, hoofing it back to Emain. The pack was heavy, and hurt places in her back where it had rested yesterday. She didn't have time now to think about it. She stood beside the horse and leapt up. But she couldn't quite get up. The stallion had jumped forward, like a rabbit chased by a dog. "Stand still!" Old Corr had never moved so fast in his whole life. You had to use a willow switch to make him walk fast. She grabbed a tuft of black mane and swung up. This time she made it.

The stallion flew forward with such speed that she almost lost her balance. She only had one rein, and the horse took off away from the water, in the direction of the stone circle. She had to get him back to the water, and she pulled on the rein, but he wouldn't budge from his direction. She pulled with both hands, and the rough rope cut her hands. Then there was a sudden, sharp whistle, and the stallion slid to such a short stop that she toppled over his head.

When she was little, MacFith had built her a small playhouse in a tree in the forest. Once she had been careless and had stepped back into the opening and fallen to the ground. It could only have taken a moment for her to have fallen, but she remembered the fall. It seemed to take a long time. She remembered that moment now as she flew over the horse's head. She remembered the heavy thud when she hit the ground, how the breath had been knocked out of her. She knew she would feel like that now, how it would take her several gasping breaths before she could actually breathe again.

She thought she would die gasping for breath. Again she

breathed, and still no breath came. She was face down in the grass, and she tried to lift her head, but she couldn't breathe. But then breath came and she knew she wasn't going to die. She was jarred but nothing really hurt, except for the grass burns on her knees where she had slid forward on them. She lay there for a moment, her face turned sideways on the grass, smelling it and the closeness of the earth. Then she slowly rolled over.

A figure ran on the other side of the horse. His body was blocked by the horse, but she saw the leather leggings of a man, and noticed the black hairs that curled above the leggings, thick and dark like black ferns. "Are you all right?" he called.

She didn't answer.

"Are you hurt?"

The horse whinnied, and Naisha, chieftain of Ulster, appeared from his side. Naisha came to Deirdre and knelt down. "Are you hurt?"

She shook her head. He ran his hands down both her arms, then gently took one leg, placing one hand on her knee and the other under her foot. He pushed the leg up to her chest, then pulled it straight. He took the other leg.

She pulled it away. "I'm all right," she said.

Immediately, the expression on his face changed. "First you steal the king's jewelry, then you try to steal my horse. You know what the penalty for stealing horses is? A man is tied to five horses, one limb to each horse and his head to a fifth. Then the five horses are whipped in five different directions."

"Lucky for me you don't have four more horses!"

He looked at her. Even in the daylight his eyes were so black that she couldn't tell where his pupils ended.

He stood up and reached to take her arm.

She pulled away. "I don't need your help. I wasn't stealing your stupid horse either. I was just going for a ride."

He reached down anyway, took her by the underarms, and stood her up. "With your packs? You were just going for a ride, were you?"

"I didn't want to leave them here in case some other thief came along."

"You're not strong enough to ride him. Look at your puny arms."

"They aren't puny."

He sneered. Or was it a smile? She wasn't sure. She tried to pull her arm away. He held it. "All right, puny arm. Pull it away. My little thief with the puny arm."

"Let go! I'm not a thief."

"Make me!"

She slapped at him with her free hand, but he pinioned her wrists behind her back. He bent his face close to hers. His whiskers brushed against her cheek, and his breath was fresh like an apple barrel. She struggled. "Tell me, Deirdre. Queen of Conor. Thief with the puny arms. How does a woman like you handle a stallion? He's ten times as strong as I am."

She looked at the ground.

"Look at me!"

She refused to look up.

"Look at me, I said," and he tucked one foot behind hers and toppled her easily to the ground. He was on top of her. His hand held her wrists. "Now you'll look at me."

"Yes. I'll look at you. I see a man with black eyes and black beard. And black hair, just as black as a horse's arse. And you might be just as strong as a horse, but you're just as stupid. Tying a horse with a rope that's big enough for a bear."

Naisha smiled. "I tie him because he's a pig. Because he always wants to eat more than he has to. And he wanders too far looking for grass." The horse was chewing again, and the crow had once again settled on his neck.

"You could always just *whistle* to bring him back."

"He comes too. All the time." Naisha hesitated. A strand of hair had blown across Deirdre's face and tickled her nose, so she crinkled it. He brushed the hair from her face, and looked at her. "You're very beautiful. The first time I heard you, you were whistling. It's ill luck for a woman to whistle."

"Are you going to tie me up, too, so I don't run away?"

"Why? Are you a pig like he is?"

She was silent.

"I told you, I tie him because he eats everything, especially flowers. I'm always afraid he'll find foxgloves and eat them. They can kill a horse." He continued. "You know how a man controls a horse? Not with strength but with wisdom and gentleness." He began stroking the area around Deirdre's lips. "He finds a horse's weakness and puts a bridle in that soft mouth. He strokes the horse, and talks to it and feeds it, so that the horse willingly accepts the bridle. A man never forces." And he whispered something, but she couldn't understand what he said, but there was the sound of his breath in her ear, like the sound of the seashell, and the rise and fall of the sea like Aya told her. His breath was warm and soft. His mouth traveled up her neck and the persistent touch of his lips brought tinglings once again to the small of her back. And his hand was there, rubbing the small of her back where it ached from carrying her pack yesterday. His hands felt good, and his breath was warm, and she arched her back so that he could rub her better. He rubbed her spine and she moaned because it was as though his hands had eyes and could find the stiffness. And the touch of his fingers and his lips brought butterflies to her body, and she turned her mouth to him. His kisses were soft; his tongue, slow and searching, touched something hidden and brought it to life, and she responded. She felt the hard muscles ripple under her hand, and felt the newness of passion. The butterflies beat in a frenzy, but now they beat with wings of flame. His mouth was no longer soft, but fierce and demanding. Now his fingers touched a place where she had never been touched, gentle probing fingers, spreading her, reaching in, and still he kissed her. She moved up to him, sliding her buttocks along his thighs. She knew she had to be entered; his fingers spread her farther. She felt him slide between her thighs. Softer than a tongue, yet relentlessly hard. The pain surprised her, and she sucked her breath in, but his mouth held hers, and something timeless, something old and timeless as the first man and first woman, made her continue. She could no more refuse him than the earth could refuse the rain, and her tongue sought his and she arched her back so that he could penetrate completely. His hands on her buttocks lifted her up to the hard, pain-bringing softness. He hurt her, a slow hurt now, gentle, each thrust pushing the pain deeper. And when he was completely in, the pain stopped, and for a long time he held her. She could feel him throbbing inside, and the fire rose again and she tilted her pelvis up to him. He began to thrust; gently, then more vigorously, and now there was no pain, only a rising wave that moved through her, and she forgot her name. She forgot where she was and how far she had come. She was everywhere and nowhere. She was a harp being strummed for the first time; she was like the white waves of the ocean breaking against the shore; she was like a flaming star falling through the night, and when he spilled into her, he spoke her name, "Deirdre," and she was like the beating of swan's wings in the dawn.

CHAPTER
21

For two nights they stayed beside the river. Naisha built a lean-to of willow twigs. And Deirdre helped him build it, and when she handed him a branch, he touched her hand and held it for a moment. And when she walked by him, she touched his shoulder or his arm. Or he slid his hand against her buttock, or he grabbed her about the waist and pulled her to him, and kissed her deeply.

And while they built the lean-to, they fell on the grass and made love, and after it was built, they made love, and they made love again, with the rain falling outside. And during the night he woke to the persistent touch of her lips, and they made love again, and when they woke in the morning, she could feel his hardness pressing against her, and they fell asleep, and when they woke, they made love once more.

But she was too swollen for him to penetrate, so he went outside and lifted his face to the rain, opened his mouth, and allowed the rain to fall in it. His mouth warmed the rain and he came to her, and she opened her thighs to him, and he bent down and filled her with the warm rainwater and then loved her once more.

The morning following the second night, Naisha woke first. It was a glorious morning with just a few wafts of cloud rising on the horizon. The sun streamed down on Deirdre's face. One of her finely muscled arms lay out on top of the cover and her left breast was bare. On the mound just above the nipple a small dark mole, about the size of an apple seed, marked the pale flesh. The nipple itself was golden pink, with a texture like an unripe raspberry. He kissed the breast and began to tongue the nipple.

She moaned in her sleep, opened one eye briefly, then her eyes fluttered back into sleep. He turned her on her side, and when he was finished, she was completely awake. She turned to him, buried her face in his chest. The hairs there tickled her nose, and she rubbed her itchy nose against his shoulder. "That's a fine way for me to be waking up. Finding your great big thing already inside of me, and not even asking me."

"Why should I ask? You would have only said yes."

She smiled. "I love it when you love me."

"You're a lusty one, aren't you?"

"Aya used to tell me that there was nothing could make a woman feel better than a man. She always used to berate MacFith. I never really understood before. Well, in a way I understood. I understood up here." She touched her head. "But now I understand here too. Poor MacFith. It wasn't his fault."

"That's the reason he was sent out there. There's been gossip for years. The king's woman hidden in the woods. And there was a prophecy, too, but I don't remember it anymore. He was sent with you. As a swordsman he could protect you, but as an eunuch he wouldn't have been able to damage you."

"Damage me?"

"All women must undergo the first forcing by the king. It's the law. That's twice I've broken the laws in two days. Three times, if you want to . . ." But he didn't finish.

"I've broken the laws too." She looked at him. "I'll break any law as long as I'm with you."

"He'll be looking for us. The Druid wouldn't allow him to come until after the Bael fires were lit and the sacrifices were made. But they would have been done this morning. The king will come looking for me. We have to leave. We're only a day's ride from Emain."

"I want to go to Ben Gulbain. Aya is from Connacht. She's told me many stories about Queen Maeve."

"I was going to Leinster. Mesgedra, the high king, has his fort at Tara. I was in fosterage there as a boy. A king always needs a good warrior. I wanted to take you with me, but we'll go to Connacht. We're closer to Ben Gulbain and to Maeve's fortress than to Leinster. A queen needs warriors as much as a king does."

"Aya tells me that she's fierce and beautiful."

"I saw her once on a far-off hill in a chariot drawn by four pure-white horses. She had white flowers braided in her long hair and white veils flew out behind her as she raced across the hill. It was during a raid. I thought it was a vision that I saw."

Deirdre sat up on her elbow. "Do you think she's more beautiful than me?"

He smiled. "No," he said.

"It doesn't matter that she be more beautiful than me. It doesn't matter if women think so, or even other men. But you mustn't think so."

He touched her face and wrapped the long tendrils of fire-colored hair around his fingers, then brushed them off her breast and kissed her nipple. "You're splendid," he said, then continued kissing her breasts, first one, then the other. He wanted her again and lifted his mouth to hers. She was sore from the constant lovemaking, but he was gentle when he pressed himself between her swollen flesh.

After, they lay side by side again. They were so close that she breathed in the air that he breathed out. "I feel as if your breath surrounds me, Naisha. I feel as if I'm wrapped in it, the way a butterfly is wrapped in a cocoon. I feel as if my arms, my breasts, my thighs—as if all of me is wrapped in fine filaments of love."

He kissed her again, tenderly, then slapped her rump. "This time we have to go."

"Don't slap my rump as though I were your horse."

"Why not?" He pushed her back down and sat on top of her. "Come on, horse, faster. On to Queen Maeve's. Faster. Conor is coming. Faster." He dug his heels into her side and began to tickle her.

"Stop that! Stop! Naisha!"

"We'll never escape at this speed."

"Naisha!"

He stopped and kissed her, then stood up and reached out his hand to her. She took it and stood. He looked at her nakedness and shook his head. "The king will never forgive me for what I've done. Never!"

CHAPTER
22

After two days' travel, Deirdre and Naisha, came to a body of water larger than any Deirdre had ever seen. The sun was just sinking, and the river spilled with colors of orange and purple and red.

"Oh, Naisha!" she exclaimed. "The sea! The sea!"

Naisha smiled. "That's not the sea. It's Lough Erne."

"I've never seen so much water. At Loughadalla I could see the other side. I could swim across it."

"You might not swim this, but look, you can see the other side. See the trees and the bank?"

"What does the sea look like?"

"Like the sea! Like a great watery beast, thrashing and churning."

Stones cropped up at the edge of the lake. Naisha and Deirdre, splashing each other and playing in the water, walked out to them. Naisha sat down on one of the stones and pulled Deirdre onto his lap. Her feet just grazed the surface of the water, but periodically little waves crested, wetting the bottoms of her toes. Frogs croaked, and a kingfisher dived, and in the distance a troop of swans glided quietly along the darkening lake. She felt Naisha harden under her, and she turned and straddled him and opened herself to him. When they were through, she felt his love-sap trickle from her. She felt a part of this place, as if she'd never felt part of anything before, part of the rocks and the water, and the wind that caught at her hair.

The moon was a thin crescent glowing in the growing darkness behind Naisha's shoulder. "Oh, look," said Deirdre. "Look there at the evening star. Two stars means evening. And three means nighttime. That's what Aya used to say. It's still only evening."

"No, it's nighttime. There's the third." Three stars hung over the hill, silver-pointed jewels in a purple crown.

When Deirdre finally saw the foam-capped sea breaking against the severe beauty of the rocky shore, she screamed with wonder and slid off the back of the horse and began to run to the water. Naisha didn't know what had happened, only that he saw her running to the sea, her hair flying. "Deirdre, come back!" he shouted, and thrust his heels into Sdoirm's flanks, but the footing was rocky, and the horse, sensing the coming storm, was stubborn and skittish, and Naisha had to fight him to descend to the beach.

"Deirdre," he said, "we have to find shelter."

But the dark seaweed known as mermaid's tresses wrapped itself around her ankles as though it wanted to claim her, and to take her to the place from where it had come.

"Deirdre," he called her again, but she was oblivious to his voice. The wind howled like a woman who's lost all her sons at sea, and dark clouds stumbled across the sky, like a herd of black bulls being chased by wolves.

She stood on the shore, dark seaweed wrapped around her ankles. The wind thrust her skirt against her body, flinging it behind her, fanning her hair like flames, then whipping it against her face. Her head was erect, confronting the wind as though it was an enemy.

He touched her arm. Lightning struck and the purple sky caught fire. She spun on him, her amber eyes burning.

"Come up to the rocks! We have to find shelter!" he shouted.

But she turned her face back to the sea. The waves were the

color of an old beaten sword, but the tops of the waves were white and churning and foaming like the mouth of an animal. The wind screamed at the earth now, and even the salt in the air had a sharp sound. The wind pressed her clothes against her, and her outline was dark and wild in front of a dark and wild sea.

He took her upper arm, but she pushed his hand away, and when she shook her head, he could feel the sharpness of her hair, like small, sharp pins as the wind whipped it against his arms. Earlier in the morning when he had made love to her, her hair fanned about her shoulders soft as silk. He had been sweating after they made love, and she had rubbed down his chest and his groin and between his thighs with the silk.

But she was a stranger now. There was a terrible beauty in her face, wild and untamable, fierce as the sea. And she kept changing. Each time he looked at her, each time the wind whipped her hair across her face, she changed. It was as though she had lived here before, and with each gust of wind, she became what she had been in generations past. One moment she was a queen, and then a witch. And then she was an eagle, and then a wolf, and then a child filled with awe and wonder, playing in the foam.

"Come back," he shouted.

But the wind slapped her hair against her face again, and again she was a stranger, something wild, something elemental.

He had to find shelter. And he raced back up the rocks, then down the shore. He found a shallow cave, and some dry driftwood that he split with his dagger and started a fire with flint sparks and dry moss, and he watched her. In a frenzy she, too, began to gather small bits of driftwood. Then she knelt down beside the sticks, her back against the wind, her cloak pulled over her shoulders so that she looked like a black outcropped stone herself, and somehow, somehow in the wind, she managed to start the fire. The wind caught it and it blazed. And then she peeled off her clothes. And the wind whipped her hair across her naked back and buttocks. And she plunged into the ocean and became part of it, rising on the waves, then disappearing in the churning, foaming waves. He screamed at her, and ran out, and then she emerged from the sea, her hair like the kelp that had caught her ankles before. And she looked over her shoulder as she walked, like a wolf in the forest. And she lay her nakedness down close to the fire, her body curled around it, her breasts close to it, and the wind blew.

He ran to the beach. Lightning split the sky. Her body was on fire. "You can't stay here," he shouted, but the thunder of gods rolled over his voice, rolled over the rocky crashes of the sea, rolled and echoed. Only the wind was louder. He tried to grab her up in his arms, but her mouth went for his. Her tongue tasted of the sea, the way a mermaid's would. Her hair smelled of the salt and the wind.

She opened her thighs and arched her back. Then he was on top of her, seeking her mouth as fiercely as she had sought his. Thrusting into her, her urgency driving him harder and deeper, until he forgot the pulse of the sea and the lightning. Only the thunder stayed with him. Its anger seemed to split the world so the stones shattered. He felt the tremor rise in her body and could no longer contain the shudder in his groin. The wind screamed. She defied it as though it were an enemy. He heard the whisper of his name on her lips.

CHAPTER 23

The storm passed as quickly as it had come. The sun came out and a rainbow joined earth to sky.

"See there," said Deirdre, "see, we just have to walk over to that cliff, and that's where we'll find the purest gold in the world. The gold of Erinn is red gold, and the gold of the rest of the world is yellow gold. But the purest gold, the gold of gods, is white gold. Aya told me that. The leprechauns guard it."

"The most precious gold in the world," said Naisha, "is the liquid gold that is the dew between your thighs." He reached down and, sticking his hand between her legs, half lifted, half pulled her to him and kissed her fully on the lips.

"Is there nothing else you'll be thinking of?" She tried to turn away from him but he held her tighter. When she tried to pull her mouth away from him, he nipped her bottom lip. This excited her, and she responded to him, kissing him harder, but he drew back.

"What do you think I am, woman? I'm made of flesh, not steel. It's not a tireless thing."

She bit his shoulder. "Then why do you tease me?"

"Ouch! Bite me, will you?" He took her chin in mock roughness and tilted it up and nipped her lower lip before forcing his tongue into her mouth.

She bit it. He drew back. "That'll be teaching you to tease," she said, "making me want you again and then not doing anything about it."

He took her in his arms and kissed her once more. It was a

tender, encouraging kiss rather than a passionate one. Then he held her, and for a moment they just stood there looking out at the sea and the countryside, which was utterly transformed by the darkness of the storm. The cliffs and hillsides seemed to be bathed in an unearthly light. The sun, which was sinking, was a finger's width above the sea. Birds sang. She heard the thrush's song, and the lark, and a piercing cry of a plover, and the shriek of gulls. She realized that she had never been happier than she was at this moment. The sea was smooth as redgold in front of her, and Naisha's arms were around her. The sun was going down, but over there, over the hills, the moon was just visible like a pale, crescent cloud.

When she was at Loughadalla, she would lie on the ground looking up at the moon at night; she would feel its power in her arms, in her legs and in her breasts, and she would long for something, but she had been unable to explain the longing. It was only now that she knew what the longing had been—love. The sky and the hillsides and the sea were soft and green and gold. The coastline was like the gentle sounds of MacFith's harp.

She wished she could pluck this moment and hold it forever. She wished she could make the sun stop in the sky where it was, and make that bird there still in midwing beat. She wished she could catch the waves of the sea at that moment when they crested over the rocks when the foam was whitest, before they spilled back to the sea. She wished she could keep Naisha's arms wrapped around her. She wished he could hold her like this forever.

But the light changed again. It was an unearthly light, like light in a dreamland. And now the coastline looked as though the rainbow had been shattered over it, and a chunk lay here and there, a rose-colored cliff, a purple hill, a yellow outcrop of stone. How different this place was now, from the darkness that had overwhelmed it earlier.

But the light changed again, and everything was greener than before, and bluer and more red. And on the hills water trickled down from the edge of a seam of peat. And the sea had turned from green to gold to red in a matter of moments, and now the cliffs were red. The light couldn't be trusted here. It was as though the fairies controlled this place. One moment you looked at a hill, and when you looked at it again, it was as though you were in a different place.

She heard voices, and saw three people coming toward the shore. They clambered over the rocks, three people smaller than herself. Three women it looked like, because they all wore long skirts. The taller one wore a dark-colored skirt with a multicolored shawl on her shoulders, crossed over her breasts and tied behind. The smaller ones wore rusty-red colored skirts and small dark caps.

Deirdre nudged Naisha, and he looked too.

"Children," he said. "Looks like they're coming to rake seaweed."

"Children?" She looked at them again. She had never before seen children. Aya had told her about them, childrens, she called them. Little adults, the same that calves were little cows. But the only child Deirdre had ever seen was herself, in a reflection in Loughadalla sometimes when she had stood beside Aya. And sometimes she had compared herself with Aya. She had laid her palm against Aya's palm: "Aya, your hand is bigger than mine." "Aie, and so's my feetsies. See, nearly twice as long they is." And then she would stand at Aya's shoulder, and stand on her toes and say, "I'm almost as tall as you." "Now, there, cheating again and standing on your tipsy toes. But you're getting to be bigger, all right." And then she had grown taller than Aya, and looked down on the top of Aya's head where the scalp lay pale beneath the strands of gray-black hair.

"Children," Deirdre said. And then she repeated the word and looked at her hands, and then at the children again.

The two smaller children carried buckets. The bigger one in the middle carried a rake.

"Hey, you there!" Naisha called to them.

The three faces started.

"Don't be afraid," said Naisha, coming out from the cave. "We're only wanderers looking for the fort of Queen Maeve."

The children had round, pale faces, simple like the moon. Deirdre came out of the cave as well. She wanted to see them more closely.

"My name is Beida," said the taller one in the middle, "and these will be being my brothers."

"Brothers?" Naisha questioned. "Why are they dressed in the skirts of girls?"

"The fairies does be haunting this place, and stealing away boy children, so we'll be dressing them as girls."

"Does this place have a name?" asked Naisha.

"This here is the earth and out there is the sea."

Naisha smiled and looked at Deirdre.

"But does the earth here have a name?"

"Up there," she said, pointing to the white cliffs to the north, "is Dhun-na-n'Gall, the fort of the strangers. The bay is called Cuan-Dhun-na-n'Gall. Me father says this is the most beautiful place anywhere that the gods ever does be made. My name is Beida," she repeated.

"That's a pretty name for a young lass. Can you tell us how far to Ben Gulbain?"

"Me Mum and me Dad is gone. Gone to the sheep fair. It's up the coast they've gone, to market. Driving two rams to buy shovels. Me Dad says the merchants is gombeen man. They always want too much for their wares."

"Merchants everywhere are gombeen," said Naisha. "Can you tell us the way to Maeve's fort?"

"I know how to spin. I spun enough already for a household. Me Mum says I'm ready to be married now. Next season at Bael-Tinne, I'll be able to leap over the broom handle. Me Dad says I've got to rake the seaweed to put onto the stones to be making earth, so as the plants will be growing, so as I can find a man who'll help work it." She motioned to her brothers. "You'd best be getting at the crottles."

"Crottles?" asked Naisha.

"Them lichens what'll be growing on the rocks. We does be using them to dye the wool. Same as what this skirt is." She touched it. "This red-brown color. Sometimes we'll be using onions. And sometimes the heather. And sometimes the broom grass or the blackberry. But a body can only be scraping off the crottles after a rain."

"Do you know how far it is to Maeve's fort?"

"I had me a sister named Maeve. But she's dead. Me Dad said she was luvelier than me. Do you think I'm luvely?"

"Yes, but—"

"Maeve was luvely. Me Mum al'ays said she'd get husbanded afore me. But I was birthed afore her. Two seasons, I was. Me sister Maeve ain't luvely no more. They buried her. I helped dig the hole meself. I got to marry soon now. Will you marry me?"

Naisha looked at Deirdre. The young woman continued. "Me Dad said Maeve was luvelier than me. But we buried her. Sick she was. She ain't luvely no more. She talks to me, she does. At night out on the furze. Do you want to come and see where we buried her?"

"We have to leave now," Naisha said.

"I have to leave. While me brothers scrapes the crottles, I got to be raking in the seaweed. We lets it dry, and then carries it up to the fields. Up there, 'cause the earth ain't good enough. Me mother boiled snails in water and gave them to Maeve to drink to cure the cough. But she died anyhow."

"Do you know how far it is to Ben Gulbain? To Queen Maeve's?"

"Me mother says that Queen Maeve is the most luveliest woman that the gods ever made. She said that me sister was almost as luvely. Do you think I'm luvely?" But she didn't wait for an answer. "If I rake up enough seaweed maybe me father will think I'm luvely too." And she turned and picked her way down to the shore where she began to rake at the kelp, raking it high onto the beach out of the reach of the tide.

Deirdre watched the simple young woman for a while. The strong shoulders and back pulling at the heavy kelp, separating it into piles so that it would dry more quickly. But it wasn't the kelp that interested Deirdre. It was what the young woman had said about Maeve. She looked at Naisha. His dark, handsome face was intent on shaking the sand from the sleeping skin. He had said that Maeve was beautiful. Aya had said it. This young woman raking seaweed had said it. Was Maeve really so beautiful? Deirdre wished there were a pool of water that she could look into. She felt uneasy.

The light changed again. The sun was sinking into the sea, turning the water brilliant red, as though it were bleeding. The clouds were on fire and pulsed like a heart. Behind the hill was even bluer now. Then the rim of the sun touched the water, and the world was still, perfectly at peace. It was the silence of sunset that lasts only a moment, and then the evening sounds begin. Deirdre looked to the south again. Tomorrow they would be in Ben Gulbain. They would see the fort of Queen Maeve.

Deirdre watched the young woman. The strong shoulders and the back pulling at the heavy kelp. She called to Naisha. "I don't think I want to go to Maeve's fort."

He gave her that same hard, dangerous look she'd seen

before. "We've come this far," he said. "We're not turning back now."

The light changed again. The sea was turning purple, and the clouds, which had been black, then red, were now gray again as evening fell.

CHAPTER
24

From the top of the green limestone mountain that was named Ben Gulbain, Deirdre thought she could see to the end of the world. The sea went on and on forever, it seemed. It didn't, though. Aya had told her that. Told her that great dragons and turtles, so big that they could swallow fifteen cows in one bite, lived at the edge of the earth, and people in boats had to be careful so that they didn't fall off when they went sailing.

"We'd better get off here," Naisha said, "and lead the horse the rest of the way in."

"Why?" asked Deirdre. She was comfortable riding behind Naisha, her chin resting lightly on his shoulder, her hands on his thighs.

"Because the fools who live on this island think a man is crazy if he rides a horse, instead of riding in a chariot behind a horse."

"But why do they think a man is crazy if he rides a horse?"

"Because it's different." He lifted one leg over the horse's neck and slid off. He reached up to help her down.

"I don't need your help," she said, and slid off the other side.

"You're getting mighty cocky again."

"Cock-a-doodle-doo." She tossed her head so the red was like brindled gold in the sun. "Cock-a-doodle-doo," she said again.

"You know what happens to a hen that crows, don't you?" he asked.

"No. Tell me."

He grabbed her and pushed her hard against the horse's leg. He ran his finger along her throat. "They get their throats cut."

"Cock-a-doodle-doo," she said. Her amber eyes were yellow and arrogant.

He grabbed her by the waist and pulled her to him and tried to kiss her. She turned her head away, and he pulled it back and kissed her hard, but she bit his tongue.

"Bitch!" He drew back. "Someday, I'll have to teach you a lesson."

She laughed. "What if I bit something else? Just lightly. You like that, don't you? Just little nips."

"Come on." He held the horse's reins in one hand, and took her hand with the other.

"Aya told me that men like it."

"Aya was right."

"Why do you like it?"

"It feels good."

"Are you afraid, Naisha?"

"No." He looked at her. "Are you?"

"Yes."

He put his arm around her and they walked toward the great gates of Queen Maeve's fort. Hers was a fort surrounded by a stone wall. Red-and-gold flags flew from various points around it.

"Why don't people ride horseback in Erinn?" she asked again. The walk up to the gate seemed interminable. She asked the question again.

"Because it's a different way of doing things, and because people are always frightened when they have to do something different. So, rather than admit their own fear, they say that others are fools and stupid. But eventually, a few more try the new thing. And soon it becomes the ordinary."

"Did the king ever call you a fool?"

"He called me a traitor. Some of his foot-lickers called me a fool, though."

"Who?"

"Men you've never heard of."

"Who?"

"Men you don't know."

"If they insulted you, I want to know their names."

"Owen Campbell."

"Did it make you feel gloomy when Owen called you a fool?"

"No. Owen's a worm. He squirms whenever the king's about."

"Sometimes Lewara used to say things to me. She would say that if it weren't for me, she would have been the mother of a king. She used to tell me that I should have died with my mother. She used to call me a stupid little fool because I didn't want to marry the king, and then I used to go away and be by myself. MacFith had built me a playhouse in a tree. I used to go there. I used to pretend that I was an eagle, and that I was high and could look down on everybody below. I used to want to cry. And I would tell myself, eagles don't cry. Eagles don't cry."

Naisha looked at her. "Yes, they do. It's just that men don't hear them."

Six soldiers stood abreast at the great gate of Ben Gulbain. Men with corn-colored hair, great flowing beards, shoulders wide as an ox's neck. They were heavily sworded, and each man held a spear.

Naisha spoke before any one of the six questioned him. It was a habit of the rank of which he had once been part. Chieftains announced their names before they were asked them. Farmers and tradesmen always spoke to soldiers only after the soldiers spoke first.

"I am Naisha, chieftain of Ulster. I seek shelter for us and for my horse."

A request like this could not be refused by any host in Erinn. Wanderers and beggars were often gods in disguise. To deny a stranger who asked for food and lodging his request meant that the wrath of all the gods could fall on the host. Likewise, a stranger who broke his host's trust would be tortured and tormented by the gods for ten times ten thousand years.

"Queen Maeve welcomes strangers, but asks that she know your business at Ben Gulbain."

"I am Naisha, chieftain of Ulster. I bring my sword to the service of Queen Maeve." He unsheathed it and handed it to the guard.

"Keep your sword, chieftain of Ulster. A sword in another man's hand doesn't serve the owner well." The guard spoke to one of the other soldiers. "You take the horse from Ulster to the stable." The guard motioned to another. "And you show them to the doors of the palace."

The doors of the palace of Queen Maeve were even more ornate than the doors of the roundhouse at Emain. They were solid bronze, as high as three men, but delicately balanced so that they opened and closed with the lightest of hands.

When one guard left them, another took them to the throne room. From the throne room came the light sounds of harp music. Deirdre had never seen such splendor in her life. Every window frame was gilded, and every beam edge in the ceiling. The wooden floor was so shiny that Deirdre could see herself and Naisha in it. She smoothed her hair and tried to smooth the wrinkles in her cloak. Naisha put his arm around her waist and squeezed.

"Don't be afraid," he whispered.

The walls were hung with tapestries, gold and red with fantastic animals that Deirdre had never seen, like huge cats with eagle's wings, and dragons the way she imagined them to be, and snakes devouring their own tails. And there were hunting scenes, men chasing deer with hounds, and hounds holding wolves at bay. And she looked up, and even the ceilings were decorated with ornate gold circles, and circles within circles.

There she was. It had to be Queen Maeve. Aya had said that there was no one more beautiful than Queen Maeve. She sat on a raised platform, her white gown spreading about her, made of so much material that it looked as though her body came out of a cloud. One breast was uncovered. She wore a gold diadem crown similar to the one that the king wore, but on either side of the crown was a silver horn, like the crescent of the moon.

Her voice was as regal as her presence. "Welcome, strangers, to the court of Maeve."

Naisha bowed low. And Deirdre, not knowing what else to do, did the same.

Naisha introduced himself and Deirdre.

"The reputation of the chieftain of Ulster precedes you," said Maeve.

"I am no longer chieftain, Majesty. That is why I have come to Connacht to offer my sword in your service."

"The son of Usna, no longer chieftain?" Queen Maeve questioned.

Deirdre looked at her. Everything Aya had said about her was right. Her hair was like the color of the sun and braided with gold cords, so that when she turned or tilted her head the gold shone. The gown was sprinkled with something that looked to Deirdre like stardust. It was as though the moon and the stars had come to the earth and settled on the platform in front of her.

"I have withdrawn my services from King Conor."

"And if you withdraw your services from King Conor, is it

not possible that you will withdraw your services from me as well?"

"I do not know how it is in Connacht, Majesty. But in Ulster, a testament is given both ways—a chieftain swears his allegiance to his king, but the king swears honor to his chieftains. Conor has broken the sacred trust of honor and makes his chieftains behave like dogs. I am a man, Majesty, and ask only that you allow me to serve you as a man. I was the best swordsman in Ulster. If you allow me to serve you, I will not dishonor that reputation."

"Naisha, son of Usna. Your father came to me as emissary many years ago when I was just queen. He was a man who did credit to his name, both as a man and as a chieftain. Is he well?"

"My father is dead, Majesty. He was killed in an accident while hunting wild boars."

Maeve looked down for a moment, then straightened her shoulders and looked at Naisha. "I asked your father to stay here with me at Ben Gulbain, but he refused. Said that he loved another woman. Your mother, I presume. . . . She did credit to your father in bringing you forth. The son of Usna is welcome at the court of Queen Maeve."

"Thank you, Majesty," he said, and bowed again.

"Tell me, Usna—I mean, Naisha; you resemble your father. Did you bring your horses to Ben Gulbain?"

"I brought one stallion, Majesty. My finest."

"One stallion to draw a chariot?"

"I didn't come by chariot."

"The son of Usna wouldn't walk like a common peasant?"

"No, Majesty." Naisha looked at Deirdre.

"I rode, Majesty." He looked at Deirdre again. "Sitting on the horse's back."

"And you came all the way from Emain"—she arched her eyebrows—"sitting on a horse's back?"

"Yes, Majesty. When I traveled across the channel to the great land that has no end, I saw great armies led by a man whom they call Caesar. His captains all travel by horseback. It's much faster, Majesty. A man sitting on horseback travels three times as fast as a man in a chariot."

"Later you'll explain more to me of how it's done. I will give you lodging. In return you will allow your stallion to stand stud for some of my mares. I have the finest soldiers in Erinn, but my horses are always taken from me at the races of Lughnasa. When your father was here, he left me a stallion. You may remember him. He was the color of the sun with a mooncolored tail and mane."

"Yes, Majesty. He was the grandsire of my own stallion. One of the finest horses in all Erinn."

"He was but a fortnight with me. It was I who held his reins in a chariot race with some of my chieftains. But there was a collision. One of the other drivers was drunk. The crossbar of the chariot pierced his stomach and he had to be destroyed. I have not had a good stud since."

"I would be honored to allow my horse to stand stud for your mares."

Maeve clapped her hands and a servant came forward. "Show them to their quarters. Naisha, tomorrow you will show me your stallion."

CHAPTER
25

The stallion whinnied shrill and loud as they neared the corral, and he pulled at his reins so that the veins in Naisha's arm strained at the surface. Deirdre sensed the horse's excitement.

As they neared the corral, the stallion raised his head and sent a piercing whinny in the direction of the stables. The wind picked up his scent and carried it to the other horses. Challenges came from the other horses in the stable as he approached, whinnies even louder and shriller than his. His head went back and the nostrils flared so that the moist redness, like a flower, could be seen. In the wind his mane was like a tossed black sea.

Deirdre could still sense the excitement in the horses and felt her breath quicken, felt her nipples grow hot. Sdoirm pulled at his reins so hard, Naisha had to grab the bridle itself and hold the stallion close. Naisha's arms pulled with the strain.

The stallion snorted and tried to toss his head, whinnied again, but low this time, a murmuring sound, almost as though he were growling. And then a groom brought out a dappled gray horse. She looked nervous, but was one of the loveliest creatures that Deirdre had ever seen.

The stallion dropped his root. It was mushroom shaped, nearly as thick as Naisha's arm, and dripping with wetness. Spinning around on his haunches, the stallion started to fight Naisha, whose tunic was soaked in sweat.

The mare whinnied and the stallion answered in a deafening frenzy. The horses in the stable whinnied and neighed, and strained at their halters, kicked at the doors, and above them all, the black stallion and the gray mare fought their handlers to get at each other. A handler tied the mare to the fence and then tied a rope to each of her legs, and then tied each rope to the fence so the mare couldn't kick back at the stallion. It was Maeve who went to the mare and grabbed the gray tail and pulled it away, exposing the wet entrance. Naisha couldn't hold the stallion any longer; the horse broke free, leapt on top of the mare, plunging his long red root so far into the mare that she shuddered underneath him. Deirdre felt the shudder go through her. She wanted to look away but couldn't. Her eyes were at that place where the stallion and mare were joined. The stallion's underbelly was sleek and arched like a bow and when Deirdre thought he couldn't plunge any deeper, he plunged again and shuddered. He bit at the mare's neck and she bowed her back and spread her legs farther, and he drew back and plunged the root in again. Deirdre looked at Naisha. She wanted him to plunge into her the way the stallion had plunged into the mare. And again he went at her, the magnificent black body rearing into the air, and that terrible red thing disappearing deeper and deeper into her. She wanted to open her legs there, wanted to lie down on the ground. *Take me, Naisha. Take me.* But Naisha was looking at Maeve. She stood there with her legs apart next to the mare, her breasts bare, her blond hair flying like a mane in the wind.

CHAPTER 26

It was the coolness on the side of the bed that woke Deirdre. When she had fallen asleep, Naisha's thighs warmed the backs of her legs, and the softness of his manhood was snuggled between her buttocks.

It was late. Through the window she could see the half moon peeking out like an eye from the lid of clouds. Then a streak of light, and a low rumble of thunder came from off the sea. Lately he couldn't sleep at night. There were too many plans in his head, he said, plans he had to discuss with Maeve. But he was with *her* again!

The day after Deirdre and Naisha had arrived in Connacht, Naisha and Sdoirm had raced the queen's chariot. When she saw Maeve driving out her horses, Deirdre sucked in her breath. Aya had spoken the truth about the queen. She was bold, courageous, and beautiful. She, Deirdre, would become like her.

Maeve had worn a leather skirt and leather leggings like her warriors. She wore a gold crescent around her neck similar to the one that Conor had given Deirdre, but Maeve's was bigger and inset with brilliant red, blue, and green enamels. Her thick yellow hair was tied back with gold threaded cords. Four stallions pulled her chariot. Four blood-colored horses with black manes and tails. Maeve herself held the reins. They were wrapped around her forearms like leather bracelets. Her breasts were bare. They were larger than Deirdre's breasts, full like bowls that had been turned over.

Maeve's warriors, men and women, had lined the plateau

top where the Queen's chariot was to race the chieftain from Ulster and his black horse. Young children dug at the ground with sticks or pushed at each other, and old women scolded them and then grabbed two of them and banged their heads together.

Naisha stood on the ground beside Deirdre. The stallion sensed the excitement and pawed the ground and pushed Naisha with his head, and pulled at his reins. Finally it was time. Naisha grabbed Deirdre around her waist and kissed her, then leapt up on Sdoirm's back. He waved at Maeve, and she nodded back. Red and gold banners at the back of her chariot waved in the breeze.

One of Maeve's captains, a giant named Camros, dropped a red kerchief to the ground and the horses leapt forward, thundering past the cheering crowd. None of them had ever seen a man sit on a horse, and it evoked in the crowd a sense of danger, and danger always brought with it excitement. Maeve's horses were powerful, and there were four of them. Deirdre watched the chariot and the dark horse, but then the crowd closed in front of her and she could no longer see.

What she did see in the area where she stood were Maeve's warriors looking at her. Particularly the giant kept looking at her. His eyes fixed on her breasts and on her legs as though she were a heifer and he were paying a price for her. And after his eyes took in her legs, he stared at her crotch. She wished Naisha were there because if he had been, the men wouldn't be staring.

She made a move to walk toward the gate, but if she did that, all the men would stare. Camros was still staring.

"Stop looking at me like I was the golden goose. I'll not be laying any golden eggs."

"You're the finest piece of woman-flesh that I've laid eyes on. Why don't you and me play us some—" But the cheering crowd overwhelmed his voice.

And the chariot came back through the gates. And Naisha was driving it. Reins wrapped around his arms. Standing beside him, the bare-breasted queen. The chariot stopped in front of the long house, and Naisha stepped out, giving his arm to Queen Maeve. Deirdre had never seen him look more handsome. The leather tunic, the green overcloak of a nobleman, the hard muscled arms, the black hair and shortly cropped beard, and the white teeth. From the look on Naisha's face Deirdre could tell that he had won. Victory made a man more handsome than any garment, and her heart flew to him. She blew him kisses with both her palms, but he was looking at Maeve, and when the chariot stopped, he stepped out, turned toward Maeve, and reached his arm out to her. Maeve took the arm, and, with the statuesque bearing of a queen who had never known defeat even when the victory went to someone else, stepped out of the chariot. She smiled gloriously at Naisha. Deirdre's lips were frozen in what appeared to be a smile, but the amber eyes weren't.

Naisha bent to his knee and kissed Maeve's hand. The queen raised her other hand and a silence fell over the crowd.

"Naisha, son of Usna, stand." He stood. The queen continued. "Do you give testament of your allegiance to Queen Maeve?"

"I, Naisha—"

"Give me your hand." She took his right hand and laid it on her left breast. Then she reached down to Naisha's short tunic and held his testicles in her hand.

"Now repeat the oath of testament. I, Naisha, pledge my sword, my lance, and my body to the service of Queen Maeve."

Naisha repeated it.

Then Maeve said something quietly to Naisha alone. He smiled, and the queen removed her hand. "Welcome, Naisha, son of Usna, to the troops of Queen Maeve." A cheer went through the crowd. Deirdre was not smiling. She turned and walked back to her and Naisha's quarters in the long house.

After, in their room in the long house, when Naisha came to her, he said, "It was nothing. It was a testament to allegiance. A king holds the warrior's testicles. I took the same oath with Conor."

"Conor doesn't have breasts," Deirdre said. "And Conor doesn't smile the way Maeve smiles."

"Surely you're not jealous of Maeve," Naisha said. "She's a great queen, but I love you." And then Naisha took Deirdre in his arms and loved her.

But Conor was planning an attack and Naisha explained to Maeve that the best way to defeat him was to have riders attack on horseback.

Maeve was not convinced. Riders were faster than charioteers, but what about the protection that a chariot afforded a man?

Naisha argued that a man on horseback was higher. He could reach down into the chariot. The lower man was at a disadvantage. He had to strike up. Upward blows were always weaker.

And then one day, Naisha came to Deirdre and grabbed her around the waist and lifted her high into the air and swung her around and kissed her. "She's put me in charge of the horse troops. Two hundred men and as many horses to defeat Conor's attack. I'll cut Conor's head off myself. Hang it from the neck of my horse, and after I'll stake it out and let the crows pluck out his eyes."

And from then on, it seemed to Deirdre that Naisha did nothing but talk about the battle. At mealtimes he sat beside Queen Maeve discussing plans with her. He had been given the position of honor on her left side. Deirdre had learned that the left side was the seat of honor, for in the war chariots, the charioteer sat on the right, while the king, lord, or warrior sat on the left. They discussed equipment.

Riders would need surcingles and light saddles. Her tanners could make those. Naisha would have to show them how. And the horses needed time to be taught to carry men on their backs. Only the best soldiers, said Maeve. No, not her best soldiers, her best horse-handlers, Naisha insisted. Men who handled horses had to be firm but gentle. Would he teach her to ride? They would start immediately.

And then more battle plans. How many warriors did Conor have? How many did she have?

He talked of nothing but the coming battle. At night when he came to bed, he talked of it. The horses had accepted the men on their backs, and some of the men could even gallop now without falling off. Deirdre was getting tired of all the battle talk, and all the time that Naisha spent discussing battle plans with Maeve. "Why doesn't Maeve just give back the black bull to Conor? She has hundreds of bulls," snapped Deirdre. "Who cares if it's supposedly descended from the very first bull brought to Erinn?"

Naisha gave her that same dangerous, unpredictable look. "It's not the black bull that Conor really cares about. It's his honor. By now he knows that you and I are here. He'll not rest until you're in his bed, or until he dies trying to get you there." And then Naisha left, stomping out of the room.

And when he came back, it was with more talk of battle. "We'll surprise him. He won't expect us to be moving so fast—"

Her kisses stopped his talk. And then his breath came too quickly to speak, except to cry out at the last moment, that cry that always sharpened her own excitement and sent her tumbling to that void where all senses were combined in one dark pleasure.

He would fall asleep before she did, and then he would

wake in the middle of the night. And at mealtimes in the banquet hall his conversations would continue with Maeve.

Conor would come in a number of small groups. Five hundred men, maybe, per group. Attack her borders at various places. That was the way he liked to fight. But Conor couldn't come to Ben Gulbain in many small groups. Connacht was divided from Ulster by the Shannon River and Lower Lough Erne. Farther south, the Shannon River ran, with the bogs and marshes and callows, the water meadows. There were only a few places where the hummocks, the low limestone hills, afforded relief from the boglands so an army could cross. These were at Magrath, the fort of the plain, and at Athlone, the fort of Luain. Dalua, the other crossing that afforded dry land, was too far south. Not only that, but Maeve herself had heard stories that the Water Sheerie had returned, the dancing flames that glided over the marshlands at night, misleading people to their deaths. Even the bravest soldiers were terrified of the Water Sheerie. Conor would come in from the north.

And then Maeve agreed to give Naisha a hundred more soldiers.

"Three hundred, my love," he said to Deirdre, the excitement evident in his voice and his handsome face. "She's sent out word to all her chieftains that they are each to bring horses, by the moon's change. Conor won't know what struck him."

Deirdre tried to share his excitement, and she herself trained harder: riding faster, sliding to instant stops, turning at full gallop, throwing a spear farther.

At mealtimes she listened to the hoops and circles that Naisha's and Maeve's conversation made. She listened for one night after the evening meal, and then for two nights, and three, then for more. The same things discussed over and over again. Conor would come in from the north. When he arrived at Es Ruaide, Naisha would go in behind him with the horse troops. Maeve's regular warriors would fight from the front. Sullivan was proving to be a superb horseman. He could be made Naisha's captain. No, Sullivan might be a fine horseman, but someone other than Sullivan had to be found. A man with any physical imperfections could not lead warriors, and Sullivan had a crooked eye. That was just fishwive's silliness, Naisha argued. A good warrior had to be able to think as well as fight. But Maeve knew her soldiers. They wouldn't follow an imperfect leader to battle.

Deirdre stopped running. Instead, she practiced riding. She practiced until the insides of her thighs were raw and aching by abrasion with the withers of the horse. She practiced till her buttocks felt as though they were being axed in half by the horse's backbone. And still she practiced. She practiced weaving in and out of stakes at full gallop, and she pulled the reins tight and dug her heels into his flanks so that he reared, and from this position she practiced throwing lance after lance at a target no bigger than a man's head.

Maeve's spies, planted at Emain, sent word that Conor's attack was coming at the waning moon. Preparations at Ben Gulbain continued. Gwion had been made captain of the horse troops under Naisha. The insides of Deirdre's thighs no longer hurt after getting off a horse. She could ride as well as Naisha. She could ride as well as any soldier in the horse troops. She could ride better than Maeve.

Three hundred horses had been trained to carry men. Horses from Maeve's own stables as well as horses from the surrounding farms. All had been brought to Ben Gulbain.

Now as Deirdre lay awake, she thought more and more of the time that Naisha spent with Maeve, and the arguments that she had already had with Naisha because of Maeve.

Maeve was having difficulty learning to ride. "Why doesn't

Sullivan teach her?" Deirdre had asked once. "Why is it always you who has to lift her up?"

"Because it's not fitting for a queen to be taught by a man of low rank."

"There are other men who are not of such low rank."

"I'm the best horseman. It's fitting that I teach her."

"But is it you who always have to lift her fat arse up?"

"You're speaking about the queen who shelters you under her roof. I'll not hear any more such talk." And then he had left. And now as Deirdre lay awake, she thought again of how Naisha spent more and more time with Maeve than he did with her. How it had started at just mealtimes, and then there were conferences with her chieftains, and then there were the riding lessons, and then the discussions in the middle of the night, because Naisha couldn't sleep, and because Maeve couldn't sleep.

The more Deirdre thought, the angrier she became. "It's because of her fat arse end bouncing up and down so much," said Deirdre out loud, and she turned over in the bed with such vehemence that the boards cracked. She threw off the down cover. The wind blowing off the sea was cool, and so she covered up again. But the cover was too heavy, and she kicked at it with her feet. She could hear Maeve's voice. It was all she heard lately, Maeve's voice. "Oh, Naisha. Naisha, Naisha. Where is the son of Usna? Where is the chieftain of Maeve's horse troops?" A voice that seemed even to penetrate her dreams lately. "Naisha!" Cajoling, but imperious. "Naisha!" And giving him gifts: a new belt corded with gold thread, a bracelet, and a gold brooch. And with every gift, he had to reaffirm his loyalty to her by giving testament. Putting his hands on her breasts. Dugs like a nanny goat. Dugs like a cow. Dugs like a great old milk cow. Deirdre kicked the blankets off and got out of bed.

The moon was hidden now. Aya had said about Maeve that

each night she took a different man to her bed. She chose them from among her soldiers.

The only soldier whom Maeve seemed interested in now was Naisha. And Naisha—all he talked about were the battle plans. Five hundred warriors. Six hundred. Nearly four hundred horse troops.

She looked out her window. It was a bitter wind that combed the sea's hair white. She remembered the night on the shores of Lough Erne, when the sun was sinking and his chin had rested on the top of her head, and his arms circled her. There was no talk of battle then, just love. He loved her, he had said.

She heard steps outside the door and jumped back into bed and pretended to be asleep. She heard the door creak. She knew from the clanging sound of metal on wood that Naisha was unbuckling his belt. She heard the rustling of his clothes as he dropped them. There was a smell of ale about him as he came into bed, and the always warm man-smell of him. She was on her side turned away from him, and he kissed her back and then slid his hand down her buttocks. She felt his hardness nudging against her, insistent and prodding. She moved away from him. If he thought that he could be up half the night talking with that cow-uddered queen and then come back and expect to love her without a word or a kiss, then he was joking himself.

The hardness grew more insistent. She slid away again, but when the hardness thrust again, it was against her tailbone, and hurt. She threw off the covers and leapt out of bed.

"That's a fine way to be welcoming your man to bed."

"That's a fine way for you to be coming to bed. Stinking of ale like a polecat. And strutting with your thing and jabbing it at me, like I was a sheep or a cow or something."

"Come here. Take a feel of this. I've got something for you."

"I'll not take a feel of nothing. You coming to bed in the middle of the night when the moon's already turned through half the sky."

"We were making plans for Conor's attack. Come to bed."

"It's all you've done is make plans."

"Battles take plans. Now come to bed. I want you."

"I'll not come to bed. You spend all your time talking to that . . . that c—"—she wanted to say cow—"her. It's as though I don't even exist for you anymore."

"That queen gave you and me shelter. And might I remind you, it was you yourself who wanted to come here. And now that you're here, you'll be acting like a child that's had its top taken away."

"I'm not a child."

"Then stop acting like one. Act like a woman. Come here, I want you."

"No!"

"Then I'll take you." And he jumped up and grabbed at her, but she avoided him.

"Go and take your queen instead!"

"I'll pretend I didn't hear that," he said. His face was hard as he looked at her, and then his voice softened. "You look beautiful standing in the moonlight. Like a goddess." He reached out his hand gently and touched her shoulder. She relaxed and let him come closer. He kissed the back of her neck, and his manliness prodded her again. She spun away from it.

"Why weren't you here when I woke?"

Naisha sighed and sat down on the bed. "There's going to be a battle, and there's going to be fighting. And I'm going to be in charge of three hundred men. Three hundred men cannot be left to their own designs. Plans have to be made." A cloud covered the moon and the room darkened.

"Ever since we came here, you've done nothing but make plans. Plans with Maeve."

"I'm not making plans now. I want to love you!"

"I would fight beside you, Naisha. I would stand with my back to your back and I would fight for you till a sword slit open my belly, but I won't let you make a fool of me with that queen."

"The only one who'll be making a fool of you, is you. Now, come to bed."

"A big yellow cow she is."

"You're not to speak about her like that."

"A big yellow cow with her cow's udders sticking out for all to see."

"Deirdre, stop!"

"Wagging her tail in your face like a bitch—"

"Deirdre!" He jumped up and grabbed her arm, and his look was dangerous as though he might hit her, and the danger excited her.

But she needed him to be gentle, and his lack of gentleness angered her. "Like a bitch in heat!"

"That's enough!"

"Next thing you know, you'll be tonguing her arse!"

The moon emerged at that moment and lit his body. The hard, lean torso, the powerful legs, the heavy rigidness of his manhood, all of him was bathed in moonlight and she wanted him. But he cast her to the floor roughly. "You can bloody well sleep alone till you apologize. If you won't love your man, I know someone who will." He picked up his robe, threw it over his head, grabbed his sword, and without a backward glance, left.

He was nothing but a frog's arse. If he thought *she* was going to apologize. He spent all his time with Maeve, and *she* was the one who was supposed to apologize. The world could freeze to a solid block of ice before *she* would apologize. Let him have his cow-uddered queen. Her army was full of men.

It was Maeve's doing. Maeve with her breasts exposed like a cow. With her smile, always smiling at Naisha. Touching him and making him touch her.

Deirdre picked up her sword and jabbed at the pillows that had been knocked to the floor. "There's one for her cow's udder. And there's another one for the other udder. Beef to the heels. All of her!"

And the wind blew through the window, and the white down feathers began to fly as though it were snowing in the room. And she threw the sword to the ground and ripped the pillows with her hands, but as she ripped, she began to cry. She just wanted him to be near her, to hold her, to touch her. Her hair and naked shoulders were covered in swan's down. "Eagles don't cry." She tried to bite back the tears. "Eagles don't cry! Naisha! Naisha, come back." But the door was closed, and no one heard, and then she felt the wetness seeping between her thighs. She looked down. The moon blood had come again.

CHAPTER 27

Deirdre was dreaming. Conor was coming after her with a great heavy sword. She had fallen to the ground and lay there, and she couldn't move, and she wanted to call Naisha, but she couldn't say his name. Conor was coming closer and closer, and smiling and he drew back his sword—

"Frog's arse! Frog's arse!" Deirdre was immediately awake. The crow had sounded an alarm. She sat upright in bed. In the same movement she reached for her sword. The transition from dream to waking was not quite instantaneous. The crow had sounded an alarm, but Deirdre could neither hear nor see anything. The door to her chamber was closed. Someone tried it. It stuck. Deirdre's hand tightened on her sword, ready to use it in a moment. The door moved.

"Why don't you be watching where you'll be plantin' your feet, you lousy, half-balled, sheep-eyed cow-brain?"

Deirdre leapt out of bed.

"Cut your throat! Cut your throat!"

"Now, Aya me loov, don't you be talking so loud. You'll be waking the dead!"

"What do you know about waking the dead? You ain't ever had much to do with the land of the living. You with your nose half-buried in the ale so much it's starting to look like an ale barrel."

"Aach, woman, will you stop pulling me nose?"

"What else is a woman supposed to grab hold? You ain't got nothing else. Now let me go first, you mooncalf. Where's your manners?"

"A man is more than the size of his pricker."

"A man is nothing *but* the size of his pricker. Now, get out of the way."

"Frog's arse! Cut your throat!"

The door swung open and in came Aya, followed by MacFith.

Aya stretched out her arms. "Child, child. But you makes me eyes happy just the sight of you. Look at you here. A regular bed in Queen Maeve's long house. Like you was a regular princess instead of in that slimy crannog where there weren't room to swing a cat! Aie, but let me look at you! And the gods'll be smiling on you brighter every day what passes.

"MacFith, you hairy-eared, baldheaded jackass gelding, come here and give Deirdre a hug. And don't you be planting your feet on mine like my toesies was a cockroach to be squashed."

"Oh, Aya. MacFith. I missed both of you so much."

"Nonsense. Nonsense. Don't you be telling Aya no lies. You ain't gonna be missing two old wrinkly prunes like Aya and MacFith when you got a buck like the son of Usna rooting your cave. Where is the son of Usna? Aie, but when he comes to me that night. Aaach! I thought the gods be blessed. They sent me a man. Oh, but to be young again and have a man like that, and not this half-balled, boiled-owl jackass what ain't even got no hair on his head what a good woman can grab and give him a good cuff from time to time, which is what it deserves."

"Aya. Don't pick on poor MacFith."

"Now, don't you go and be telling me how to do me business. The only reason that skinny-arsed cow-brain is putting one foot on this earth in front of the other is because of the digitalis in Aya's foxglove tea, what keeps his heart beating in that skinny chest!"

"Frog's arse! Rawwwk!"

"Ain't you or anyone else in this fort had the common sense to cut that crow's throat yet?"

"Aya!"

"Cut your throat! Cut your throat!"

"I'll cut your throat, all right. First chance I'll be getting!"

"Aya!"

"Any Connachtman knows what to do with a crow. Crow stew. Onions, garlic, carrots, and your black arse simmering in the middle. And get a wrap on you, child. You'll be catching your death in this rain. Doesn't Naisha look after you? If'n I was a man and you was me woman, I wouldn't be leaving your side, and you so lovely you make the sun smile when he gets up in the morning. MacFith. What the blazes you be doing? You're in the long house of Queen Maeve, and there you go scratching where you ain't got nothing to scratch, like you was in the field with the cows. Where's Naisha that an old woman can smile again in her heart?"

Deirdre looked away. Out through the window. The sky was a gray mist. The feathers had settled like a carpet on the floor.

Aya looked at the window, then at the door, then at the feathers scattered on the floor, and sniffed loudly. "Oh, well, don't you be minding a thing like that. You got lots more than the son of Usna to choose from. You got your choice now of the warriors of Connacht. Ain't a man in Connacht what won't put an Ulsterman to shame on the battlefield or in the bed. Makes me heart glad just to see them all out there. I'll sample me one or two this afternoon. Aaach. A real man. Not just a half man. Blamed half-wit that he is. Kills his brains with ale. Stop scratching, will you? Scratching your arse, which is so skinny you almost ain't got one. Scratching your balls, which you also ain't got. And scratching your feet. If your feet'll be itching it means you'll be treading on strange ground, and I already is on strange ground, and I've been hoofing it around this bogland long enough, and I ain't going to be hoofing it no more.

"We'd've been here a fortnight ago excepting as what I had to go a hunting for him in the bleeding forests. Oh, would Tethra come and end me miseries and take me away to Tir-na-n'Og where there are soldiers and warriors and everlasting dancing and singing instead of blamed half-wit half-men. A shepherd's got an easier life than old Aya. At least the sheeps got sense enough not to hide when they runs away. But I knocked that out of MacFith in a hurry! He won't be hiding again in a while."

"Aya, me loov. You'll not be telling lies about MacFith again. The reason we is not arriving as early as what we expected is because the old woman canna walk as far as she used to. Bunions on her feet, she's got. We had to keep a stopping and put poultices of fish oil and warm cow dung—"

"Liar! MacFith, I'll knock your head off, I will. Use it as a drum, I will. I ain't no more got bunions than cows can be flying. Corns I got, not bunions. Fools. I spend my life with fools. Where's the son of Usna? There's a man if I ever laid me sweet eyes on one."

"He spends all his time talking to Maeve."

"And why shouldn't he be spending his time chewing the fat with Maeve? She's a proud, amorous woman, all right. There ain't a time but that she's with a man and two or three more hanging in the shadows. She's queen. Ain't another queen in the whole world the likes of Maeve. Aie, it'll be doing my heart good just to look on her again."

"Well, you can look on her. I'm tired of looking on her."

Aya clapped her hands and rolled her eyes to the ceiling so the whites showed. "Well, well! Listen to the child, will you? Jealousy, is it? The whole troops of Maeve's army standing outside her door, and she'll be whining over *one* man. By the soles of me aching feet, child, but you're a silly goose. A man's

a man. And all mens are more or less the same"—she gave
MacFith an irritable look—"except for some what's got a
whole lot less than others, and ain't good for nothing. You
listen to old Aya. You be taking some clothes and putting
them on and then Aya'll braid your hair. Then you be taking
yourself out there, one hand on your hip, your head in the air.
And the moment another man's hand is on your body"—Aya
clapped her hands—"you won't even be thinking of the son of
Usna!"

CHAPTER
28

Tomorrow morning at daybreak the troops would be going out. There was no further training. The men were relaxing, but young men relax by moving their bodies. On the courtyard in front of Maeve's house, about thirty men played a game called hurling. The hurlers were all naked; each held a stick, and with the stick they beat a wooden ball from one end of the field to the other. The rules of the game were simple: there were none, except to beat the ball past the opponent's line. One young warrior had already been carried out after his leg had been broken when someone hit it with the hurling stick. He had been taken away and given cranberry tea, and the rags soaked in vinegar were lain on his leg. Another had had his head split open.

Some soldiers polished their swords and spears, while others whittled pieces of wood. They whittled ducks, or eagles, or the faces of gods, or wolves, and some whittled man-roots, and Deirdre could hear the teasing among them.

"Will you be carving that, in case yourn won't work?"

"Mine'll be working right fine like. Mind yourself to what you'll be whittling. Wouldn't want you to be having an accident. Cut off what you don't mean to."

"Even if I was to shave a bit off, I'd still have a lot more left than what you got."

"Now, don't you be bragging," came another voice, "just because yours hangs clear down to your knees."

"Arrrch. It's not size what counts. You could have one as

big as a horse; if it don't get stiff, might as well have a dead fish, I say."

"Is that what it is that you'll be calling that thing of yours—dead fish. No wonder your wife left you for Drury. I hear tell he makes the women leap, like a salmon being pulled in. Hard like a fence pole, old Drury is, and nearly as long as a man's forearm. Puts even horse cocks to shame."

Other men played games with the young women who went to the well. The men would hide behind some of the houses, and catch the women as they carried the pails of water. They would hold them down and tickle them lightly before claiming them.

Deirdre practiced with her sword. She had set a block of wood on a pillar, and kept aiming at it with her sword.

In the hay pile close to the stables a steady stream of couples came and went, the women coming out with flushed, happy faces. She'd seen Aya disappear behind the bathhouse with a man, and when Aya came out again, she, too, was smiling.

Deirdre had seen Naisha briefly. He had come to the window in Maeve's quarters and looked out on the hurling match. Then he had turned his back. She had seen his shoulder muscles ripple under the skin, as he had left the window.

Children were playing tag and five-stones, and throwing sticks to dogs, which yelped excitedly.

"Hey, the world's upside down," shouted a small voice, and Deirdre looked and saw a boy hanging from his heels upside down from a crossbar above the corral gate, and he waved his arms and they made great shadows on the ground, like spiders.

"Mikla," shouted someone, "get down from there or you'll be breaking your neck."

"No I won't, it's fun."

"The blistering I'll be giving your arse end won't be much fun. Now, get down!"

Deirdre hadn't noticed Camros come up, and he stood now and leaned against another pole. She knocked the block off with her sword, and he reached to lift it up for her.

"I can do it myself."

"You've got a fine arm for a sword," he said, but it wasn't her arm that he was looking at. She tried to ignore the giant, hoping he would go away, but he simply continued standing there and staring at her. Finally he said, "You're the finest piece of woman flesh I ever laid eyes on. It's a shame, it is, when a woman like you is alone." He licked his lips. "How about you and me playing a little game of bull-and-cow?"

"You want to play bull-and-cow, then find yourself a cow."

"Uppity wench, aren't you? Especially considering . . ."

His voice trailed off, but he lifted his eyes to Maeve's window.

She made a thrust with her sword and knocked the block off the pole. "Excuse me," she said, as she bent down to pick it up. "If you stand there, you might get hurt."

"I'll be taking my chances."

She thrust again.

"You were supposed to be King Conor's woman, weren't you?"

She didn't say anything.

"You know what some of the men'll be saying? They say we oughta hand you back to Conor. They say your coming here'll be angering the gods and bringing ill luck."

"Bugger a frog's arse with your ill luck," she said, and then knocked the wooden block off the pole so it flew at Camros and he had to duck.

She walked to the other side of the stables. The horse she had ridden for the last several weeks, a handsome dappled young stallion, stood outside in a corral. When Deirdre went up to the fence, several horses came over and hung their heads over the poles. Her horse was not among them. She scratched behind their ears and patted their long bony faces, and the soft velvet noses. She looked at her horse. It stood head to tail beside another horse, lazily brushing flies from the other horse's back with its tail. Other horses stood together, gently nipping at each other's mane or rump. Over by the hay pile she saw feet sticking out, a man's large, splayed, horny toes, and a woman's smaller, tightly curled toes. From somewhere she heard the giggle of a woman and the deeper, subduing voice of a man. Suddenly it seemed to her that the entire fort had broken off into groups of two. Two, two, two, even the dogs lay in twos. And among all the twos, she was alone. A well of sadness rose in her. She could almost taste it, like bile at the back of her tongue. She wanted to be held. More than anything, she simply wanted Naisha to hold her again the way he had held her that night as they watched the sun go down. She wanted to feel his arms around her. She wanted to hear him say "I love you," and she looked at the window where she had seen his back, and he appeared in the window again, and she called out his name, "Naisha!" and began to walk in the direction of the window. And Naisha glanced outside and she smiled, but a horse whinnied at just that moment when she called out, and her voice was lost in the shrill animal sound, and Naisha turned away again, and the moment was gone, and she stopped walking. *I won't be returning to your bed until you apologize.*

Two flies lighted on a corral pole. They were coupled, one on top of the other. She picked up a rock and smashed them.

CHAPTER
29

At daybreak six hundred men and women stood beside their mounts. Adrach, the High Druid of Connacht, moved through the ranks of warriors, touching the swords and naked bodies of each warrior with the sacred mistletoe. He recited as he moved among them:

> "Morrigan, goddess of war,
>   fill their bodies with powerful valor
>   make limbs light
>   make feet and hands
>   burst into winged flight
>   like a hawk with quick wings
>   who from the huge height
>   of an impassable rock
>   lifts, then leans to flight
>   to pursue some other bird. . . ."

The night before the Druid had sacrificed black bulls to Tethra, god of death, so that he would not claim more of Maeve's warriors than was necessary for victory. Twelve bards strummed their harps and sung an incantation to the Triple God of Bael, Cromm Cruach, and Mam Caellach. The Triple God was the moon by night, the sun by day. The bards sang of how once the sun and the moon were not separate, but together the way that blood mixed with water, of how once, the four elements, earth, wind, fire, and water were all joined together in a sacred circle of timelessness that included past, present, and future. The twelve bards in turn sang their prayers to each entity of the Triple God that He/She would not raise the elements in bad forces against the troops of Maeve.

The warriors were naked, but the bards wore the striped plaids of blue, green, and yellow, and the shoulders of their cloaks were decorated with the sacred feathers of eagles, for the first bard in Erinn had once lived as an eagle before he was transformed into a man. After the bards sang their incantation to timelessness, they changed modes and sang the war anthem:

> "Shower thine mights upon the foe!
> Lay their pride against Gulbain low!
> Thine the sway of contested fields
> To thee for aid these Connachtmen fly;
> On brave arms this country's hopes rely,
> From every foe this seaside land to shield.
> Wide our vengeful ruin spread!
> Heap the groaning field with dead!
> Furious be our gleaming swords!
> Death with every stroke descend!
> Those whose fame earth can no match afford;
> That fame which shall through time, as through
>   the world, extend!"

Maeve was resplendent in a delicate linen dress, interwoven with the red-gold of Erinn. Her breasts were bare. She wore a gold torque and a gold diadem in her corn-colored hair. "May the gods go with the son of Usna and with Gwion, and with all my warriors." Naisha and Gwion bent to their knees and kissed her hand.

Now the war cries of the clans, wild, fierce shouts rising from the lusty lungs in defiance of the enemy. *"Faire! Faire!"*

they shouted, "On guard, on guard," and then, *"A buaidh! A buaidh!"*— "To victory."

Six hundred horses galloped out of the gates of Ben Gulbain and the sound of their hooves was like thunder along the sea and across the misty hills.

Sadly MacFith watched the flying tail of the last galloping horse and the last banner disappear out of the gate of Ben Gulbain.

"Ach! It'll be a fine thing to be swording again," he had said to Naisha when he saw the battle preparation of Maeve's troops. "There was a time never a day was passed without me swording a Connachtman's gullet. Or a night without me plundering by fire. Used to use their heads to pillow me head at night. Ach! But it was a fine thing."

But Naisha had said, "It's better that you stay here at Ben Gulbain. You're no match anymore for Sean or Owen or any of the others who'll be fighting for Conor." And then, after he had told him that, Naisha had tried to comfort him with memories. "Remember, MacFith. You had your glory. My father told of how you could fight ten men at a time."

"I wouldn't be giving a pig's grunt for memories. I'd be trading every memory I got for a good swording match. I still got lots of fighting in me."

"You fight here," Naisha said, touching MacFith's bald forehead, "but here, you're weak." And he touched MacFith's heart.

" 'Tis an honorable way to be dying, it is. On the battle-field."

"You've had your honor. Leave honor to the younger war-riors."

"Why is it that always the young will be getting the best of everything?"

"You can't ride a horse, MacFith."

"And what is it I'll be needing a horse for? No horse can swing a sword for me. I can fight with the best of them."

"Once upon a time you could fight with the best of them, all right. But Aya would never be forgiving me if I took you to battle with me. Now, come and tell me the story of how you collected the heads of twenty of the blue men from Alba."

"Bah! Stories! Stories!"

Even the banners had disappeared now beyond the horizon of Ben Gulbain, and stories and memories were small comfort for a man who had been the best swordsman of the Red Branch of the Ulster warriors.

Because of the curse of Macha, which passed into nine generations, the warriors of Ulster grew weak in battle, and it came to pass that the kings of Connacht came to rule over Ulster. The upper half of Erinn came to be known as Leth Cuinn, the half of Cuinn, after a Connacht king by that name. Ulster was allowed to keep its kingship as a figurehead, but each year Ulster had to send a prescribed number of cows, bulls, slaves, horses, and measures of grain to Connacht.

Originally, the Red Branch was the name of the descendants of Burke of the Red Beard, a chieftain in the time of the great Lugh, when Erinn was ruled by just one king. But in a vengeful attack from the Firbolg descendants, who lived off the coast of Erinn, all the descendants of Burke of the Red Beard were killed. Not even a child was left. Eochaid the Fair, who was king before Fergus, held swording and spearing competitions in Ulster in an attempt to bring spirit back to his warriors, and the winners of the competitions were named to a group of men that he called the Red Branch in memory of the Burke clan.

Although the rest of the Ulster warriors continued to suffer from the curse of Macha, the Red Branch seemed to come under the protection of the spirits of the Burke clan, and no individual warrior of the Red Branch was ever killed in battle.

Because only twelve warriors were allowed to become members of the Red Branch at any one time, they could not fight against the entire army of the Connacht king; nonetheless, the Red Branch was extremely successful in small, quick raids against individual Connacht troops and against Connacht farmers. The spoils in slaves, cattle, and gold grew to such a large amount that King Eochaid was required to build a special house to accommodate the Red Branch and their spoils, which he called the House of the Red Branch.

The Red Branch attacks became so frequent and so successful that King Og, father of Queen Maeve, threatened utter destruction of Emain if the raids did not stop. King Eochaid the Fair ordered the Red Branch to stop raids into Connacht, so instead they turned their attentions to Alba.

MacFith came into the Red Branch when King Eochaid was nearing the end of his reign. MacFith never left a battle with the blue-painted men without at least a dozen heads hanging from his belt. The warrior who carried off the head of a defeated enemy had more than just proof of his victory—he caused the power of the sacred that dwelt within the other warrior to work for him. And MacFith's power had grown with each subsequent raid, as he gathered more and more heads. His power continued to grow when Fergus took over the kingship from Eochaid.

When Fergus lost his hand, and Conor took the Ulster throne, the curse of Macha seemed to fall from the rest of the Ulster troops and the Connacht soldiers who were posted throughout Ulster were defeated. War was declared on Connacht and hundreds of cattle and sheep were brought back in successful raid after successful raid, and the House of the Red Branch swelled with booty and slaves. Nonetheless, losses in warriors were severe to both Ulster and Connacht, and when her father died, Queen Maeve of Connacht declared a truce with King Conor.

The blue-painted Picts, who were angered with Ulster raids on Alba, attacked Ulster and landed on Giant's Causeway on the north shore of Ulster. However, when the curse of Macha fell from the rest of the troops of Ulster, the protection of the spirit of Burke fell from the Red Branch, and it was at the battle of the Giant's Causeway in which MacFith was wounded.

Like the men of Erinn, the Picts of Alba went into battle naked, except that the Picts painted their bodies blue so that none of the natural flesh tones showed through. The Picts had long black hair, nearly to their waists, and over the dye, they had painted the ferocious faces of men and animals. They had black, ferocious faces painted on their knees and thighs, and yellow dragons on their pectoral muscles, and orange eagles on their shoulders and snakes winding up their forearms. Even the man-roots of the warriors were painted with the fierce beaks of birds.

MacFith had lost track of how many men he had killed. Two times ten. Three times ten. And then five painted Picts came at him at once. But the *boss,* the wooden handgrip, had come loose from his shield and it fell, leaving him without protection. The sword of one of the Picts caught him on the inside of the thigh and ripped upward.

It was Usna, father of Naisha, who had come to his rescue, and slit open the bowels of two of the Picts. Then Usna had carried him from the battlefield and laid him on the rocks, on the perfect, six-sided columns* that had been built by Finn MacCoul to attack Far Rua, the Alban giant. The blood had spurted from MacFith's thigh, and his plumbs were cut away and hung only from a thin piece of skin. The Druidic novices

---

* In myth, Giant's Causeway was built by the Irish giant, Finn MacCoul, to attack his rival in Scotland. In fact, it is an area of thousands of hexagonal, basaltic columns formed by the slow cooling of lava.

had tied rags tightly through the groin to make the blood stop flowing. But the wound grew swollen and red and they applied poultices of three parts milk and one part seed oil.

After being wounded MacFith was no longer allowed to be a warrior, nor was he allowed to teach swording to the boy troops, because having a man who was not a man might bring ill luck to them.

He listened to the bards and their songs, and decided that he would learn to sing and recite ballads and to play the harp or *durdable,* as the bards called it, meaning the murmur of the sweet apple tree. He looked carefully at the harps that the bards used to see how they were made. He found a black willow not far from the bank of the Blackwater River and felled it. He cut it into a suitable sized plank, and hollowed out the soundbox and then waited for three seasons to pass while the wood aged. In the meantime he carved out the forepillar with a chisel, and the harmonic curve. When the wood was properly aged, he fitted the three pieces together and strung them with brass wires. Finally, he stained the wood with beeswax and tree resin.

Although he had lost two fingers in an old battle, MacFith had a talent for the harp and storytelling, just as he had a talent for swording, and he began to sing:

> "Should any inquire about Erinn
> It is I who can give the truth
> Concerning the deed of each daring
> Invader, since Time was a youth."

The bards made fun of him and ridiculed him, but MacFith would simply take another drink of ale and continue with his playing and singing.

By listening to the bards, MacFith learned to recite the tales from the beginning of time. But MacFith was never allowed to wear the sacred cloak of the white-tailed eagle that the other bards wore. The time occupied by the education of the bards was twelve years, spent in the bosom of the deep woods of the oaks. Because MacFith had never studied to be a bard, he was excluded. He could not accompany the *orfidigh*, the musicians, nor the *seanachies*, the tellers of historical tales, although he knew the story repertory and musical modes of both groups of bards. But he never learned to speak the Feni, the hidden language of the poets, which they learned in their secret schools in the fifth year of their studies, and which they used to speak among themselves. So the bards jeered him and called his words *cronan*, which meant buzzing of flies. And because no one listened, he would drink his ale and sing the stories to a wall, using all the gesticulations and bardic language of the story as though he were surrounded by people who listened to him.

Then MacFith was sent to Loughadalla, and Aya and Lewara listened to him for a while, until they tired of it, and then he told his stories to Deirdre. And if Deirdre was not about, he told his stories to his old horse, or to the goats or the cow, or the sheep.

MacFith could recite the lineage of the kings from King Nuada to King Fergus, and finally, King Conor, but no one wanted to hear him sing anymore, and no one wanted him as a warrior.

MacFith took another drink of ale, but his pouch was empty and he threw it to the ground, and then he threw his harp to the ground, and then he threw his sword to the ground.

CHAPTER
30

Conor grasped for the sides as the wooden wheels of the chariot lurched over a stone.

"Fool! Can you not watch where you're going?" he shouted at his driver.

"Pardon, Sire!" came the reply.

"Pardon you'll ask, if it happens again. I'll stake you out for the wolves to eat."

"Yes, Sire."

In the hills behind the way Conor had come, dark smoke billowed. The army burned thatches and crops as they came. Unlike his other campaigns, his soldiers consisted not just of warriors, but of farmers and even the slaves of other chieftains. Conor had gathered men from all over Ulster; every able-bodied man who could pick up a sword, lance, blackthorn club, or rake had been ordered to come.

"The king's lost his bleeding mind," grumbled the farmers. "Let him find himself another bitch." It was nearing the end of summer. Crops had to be tended for the approaching harvest.

"Imagine fighting a war for a woman."

"War is war, no matter what the reason. You'd complain if you had to fight for your own sweet mother."

"What's he think, that there ain't enough women in Ulster good enough for him?"

But the farmers voiced the complaints quietly and only among themselves, for they'd heard what had happened to the chieftains who argued with the king.

"The harvest is approaching, Sire. If the campaign into Connacht is long and the rains come, the farmers will not get back in time to take in the corn and wheat. There are other women in Ulster. They can all be brought to you," one of the chieftains had said to him.

Conor ordered the chieftains killed as traitors. Owen had killed them. The king relied more and more on Owen these times, and Owen was proving to be a most valuable member of his private guard. When this campaign was finished he would reward Owen well for his loyalty. He would bestow on him the title of chieftain of the Tuatha na Delga. The chieftain of Delga had been one of the dissenters. Dogs. Didn't they know a king's word was command? *Sire, reconsider. A king must be without jealousy and without niggardliness. Jealousy is acceptable in a ploughman, not in a king.* Owen had killed him too. Three chieftains had been named as traitors.

"I will have my queen," Conor shouted, and slammed his hand against the chariot side.

"Yes, Sire," said the charioteer.

"Can't you move any faster, fool?"

"Sire, the foot troops are already far behind—"

Conor struck the charioteer with the back of his hand. "Your job is not to direct the battle!"

"Yes, Sire."

"Give me that whip. I'll show you how to drive."

The king glanced over at the chariot beside him. Owen, too, was whipping his horses.

It was at the foot of Knocknageeha, the hill of the wind in the Curlew Mountains, that the chariots of Conor and the horse troops of Maeve came together. The Curlews, so called because of the long-necked, slender-beaked birds of that name that frequented the area, were not really mountains so much as great, bleak highlands of a boggy character. The hillside was studded with yellow and a small winding road that resembled a well-bent bow curved down the hill.

The horse troops of Maeve came down the hill in a pack and Naisha led them like a great rolling stone that a river swollen with winter rain has wrenched from its socket. The swordsmen of Conor stood with wide eyes in their chariots, incredulously staring at the boulder of warriors and horses that thundered down the hill. And the multitude of thundering hooves spread when it encountered the chariots, like a river that forks, and the river of running horses circled the chariots. The air was filled with the war cries of Connacht and Ulster, and the screaming of horses. And on all sides the battle began. Spear locked against spear, and swords were thrust into the bellies of the horses, so that they stumbled under the weights of their riders, or in the chariot stays, and collapsed, bleeding and coughing blood. The chariots couldn't get turned around quickly enough, and Naisha saw the face of Fathman MacRoi, with whom he had been in the boy troops, and for a moment Naisha felt in his belly the sharp regret of fighting his own countrymen, and he had stayed his sword, but Fathman threw his lance, and had Sdoirm not reared so that the lance passed under his black legs, it would have pierced his belly. Naisha angrily struck with his sword at Fathman's head, and hewed it away from the soft neck and it fell to the chariot floor and rolled like a ball to the ground. And the terrible clanging of metal rose like a din and echoed off the hills, and the ground became like red grease with the blood of horses and men, and the horses lost their footing and slipped and some struggled to their feet again, and others shuddered from the surprise of sharp metal in their bodies and fell never to get up again. And as the sun moved into afternoon, men drowned in pools of their own blood.

Earlier, Deirdre had been unseated from her horse by a heavy lance blow against her shield, and she had been fighting on the ground ever since. Her arms ached from swinging the sword and from bracing the shield against the blows of others, and at some point she had been conscious of the pain, but now it was as though the pain were somewhere outside of her, as though her arms and shoulders no longer belonged to her, but belonged to a woman carved from wood and she herself stood hovering in the air, watching the woman of wood jab and slash and jab. Other warriors had slipped off their horses or leapt out of chariots, or had their horses killed under them, and men and women fought shield against shield, head against head.

She no longer saw the faces of the men she fought, they were just vague shadows that made her teeth jar when their swords collided with hers. A warrior approached, and he stabbed at her but she was quick with her shield and lifted it to protect her breasts, and then from under her shield she lunged up with her sword and stabbed him under the ear and wrenched her sword out again, and the Ulsterman dropped like an ash tree, hewn with an axe.

And then another was in front, holding the perfect circle of his shield before him for protection. He shouted at her, "Fire-headed woman of Conor! It is time to return to your rightful husband, and I, Owen Campbell, will take you to him."

She looked at him briefly; he had a crooked, sinister smile. He held the perfect circle of his shield in front of him, moving lightly on his feet as he walked in the shield's protection. She threw a blow and struck the shield in its circle of bull's hide, and he slammed his sword on hers, and hers broke with the blow.

The man lifted away his shield and smiled more broadly at her with his crooked mouth. "Conor will reward me richly for you!" And he came at her with his weapon, and backing up, she fell backward over the body of a dead man, and the one called Owen approached, his sword point aimed at her breast,

and she lifted her arms in a gesture of surrender, and then
when he was close, she kicked him with full force in the groin,
so that he fell back screaming louder than if a spear had been
thrust in his heart.

And then another came at Deirdre, and he lunged at her
throat, but one of the warriors from Queen Maeve's horse
corps, Cet, with whom Deirdre had spoken on the ride to
Knocknageeha, thrust at her attacker from the back so that
Cet's sword came through the attacker's chest. And when Cet
pulled out his sword, the attacker made an effort to turn
around, as though he didn't believe that he had been
wounded, and then he reached out his hand to Deirdre and
stumbled to his knees.

Then Cet walked to Deirdre and reached out his hand and
helped her to her feet, and smiled at her. Then he took the
sword from the dying Ulsterman, and handed it to her. She
smiled at him, but only for a moment, for they were under
attack again. And then there was another who came at her,
and another, and her mind went dead, and only when the
ground was stained the color of the sunset itself did she become aware again, aware that the fighting was easing: that the
Ulstermen were withdrawing in their chariots. On the plain of
Knocknageeha she saw the backs of men and chariots retreat.
On a low drumlin she saw the white stallions of King Conor
and his moon-colored hair, and beside him, in his stopped
chariot, was the one who was called Owen.

Conor looked directly at her. She saw his mouth move as he
shouted something. "I will have my queen" was what he
shouted, but Deirdre had no way of knowing what his words
were, for they were lost in the din of retreating chariot wheels.

Deirdre turned, and for the first time noticed the terrible
stench of death. She had been in the midst of it all day, but
had been oblivious to it; her attentions had been focused only
on staying out of the way of the swords of others, and except

for the immediate threats to her own life, the rest of the battle might just as well have gone on in another country. But now, for the first time, she noticed the carnage. It was everywhere about her, the torn, destroyed, dead bodies of men, women, and horses. There was the terrible howl of pain, and from over the hills came the howl of a wolf as if in answer, and suddenly the great fatigue of battle was on her, and her legs and arms began to shake so that she dropped her sword, and the shaking continued so that, instinctively, she reached out for something to hold on to, but there was nothing there, and just as she was about to collapse, Naisha was beside her, and he caught her up in his arms.

CHAPTER
31

According to the laws of the ancients, a person who had
wounded another had to take the victim into his own house
and look after him till he recovered. But it was not to be done
until the proper time had passed: "Not removed before the
ninth day is any person transfixed by a spear or any invalid of
whom it is not known whether he will live or die. For it is
wasted labor if anyone maintain a doomed person." Not all
were entitled to care: "There are three men in the territory
who have no right to nursing: a man who refuses hospitality to
every class of person, a man who is false to his honor, a man
who steals property."

Naisha and the horse troops stayed in the Curlew mountains, and after the ninth night the ill and the wounded were
loaded onto chariots and horses and carried back to Ben
Gulbain. The enemy warriors who died were decapitated and
the heads were strung from the belts and saddles of the Connachtmen.

Victory brought Maeve's horse corps back to Ben Gulbain
with green banners flying, and the heads of Ulstermen tied to
the manes of their horses. The twelve bards who had accompanied them, but who had stood aside from the battle, came
at the forefront of the victory celebration, now singing the
lilting modes of victory. Immediately behind them rode
Naisha and Deirdre, and as they rode, they talked with each
other and smiled at each other and their hands reached out
and grasped each other's fingers.

And behind them in the ranks, other warriors talked and touched, too, for victory excites the desires of men and women. Those men who didn't have a woman to talk to, talked among themselves about women and the battle.

"You ever seen such a splendid, straight back in your days? And the hair curling round the shoulders. Every time I sees it, I want to reach up me fingers and touch it."

"Aie, she's a lovely one, she is. See how her waist'll be thinning. And them hips. A man would die to feel them hips under his."

"A man *would* die trying to feel them hips under his, unlessen she was a-wanting it too. Fierce like wildcat, she is. I seen the way she handles a sword. Ain't never seen swording like it. Man or woman."

"Fierce! Pssha! Look at the way she touches the Ulsterman. That ain't fierce."

"Aie, but Maeve'll be looking at them with anger in her green eyes."

"Pssha! Do you think Maeve'll be caring? Maeve's always got one man in the shadow of another. You'll be knowing that sure as I do." And they elbowed each other, for each of them had shared pleasure with Maeve at one time or another.

"Still. 'Tis always Maeve who'll be deciding when she's finished with a man, and not the other way around."

"Pssha! 'Tis the same to her, one as another. Three or four in the same night ain't being uncommon for her."

"Aie. Or even more sometimes, when she's in a gamy way. But she looked favorably on the Ulsterman."

"Pssha! You ever seen a Connachtman what couldn't keep up with an Ulsterman? We showed them how back at Knocknageeha. Them running away like deer afore the hounds."

"Them what was left of them! We killed off half of them."

"Acch, stop your bragging, will you? Making it sound like you did it with your own sword."

"I must've killed fifty by myself. Smashing the bones in their heads under me foot!"

"Is that why you only got one Ulster head tied to your horse? You smashed the rest with your feet?"

"I killed fifty of them, I tell you! There was once, must've been ten coming at me at one time. Shoulders like bulls—"

"Psha! Bull flies, that's the only thing you ever killed fifty of. . . ."

Maeve waited for her troops on the top steps of her long house. Her gown was of the finest silk, the color of the sun. In her hair she wore a cut crystal diadem, which caught the sun and threw a thousand rainbows on the ground about her, transforming it to sky, so that she seemed to be queen of heaven. Her breasts were bare. "Welcome, warriors of Maeve. Bards, your chants and songs have turned the frowns of gods yet another time to smile on Connacht. Go now to Adrach. The Druid waits for the ceremony of the solemnization of the eagle feathers. After the ceremony, those of you who are well must help carry the wounded and injured so that they might be cared for."

The wounded would be taken and treated with poultices and herbs. The green leaves of the hedge woundwort would be applied to the wounds, since the leaves contained a volatile oil with antiseptic qualities. Poultices of wheat oil and milk would be applied to infected wounds to draw out infections and teas of garlic would be administered to keep the blood pure.

Wounded who could not walk would be carried to the sacred well; and those who could, would limp and stumble there.

At the sacred well outside the gates of Ben Gulbain, the wounded ripped strips from their bandages and tied them to the sacred blackthorn tree that grew next to the well. The blackthorn tree, because its white flowers were among the first

THE CELTS

203

blossoms of spring, had magical powers of rejuvenation. Wells
that sprung beside blackthorn contained the same magic, and
the sufferers, those who could, reached their hands into the
sacred spring, and drank of the magic water and poured it on
their ailments, and prayed to the goddess Dana, goddess of
healing and magic, that she would see their suffering and cure
them.

Those severely injured who could not reach the water by
themselves would be cared for by wisewomen and Druids.
They would lift the sacred water in clay cups to the lips of the
wounded so that they might drink, and then the water would
be poured over the wounds. Then the wounded would be
carried back to the houses inside Ben Gulbain and cared for
according to the laws of the ancients.

Then Maeve turned to Naisha. "And the gods have smiled
on Naisha, son of Usna."

"The gods have smiled on all your warriors, great queen.
Men *and* women warriors," Naisha replied. And he reached
up, put his hands on Deirdre's waist, and pulled her from her
horse.

Queen Maeve looked at Deirdre. It was a direct, appraising
look, but without malice.

Deirdre stood straighter. Her head proud. This queen
would not claim her man a second time. She moved closer to
Naisha, not in any perceptible way. Her feet didn't move, but
she turned her shoulder slightly toward him.

Maeve looked from Deirdre to Naisha again. "That is the
way in Connacht. Just because a woman is a woman does not
mean that she lacks courage or strength. Go now to the bathhouses. There will be much festivity tonight. There will be
dancing and roasted meat from fatted calves and goose stuffed
with chestnuts and creams sweetened with honey."

But Deirdre and Naisha didn't go to the bathhouse. They
returned to their quarters. There had been a tension between

them all the way back on the road from Knocknageeha; it was the tension of want: it was the tension of two people who had known each other, had found pleasure in each other's bodies, and then been separated, with the memory of pleasure lingering in each of them, pleasure remembered but unable to be consummated.

The laws of the ancients stated that no pleasure could be taken until the wounded were cared for, but on the road home from battle, anticipation had grown. Anticipation grew with each landmark announcing the nearing of home. Anticipation made them reach out to touch each other, and anticipation made Deirdre suck in her breath when the troops stopped to water the horses and Naisha grabbed her and pushed her against the horse, and kissed her fiercely. Anticipation made his manhood rise against her. But then it was time to move on again, and after that he looked at her with blatant knowing, and she looked at him in the same way, the tawny crystal of her eyes filled with want.

Now the intensity of want churned in her. She was urgent in her need, her hands grasped his hips, pulling him to her. He picked her up and carried her to the bed they once had shared.

She was as fierce and impatient in pleasure as she was in anger, but Naisha refused to indulge her impatience. "Love, like anger, needs to be taught control," he whispered, and he teased, and made her wait. His mouth tasted her nipples, and she arched under him, her body demanding that he take her. His fingers pleasured her, but he withheld the thick hardness that she wanted. He tongued the thin, lithe waist and the hard belly, and she felt the thick, soft hair of his head curl densely against the inside of her thighs. She felt the brush of his lips against that part that ached for him, but his lips were not enough. They were softness when she wanted hardness. Yet, their soft searching was pleasure in itself, and when he went into her with his tongue, she cried out. Her hands grasped his hair, and in the same instant that she wanted to pull his head up to hers, so that the hardness of his cock could replace the softness of his tongue, she wanted to press his head down between her thighs, so his tongue would go further, deeper into her, search out that essence. And then he made her come. And she bucked with pleasure, her body leaping skyward, like a rainbow, each spasm of pleasure sending her higher and higher until she was afraid the spasms would throw her off the bed onto the floor, and when she was still in the spasms of the first pleasure, Naisha covered her with his body. He grasped her buttocks and plunged into her, and her contracting, pleasure-giving muscles contracted against the hard thing in pleasure, and pleasure brought her higher and higher, into a place where her body was convulsed as though struck by lightning. Her body was a pure white thing flying through the dark voids of pleasure. And his finger nudged at her, as though he wanted all of her, as though no part of her was going to be secret from him anymore. She was a circle of pure white pleasure where the darkness of the world began and ended, and each part of him searched deeper in her, and her pleasure grew and grew until it exploded like a shower of stars.

CHAPTER 32

When Naisha left their quarters to go to the stables, Deirdre rose quickly from the bed. From the pack that she had brought from the Lake of Two Swans, she pulled three gold bracelets. These she tucked into her pocket and left her quarters.

News of victory always brought with it commerce. Merchants had a nose for victory and they seemed to have appeared from nowhere and had set up their stalls just inside the gates of the fort. Some of the captured soldiers from Conor's army were already being auctioned off as slaves. In another area, horses and some of the chariots were also being auctioned off.

The people gathered round: the old women with their heads tied with woolen scarves, their noses almost reaching to the ground as they walked; and the farmers, with their faces rough as oak barrels. Small boys pushed each other and called each other names. "Fish bellies! Cowards! Traitors! Ulstermen! Liars!"

Auctioneers haggled with the citizens. "Am I bid half a cumal for this fine piece of horseflesh?" A cumal was the trading currency. One cumal was worth a female slave.

"Half a cumal for that nag. She's fit for nothing but crowbait, she is."

"Shut your mouth, I say. If you're not interested in bargaining, move on."

"Shite—poker. You'll not be telling me where to walk and where not to walk."

"I'll call the soldiers. They'll be showing *you* where to walk in a hurry."

"Half a midin. That's all that nag is worth. Chop it up to feed my swine." A midin was the worth of a fat chicken.

"Half a midin. That's all your mother was worth when she was bought by your father to plough the corn."

The farmers had brought cheeses and goats to sell, cows and horses, and leeks and cabbages. The men scratched their beards and talked of cattle and the corn crop. Against the voices and shouts of the crowd were the bleats of the sheep, and more shouts from children, and the whinnying of horses. There were jesters and jugglers throwing bright, painted balls of red, green, and yellow; musicians, too, vagabonds who played flutes and harps and drums called *bodhrans*.

Deirdre had seen how Maeve's musicians made their drums. How they took goat- or deerskin, which they cured with hydrated lime, and some secret ingredients. Then the *bodhran* makers soaked the skin in a liquid lime solution for seven to ten nights so the skin would soften and the fatty tissue would be dissolved. Then the skin was stretched on a frame and the hair and fat scraped off, and then it was tacked to a beechwood frame. And finally the cross pieces were fitted. Then she'd seen how the *bodhran* makers would carve the beater from holly wood, oak, or beech.

Deirdre moved through the smells and noises of the market. The smell of roasting corn, and fresh cow dung, the malt smell of ale bittered with meath, and the smell of spruce beer. And the smell of horse sweat and burning feathers as chickens were plucked and their pin feathers burned off.

Deirdre looked for the cloth merchants. Linens were made in Erinn and Aya had described to her how back at the fort of Emain, farmers went out and pulled the blue-flowered flax by hand and tied it into bundles and then tossed the bundles into a flax dam to "ret" or to rot. Then the bundles were removed and dried, and then the fibers were "scrutched" or broken to prepare the fibers for spinning or weaving. Then the cloth was laid in the sun to be bleached.

There were the wool merchants, men who went around to the farms and bought the cloth from women who were too far away to ever sell their wares.

At Ben Gulbain Deirdre had seen the old women weaving the wool and staining it in so many colors. She had watched them take the wool and wash it, scour it so that the grease didn't come between the fabric and the dye. She had seen them prepare the wool with the mordants, the metally salts, that made the dyes permanent. She had seen them make mordants from the alum obtained from wood ash, sheep manure, and even human urine, and then plunge the mordant-treated wool into vats of dye. Plants and roots were used to make dyes: black made from sediments of bog pools, or dirt containing iron, or the bark of some trees; brown made from crottle, a lichen that the children were sent out to scrape off the rocks, or from the seaweed called dulse, or peat soot, water lilies, or onion skins; blue and blue-black were made from indigo or frauchens (bilberries), or blackberries, sloe, or blackthorn; red was made from the roots of the madder; and yellow from the heather or autumn crocus, or bracken or weld.

But it was not wool or linen that Deirdre was interested in. It was silk she wanted. Silk that came from a far, far place, a cloth made from worms, Aya had told her. She wanted silk, the kind of material that Conor had brought for her when he visited, and that Aya would sew into dresses. It was funny, Deirdre thought: back at Loughadalla she had such fine clothes and gold to wear, and no one that she wanted to wear them for. And now that she had met Naisha, and wanted beautiful clothes to wear for him, she had nothing. She had one ripped dress. She wanted to find a silk merchant now. She wanted a dress as fine as any that Maeve wore.

"Have you any silk?" she asked the man behind his stand of bright bolts of linen. His head was bent down behind the counter as though he were looking for something, and she talked only to his back.

"Silk? Silk? At a market next to the stinking swine and smelling sheep?"

"But merchants must sell silk."

"Merchants sell what they can sell. In the likes of this crowd, you ain't be seeing much silk."

"But the queen must get it from somewhere."

"If you was queen, you'd have it too. Now, move your carcass out of the way. You're blocking me wares from people who are interested in buying and not just dreaming." At that moment he looked up, stopped in midword when he saw Deirdre, and looked at her up and down, the same way that Camros did. Immediately, the tone of his voice changed. "Well, now." He licked his lips. "It's silk now that you'll be wanting, is it?" He was a very round-faced man resembling a pig. Deirdre thought of what the girl raking seaweed on the beach had said about merchants. "Gombeen-men," she had called them.

"Yes, silk."

He looked her up and down again, and Deirdre was vaguely self-conscious about her torn, ragged dress. Only vaguely, though, because although the merchant looked at her clothes, he looked more at what the clothes hid underneath. "I can pay," she said.

"That's silk you're wearing."

"What I'm wearing is none of your concern. Do you have more cloth?"

"I might have some"—he looked her up and down again—"if I'm paid the right amount."

"Is this the right amount?" She pulled a gold bracelet from her pack and laid it on the counter.

He lifted the bracelet and examined the ornate circular patterns in it. "Where'd you get this?" He was going to put it in his pocket, but Deirdre grabbed it from him.

"First the silk," she said.

With a nod of his head he motioned in the direction of a cart pulled by a sorry-looking mule. The merchant had a young lad who, judging from his thin and neglected look, Deirdre took to be a slave. The merchant shouted at the slave, "Hey you! Watch over here! And don't you be taking nothing what ain't yours." And for emphasis he gave the boy a sharp cuff to the ears. Then to Deirdre the merchant said, "This way," and he led her to the cart behind his stand. When Deirdre walked past him he slid his hand down her hip and made a grab at the inside of her thighs. Her hand went immediately to her dagger. He stood back, his palms facing her, raised in front of his chest. "Just checking. Just seeing if what you're wearing is real silk. I could be offering you a little saving. Just a little one, mind you. There's still some wear left in it. I could sell it for a little something."

"Don't touch me. I have plenty enough to pay for a bolt."

He rubbed his beard, then scratched underneath his chin. "Well, I'd be hoping so. Cloth like what I'm going to show you don't come cheap."

He reached to the bottom of his cart, and under bolts of fabric, he lifted out a wooden box. Inside the wooden box were more bolts, and he unwrapped them, and inside them was a roll of green silk. The merchant lifted a length over his arm. The cloth was green, but like a leaf that is turned in the wind when the sun shines, that one moment is green, that one moment is silver, that one moment is blue, that one moment is gold, that is how the cloth was.

Deirdre reached out to touch it, but the merchant pulled it away. "Cloth like this . . . is fit for a queen. Was going to take it over to her after I finished here. She's waiting for it.

Course, now"—he pursed his lips and looked at Deirdre again —"I could always tell the queen that I wasn't able to find nothing for this trip. I could tell her that providing someone was able to pay me enough to make it worth my while." He reached out to touch the ragged arm of Deirdre's dress.

She pulled away. "I have more gold," she said, and she reached into her pack and pulled out the other bracelets.

"That's a lovely lot of gold for one who's so raggedly dressed." He reached for the bracelets.

But she drew them back. "Give me the material, then I'll give you the other bracelets."

A smile came over his round, pig face. "Cloth like this. Three bracelets. I don't think I can let you have it. Even for three bracelets, even if you threw in that rag you're wearing. The king of Leinster is waiting for this very bolt for his queen. I even had to keep this hidden from Maeve. Material like this, you see only once in a lifetime."

"How much more do you need?" Deirdre thought of the gold torque still in her quarters.

"Not how much. What. You see, the king always gives me gold. But he always gives me a little something else."

He scraped his beard again, then pursed his lips and looked at Deirdre. "He lets me enjoy a couple of his slaves each time I come through. But none of them ain't as lovely as you. Now, if you was to . . ." He looked her up and down again. ". . . I could . . ." He reached out to touch her.

"Bugger a frog's arse," said Deirdre, cuffing him so hard across the ears that he dropped the material. She grabbed it up and threw the bracelets at him. "There's plenty there for you."

"Now, who'd you go and knock over the head to be stealing that?" asked Aya when she saw the bolt of silk that Deirdre brought back to her quarters.

"No one. I paid for it. Well, only a little knock. He wanted more than gold, the gombeen swine."

"Well, only a little knock? Silk like this, fitting for a queen to wear?" said Aya, running her hands over the shimmering green.

"That fat pig wanted my favors as well as my gold. I paid for it. Three of the bracelets that Conor gave me. I want you to help me make a dress. I want it to be like one of Maeve's. I want both my breasts to show."

"You can't go around having your breasts showing."

"I did yesterday."

"Yesterday was different. Yesterday was battle. The Morrigan war goddess can best bless warriors if they're naked."

"Maeve has bare breasts all the time."

"Maeve can do what she bleeding likes. She's queen."

"I want my breasts to show. When she's around, Naisha never looks at me. His eyes are always on her."

"And can't you be finding another man to be looking on?"

"I don't want another man. I want you to help me make this dress."

"Thick headed as a cow, you'll be. All of Maeve's soldiers to pick from and—"

"I don't care."

"Look at this." Aya pulled at the chest of Deirdre's tunic, exposing a mole on her left breast. "Is that what you'll be wanting all to see—the mark of ill luck?"

"Why should a mole be ill luck?"

"Because it's being so."

"It's never brought me ill luck before." Deirdre hugged Aya. "It made you come out to Loughadalla with Lewara. And it brought MacFith with you. And it brought Naisha to me. How can you say that this mole brought ill luck?"

"Child. Child. If you could see yourself. The ill luck you'll be having is from your own loverliness. Too much beauty in a woman will be turning men against each other."

"And not enough will be turning men to other women. If you won't help me make it, I'll do it myself."

"And what will you be knowing about sewing? Not so much as me big toe. Always running with the lambs, you were, and picking up sticks, and feeding the crows like a wild thing."

"You'll help me make it, then?"

"Help, me arse. *I'll* make it, and you'll be knocking the eyes out of anyone who sees you. Ill luck and all!"

CHAPTER 33

Silence can move through a room in waves, just as noise can. Maeve's banquet hall was filled with the noisy revelry of victory, music, dancing, and loud laughter. As Deirdre walked into the banquet hall, heads turned, conversation stopped in midword. Her tawny red hair was braided like a tiara on top of her head and decorated with ash leaves, so that her amber eyes caught the color and sparked with green. Her proud head was high.

The dress she wore was slim across her hips and stomach, and rose with a high back to the front of her neck where a swatch of the magnificent silk folded under her chin like a choker. The dress had no bodice. Deirdre's breasts were bare. The magnificent shoulders were bare, too, except for a wide gold bracelet that adorned her naked, taut arms. She wore a sword girded to her waist.

Like Conor's banquet hall, Maeve's was a long hall with fires burning along its length, and the vermillion flames turned the green shimmery dress into gold. People parted to let her pass. Men stopped chewing their mutton shanks and gaped at her with open mouths.

Camros stepped in front of her.

"Excuse me," she said.

"I might and I might not."

"Excuse me, or you'll feel my sword point in your heart."

"That's what I like, a woman with spirit."

Aya came up from behind. Camros was one of those men who didn't like women, and Aya had already had a taste of his meanness, and she had the bruises on her arms to prove it. He was strong as five horses, but had the disposition of a wild pig. She knew what to do with men like that. Deirdre didn't.

"You're a tasty bit of woman flesh," Camros continued.

"Woman flesh," piped Aya from behind. "You want a woman? Here's a woman, right here." She pointed to her own chest. She took Deirdre's arm. "This here is nothing but a child, and a spoilt, headstrong thing at that. Not once is she listening to what Aya'll be telling her."

"I wasn't talking to you, old woman."

"Mind who you'll be calling old. Females is of two natures. A pretty girl is like a willow. A woman is like an oak. Any fool can make a willow tremble. Even a boy. To make an oak's branches sing . . . it'll be taking a man." Aya's head was thrown back. Her hands were on her hips, and she nudged her thigh against Camros. She toyed with the ties of her bodice so that he could see her breasts. Aya had a face that told of many harvests, and many men, but her breasts were sure and firm and smooth as a young woman's. She took Camros's hand and brought it to her left nipple. "What'll you be doing with that thing? See the mole of ill luck on her left dug? You'll be finding no such mole on Aya. Woman flesh what's willing is always tastier than woman flesh what's not."

Camros removed his hand and reached out to touch Deirdre's shoulder. Deirdre's hand went to her sword.

Camros's eyes went from Deirdre's breast to her shoulder and back to her sword. "I watched you on the battlefield. You'll be doing a man a lot of damage with that sword."

"Woman flesh what's willing is always tastier than woman flesh what's not," Aya repeated.

"She'll be willing soon enough. The Ulsterman is already swooning about with the queen."

"He is not swooning with the queen. He had to talk to her."

"Not swooning, ain't he? Take your haughty Ulster eyes and look there." Through the crowd of men and women Deirdre could see Naisha. He was sitting on the throne beside Maeve's and hugging her. His hand was on her breast and her arm was behind his neck and now Maeve was kissing him.

At that moment a figure, bent over double, lurched through the crowd and stumbled in front of Aya and Deirdre. He rolled over on his back and looked up at Aya.

"Aya, pulse of me heart, soul of me soul. Where you been hiding from me? I been looking under every stone for you."

"MacFith! I'll be leaving you out of me sight for a rooster's crow and there you be, falling down drunk again. I'll be pumping you full of foxglove tea, and you'll be countering it with ale."

"Aya, pulse of me heart, soul of me soul."

"Die and give a crow a pudding, will you? Why do I even bother with one such as the likes of you? Half man too. One that ain't even got his plumbs no more."

He rolled over slowly and got up on his hands and knees and grabbed hold of Aya's leg. "Aya, me loov. Was I ever telling you you got the loovliest legs?" And he began to kiss her shin, and his lips traveled down to her ankles and the tops of her feet. "And the loovliest little toes."

"Bugger a frog's arse, will you!" And she shoved him so that he fell flat on his back again. But a strange stillness overcame MacFith, and he lay there without moving. Aya slapped at his face, and still he didn't move. And then Aya's voice took on a panicky, desperate quality. "MacFith, you half-balled dimwit. Don't you go dying on me now." And she plucked in her pocket for a foxglove leaf. But when she touched his mouth, he grabbed her around the head and pulled her mouth to his and landed a kiss fully on her mouth.

"You bleeding dimwit. I'll be teaching you to trick me.

Next time, I'll be letting you die." She gave him several cuffs to the head.

In the meantime Camros had stepped between Aya and Deirdre and put his hands on her shoulder. He turned her so that she could better see that Naisha's hands were on Queen Maeve's breasts.

"Come," said Camros, "the Ulsterman isn't deserving of one so lovely as you."

There was an ache in Deirdre. She felt now as though she were an apple, and her core had been removed.

Camros's arm was around her shoulder now and he guided her out of the banquet room. The pipes and harps of feasting, and the laughter of men and women grew distant and vague. Camros stopped, pushed her up against a polished oak pillar. His tongue was bitter with the taste of ale, but she didn't try to turn away. It was easier to go through the motions of kissing him. And why even would she want to pull away—to run to Naisha's arms? Aya was right. Why think about Naisha when there was all of Maeve's army to think about?

Camros's tongue was larger and wetter than Naisha's. And his hand was already pressed against the inside of her thigh. Somehow she seemed oblivious to the hand and to the tongue. It was as though some other woman were standing here, pushed against the pillar and kissing Camros. Just the shell of a woman. Aya used to decorate eggshells, and had shown Deirdre how to nick a small hole in the top and in the bottom of an egg and blow the contents into a bowl. Now Deirdre felt as though the creature standing here with Camros was just the shell of Deirdre and if Camros squeezed too hard, that shell would collapse on itself, and she didn't care.

The real Deirdre was back at Loughadalla, back in a happier time, when her world was complete and clear without Naisha. She remembered the smooth green surface of Loughadalla, and the way the trees were reflected in the lake surface along the shoreline, the way the clouds and the sun and the moon at night were reflected in it, and the way her own face was reflected in it, and the way the reflection of her face was disturbed when she dipped her finger into the water, or the way the reflection of the clouds grew ripply and askew when she threw a stone into the water. Why wasn't love like a stone thrown into the water? A sort of rippling, a disturbance for a while that went away, and then the surface was smooth again.

But love wasn't like that. She remembered how when MacFith butchered a calf, he always washed the meat. She remembered how he had plunged the calf heart into cold water, and how the water had turned red. Love was like blood in the water. Once it was there, it couldn't be taken out. But she didn't want to think about it now. Better to think of nothing, the way she had done as a child. And when she thought of nothing when she was a child, she thought of clouds.

Sometimes there had been shapes in the clouds, a dove, or a horse's hoof, or a partridge, or a dog's snout, or a spear. And she had asked Lewara how Loughadalla had gotten its name. There had been a time when Lewara answered her questions. There had been a time when Lewara was gentle and kind as Aya, and there had been a time when Naisha held her in his arms, and kissed her as though he were never going to stop. But she didn't want to think about that now. You couldn't stop time, no more than you could make the wind stop from blowing the clouds into another shape, and another shape, and still another shape. A horse's hoof was spread out into a spear, and then into a leaf, and then into a cat's face, and it joined with another cloud and became a tree. Love was like that. It was here and then it was gone. Tomorrow she would leave Ben Gulbain. She would return to Loughadalla. Maybe she would even return to King Conor. She was not in love with Naisha. She was vaguely aware of being lifted and carried and then pushed to the ground, but she was not Deirdre, and she was not at Ben Gulbain. She also was vaguely aware of having her thighs pushed apart roughly, but what did it matter? She was not Deirdre.

"Leave her alone," an imperative voice came vaguely into her numbness.

"Says who?" came Camros's rough reply. Deirdre opened her eyes and saw Naisha standing beside them.

"Says I," he said.

"Go back to your queen," she said, and she turned from him and lifted herself to Camros, putting her arms around his neck and tilting her hips to him.

"Get up!" Naisha ordered.

"You bitch's bastard. Arse-worming, bog-trotting dog vomit. I'll show you to interrupt," Camros yelled, grabbing for his sword.

Deirdre felt the coolness on her breasts where Camros had lain. Naisha's hand flew out to Deirdre's arm and jerked her roughly to her feet. For the first time she was aware of where Camros had brought her. It was a large communal sleeping room, with cots and pallets, and gray-colored blankets and comforters and dogs. Elsewhere in the room, couples were in various states of copulation. The room smelled of lust and dogs and drunkenness.

Camros came at Naisha. "All right, Ulster vomit. Let's see what you can do without your horse." Camros was a whale of a man. He was half a body higher than Naisha and twice as big around. Aya had told her it was because he was made from the seed of two men. He was like twins except that he was all in one. Naisha lunged at him, but although Camros was a big man, he moved as quickly as a wild boar, and Naisha's sword stuck in a wooden pillar behind Camros. Naisha tugged at it, but it was stuck fast. Camros was at him now. Naisha let go of the sword, but too late; the great hairy giant had his arms around Naisha and was squeezing. Deirdre watched. Camros could break Naisha's neck like that. She hated Naisha. She didn't care. Then Naisha let his arms relax and he slid through the giant's arms to his feet. Naisha shoved a foot as hard as he could into the giant's groin. Deirdre hated Naisha, but in some strange way, she found now that he had dispatched the giant, she was going after Camros. She drew her sword and lunged at him, but the giant rolled to the side.

"Deirdre," Naisha said. "Listen, I love you."

"I don't want your love. Go and love the queen."

Naisha made a move to take her arm. "Come, let's get out of here."

"Go to your queen. I don't want any part of you."

"Deirdre, I love you. You're coming with me whether or not you—"

But the giant had grabbed Naisha from behind and held him and squeezed him in a bear hug. Naisha rammed his elbows behind him into the giant's belly, but to no avail, and he kicked at Camros's knees, but the giant held fast. An unlit torch hung on the wall. Deirdre grabbed it and slammed it down on the giant's head, but he held fast to Naisha. She leapt up on the giant's back, caught his throat between her elbow and forearm, and began to squeeze. She felt his throat wriggle as he swallowed, but he didn't loosen. She slammed the palm of her hand up against the base of his nose; Camros bellowed and Naisha slipped from his arms. She leapt off his back. The giant, holding one hand to his nose, came after her. She was backed into a corner and went for her sword. Suddenly, the giant stopped in midstep, as the point of a knife came through his throat, from one side to the other. Naisha had thrown his dagger, and his aim had been true. The giant reached up with his hand, pulled the dagger out, gave a horrible smile, and came at her with the bloody dagger in his hand. Blood ran down the sides of his neck and she screamed, and the giant toppled.

Naisha pulled his sword from the pillar, then stood over the giant. "He won't bully anybody anymore. Come."

"Don't touch me! I'm not going with you."

"I said you're coming." And he grabbed her up, kicking and screaming, and carried her back to their quarters and kicked open the door. Inside, he put her down.

"Deirdre, I love you," he said. "I've spoken to Maeve. I want to leave here . . . go away with you."

But she wasn't listening. "Bugger a frog's arse!" An arm had come free and she pounded at his chest and face. He grabbed her hand and pushed her back onto the bed so she was under him and he kissed her.

She hated him then. Hated him more than she had ever hated anyone or anything in the world. No, she didn't hate him. She loved him. Was there a word that mixed the notion of love and hate together? But she would not be made a fool of. She bit him—hard. He drew back.

"Go and kiss your queen. I can taste her on your mouth."

"You're a fierce, implacable woman. I—"

"I hate you. I despise you. I'll kill you the moment you let me go."

"Listen to me. I love you!"

She spit in his face, and when he let her arm go to wipe it away, she scratched him with her free hand. He grabbed it roughly and pinned her arm. His face was bleeding.

"For once you're going to listen to what I have to say."

"Say it to the queen."

He grabbed her hair and knocked her head against the mattress twice. "Listen to me! I love you."

She spit at him again.

"Stop struggling!" he shouted. "You can't get up without my letting you up. Look!" He let her struggle, then subdued her roughly. "You can't get away from me. You can kill with your sword. I watched you. You're an excellent swordswoman.

But you've met your match. You're not getting out of here until I decide to let you go."

"You can subdue my body, but you can't control my soul. My soul hates you."

"You're a woman of spirit. You're a fierce, passionate woman with more courage and beauty than any woman I've ever met. But you're stubborn and violent. Anger and violence have to be controlled, Deirdre, or you'll destroy yourself and those who love you!"

"I don't care. I don't care about myself. And I don't care about you. I thought I did, but I don't."

"Look at me."

She turned her head.

"Look at me, I said," and he grabbed her cheek. "I love you!"

Her hands were powerless, but she bucked with her pelvis, trying to throw him off. His knee came down hard between her thighs, and she cried out from the pain, but anger took over again. "I'll kill you. The moment you let me up, I'll kill you."

"For once, you're going to listen. When you saw me with Maeve, I was saying good-bye. I was telling her I was taking you and leaving for Leinster. We're leaving tomorrow. We would have left tonight but my *geisa* doesn't allow me to travel when the moon is full."

"Is that how you say good-bye, by pawing?"

"I wasn't pawing, I was giving testament of my allegiance to her."

"Your hands were on her breasts."

"That's how a warrior gives testament. Testament—that's the meaning of the word. To touch the testicles of a man. Maeve is not a man so a warrior touches her breast. You grew up on a crannog with two old women and a eunuch. You know nothing of testament. Try and understand."

"Did you give testament in her bed too?"

"I went to her bed because your stubbornness enraged me."

"Well, I'm still stubborn." She struggled. "So you can bloody well go to her bed again."

"I don't want her. I want you. And by the gods, I'll have you. And if I can't tame you with words, I'll tame you with the only language you understand." And he pushed her thighs apart and plunged into her. "If you won't listen to reason, you'll listen this way." He plunged in again as though his root were a sword, and she the enemy. "To tame a woman's heart you have to tame her there, and I'll tame you. And if I have to lie here and fuck you till the sun and the moon become the same thing, I'll fuck you! And if I kill myself, and kill you doing it, I'll do it. When I slept with Maeve, I dreamt of you. The night before battle, I kissed her in sleep . . . called your name. 'Deirdre,' I said, 'I love you.' And she woke. 'Go to her,' she said. And when you're not with me, my soul is gone. And if I have to die, forcing you to love me again, I'll die, and if I have to kill you doing it, I'll do that too."

"Naisha." She began to cry. "Naisha. I just wanted you to love me. I just wanted you to touch me. I just wanted you to be near me. It's all I've ever wanted. I love you."

He loosened her arms. "I love you, Deirdre. I love you like breath itself."

"I love you!" she uttered between kisses. "I love you." But their words grew fewer, and then their words went from them completely. Words of anger, words of love, words of endearment, gave way to the urgency of desire, and he thrust into her, deeper and deeper, and it was as though their souls swirled and caught the moon and flew as one.

CHAPTER 34

The morning of Naisha and Deirdre's departure, Maeve stood on the front steps of her long house. She was resplendent in a gown of silver silk. Her breasts were bare. Naisha and Deirdre stood in front of her.

"Naisha," she said, "son of Usna. You have served me well. It saddens me to see you go."

"Great Queen, when I lifted my sword against Conor, my kinsman Sean reminded me of the laws of the ancients. There can be no peace for a man who lifts his sword against his king."

"I can promise you peace here in Connacht, just as I promised it to your father before you. I could promise peace to you and to Deirdre." The queen looked at Deirdre, and for a moment the eyes of the two women were locked. The amber eyes of Deirdre held the green eyes of the queen in an unwavering look. But there was no animosity between them. "She is a powerful warrior. She would make a good captain of Maeve."

"My foster father, Mesgedra, king of Leinster, would also welcome Deirdre."

"May your love for each other grow. May Aengus bless the love that you have for each other and may your kisses be as numerous as his children, the doves who fly and warble in the woods. May you always love each other as you do now. Love him, Deirdre. I have loved more men than the men who number my army. None have pleased me as much as Naisha, son of Usna, except for Usna himself. Treat him as you would life itself. For he is more precious than life. Living without love is like being in a garden where the sun doesn't shine. All the flowers are dead." The queen looked out across her courtyard for a moment, then continued. "Naisha and Deirdre, if ever you have a need of the troops of Maeve, send this ring to me." Then she slipped a ring from her finger and reached for Deirdre's hand and put the ring on Deirdre's index finger. "Go now. The Druids have seen the flights of the wild geese this morning and tell me that your journey will be auspicious if you leave before the sun moves to midday. May the gods speed your journey, and may your days begin with sunshine."

Then she reached down and touched Naisha's testicles, and Naisha placed his hand on her breast. Then she turned to Deirdre, and placed her hand on Deirdre's chest. The gesture surprised Deirdre and she looked at Naisha. Naisha nodded, and Deirdre reached out her hand and touched the queen's bare breast. It was the softness that surprised her. She had touched her own breasts often enough, but touching those of another woman was different. The large nipples and the fleshy heaviness, like a pear, but heavier, yet lighter and smooth, so smooth. And for a moment Deirdre wondered what it would be like to kiss and tongue a breast the way that Naisha did. But the curiosity passed, and this time it was Deirdre who spoke, "The gods bless you, Great Queen."

"The gods smile," said Maeve. "Go now."

Deirdre and Naisha mounted their horses. MacFith and Aya were waiting to follow in a chariot and would arrive at Tara, seat of the kingship of Leinster, several nights later than Deirdre and Naisha.

"If you were both to learn to ride horseback, you could travel as quickly as Deirdre and I."

Aya's response was immediate. "If the gods would've been wanting for me to have a horse attached to me arse end, they would've birthed me with one stuck to it!"

"Frog's arse. Frog's arse," mouthed the crow.

The aspen leaves were touched with yellow as Deirdre and
Naisha made their way from Ben Gulbain, and the yellow
mountain saxifrage was in flower. The mountain avens that
grew in the rock crevices had turned. The small flowers that
once were white had dried and looked like an old woman's
hair.

CHAPTER
35

Deirdre and Naisha came to the Hill of Tara at sunset on the third day's travel. The quiet, weedy river was in front of them; the sun behind them, low in the west, and soon the mists would fall over the grasslands over which they had traveled. There was always a quiet that came at sunset, and even the wind in the grass stilled. The quiet bleating of the sheep in the hills had stopped. From somewhere distant came only the gentle sound of a sheep bell as its carrier nosed in the deep green grass.

The passing light was throbbing now, and a lark sang out to its mate. And the light changed from red to blue to green at the base of the hills.

Tara was the largest and oldest seat of kingship in Erinn. It was to Tara that the Tuatha de Danaan came, bringing with them their knowledge of magic and music, and the golden harp of Dagda. It was to Tara as well that they brought the four magic talismans of Erinn: the spear of Lug—no victory could be won against it, nor against him who had it in his hand; the sword of Nuada—no one escaped from it when it was drawn from its scabbard; and the cauldron of Dagda, from which no company would go away unsatisfied. They also brought with them the Lia-Fail, the stone of destiny. The other talismans had all been buried deep with Fergus's body along the River Liffey. Only the Lia-Fail remained, standing on the Hill of Tara. It was called the "stone phallus," or the "member of Fergus." It was on this stone that the kings of Tara were crowned.

It was on this same hill that the signal fires were lit at Bael-Tinne on the first night of no moon, after the three nights of dead embers. It was forbidden by the ancients to light a fire anywhere in Erinn until the signal fire from Tara had been lit.

The great house of Tara was built of seven oak ramparts so that the King of Tara could walk out and look in seven directions. The *rath na rioch,* the royal enclosure, was divided into five parts. The great central hall of lights, which was so named because the ceiling was partitioned with windows made from the birth sacs of mares, so that the light of the sun, or the moon and the stars, were always upon the great gold throne. Thirteen huge prisms of cut crystal, one for each moon change in each year, hung by silver chains from the ceiling, and these prisms caught the sun and the moon, and threw thousands of rainbows across the hall of light, rainbows which, in turn, were caught by other crystals and split again and again into spectrums of color.

The center hall was surrounded by the four halls of the seasons: summer with its walls of gold leaf, fall with copper inlay, winter with the walls made of silver, and spring where the walls were covered in emerald tapestries.

It was here at Tara, under the tutelage of King Mesgedra, that Naisha had spent his fosterage until he was ten years, at which time he was returned to Emain to enter the boy troops of King Conor.

Because Naisha was a chieftain, he spoke first to the guard at the rampart. "I am Naisha, foster son of Mesgedra of the hairy arms. I seek shelter for myself, my woman, and my horses."

"You come from a long way," came the answer from high among the ramparts. "Mesgedra is dying. But you are welcome to lodging here."

The enormous gate was opened and Deirdre and Naisha were met by curious looks from the guards, who had never seen people riding horseback before. The laws of the ancients ordered that the horses be given grain and water. When Naisha handed the reins of his horse to a stable guard, a man with great horny hands and one eye that looked at the sky and one eye that looked at the ground, he said to Naisha, "You been the ones what was a-causing Conor of the yellow eyebrows to be put to running. And you got the she-warrior with you."

Naisha looked at Deirdre, then at the cross-eyed stabler. "What's the matter with King Mesgedra?" asked Naisha.

"What's the matter with all of us?" The stabler rubbed a horny hand under his nose. "We all of us is heading in the same direction one day sooner or later. You been the ones what was a-riding horses instead of yoking 'em into chariots."

"News travels faster than we do," said Naisha.

"Niafar says what we is all to start learning how to ride."

"Niafar?"

"Niafar, chieftain of the clan of Morna. It's he what'll be keeping the gold brooch of Tara until a new king gets chosen at the feast of the Bull's Blood."

The brooch of Tara was the finest brooch in all of Erinn. It was said that it had been fashioned by Credne, the artificer of the Tuatha de Danaans who brought to Erinn the art of goldsmithing and enameling. The brooch of Tara was nearly as large as the palm of a large man's hand. It was made with panels of silver, overlaid with the finest lacelike gold, carved with intricate circles, and inlaid with precious stones.

Naisha asked to be taken to the bedchamber of Mesgedra. Already the king had been removed from his couch and laid on the floor on a pallet, for this was believed to ease the escaping spirit. Death was imminent. The king's face was dangerously brilliant with fever, and his breathing was raspy, so that he sounded as though he were gasping with each breath. The face that once had been robust with calm energy was now sapped and frantic at the same time. The blue eyes, once as alert and hard as an eagle's, were now heavy lidded and closed.

Harpists played to ease the passing: soft, melancholy tunes, accompanied by the soft wail of pipes. Mesgedra groaned and clutched at the fire in his belly. An agate stone had been placed on his head to draw out the fever, and all the fires at Tara had been put out, so the fever of Mesgedra would not spread. Hairs had been plucked from his head, and these had been smeared with goose grease and then fed to his wolfhound so that the dog would catch the fever and Mesgedra would lose it. Other remedies had been tried. Human bones had been powdered and mixed with ale and he had been forced to drink this, but nothing helped. The fever grew worse, and Mesgedra clawed at his belly with his fingers.

Sabine, Mesgedra's wife, and Naisha's foster mother, knelt on the floor beside her husband. She was as gray haired as her husband, but with complacent, plain features. Her hair was parted in the middle and braided down both sides of her head. Naisha touched her shoulder, and she looked up, and reached to hug him.

Mesgedra's three daughters stood to the side of the room, three women, although Naisha remembered them as girls, for he had not seen them for . . . it was over a dozen years now. All three women had the same complacent look of their mother, and the same sallow hair that their mother had when she was younger. Naisha nodded at them, and the youngest smiled and looked at the ground.

Naisha knelt down to the old man's cot. He reached out and took the fingers that clawed at the belly. The king's fingers were hot against Naisha's palm. A moment of lucidity came over the king.

His eyes wavered and tried to fix on the handsome, dark face. "Naisha?" he questioned, and his eyes closed. A small mole edged the left eyelid of the king. And then the eyes opened. The blue irises swam, not able to focus on anything for a moment. Then they stopped swimming. The whites were red with fever. "Naish—" The voice didn't question now. But pain caught the last syllable and carried it away so that it was unrecognizable. Mesgedra's fingers tightened around Naisha's. Naisha remembered arm-wrestling with the king when he was just a child. The arms had seemed so formidable to him then. Now, in pain, Mesgedra's hand was still strong. Naisha clutched back, as though trying to draw some of the pain from the king into his own body. The Druid came and placed the agate stone, which had slipped off, back onto the king's forehead.

The fingers relaxed. "Naisha, my son. You have come at a bad time. Your foster father . . . the pain in my bowels. Like fire."

"Don't talk."

"I know why you have come. Let me see your woman."

Naisha reached out his hand to Deirdre, but she didn't want to come closer; a strangely hostile look in the frantic, pained eyes of the king frightened her. But Naisha let go of the king's hand and stood, and put his arm around Deirdre's shoulder and led her forward.

The king turned his head, and the agate stone fell off again. "She's a beauty, my son." Deirdre felt all eyes on her. "But she belongs to a king."

"She belongs to me." And Naisha pulled her closer.

"The traveling minstrels brought news of your flight many moon changes ago."

"Conor has chosen to ignore his responsibilities to his chieftains. A king is wedded to his kingdom, as a man is wedded to his wife. A king does not subjugate his chieftains as though they were slaves."

"The power of a king is divine." Mesgedra spoke in rasps. "It comes from Cromm Cruach at the . . . sacred ceremony of the Bull's Blood. . . ." But then he was clutched by another spasm of pain, and screamed out, "Tethra! Tethra! Don't leave me here to suffer. Take me to the land of youth. Take me to Tir-na-n'Og." It was some minutes before he spoke again. "Wrongful marriage and wrongful succession bring calamity and famine to a land. Cairbre Caitcheann . . . a usurper. The ancients tell of him—his marriage with the adulterous Becuma, and after, there was no corn or milk in Erinn. And only one acorn on each oak . . . and the rivers, empty of fish."

"Justice is the primary attribute of a king. Conor has betrayed his trust. A chieftain, if he is to keep his honor, cannot obey unjust laws."

"You are fired in your heart with strength and courage and invincibility. Listen to an old man who no longer has fire in his heart, but only in his belly. Listen, my son. I loved you as I loved the sons of my own loins." He grasped Naisha's hands again, looked momentarily at Deirdre, then spoke to Naisha. "She is very beautiful. But look at my own daughters. They are good natured. Look at Brigh or at Rhiannon or at Deoca. They are virgins, all of them. Waiting to open their thighs to a chieftain. And they are not betrothed to kings. Take one of them. Take your choice. Each of them is a wealthy woman. Each of them has large tracts of land along the Boyne. Lands where the grasses grow to the bellies of cows. River sections where the salmon are so thick they leap into a man's boat. Send the fire-headed woman back to her king. Live in peace here in Leinster."

"I will not send her back. I love her," Naisha said, withdrawing his hand from the old king's grasp. He stood beside Deirdre again and put his arm around her waist. The king's face grew contorted with pain. A slave took cloths soaked in

tepid vinegar water and wiped the sweat from his shoulders
and neck.

"Listen. I am dying. Listen to an old man who has lived
much longer than you . . . has forced more women, and had
more concubines, than you could ever imagine. Love is nothing but a young man's desire, a middle-aged man's habit, and
an old man's need. For more harvests than I can think, I've
lived with the same wife. Look at her." He reached up and
touched Sabine's head. "Desire gives way to habit. One
woman, if she's good tempered, serves as well as the next.
Love is the subject of the bard's songs. But the laws of kings.
The law of the ancients. Whoever transgresses the laws of
kings should die. You'll have no homeland, Naisha. None.
Ever. Know where your choice will lead you. You'll be a wanderer sleeping in ditches and caves for the rest of your life. You
bring dishonor to the name of your father, and your father's
father, and your father's father before him. Send her back.
Conor is a reasonable man. He will forgive."

This time it was Deirdre who spoke. "I have listened to you
because you are a dying man. But I'll not listen anymore.
What do you know of love? You've had so many women, not
one of them is important to you. In a garden where there are a
thousand flowers, there are no special ones. In a garden where
there is only one, it is precious. I would rather sleep in a cave
for a thousand nights than spend one night in a house without
love."

Mesgedra ignored her. "Conor is a reasonable man. He will
forgive. Think of your honor. Send her back."

"I will not send—" But Naisha's words were lost on the
king. This time it was not only his face, but his entire body,
that contorted in spasms of pain. He quivered like a deer when
an arrow pierces its heart, then was still.

Immediately, a great keening went up from among the

women. The windows and door were flung open so that the soul could pass on, and two men left the chamber to tell the news of the death to the warriors, to the bees, to the cows, and to the oak grove.

CHAPTER
36

Mesgedra was dressed in a green silk cloak embroidered with gold harps, and an overcloak of crimson silk, bordered with gold. A gold crown inset with precious stones, garnets and emeralds, ornamented his head. All signs of the fever had disappeared, and his face was at peace. The skin was cold. He sat absolutely straight on his throne, peacefully watching the raucous gaming, teasing, brawling, and feasting that was going on. The fine raiments covered the board that had been tied to his back with buckskin thongs around his torso to keep his body from falling over. A plate of food had been set on a small table at his left hand. His queen sat on his right, occasionally smiling at the festivities. The thrones were on the north side of the hall of lights, so that as the sun moved across the sky, it shone on them through the day. The two thrones were on a raised bulge in the center of the hall, edged on each side by the thirteen princes of Leinster. The lesser nobles and warriors ate and danced and drank on the lower floor.

The lesser nobles were arranged by order of rank in a sun-wise direction, and even food was distributed according to rank. Only nobles were allowed to eat the tender rib portions of the bulls. The warriors fought over fatty back pieces, while the gristly, tough legs went to the freemen. Knucklebones went to the stonecutters and to the harness makers. The great hall of lights was packed with men from all across Leinster who had come to pay their respects to Mesgedra.

Mesgedra's jeweled sword was sheathed to his waist. His spear was tied to his right hand. His shield lay at his feet. His scepter had been placed between his knees. A buckskin thong, hidden under the gold silk, held Mesgedra's knees together so the scepter didn't tumble. Two invisible threads had been sewn into the lids just behind the lashes and these were sewn into the skin just under the eyebrows so the eyes didn't close. The laws of the ancients said that a dead king must watch his own wake.

In the afternoon there had been chariot races and hurling games. Naisha and Deirdre had been invited to take part in the chariot races, and on horseback, they had easily beaten the chariots of Niafar and the other nobles.

Mesgedra had taken ill very suddenly and died in the space of two nights. A message had gone out to all the nobles of Leinster as soon as he grew ill, that an assembly was to be held. A king, because he was the divine presence, had to be of sound body. Illness of any kind was considered weakness and a king who showed weakness had to be replaced by a vigorous successor immediately, before the divine powers, which were manifested in him, became seriously impaired by threatened decay.

A Druid had stood on the rampart of Tara waiting as the sun climbed to midday. He stood with raised arms and dropped them when midday came. This was the signal for the wake celebration to begin. There had been games, hurling and foot races, and roaring matches, and swording matches, and spear throwing, and ale-drinking contests. And the men waited to see who had the strongest bladder, for the men with the strongest bladder could give the most pleasure to women. And the women cheered their champions.

And then there were wrestling matches, and leaping contests. And more ale drinking. And the warriors and their women who sat down to the meal in the hall of lights were a bruised, bleeding, drunken lot. The drinking continued. And after the meal the tables were pushed to the edges of the hall so that more games could be played and the dancing could begin.

Naisha had wanted to leave right after the banquet, but the dancing and the music had moved Deirdre. She had never seen the likes of so much swirling, and leaping and laughing. Sometimes Aya used to dance while MacFith played and sang, and Deirdre would dance with her, and they would laugh and laugh. And even Lewara, in early times, had joined them. But that was so long ago. Deirdre had refused to leave, and took Naisha's hand and led him down to the dancing floor.

"This is a wake," shouted Naisha above the music and noise. "You won't like what's going to happen."

But the excitement of never having danced with a man caught her up. "I want to stay," she'd said.

"Your stubbornness—" But she pressed his lips quiet with a kiss.

"Dance with me," she had said. "Dance with me." And the music moved in her body as though she herself were an instrument being played. She whirled and twisted, lithely as a reed in the breeze. She was part of the music and it was part of her. She whirled and her red hair spun around her waist, lower than her waist, like a fire.

The nobles grabbed the king's corpse and took him down to the main floor and began to lead him in a wild dance round and round the central fire. More and more people joined in, some leaping, some stumbling. The noise of the tympans, harps, flutes, and pipes was deafening. The crown fell off the king's head, and it was stuck on the head of the cross-eyed stabler. He was given a broom made from a heron's wing, as a scepter and placed up on a table. Someone put a cloak of straw rope around him.

They sat the dead king on the lap of the fool-king. A man in a straw hat and straw suit went through the room pairing men indiscriminately with women and leading them to leap over a small turf fire, in a mock marriage ceremony. "As the wheat was once joined to the chaff, I join you." Hand in hand, the men and women leapt over the small fire, and then found a corner of the hall of lights where they could lie down and begin coupling. As soon as they were finished, they leapt up, took another drink of ale, and found another man or woman to leap over the fire with before they coupled with them.

Then the revelers played a game called search. The men were blindfolded, and the women, most of whom were naked now, had to kneel on the floor on all fours, while the men explored the women to find their wives and concubines. Then it was the women's turn to be blindfolded, and to search out their men by touch.

Then there was a call for the king of the wake. The cross-eyed fool was brought down from the table, and his crown and straw cloak were removed, and he was slapped a few times for being so presumptuous to think he was king of the wake, for now the real king of the wake had to be chosen. The men lined up and paraded in front of the women, who shouted and clapped at the sizes of the men's roots. The man with the largest root, a thin man with knobby knees, a round stomach, and red pubic hair, was named king of the wake. The crown was put on his head, and then the women were told to kneel down so that he could exercise his right of a first forcing. As soon as he could no longer continue, the crowd stripped his crown and his heron's-wing scepter and gave it to someone else.

Then it was time to find the pisser king. The men lined up and whoever could piss the farthest was declared the winner. He was given two gold goblets, so that he could drink even more ale.

Now someone began to shout, "Bulls and cows," and then the whole crowd shouted, "Bulls and cows! Bulls and cows!" Tanned hides of bulls and cows were brought in, and the men pulled the skins of bulls over their heads, and the women put on the robes of cows, and they began to walk on all fours. There was great laughing and shouting and drinking, and then someone came in with the long root and testicles of a bull, hanging from a belt at his waist. He grabbed the bull skin from someone and began to crawl over others, lifting the backs of their cow hides and plunging the bull root into the women, who screamed with drunken surprise.

Deirdre watched the drunken frenzy from the balcony, and waited for Naisha. They had been jolted apart in their dancing when the man in the straw cloak and straw mask had grabbed her hand and pushed her against the nobleman called Niafar, the one who Naisha said would most likely be chosen by the council as king. Niafar had held tightly to her hand and had pulled her across the turf fire. She had refused to leap, and had nearly been pulled head first into the fire, so at the last moment she had been obliged to leap along with him.

He pushed her to the floor almost immediately, ripping at her clothes, his big wet tongue like a frog in her mouth. She bit him as hard as she could, and he drew back. And then Naisha was beside her, helping her to her feet.

"Are you mad," said Niafar, "disrupting the wake celebrations? Ill things will befall Leinster if the king is not sent to Tir-na-n'Og with proper ritual."

"Save your rituals for your own women," said Naisha. He turned to Deirdre. "Come. I'm taking you away from here."

But then Sabine called to him. "Naisha, my foster son. Come, you must help us with your father."

Naisha looked at Deirdre, and then at his foster mother, and back at Deirdre.

"I can't refuse if I'm asked. It's the law of the ancients. It's the family that must salt the body and the turf to preserve it. Otherwise, the spirit will not pass with tranquillity."

Deirdre was silent.

240 *Elona Malterre*

Naisha continued. "He was my father for five years. I cannot refuse."

"Go with her," said Deirdre. "I'll wait for you up there." She pointed to the balcony where they had dined during the banquet.

"You should return to our quarters. You won't—"

"I'll stay!" Deirdre's response was sharp. She felt the antagonism of Mesgedra's wife, had seen how the daughters of Mesgedra had looked at Naisha during the banquet, and was convinced this request was nothing but a ploy by Sabine to get Naisha closer to her daughters. If Naisha was going to go with Sabine, she would stay here at the wake.

But Deirdre was now regretting her decision. She had no idea how long she had been waiting, but the frenzy continued. She wished Naisha would come. There were great roars of laughter, and the screams of women. Yet, what was the pleasure in such excess? Some lay in their own urine. Some of them in vomit.

There was no exit from the balcony itself. The only way to leave was down the stairs and through the crowd. It was a crowd that was hostile toward her. She had felt the unfriendly eyes of the women each time they looked at her. It was as though they echoed Mesgedra's words with their eyes. *"No corn . . . and the rivers were empty of fish."* And the men looked at her, too, but in a different way.

Now Niafar was coming up the steps. He was a heavyset man, as muscular as Naisha but not as tall, with ash-colored hair and brown eyes. He was the handsomest man in the court of Mesgedra, but a sneering, arrogant man.

He didn't try to hide the way that he looked at her. "It's ill luck not to participate in the wake games."

"Who for?"

"For the dead king. His soul doesn't pass easily to Tir-na-

n'Og. Our voices, and the singing and the dancing, send his
soul along."

"There are enough voices. You don't need mine."

"A pity. Yours is sweet as a thrush's voice."

"Yours is the honk of geese."

He paused, pursed his lips, then looked at her again with
that look. "I could have you sent back to Conor. My word is
law here now."

"You're not king yet."

"I will be so named tomorrow night."

"If the gods are willing. They may smile with favor on the
fool king."

"I have my choice of women in Leinster. That is my right
as king." His look and the tone of his voice were obvious.

"You will not have *this* woman unless she wishes it." And
she spun and turned to go.

Niafar grabbed her elbow roughly and spun her back again.
"I will be king. You can come to my bed of your own accord,
or I will have you brought there."

"Bugger a frog's arse!" she said, pulling her elbow sharply
from his grasp.

Then through the crowd she saw Naisha coming back and
she ran down to him, pushing at the drunk, stinking, boister-
ous, naked bodies as she went. To escape them, she ran close
to one of the fires, but just as she ran past, a spark exploded in
the fire and landed on her forearm. She stopped suddenly,
screaming out from the burning, which felt as though someone had pressed a burning pin into her flesh. She rubbed her
forearm, and then a fat, naked man grabbed her and pinched
her breast. She slugged him. He teetered drunkenly for a moment, then half smiled as though dreaming, and collapsed on
another naked drunk.

Deirdre ran to Naisha's arms.

"I told you you wouldn't like it," he said.

"I want to leave here, Naisha."

"I wanted to leave earlier. You wanted to stay, remember?"
But he put his arm around her shoulder and led her away.

How could such a beautiful hall be filled with so much
ugliness, she wondered. Whenever MacFith went fishing, he
put worms into a clay cup. That was what it felt like when she
was up on the balcony. Looking down onto that moving,
sweating, copulating mass of human bodies was like looking
down onto a mass of writhing pink worms.

CHAPTER 37

The day of the burial was cloudy, but the Druids, with their secret skill, could tell when the sun was at high point, and it was then that the burial entourage made its way from the great house to the passage tomb.

Thirteen Druids, signifying the number of moon changes in a year, led the way, followed by bards and musicians. There were thirty-nine bards and musicians, three times the number of Druids. The tripling signified time past, time present, and time future. All time came together in a timeless unity when a spirit transmigrated after death from one body to another. All life came from death. Thus it had been from the beginning of time, and thus it would be for always. This was the law of the ancients.

The entourage passed out of the gates of the fort and made its way along the outer bank of the rath on the north side. They passed the Lia-Fail stone, on which the new king of Tara would be crowned tomorrow morning at sunrise, after the festival of the Bull's Blood tonight. Only the clan heads of Leinster would participate in the ceremony of the Bull's Blood. The Druids would mix secret potions into the blood of the sacrificial black bull. Visions would be brought to the thirteen clan heads of Leinster, which would help them decide on the new king.

The entourage moved slowly past the Lia-Fail. It was a dark gray stone, half as tall as a man's waist, and carved at the top to resemble a man-root. It was a forceful stone, evocative of the power of the new king.

A short distance from the Lia-Fail a wicker construction was being built by slaves. It was a tall wicker figure, taller than ten men. As the entourage walked by, the slaves looked, their eyes a mixture of sullenness and pleading. Their hands were manacled by long chains to collars around their necks. Aya, too, had been a slave. And Lewara still called her only by that name, slave, yet Deirdre had never seen Aya in shackles. Her Aya in shackles, chained and tied like a cow or a goat. The thought filled Deirdre with horror.

"What are they building?" asked Deirdre. The figure vaguely resembled a man, but why would they build a wicker man?

"Sssh," said Naisha. "Only singing must be heard on the way to the court tomb. Otherwise, the journey for the soul will not be pleasant."

"Why would they build a wicker man? Naisha," she whispered, "tell me."

"For the sacrifice. Now, be quiet or the Druids will grow angry. They say it's ill luck."

"Everybody is always getting angry in this place. Ill luck this, and ill luck that. Life is more than ill luck."

"Deirdre, hush."

"What are they going—" But before she finished the question, she knew the answer. It was a wicker man, hollow inside.

Every year, at Loughadalla in the spring, MacFith had killed the firstborn calf and then burned it and sprinkled its ashes over the backs of the rest of the herd to secure good health and continued fertility for it. But Cathbad had come out once, and he had insisted that the calf be put in a wicker cage and burned alive, for that was how it was written in the laws of the ancients. Deirdre was just a small child, and had screamed and kicked and torn at the cloak of the Druid when he torched the fire, but he cast her aside.

It was Aya who had been ordered to take Deirdre away, and

Aya had carried her, kicking and screaming, to the tree house that MacFith had built for her. "That bleeding, bloodthirsty frog's arse of a Druid. What's them gods going to know if a calf be alive or dead before it's roasted?"

Cathbad left orders with MacFith that no sacrifice was to be made unless the animal was burned alive. But MacFith, when the Druid wasn't around, didn't listen. "There ain't no point to it. Making a little calfy suffer more than what he already has to." And with a swift and skilled sword he pierced the small animal's heart so that it crumpled and lay down as if it were going to sleep.

To ensure continued prosperity and good crops in Leinster, people were going to be burned in the wicker man.

"Naisha!"

"Ssssh!"

"But they're going to—"

But she was silenced by a rough jab in the side with a staff. Her immediate reaction was to reach for her sword, and she spun, but left her sword in its scabbard when she saw that the person jabbing her was a Druid. She knew that a Druid's person was sacred. To attack a Druid meant instant death for the aggressor. It was only because she was the betrothed of the king that she had been saved when she was small and attacked Cathbad. And after, MacFith had warned her. "Better to kill a king than a Druid, for if it's a king you'll be killing, you can always seek shelter among his enemies. But if it's a Druid you'll be killing, all people will be your enemies, and all things, too, even the trees and the stones."

"Bugger a frog's arse, MacFith," Aya had interjected. "Trees and stones, me arse. Druids is got power 'cause men is cowards. Their mumbo-jumbo pocus-hocus, putting fear into the hearts of the likes of you. Anybody can be a Druid. Even me. It's just learning, is what it is. Same as what one learns to spin the wool. One learns to say the words a Druid'll be say-

ing, and learns to mix their magicings same as what I learn
with the foxglove tea. I could learn to be a Druid same as I
learned to be a slave."

MacFith had laughed. "Mumbo-jumbo, you'll be calling it,
will you? You wouldn't be saying mumbo-jumbo if he was to
be standing here. You'd be fearing him same as me."

"Bugger a frog's arse," Deirdre whispered under her breath,
but for the rest of the funeral procession, she was quiet.

The bards were followed by the body of the king laid out in
his emerald and crimson silks for his life in the next world. His
sword was at his side, as well as his spear and shield, and his
dagger was in its sheath. Other articles lay on his chariot
around him, some more clothes, another pair of pampooties,
in case the ones he was wearing wore out, cups and dishes, and
Mesgedra's favorite game of *brandub*. (This was a board game
in which the king piece, playing against four hostile pieces,
tried to capture the center of the board. The board itself was a
square piece of highly polished oak divided into forty-nine
squares, seven on each side. The forty-nine squares were divided into four segments indicating the four kingships of Erinn. Mesgedra, while he was king, amused himself night after
night by playing with his opponents around the fire.) Clay
pots were filled with grain and other foodstuffs and these were
on the chariot as well. Sabine followed on foot, as well as her
two sons and three daughters.

Naisha followed, with Deirdre beside him, and behind
them the thirteen chieftains of Leinster with their sons. The
entourage turned three times around the court tomb in which
Mesgedra was to be buried. They turned in the direction of
the sun. Like Bael, who was king of the sky, Mesgedra had
been king of Leinster. Mesgedra's soul would pass to other
kings, just as his soul had come from the bodies of other kings
before him. This, too, was the law of the ancients.

Deirdre had never seen a tomb. She knew, from Aya and

MacFith and Lewara, that the souls of men lived in Tir-na-n'Og, the land of youth, for some time, and then they returned to earth again, sometimes as men or women, sometimes as animals. MacFith would sing, "The spirit wanders, comes now here, now there, and occupies whatever frame it pleases. From beasts it passes into human bodies, and from our bodies into beasts, but never perishes." That was why it was *geisa*, forbidden, for certain men to kill certain animals, because their forefathers had returned to earth as animals.

Before the curse of Macha fell on Ulster, even the great CuChulain, the great hero of Ulster, fell victim to his own *geisa*. When CuChulain was just a boy, he killed the ferocious, huge hound of the nobleman Cullan, and so the boy became known as CuChulain, the hound of Cullan. But unknown to the boy, it was *geisa* for him to kill dogs, for his own grandfather's life had once been saved by a wolfhound, who appeared from nowhere to save him from an attack by a wild boar. The wolfhound contained the spirit of his ancestors. CuChulain, as he grew to manhood, seemed to have escaped the curse of his *geisa*, for victory after victory became his, and he was loved by many women. But one day, while fighting on the beach called Baile's Strand, CuChulain killed a young enemy warrior who, he later learned, was his own son from the warrior queen Skeena, who lived on the rocky islands off the coast of Erinn. And so CuChulain lost his will to live and was injured in battle. But because he was of great courage and strength, the enemy feared him more than it did all the other warriors, so CuChulain ordered his slave to tie him to a tree so that it would seem to the enemy that CuChulain was still standing and fighting. It was only after one more day of fighting, when a raven settled on CuChulain's head, that the enemy realized that he was dead, and came and cut off his head and carried it away as a trophy.

Other heroes had other animal *geisa*s. MacFith told her

that Konaire was not allowed to eat the flesh of birds, Echebel
was forbidden to eat horseflesh, and Oscar's *geisa* forbade him
to hunt deer. Sometimes *geisas* included the necessity to do
something. The king of Tara was forced by *geisa* to walk his
seven ramparts seven times each day, and it was forbidden for
him to be in bed after sunrise. Diarmud's *geisa* had forbidden
him to deny a request from any maiden, and Ingcel was forbidden every ninth night to leave his residence. King Fergus's
geisa had forbidden him to deny a request to a corn-haired
woman, and that was how Conor had come to be named king
of Ulster.

Naisha had told Deirdre that his *geisa* forbade him to travel
when the moon was full.

The court tomb was a series of tombs built into the side of a
low mound. The entrance to the court itself consisted of two
huge vertical stones, almost as high as a man and as wide.
They were capped with a horizontal stone, as large as a fat
bull. The two vertical stones themselves stood on a big, flat
stone, about as high as an adult's waist and as long as a cow or
horse. On this were carved a series of double spirals to indicate
the journey of the soul moving through death to find rest and
rebirth in the central chamber. The inside of the passage was
dark, and already Deirdre hoped she wouldn't have to go in.

The horses were stopped and unhitched from the chariot.
The body was lifted off. The bards changed their song and the
Druids who had brought sacred water in skin sacks sprinkled
water on the corpse and on those who stood watching.

The foodstuffs were lifted off the chariot. The sun came out
from behind a cloud and lit one side of the tomb. Deirdre saw
the curving loops of more spirals carved on the walls. A Druid
spat on his hands, lifted them to the sun, and then entered the
tomb.

Then the body of the king was carried into the darkness.
The sons and daughters and wife followed. Naisha took Deir-

dre's elbow and led her gently into the stone corridor. She hesitated at the first step. She was afraid of the dry, acrid taste of the air that had been untouched by the sun for . . . how many harvests?—but Naisha's hand was at her waist nudging her gently along. She followed the corridor and saw that some of the stone carvings were not just spirals and double spirals, but actually looked like the frames of boats, crescent shapes with the sun pictured above.

The passage narrowed; her shoulders didn't brush against the stones, provided she stayed right in the middle of the corridor, but each time she veered a little, her shoulders struck the carved, rough rock. The air smelled of stones.

Naisha's broad shoulders continually brushed against the corridor sides. Then the corridor narrowed even more and she had to go through sideways. Back, back, deeper. A pressure grew inside her head, as though there were a sac of air there being blown up. When she was small, when MacFith butchered a pig, he would show her how you could blow up a pig's stomach. Now she felt as if there were a pig's stomach being blown up inside of her head, pressing against the backs of her eyes.

How many kings had been buried here? She seemed to hear their voices coming at her through the stones, saying again, *No corn in Erinn. No corn in Erinn. No corn in Erinn.* First it was the voice of Mesgedra. And then the voice of Conor. *I am your king, Ceantine. No corn in Erinn. I am your king, Ceantine.*

The passage grew darker, and the only way she could make her way was by touching Naisha's back in front of her. They felt their way back, deeper and deeper into the hillside, back and darker, and she felt as though they were entering the womb of the earth itself. Then Naisha's back suddenly disappeared from her touch and she felt nothing but the cold, rough stone.

"Naisha," she called out.

"Ssssh, I'm here," he said. The passage had suddenly veered. "Here," he whispered. "This way."

She reached out with her right hand, and at the same time, with her left hand, she felt that two other passages separated off from this main corridor.

"Come," whispered Naisha.

"I'm afraid," she said. "I want to go back."

"Sssh! Not so loud."

"I want to go back." But at that moment something hit her sharply in the small of her back, and she was knocked forward, bruising her elbow on the stone in front of her. She couldn't go back now: others were following, carrying personal articles and food to be buried with the king. And now the voices came louder. They came at her from the stones and from the spaces between the stones. *No corn in Erinn. Whoever should trespass against the laws of the kings will die . . . will die . . .* The terrible echo hurt her ears, and she covered them with her hands, and still the echo kept coming, like a stick beaten against her ears.

"Naisha—" But there was a jolt in her back again, and she was thrown forward. This time she saw light ahead and bolted toward it.

Suddenly, the narrow, dark passageway opened into a lit room. A shaft of sunlight came from a hole in the ceiling. Naisha was waiting for her in the chamber and she ran to him. The others had disappeared into one of the three other dark passageways that led away from the chamber.

There were more carvings on the walls, and these sprang out at her. They were no longer just crescents and spirals as they had been at the entrance, but herringbones and complete circles, like the top of gablets.

Now more people followed her into the chamber, carriers of the king's possessions. None of the carriers stopped, but they all gave her a sideways, condemning look that seemed to ask what she was doing in Leinster and what she was doing in the tomb.

"Naisha, I want to go back!"

"Shhhh. You must whisper in here. Look! It's a magic opening," he whispered. "The day of the summer solstice, the sun shines directly down through that opening at midday. The ancients have constructed the hill over us in such a way that the sun can shine in but no rain ever comes in. They have lipped the earth around it outside to protect the opening. Look there!"

There was a great circular carving on one of the stones, concentric circles, all of which were open at the top.

"That is where the soul passes for its journey from dark to light," said Naisha. "Come now." He moved toward one of the dark passages.

"Naisha, I don't want to go. I want to go back. These people hate me. I hate this tomb. It terrifies me. I feel as though the walls are crushing me."

"Deirdre, you mustn't shout. Please. I have to go. Mesgedra was my foster father. Come. There's nothing to be afraid of. It's just a little way farther. Please?" And he took her by the waist and then, holding her hand behind him, led her into another dark passage.

Naisha was right. It was only another short distance in the dark passageway. Once in the darkness, Naisha grabbed her and kissed her. "Remember. It's forbidden for anyone but the Druid to speak in the burial chamber."

Two torches had been lit in a square anteroom to the burial chamber itself. A pile of loose stones was on the floor. Through a low opening Deirdre could see that the king had been seated on a chair of stones. She saw that his sword had been put at his right hand, his spear at his left, his shield at his feet, as well as the foodstuffs, and the extra clothes and pampooties.

His wife went and sat beside him, and all the time the Druid chanted an incantation in some secret language that Deirdre didn't understand.

The woman's two sons and her three daughters went and kissed her. And then Naisha went and kissed her cheek. All the members of the family then left the burial chamber and the Druid, chanting an incantation that was half sung, half spoken, entered the burial chamber. He sprinkled the dead king and the queen with sacred water, raised his arms up, lowered them, then left the chamber.

A *bhodran* began to beat now as the Druid left the chamber. Thump, thump. Thump, thump. The drum sound caught in the chamber echoed off the wall, so the inside of the tomb sounded like an enormous heart. The Druid stood over the pile of loose stones and sprinkled water over them and the *bhodran* kept up the sacred rhythm of the stones. Thump, thump. Thump, thump. The Druid nodded to the two sons and they began to pick up the loose stones, and in rhythm to the thump, thump, began to wall up the entrance to the king's burial chamber. Thump, thump. Stone by stone, the entrance was slowly blocked, except for a small circle the size of a fist.

The loud echoes disturbed Deirdre. She felt as though the stones were going to swallow her up, wall her up, the way they were walling up the live queen. The echoes grew louder and louder. The echoes began to deafen her. Other echoes came back with the heavy, repetitive thump, thump. *No corn.* Thump, thump. *No corn.* Louder and louder the echoes came, almost bursting her skull. She couldn't breathe. The pain behind her eyes, inside her ears, was immense. She couldn't breathe. NO CORN! NO CORN! Covering her head with her hands. *Stop the noise!* Stop the noise! Thump. Thump.

But the noise grew huge. NO CORN! NO CORN! Her skull bursting. *"Naisha!"* she screamed, *"Naisha!"*

"Silence!" shouted the Druid, his face contorted and ugly, with a kind of fury that Deirdre had never seen. "You have broken the sanctity of silence of the burial chamber. Only a Druid's words must be heard in here. The king must be carried out again, his body must circle the tomb three times before he can be brought back in. More sacrifices will be needed for the wicker man to appease the gods. Leave! Leave immediately! Leave this chamber! Leave this kingship!"

Deirdre ran from the chamber into one of the dark passages. This was a place for the dead, this was no place for the living. She wanted to be where there was light again. Where she could breathe again. The air was close and suffocating. She ran through the corridor, faster and faster, but the corridor seemed darker going out than coming in. It narrowed sharply, and she scraped her arm. Now there was just blackness, and the closeness of the stones, and still she ran, faster and faster, feeling her way with just her hands, for her eyes were frantic but useless. She touched the rough edges of the stones, gripping at them. Her breath came more and more quickly, but there was no air in here. She clutched at her throat. Breath coming faster and faster. *No corn.* No corn. The passage forked three ways. Which way? No corn! No corn! Which way? "Naisha! Naisha!" Her voice shattered around her like a clay pot hurled against the stones, then echoed down the passages, "—shaa-shaa—shaa—" Panic took her into the left passage. Running in the blackness. She had to find the light. "Naisha!" *No corn!* LEAVE! LEAVE! NO CORN. Running, she slammed her forehead into an overhead of stone. A splatter of brilliant white light, falling, falling, trying to get up, her head reeling, now crawling. Backward the way she had come. NO CORN! NO CORN! Knees scraping on the stony floor. NO CORN. NO CORN. NO AIR! NO AIR! And hot! Getting hotter, and blacker. Another passage. Crawling into it. "NAISHA! NAISHA!" NO CORN! NO CORN! Stones compressing. Her voice echoing. Stones breathing. She heard them. Like live things. She felt them closing in on her as the passage got narrower and narrower. She made another wrong turn. She was lost. Going to die in this labyrinth of stone. "NAISHA—shaa—shaaa—shaaaaa . . ."

"Deirdre!"

"Naisha. Where are you, Naisha? Where are you? Help me! The stones—"

"It's all right."

"Naisha! The stones are closing in. Help me!"

"Don't scream. Your voice echoes." And then his voice was caught in the echoes and her screams, and their loudness drowned out Naisha's voice. She screamed even louder, calling to him to help her. "I can't get out!"

"Yes, you can come back." His words were engulfed again by a wave of echoes, and she called even louder. But hysterics had hold of her. "I can't breathe." They were clogging her windpipe, and her nostrils, and her chest heaved in spasms. "Naisha! Help me." And then she felt his hand on her. "Naisha! Naisha!" She clutched at it as though it were a rope and she were drowning in a river. "Help me get out! I can't breathe. Help me."

"Don't scream!"

But hysterics had pitched her voice into panic, and she screamed again and again, once more breaking the sacred silence of the burial tomb. Then in the darkness, she felt Naisha's hand in her hair; then she felt it draw away and she screamed again; and she felt his fist strike and she collapsed into a darkness that was silent and still.

CHAPTER 38

When Deirdre awoke, she was in her bed, back at Naisha and her quarters in the royal enclosure. Naisha was kneeling beside the bed, and he had a bowl full of cool water from which he was making compresses for her head. He smiled at her.

"I'm sorry," she said. "I guess I've spoiled it for us here, haven't I?"

"What have you spoiled?" he asked.

His eyes were very dark. When she looked into his pupils, they reminded her of the black tomb.

"You came here expecting to be taken in as one of Mesgedra's sons. Now we have to leave again . . . because of me."

He stroked her hair and smiled. "We have to leave as much on my account as yours. You heard Mesgedra's words. 'A man who trespasses against his king is doomed.' We'd have to leave anyway. Tonight, Niafar will be named king, and I've seen the way he looks at you. He spoke with me already this morning. He wants me to take some warriors and go to the south to Shillelagh. One of the chieftains, Llevelys, son of Beli, has refused to come to the assembly that will name Niafar king. Niafar suspects treachery, and with good reason too. He wants me to take troops and horses and train them to ride and then root Llevelys out of the oak forests at Shillelagh as an act confirming my loyalty to him. When I told him that I would agree provided that you could accompany me, he said that you were to stay here and learn the ways of the women of Tara.

The ways of the women of Tara include warming the bed of Niafar."

Deirdre loved this man. She loved everything about him. She loved the dark, swarthy look of him, the smell of him, the mixture of horse sweat and horse smoke and leather, the feel of him, the roughness of his hands, and the coarseness of his beard, and she opened her arms to him, and when he bent to her forehead, she reached for his lips and kissed him, desperately, for she suddenly remembered what had gone on in the tomb, and she wanted him to drive the memory from her.

And after, when he lay beside her, she buried her throbbing head under his arm, close to his heart, for she wanted the sound of his heart to heal the hurt in her head. They stayed like that for some time, and for a while she slept, and when she woke, she began to pull lightly on the black, wiry hair that grew from his armpits, and she twisted her fingers in it. Then she traced the hard muscles of his chest and arms, and she kissed them, too, tracing her lips along the arm to his shoulder and to the square, hard bulge of his chest.

Then she lifted her fingers to his face and touched the black beard and traced the firm, thin lips.

He touched the side of her chin. A good-sized bump was on the top of her head where she had collided against the stone overhang, and then he brushed his hand against her chin. "I'm sorry I had to hit you. But your voice in the sacred tombs was sending the Druid into a frenzy. If I didn't get you out, he would have ordered you entombed in there."

"I was frightened," she said.

"As soon as Aya and MacFith arrive, we'll leave here. I think you should stay here in our quarters until then. No one will bother you here."

He got out of bed and fastened his tunic, sword, and cloak. She watched him as he dressed.

"What about you? she asked. "Won't they harm you?"

"I'm still the foster son of Mesgedra, and it was not I who screamed in the court tombs."

Some apples were stacked in a clay bowl on a table under the window. Naisha took one and came and sat down on the edge of the bed again. "I'll begin preparations for our journey to Munster." Taking his dagger, he made several lengthwise slits in the apple down to the core. Then he cut around the apple near the top in a circle. He stuck the point of the dagger into a section, and pulled out a triangular section of apple stuck on the knife point. He pulled the apple chunk off with his teeth and began to chew.

"Aren't you afraid of cutting your tongue?" asked Deirdre.

"Then I would be just like your raven," Naisha said with a smile.

"Cut your tongue out! Cut your tongue out!" squawked the raven.

"See," laughed Naisha. He stuck another piece of apple and offered it to Deirdre. "It's good, but not as sweet as the apples of Ulster."

She looked at the dagger point with hesitation.

"What's the matter?" asked Naisha. "Don't you love me? Love, after all, is nothing more than trust." His eyes held hers, but they had that dark, unpredictable quality that she'd seen in them other times. "I didn't save you from Conor and from the Druid, to cut your throat. Besides"—he pushed her back gently on the bed—"I love you too much to cut your throat." He pressed the knife point with the apple on it to her lips. "I won't let you up until you take it."

She opened her mouth and carefully closed her teeth down on the apple chunk and pulled it off the dagger.

"Cut your throat!" squawked the raven. *"Frog's arse!"*

Naisha kissed her. "See, that wasn't so dangerous."

When he left their quarters, Deirdre got out of bed and went to the window. In the distance she saw the gray mists rolling in, changing the wide plains of Meath into a frightening, uncertain spirit land. Hillsides and corn stalks and cattle disappeared before her eyes. The landscape disappeared before her eyes, as though swallowed by the mist. Only rocks loomed larger than before, and the Lia-Fail took on a brutal, primitive force rising through the mist. The wicker man stood tall now, like a giant. He looked as though, any moment, he would reach down and claim as his whatever lay beyond the edge of the mist. Deirdre thought of the slaves she had seen working, and of the sacrificial fire, and she was overcome by a shivering coldness, as though the mists that enveloped the land were freezing it, as though all the waters of Erinn had turned to ice.

CHAPTER
39

"**B**ugger a frog's arse. May the sky fall down on your heads, if you don't be letting go of me." Aya whacked a Leinsterman across the ear with a solid cudgel made of an ash branch.

"That's me loov of me life," said MacFith. The two of them stood back to back, beating away the soldiers at Tara.

"That's a fine way for you to be welcoming wanderers to this place. Tara, seat of kings, me arse. Tara ain't nothing but an arsehole full of bandits!" And she whacked out again, cracking a Leinsterman full in the belly. And then, out of the corner of her eye, she saw MacFith crumple. She dropped her cudgel immediately and ran to him. "You bleeding, half-balled cow-brain," she said. "You picked a fine time to—"

"Grab her! But not with your swords. The Druid says they must be alive."

"Aya!" whispered MacFith, clutching his hands at his heart. "Aya."

The soldiers grabbed her roughly by the shoulders and lifted her up, so that her feet kicked at midair. She managed to land one foot against a soldier's thigh, but he was as muscled as a bull, and she was vaguely aware of having hurt her little toe.

"You want us alive? You want me and him alive? You'd better be letting me *adminsister* to him."

"Aya! Aya!"

The soldiers looked at MacFith with a curious, distrustful expression. When a man fought and dropped from a sword wound, they understood, but this sudden weakness left them bewildered.

"Leave me hanging here with me legs in midair, like I was a half-flying thing, you bleeding fools. That man is dying, unless you'll be letting me *adminsister* to him. It's his heart." The soldier who held Aya by one arm looked at the soldier who held her by the other side, and they both looked at their captain, who nodded to put Aya down. In one leap she was at MacFith's side, kneeling over him. She reached into the pockets of her billowy skirt and pulled out a handkerchief and carefully unfolded it to the center, which was stuffed with dried foxglove flowers. She lifted out a tiny amount, for too much foxglove could kill a man as easily as it could make him well, and dropped a few crumbs into his mouth.

MacFith felt the shreds of dried blossoms, closed his mouth, and began to work his tongue around them, mixing his saliva with the blossoms.

"You'll always be choosing the bleedingest fine time to have your attacks. Can't have them when I'll be having nothing else to do, can you?"

She gave a hostile, warning look to the soldiers. "It'll be a fine thing for you if he dies. I'll be knowing what Druids is like. They'll be skinning you alive." She held an imaginary knife in her hand and went through the motions. "From the tips of your Leinster heads, to the soles of your flat Leinster feet." She took particular relish in this last statement. When she saw the soldiers wince, she knew her remark had struck. All Druids were the same—bloodthirsty, the whole bleeding lot of them.

One of the soldiers, who had huge, scarred pores on his nose, bent down and took MacFith's hand and started gently slapping the top of it.

"Keep your Leinster paws off him! Any curing what gets done, I'll be doing." A tear rolled off her cheek, like a drop of water off a leaf, and fell on MacFith's bald scalp. She quickly wiped it off and continued her tirade. "I ain't been keeping you alive since the last two harvests to see you done in by a bunch of Leinstermen what calls themselves soldiers." She shook him. "MacFith! MacFith! Open your eyes, you scrawny half-wit. Where's your pride, man?" and she shook him again.

MacFith opened his eyes slowly. He had the clearest, bluest eyes of anyone, but his pupils were large now, and only a small area of blue showed. Aya saw her own face, small and concerned, darkly reflected in his pupils. "Aya, heart of me heart. Soul of me soul!"

The soldiers shuffled their feet with relief. What Aya had said about taking her and MacFith was very near the truth. The soldiers themselves would have been put to death if Aya and MacFith were killed. Aya's expression relaxed, too, and she saw the brief reflection of her smile in MacFith's eyes, but she squelched it immediately and continued upbraiding MacFith. "You half-man half-wit. Fine time you'll be picking always. Next time, it'll be serving you right if'n I was to let you die."

But Aya would not have been so relieved if she knew why she and MacFith were to be unharmed. The reason was that she and MacFith were needed as sacrifices.

The funeral services for the old king had been disturbed, and had to be changed and redone because of the fire-headed woman who had come with the foster son of Mesgedra.

But the inauguration ceremony of King Niafar had been marred by ill portents as well. King Niafar had stood, balancing on the top of the Lia-Fail, and in the sacred words he swore that he would be ever faithful to his trust as king and defend his territory against all foes, no matter from what quarter they came from. While making his declaration, he cut with his sword successively to the east, west, north, and south. He was surrounded by the chieftains and warriors of Tara, all

of whom were equipped with their implements of war. But as
he cut to the west, an eagle flew over, suddenly dropping like a
stone to the ground, where it grabbed an unsuspecting hare
whose cry pierced like a child's scream through the sacred
words of the king.

A look of horror came over the crowd and the Druid immediately lifted his arms and eyes to the air. He spun quickly
three times, throwing sacred ashes in all directions. More sacrifices were needed to stave off the evil omen. The first three
people coming from the west on the third sunrise after the
inauguration would have to be burned so that the smoke from
their fire would appease Cromm Cruach, god of all things.
Along with them a ram, the sacrificial animal of the Morrigan
war goddess, would also have to be burned. An unsuspecting
Aya and MacFith were the second and third strangers to have
come through the gates.

The soldiers lifted MacFith to his feet. But there was some
disagreement among them. "The gods will not accept a feeble
sacrifice."

Aya was incredulous. "Us, sacrifices? Him and me?" She
leaned forward, her face sharp as a hawk's. Her head turned,
following the semicircle back and forth where the soldiers
stood. "Not only is he feeble, but he's a half-wit and a half-
man as well! Look at him." She grabbed one of MacFith's
arms and shook it lightly. "Like a chicken's feet! Would you
be sacrificing an old crow to the gods instead of a young cock?
The gods' anger will be falling on your heads." Her voice
reached a shrillness. And her face now was that of a crone.
"Look at him!" she insisted. "Look at him! Is this what the
gods of Leinster will be after?" And she reached down and
pulled away MacFith's tunic and showed the mutilated stump
that had once been the symbol of MacFith's manhood.

CHAPTER 40

It was MacFith who brought the news to Deirdre and Naisha that Aya had been taken as a sacrifice. MacFith came with slumped shoulders and a look of utter dejection, as though his bald scalp weighed too much on his skull. His lower lip quivered as he talked, and there were tears in his eyes. "If only I hadn't . . . If only I'd been able to fight like the man I once was." And he slammed his right fist into his left palm, and then slammed both fists against the wall.

Naisha went to him and led him to a chair. "Come sit down."

MacFith's shoulders shook as he sobbed. "The seasons change. An oak just grows stronger, and what'll be happening to a man? His muscles grow soft and his heart feeble. She's right. I'm nothing but a useless old half-man."

He held his temples with his hands. His knuckles were skinned where he had hit them against the wall. Deirdre grabbed her sword from against the wall, and buckled it on.

"Where are you going?" asked Naisha.

"Where do you think I'm going?"

"You can't take on the warriors of Tara by yourself."

"And what is it that I'm supposed to be doing? Watch while they burn her?" He blocked her way and wouldn't let her pass through the door.

"Let me go."

"Don't be a fool. You might kill one or two or three, or even half a dozen. But there are three hundred sixty-five guards posted around Tara at all times, one for each day of a year.

You. Not even you. As good as you are with"—he pointed to her sword—"can do that."

"Let me go!"

"No!"

"Naisha, I'm going. I can't stand by and let her die." And she pushed at his arm. He stood, legs akimbo, his arms crossed on his chest. He was a head taller than she was, and as she pushed at him, the top of her head came just to the tip of his black bearded chin. She pushed again, but he was immovable as though he were made of rock.

"Deirdre, listen!"

"I'm listening. I'm listening to MacFith. Aya's going to be burned! My foster mother! And you expect me to stand by and watch them. I won't. And if I die trying, at least I've tried something. Which is more than I can say for you. Now leave me to go."

"Stop pushing me. You can't get by."

"I will get by," she said, throwing herself at his stomach. But he grabbed her wrist, spun her around, and caught her other wrist behind her back, so that now *her* arms were crossed on her chest. She brought her foot down hard on the arch of his foot, and he yelled and let her go. She ran past him, but he grabbed her wrist again and dragged her back.

She was kicking and screaming. "And you're a coward! You won't fight. Coward!" She spit like a cat confronted by a dog. "Coward! Coward! You're nothing but a coward!" She started to slap at him, at his arms and at his face. "At least if you won't fight, then let me. I'd rather die anyway than live with a coward!" She stood back a moment, taking aim with her words. "No wonder Conor threw you out of his army. You're nothing but a coward!"

He struck her across the face.

"That's right! That's what you're good at! Striking women. You're afraid to fight men, but you're good at striking women.

Since you're afraid of women, hit me again," and she turned her other cheek to him.

He stood still.

"Come on!" she taunted. "This side too! Hit me, coward!"

"Deirdre, stop. You're not reasonable now!"

"Hit me! A big man like you." She shoved him. "Once more! Twice! A dozen times across the face. If you hit me hard enough, maybe I won't even hear Aya screaming when they set the torch to the wicker. Hit me!" And when he didn't respond, she slapped him. Again and again.

He grabbed her and threw her on the bed, and then his powerful fingers grasped her shoulders and shook them. "Listen! For once, just listen. You're always so bloody fired. Always working yourself into a frenzy. Now, stop! Stop it! Just stop slapping and fighting and pushing, and think!"

"I am thinking. I'm thinking they're going to burn Aya. That's all I've been thinking since MacFith told us." She was crying now. "I need your help. Please! Naisha, they're going to burn Aya! Oh, Naisha!" And all the fight went out of her and she shook with sobs under him.

He rolled off her and cradled her against his chest. He pulled her close and kissed the top of her head and began to rock her. "You're so fierce and passionate, but you can't fight without plans. You can talk back to Aya and you can slap me, but you can't take on the whole guard of Tara."

"But I have to—"

"Not you—us. We have to. And because there are a lot more of them than there are of us, we have to use this." He touched her forehead. "It's fine to fight with this." He touched her heart. "You have to fight with this, but it's not enough. You have to slow down. You have to make plans."

CHAPTER 41

The wicker man stood waist deep in a gray, billowy mist in the early dawn the day of the sacrifice. Because he was just the rudest shape of a man, his face without features, it was impossible to ascertain whether he faced in the direction of the sun that had set the previous night, or whether he faced in the other direction, toward the sun that was about to rise. Perhaps he was like a two-headed god who faced both directions at once. Although the wicker man had no features, five branches were attached to the stump of each hand, to signify fingers. Each of the branches was approximately as long as an adult's leg. The mist swelled, engulfed the wicker man's fingers, then dropped like a gray, dismal sea to the wicker man's knees. The mist was like a living thing, risen out of the hills, coming to touch each blade of grass, each tree, each stone, each strand of wood-sorrel, coming quietly, then passing unnoticed as day broke.

Deirdre had not slept, but just before the first red fingers of dawn reached through the darkness, fatigue caught her up as a river picks up a branch, and carried her along in a half dream, half memory in which she relived the past three days and foresaw the coming day.

Naisha had gone to see Niafar, and pleaded with him for Aya, but Niafar said that he was powerless to do anything to change the Druid's commands. Unknown to Naisha, Deirdre herself had gone to Niafar. She plaited her hair so that the thick braids ornamented the top of her head like a crown. She rubbed essence of rose petals at the base of her neck, across her shoulders, and under her breasts. Two soldiers led her into the hall of lights, where Niafar sat on a crystal throne, embedded with emeralds and rubies.

Deirdre bowed low. She wore the silk dress that Aya had made for her in Connacht, but into the bodice, which was bare, she had inserted a piece of red silk that she'd brought with her from Loughadalla. She put a gold bracelet at the top of her right arm and put the gold torque with her name engraved, *Ceantine,* across the edge.

She was admitted to the king, and in her dream she walked down the great hall of lights. It was a journey that seemed to take forever. The prism colors from the cut crystal leapt like barriers in front of her: barriers of red, of orange, yellow, green, blue, and violet. Each time she came to a barrier, a soldier came and pulled it away, but each time he took so long. "Can you hurry?" she said, and her voice echoed in the great hall. "I don't have much time." And when she passed one barrier, another one rose up in front of her. Her silk skirt rustled as she walked, but the sound hurt her ears, like the crackling of fire. And as she walked, she held her hands over her ears. There were voices in her head. Aya's voice. "Child! Child! Isn't that a fine thing now? Burning a fire, and me arse right in the middle of it. Like a roasted goose, I'll be. Help me, child. Help me!"

Then Niafar rose and reached out his hands to her. And she knelt in front of him and took his hands and kissed both of them. He had chestnut-colored hair and a chestnut beard, and his tongue and lips seemed very pink between the dark hairs of his beard.

"I know why you've come," he said. "I told you you would come of your own volition to my bed." He led her to his bedroom. The green silk covers of Erinn, ornamented with gold-embroidered harps, covered the bed. The headboard was a huge gilt harp with a crown on top. A canopy rose over the bed, and it, too, was green embroidered with gold harps.

"Pull back the covers," Niafar said. Deirdre did as she was ordered. The king reached into the bodice of her dress and ripped out the piece of red silk. "What splendid breasts you have. You would make a king a fine concubine. Pity you have the mark of ill luck." He pointed to the dark, pea-sized mole under her left nipple. "Slaves and servants talk among themselves. Talk gets out. It would not do to have the warriors of the king know that his concubine wore a mark of ill luck."

He took his dagger and held the tip of it just at the mole. Deirdre sucked in her breath and involuntarily straightened her shoulders. She thought of Aya. She thought of the fire that would flare up around Aya's feet, blistering them. She thought of Aya's voice. "Aie, child, but you're loverly. Why do you always want to be bothering me about your mother for? I'm your mother." The dagger point lifted at the mole. Deirdre clenched her teeth so her jaws ached. She pushed the dagger out of her mind, far far away, and thought of afternoons when she ran to the hills of the three sisters. She pushed her mind back there, to the path that she had worn, past the stone in the shape of a dog's head that she passed each day, past the purple clover flowers and the keen smell of bog myrtle. Then she thought of Naisha, of the time they sat on the rocks of Lough Erne. Of the way the moon had hung in the sky like a crescent with two stars below it. "Two stars is evening, three nighttime." That's what Aya always used to say. She would not feel the dagger as Niafar cut the mole from her breast.

"King Niafar is not a cruel man, Deirdre. You have great courage. I have no wish to harm you, and it would be a pity to see blood flow from such perfect breasts. I wish that I could claim you for my queen, but you are ill fated and would only bring the wrath of the gods to Leinster. I can do nothing for your old nurse. Go now, before my desire for you overtakes my good sense. Take Naisha and go your ill-fated ways."

She ran from the king's bedroom and through the hall of lights. Now, instead of colored barriers, the hall was a labyrinth of colors, as though it were a maze. First she got lost in the corridor of purple, and then couldn't find her way out between the walls of orange, and the yellow loomed large and seemed to swallow her.

And then the red walls melted like heated butter, and the red walls grew liquid like a sea of blood and she bobbed like a cork on a sea of blood. She was swimming through blood, her arms thrashing in it, and then the green shore reached out to her and pulled her in, and she closed her eyes, thankful to be at rest, like a dove on the sand, and then she saw a shadow on the green shore. A great shadow moving slowly but inevitably toward her. She looked up and saw the faceless wicker man coming, reaching out for her, and his hands were on fire.

She tried to scream but nothing came out, only a small kittenish mewing sound, but that was enough to wake her. The room was exactly as before. Naisha stood by the window waiting for morning. MacFith sat in a chair, playing his harp. He played with his long, crooked nails, and even though he missed two fingers from his right hand, the melancholy tinkling of the small wires and the sorrowful words brought an infinite sadness over the room.

"How I long to muse on the days of my boyhood.
    Though fourscore years have flitted since,
    Still it gives sweet reflections, as every young
                                    joy should,
    That merry-hearted boys make the best of old men.
    The falcons of the wood are flown,
    And I am left alone—alone;

Dig the grave both deep and wide
And let me lament no more, no more."

It was in a matter of moments that a lifetime changed. If
only she hadn't called out in the tomb. If only she hadn't
become frightened. If only she had kept her wits about her. If
only Aya and MacFith had not arrived the day they did. If, if.
Such a small word to hang a lifetime on. Like hanging the roof
of a house on a twig the size of a toothpick.

CHAPTER 42

Preparations for the sacrifice began at midmorning. The Druids came and dropped leaves of the all-healing mistletoe into the woodpile. The smoke would rise across the land and protect the crops and cattle from disease and from invaders to the west. A ram with two great curled horns shaped like huge shells was led to the wicker man. His two great horns, twisted spiral horns, were draped with green ribbon, and he wore a collar of mistletoe. Steps led up to the body of the wicker man and four slaves picked up the bleating, kicking ram and carried him up the steps.

The human sacrifices followed. They, too, had been ornamented with mistletoe leaves and green ribbons. For three days they had been given whatever foodstuffs they wanted, and whatever amusements they asked for. Aya had asked for a dozen of the young soldiers from Niafar's army to attend to her. She had a soreness in her cave from the almost constant use. But it was not an unpleasant hurt, and as she walked and felt the soreness, she was reminded of the three days she had had with the soldiers. They were all young men, with plenty of spunk in them. For the first time in her life she had felt satisfied. There had never been enough before. It was like a hunger in her, like never having enough to eat. It was like eating one apple, and wishing that there were another and another, or like eating one morsel of roast goose and being told that that was all you were allowed. There was always a desire in her, as though if there were another man, then maybe she would have enough. At feast days at Emain she would have five or six men in an evening, and even then it wasn't enough.

And then, of course, Lewara had always come looking for her, and beaten her when she found her with Geena, the cowherd, or Bov, or any of the others. But for the past three days she had done nothing else but eat, love, and sleep. Tir-na-n'Og, the land of the dead, would be more of the same. Aya was not unhappy about dying. Death was just a continuation of life. Life and death were one. Besides, she'd spent enough time in this same old skin. The index fingers on both hands were twisting away from the other fingers, and often the pain, especially at night, was so bad that she wanted to take an axe and chop the fingers off so that they wouldn't hurt her anymore.

She had caught sight of her own reflection in a lake coming to Leinster. Her hair was gray, and her forehead was furrowed and gnarled like the bark of an oak. Her lips, which had once been full and bright like the yewberry, were now thin and colorless. The cheeks had grown gaunt. Her body was like a cloak that covered her spirit. Once a cloak wore out, you discarded it and wove yourself another one. It was the same with a body.

How old was she? She didn't know. She had been eighteen when she was stolen away by Lewara's father from Connacht. But it didn't matter. Life was not like a merchant's stall in which a body counted up the cabbages. Life was a river. Some years the river rose higher with water, and some years it fell. But you didn't go about lifting water out of the river with buckets to measure how much was there. A river eventually reached the ocean. That was where it was meant to go. A body eventually died. That was where it was meant to go.

But she would be the one to decide when she was going to die, not some fire-happy, hoity-toity Leinster high Druid. They were not going to burn her arse in a fire, roast her like a common goose. That was fine in Leinster. Let them do that to Leinstermen, none of whom had more brains than a goose, but they were not going to do it to Aya. When she raddled her cheeks with berry red, and when she put on her best smile, she could still make the men look at her. These young bucks she had been given, she could put a smile on their faces that women half her age couldn't do.

And especially now that she had been dressed in some of the finest clothes she had ever seen. It was a fine thing that Leinster Druids did. They put their finest clothes on the sacrifices to be burned in. Bloody, arse-forward Druids. Always doing things backward. Putting the living to death, so as to bring life to them what was already dead. Why not burn the dead that was already dead? Why not burn the king what died, and his goose-brained wife what wanted to die along with him? Why not burn a sheep what had died from natural causes instead of burning a ram what was perfectly healthy? And why not give these fine clothes to them what was living instead of putting them on the backs of those what was to be burned?

But Druids never made sense of nothing nowhere. Burn alive, skin alive, bleed alive, cut throats, sacrifice. Bloody, bleeding, bloodthirsty, hoity-toity Druids, the whole lot of them. Take a few Druids is what they needed to do. Burn their arses in a fire.

Oh, but they'd brought her some sweet young men. Especially the one called Treon. Hung like a bull, he was. Just as dumb, he was, too, but what did it matter? It wasn't on account of brains that she'd asked for the young men. Pity she'd have to be leaving him behind. Him she would be missing. The rest were no different than any of the others she'd had. Soldiers, slaves, cowherds—with their clothes off, they were all the same.

CHAPTER
43

Deirdre stood in the crowd that watched the ram being carried up the steps to the body of the wicker man. The sun was just the foreside of midday and the wicker man's shadow darkened the ground for only a short distance. MacFith stood beside her, chewing at a hangnail on the little finger of his left hand. His right hand appeared resting nonchalantly on his sword hilt. His harp hung over his left shoulder.

Deirdre's face showed more concern, and her eyes traveled constantly and quickly along the distances between the house where the sacrifices were being kept and the stables. She gauged the distance between the sacrifice house and the wicker man. And then she gauged the distance between the stables and the wicker man.

The shadow of the wicker man was growing shorter, and she, too, filled her time with apparently nonchalant gestures: she twisted a strand of hair around her left fingers and brushed imaginary specks of dust from her tunic. Periodically, she touched the dagger at her waist and her sword handle. Duff sat on her shoulder, and as he groomed her hair, she touched his black silky head. He made low, contented warbling sounds in his throat, as he surveyed the crowd with his bright black eyes. The crowd talked among themselves. People shuffled their feet and babies cried.

Then there was the sound of the drums and harps: the sacrificial parade had begun. Deirdre and MacFith looked at each other and both touched their swords lightly. Deirdre's eyes shot in the direction of the stable. The raven sensed the surge of energy hidden beneath the seeming stillness of her arms, and complained obscenely. *"Bugger a frog's arse."*

"Sssshhh."

People in the crowd turned and looked at her. Deirdre gave them a wry smile. "Ssshh," she said again to Duff, and petted him. A small girl with blond hair, no higher than Deirdre's waist, stared at her. She was a pretty child with freckles sprinkled across her nose. The child asked, "How'd you learn him to talk?"

Deirdre's eyes moved in the direction of the sacrifice house. She saw the first banners—the red and green banners with the gold harps of Tara. "My foster mother split his tongue," said Deirdre.

"Split his tongue?" asked the little girl, trying to understand.

"Cut it in half," answered Deirdre.

The little girl pursed her lips as though she were trying to imagine what that would feel like. Then she said, "My little brother can't talk. Maybe if they split his tongue . . ."

"Ssshh," quieted the child's mother. The child looked at the small boy standing beside her mother, and then back at Deirdre.

But Deirdre was no longer paying attention to the child. Behind the harp banners of Tara she saw the bobbing heads of the sacrifices. Without seeming obvious she stood taller, as though trying to peer over the heads looking for the top of Aya's head. In the same motion her eyes traveled to the stable.

The crowd was quiet now, and only the sound of the harps, pipes, and drums filled the air. Duff made low *rawwks* in his throat. Then, out of the stable doors, Deirdre saw the black head of Sdoirm emerge with Naisha astride, leading the gray that Deirdre would ride. Naisha had been successful in silencing the guards in the stable. All eyes were turned away from

Naisha in the direction of the sacrificial parade. Deirdre motioned with her eyes to MacFith, who also looked at Naisha.

The drums and music beat loudly, drowning out the urgent beating of the hooves of the galloping horses. Deirdre readied herself, and as Naisha came galloping up, Deirdre grabbed the mane of the gray and leapt up. She reached out a hand to MacFith, and in a moment he was behind her. The raven responded with a string of furious obscenities and flew, following Deirdre.

"Look, Mammy," screamed the child at the horses and riders, but then all words were lost, and there was only the thundering sound of the horses' hooves. The smooth, hard muscles of the horse slid between her thighs, and Deirdre fixed her eyes on the gray-black head that bobbed in the procession.

An alarm went up, and suddenly soldiers were scrambling at the mounted threesome. Swords were drawn, and spears were hurled. A spear flew at Naisha, and he reined in Sdoirm suddenly. The horse reared, and instead of passing through his belly, the spear passed harmlessly beneath his hooves and fell with a clunk to the ground.

The soldiers were confused about how to fight people on horseback. But those who had bows drew them and began shooting arrows. The horses galloped at the procession and the soldiers came at them with spears. The riders' swords were drawn and they hacked down against the spear heads, and shouts went up from the crowd. Aya was in the middle of the procession, behind two rows of soldiers. There was no time to waste. If more soldiers came, all would be lost. An arrow whizzed and Deirdre ducked. MacFith lopped off a soldier's head.

Naisha stabbed at the procession with his long spear. Soldiers who fought only with swords leapt out of the way of the black hooves.

Then Naisha was beside Aya. "You ain't expecting me to lift

my arse up there on that thing. I'd rather have it baked in a fire—" But Naisha reached down and grabbed her, swinging her up in front of him.

The Druid was suddenly in front of them, looking like a large kite with his wide, white-robed arms outstretched. He yelled a curse at Naisha. "On you and your kin descend the wrath of the gods. May you know nothing but afflic- tion. . . ." Naisha dug his heels into the stallion's flanks, and the horse bolted forward at the Druid, who had to leap to one side to avoid being knocked down. Deirdre, seeing that Naisha was free of the crowd, reined the gray in the same direction and, swiping at the heads and chests of the warriors, followed the flanks of Naisha's horse.

An archer took aim. Naisha was speeding away, his dark back a broad square against the green. The wicker man stood silent, overlooking the plain. The archer fixed his aim, sighted along his straight left hand, closed his right eye, pulled his left hand back against his cheekbone. He felt the arrow feather brush against his fingers, the bow strained against the muscles of his arm. The dark square was moving away. The archer released the arrow.

The raven flew above Deirdre, his black wings flapping ex- citedly above the noisy clanging of metal and shouting on the ground. When he saw Deirdre speed away on the horse, he squawked his complaint at being left and swooped down after her. The arrow pierced him through as easily as if he weren't there, and for a wing beat, Duff continued to fly as though nothing had changed, as though he were free with only the air to pass through. But the second wing flap only rose halfway, and then the wings stopped, and Duff plummeted to the ground. He fell neck first, and the rest of his body tumbled in a heap over it. The body flipped once with the momentum of the fall, and then was still.

PART III
The Lovers

CHAPTER 44

The rocks of Caiseal rose dramatically above the plain of Tiobriad-Arann, the well of Ara, from which flowed the sacred clear water. Here and there, moss grew out of the gray limestone mass like tufts of hair on a bald man's head. Caiseal was the seat of the kingship of Munster, and King Olum ruled from there with justice, in keeping with the direction of the ancients. The symbol of his kingship was a chiseled gold ornament called a gorget, made to be worn under the chin and secured at the shoulders with discs.

King Olum was not a tall man, but like some of the wild ponies that roamed the mountains, he was fleet of foot, with a courageous heart and a proud, good mind. His hair was receding slightly off his temples, and the dark was becoming salted with gray, but he had bright brown eyes that spoke of kindness, justice, and truth.

Munster prospered under him. The wind off the great ocean blew fierce in Munster and many of the trees were permanently bent and bowed from the onslaught of the wind. But despite the fierce storms that could uproot trees, the quiet sounds of prosperity were everywhere in Munster. The quiet, weedy Suir flowed sluggishly between the green banks. Herons chattered to each other and crossed the river in their leisurely, flopping flight. At dusk the salmon leapt, making small splashes and plunking sounds in the silver-green surface of the Suir and in the dark the black-waters of the Abhain Mhor. Like the Abhain Mhor of Ulster, the Abhain Mhor of Munster was named after black stones at the bottom which gave the rivers a profound color. Thrushes sang with their particular sweetness, and the scythes and sickle blades whispered through the hay and the rye with the even speed of unhurried harvest. Cows grazed contentedly, their rough tongues stained green with abundant grass. Lambs bleated quietly, and the corn, when the husks were pulled, was fat and yellow.

It was to Caiseal that Deirdre and Naisha fled with Aya and MacFith, and despite the hostility of Maeldun, the Druid who warned against sheltering the fugitives, under the just kingship of Olum, Deirdre and Naisha found peace. Naisha was admitted to the troops of Olum and quickly established his reputation as a fierce, able swordsman and horseman. He was made a cavalry chieftain. Two hundred horses were put in his command; he was given a suite of rooms in the king's house. Maeldun warned against the giving up of royal rooms to fugitives, but the king replied that it was the king's house that had been given, and the king's house, even when it passed to the hands of another, was still the king's house, and Maeldun frowned but he remained quiet.

It was in the winter of the sixth harvest, at the festivities of Nuadhullig, the new healing when the magic mistletoe was harvested with a golden knife from the crotch of the oak trees and given to each inhabitant to hang on his door, that something in Deirdre's belly fluttered. She woke in the morning before the snow had melted in the sun. She felt the first tremulous flutter of the child she carried. "You got a belly full of marrow pudding," Aya had said. And as Deirdre swelled with the signs of motherhood, Naisha pulled her close to him at night and rubbed his hands down the silken, swollen skin of her belly. And as she grew bigger, he laid his head on her stomach and listened to the heartbeat of their child.

Aya's hair had turned from black to the color of the mists that rolled across the plain, and when she sewed she had to hold the bone needles in peculiar, askew directions, away from her eyes. "Aya, me loove. Your eyes won't be seeing as clear as they used to be," said MacFith. But her eyebrows stayed black. If she came across a quiet pool of water when she went out to the streams to pick watercress, she would look at herself, and wet her fingers and draw them across her eyebrows and make them into a smooth arc. And she would smile at her own reflection.

The years had been kinder to Aya than to MacFith. Age had crippled his back so that he walked bent over, like a thistle in the snow. But Aya never relented in her tirades. MacFith could no longer see the two stars in the Great Bear. "Not only are you a half man and a cripple, but you're getting to be blind too." But he still sang and continued to play his harp. Sometimes the small children would listen to him, but the bards of King Olum called him a honking goose because he didn't have a cloak of the sacred eagle feathers.

Once a year, at Samhain, at the anniversary of the sun, when the harvest was taken into the graineries, Olum called his chieftains to council at Caiseal. It was here that grievances were heard. The grievances of the chieftains were not heard by the king, but by the grievance council, made up of nine chieftains. Each year the chieftains, among themselves, would elect the nine members. In this way the kingship did not fall prey to hostilities.

In addition, King Olum, once a year, journeyed through Munster to visit the raths of his chieftains. Naisha had taught the king how to ride horseback, and many of the king's men were mounted. But King Olum was a man of custom, and although he acknowledged the speed advantage of mounted warriors, he himself preferred the comforts of the chariot when he traveled. He was a man who believed in unity in his kingdom, but he was a man who believed that real unity tolerated differences. He was a man who believed that if a king forced men to do what they did not wish to do, then the king was in danger of losing his kingship. He was a king who always listened before he spoke.

Just as there were mountains, and rivers, and streams, and grassy meadows in his kingdom, so, too, he acknowledged that there were men of different temperaments and of different persuasions. Some men were melancholy, and their eyes showed large areas of white underneath the eyeballs. Some were jovial, and the outer edges of their eyes were marked by the deep lines of their mirth. Some men were high colored and quick to anger. Some men had sly, narrow eyes like the fox. But even the fox, if given enough to eat, did not chase the hens fluttering about the hen house. Each year King Olum toured his kingship, making sure that his foxes had enough to eat.

King Olum took his journey each spring through Munster to be hosted by his chieftains. Naisha traveled with him, as had Deirdre in the past. This spring, because of her close time, she stayed at home and waited. The king's visitations began on the channel side, at An Charraig, which meant rock, where the Suir River emptied to the sea. The river was tidal here, and the land a marshy flat where willows grew in abundance. A great trade in wickerware flourished here. At high tide these willows were completely covered, and at low tide they emerged from the water like thousands of thin, swimming men swept up on the shore.

At An Charraig the king's retinue stayed for two nights and feasted on eels fried in the gamy fat of wild geese seasoned with garlic. Then its journey continued back along the coast, where its way was blocked by the wide estuary of the Abhain Mhor, the black-water river. The retinue followed the river north to where it made a sharp elbow, and then the travelers continued to follow the Abhain Mhor in the direction of the sunset.

Naisha felt moments of longing for Ulster each time he saw

the sunlit, lazy green river, for how many times had he himself traveled along the river of the same name that flowed through Ulster?

And then at the foot of a shallow rapid he saw a crotched stick caught against a rock. It was a double-forked branch, for the right fork near the end, again forked into two. When he was a boy, he had floated sticks such as those down the river. He and his friends had drilled small holes into the tops of the branches and plugged the holes with smaller twigs and pretended that they were sea voyagers traveling to the ends of the earth as the sticks navigated the deep black pools and the small waterfalls edged by a luxuriance of leafy ferns. And then homesickness was more than just a yearning. It grew to an aching deep in his belly for the hills of home, and he began to wonder what would have happened if he had made a challenge to Conor's kingship.

The king's retinue forded the river and moved south along the coast to Kinsale, where green mossy rocks that fell abruptly to the sea alternated with wide sandy beaches. Kinsale meant head of the saltwater and behind the head, low green hills rose and fell in easy, sheep-speckled slopes. The king was invited by Drury, chieftain of Kinsale, to go shark fishing, and the chieftain and his king went out in a boat oared by the slaves of Drury, and after a long fight in which the sweat ran in rivulets from the king's brow, he brought in the shark. It was a huge animal, taller than himself, and when the king left Kinsale, he waved and smiled broadly.

Rain followed, days of rain, with the sky, ground, and sea shrouded in mist, forming an indistinguishable leaden wall. Rain and droplets of water formed by the mist dripped down the travelers' eyebrows into their eyes, down their noses. Rain and mist dripped into the backs of their necks. The retinue was hosted at the stone fort of Neil of the horse's foot, so named because of his club foot. The fort circled an area along the estuary of the Kenmare River. A great fire blazed in the dining hall, and dogs stretched lazily and yawned widely in front of the fire. The next day, when the household awoke, a thin mist clung to the coast, but as the sun climbed, the mists burned off and the day was glorious and blue. Cormorants and gulls shook themselves in the sun, and their cries rose above the lazy slapping of the sea against the shore.

The retinue climbed, and then stopped to look out at a valley to the north of them. An outcropping of rounded mountain, gray and bald except for the scattering of yellow, flowering plants which sprouted from the minute crevices, lay to the immediate left of the travelers. Directly in front of them, in a long, deep valley, lay a chain of lakes, brilliant and still, and blue against the patchwork of green and darker green, of gray and silver, and still more blue.

"Look out there," said King Olum to Naisha. "There is my kingdom. Lakes like jewels in a giant's crown." The king stepped out of his chariot. "We'll stop here to rest the horses," he said, and leather creaked and swords clanged against their sheaths as men dismounted or stepped out of chariots. Horses snorted and twicked their ears against the flies. A cry pierced the air, and Naisha and the group of men looked up.

A white-tailed eagle flew from a distant rock, its great wings beating against the sky. Up higher, another eagle soared. The king, adjusting his tunic, pointed to a great face of the round, smooth mountain. "It's called the Eagle's Nest," he said. "In ancient times it is said that Prince Behan was besieged. He had two children, but he succeeded in smuggling them out of this fort with a slave. The slave brought them here to this remote, formidable place, and then went to search for food. Being an old man, his heart was tired from the climb, and as he was descending, the slave slipped and fell . . . there"— the king pointed to the steeper front—"and died. Eagles were nesting nearby and heard the cries of the children, and when

the eagles flew over and saw the children rubbing with their
fists at the tears in their eyes, they were moved to go and hunt
for the children. They brought back hares and grouse and
dropped them to the children. Peace was eventually restored
when Oliol Olum, king at Brugh ria, sent troops to Prince
Behan. The princess, Don, was betrothed to King Olum's son,
and since then it is *geisa* for any king of Munster to kill an
eagle."

Naisha looked at the two soaring eagles, and as he watched
them he thought of many things. He thought of the fierceness
of Deirdre, of how she held her head, of how her approaching
motherhood had softened her. He thought of his own *geisa*,
which forbade him to travel when the moon was full. Once
already during his trip with the king, he, Naisha, had been
obliged to wait behind, and then catch up the following day
with the retinue. He thought of MacFith, who had been the
best swordsman of any in Ulster, who was now bent and growing thinner by the day, of how the old man would smile if he,
Naisha, could present him with a cloak of eagle feathers.

He watched the eagles soaring. Their nests had to be somewhere in those rocks. As the king's retinue lunched on cheese,
bread, sausage, and fresh berries, Naisha began his climb to
the eagle's nest. The climb up the rock face was not difficult.
But when he looked down to where the eagles had nested, he
realized it would be impossible to cross there without a rope
ladder. Naisha tied his spear to the rope and, hiding in a
crevice, waited.

Judging from the size of the nest, it was an old eyrie. Each
year eagles returned to the same nest, adding new twigs to it
with each nesting. A really old eyrie could be as wide across as
two men, and nearly as high.

He would have to stay well hidden in the crevice. If either
of the adult eagles saw him so close to their nest, they would
attack him. An eagle's claws could rip a man's hands to shreds.

He would have to be ready with his spear for the plunge. He gazed down into the nest. Only one eaglet stood there. Eagles usually hatched two eggs, but since one egg usually hatched two or three nights before the other, the older eaglet would often attack the younger one and kill it. This eaglet was largely still covered in an ash-colored fuzz, although some brownish feathers were beginning to sprout on its sides. *Eagles don't cry.*

And then as Naisha stood there, he thought of the eagles. He thought of the eaglet in the nest. Eagles mated for life. He looked at his spear, and the rope tied to it, and he looked at the sky. Over on the distant mountain he saw the slow, soaring circle, the outspread wings, and he untied the rope from his spear and walked down from the eagle's nest.

CHAPTER
45

Deirdre had not slept during the night. She wasn't certain why, but in the middle of the night she had woken as though the baby she carried had turned suddenly. There had been no pain. She wasn't even sure that it had happened. It was a feeling more than knowing. Outside she heard a lone wolf howling, and an owl cry. *No luck in owls,* Aya always said.

Naisha was close to her, and she felt his breath on her shoulder. She tried to turn so as not to disturb him, but the heavy, pregnant discomfort of her stomach made any turning movement into a major effort. She thought of the stories that Aya had told her as a child. The story of the wolf who had eaten up the seven children of the mother goat. How one kid had survived by hiding in the flour bin, how the mother returned to find all her children devoured except for one. How she and the last remaining kid had found the wolf asleep on the sunny bank beside the river, and how they had cut open the wolf's stomach, and pulled out the kids, and then put big stones back into his belly and sewed it up. How when the wolf awoke he felt a terrible thirst, and when he bent over to get a drink from the river, he fell in because of the weight of the stones, and drowned.

A silly story. A child's story. She had seen on the battlefield what happened to men when their bellies were opened. They screamed in agony. You didn't open a body's stomach without it knowing. Still, she felt now as though her body had been filled with stones. She felt that heavy.

Was it a boy or a girl she would have? Aya had told her the

child would be a girl. She had made Deirdre clear a shoulder
of mutton of every bit of meat. Then she had told Deirdre to
hold the blade bone to the fire until it was scorched. Then
Deirdre forced her thumbs through the scorched thin part,
and through the holes she passed a string, knotted it, and
hung the bone over the door. Since the first person to come
through the door had been a woman, a young milking maid,
Aya predicted the babe would be a girl. Had the first person to
come past the mutton bone been a man, the child would have
been a boy.

She thought of the lullaby that Aya had sung to her. "*Suan-
tri*," it was called, hush song. The words and melody went
through her mind.

> Sweet babe, a golden cradle holds thee;
> Soft a snow-white fleece enfolds thee;
> Fairest flow'rs are strewn before thee;
> Sweet birds warble o'er thee.
> Sho-heen . . . sho-lo. . . .

> Oh! Sleep my baby, free from sorrow,
> Bright thou'lt ope thine eyes tomorrow;
> Sleep while o'er thy smiling slumbers
> The gods chant happy numbers.
> Sho-heen . . . sho-lo. . . .

Why was it that lullabies always had an air of melancholy to
them? She would hear some of the servant women singing to
their children. The words were different than the lullaby that
Aya had sung to her, but the tunes were always verging on
sadness, and if you listened to them long enough, they
brought tears to your eyes. She thought now again of Aya's
voice singing to her, and sometimes MacFith accompanying
her on his harp. And again she thought of her own mother.

Lewara told her her mother had died giving birth to her. All of this raised a well of sadness in her, and tears streamed out of the corners of her eyes onto her pillow. She wiped at them, and Naisha sighed in his sleep and reached out to touch her.

Even now, even after seven years of sharing the same bed, they reached out for each other in sleep. Often Naisha cupped her breasts as they slept, and if he turned he would kiss her shoulder. Sometimes just their thighs touched against each other, or a foot, but unless the night was extraordinarily hot, as it sometimes was in the middle of summer, at least one part of each of their bodies touched the other.

She wished that Naisha would wake, and wondered if her time had come. How did a woman know when her time came? She had seen the cows and the horses in the pastures. They, when they sensed their time near, left the herd and found a hawthorn bush or larch stand to give birth in. But she felt nothing. The owl cried again. *No luck in owls.* Aya was always seeing good luck and ill luck in everything. Naisha stirred again, and this time, instead of just touching her, he closed his arm around her and pulled her close against him. The hairs of his chest momentarily tickled her nose, and she rubbed it against his chest. He patted her head lightly, and then was still.

Sadness left from her. Her heart suddenly filled with an enormous love for Naisha. She loved him more now than she had ever loved him before. This was how the gods had meant man and woman to be. If she were to die now, this moment, if breath were to stop coming, or if poison made her heart stop beating, she would welcome it. What was death? Aya said death was a land of perpetual youth, of dancing and singing. Deirdre was overcome by a great, weighted heaviness. Maybe death was like sleep, and dreaming of death, she fell asleep.

It was Abran, the budding season, and the day was glorious, bright and crisp as a daisy, and it was just after midday when the ground was without shadows that the first pangs of labor came to her, and instinctively she knew. Deirdre was weaving and the spindle fell from her hands. Aya was in the room with her, and when Deirdre clutched her belly, she rushed to her. "Well, it's about time, it is. I thought you was going to be carrying that babe around inside you for the rest of your days. MacFith! A curse on your bald head. Where is that man? Ain't ever around when you'll be needing him. MacFith!"

"Aya, me loov." He stooped in.

"Don't you be Aya-me-looving me now. You half-wit. You been in the ale again, haven't you?"

"Aya, me loov, a few sips of *usquabaugh*. The water of life to be taking away the pains in me back."

"Pains in your back, me arse. The only pains you'll be having are the ones what I'll be giving you if'n you don't be running and telling Naisha the birthing time has come."

"Aya, me darling, heart of me heart, soul of me soul, I can't be going and telling—"

"Don't you be telling me what you can be and can't be doing. Just because you're old don't mean you can't be walking to the stables. It's your back what's sore, not your feet. Naisha was here to put this babe into this woman. If he's a man, he'll be here when this babe comes out."

"It's ill luck for a man to be with a woman who's birthing. He'll be growing weak like a woman with birthing pangs—"

"Lame-brain," she said, raising her hand to cuff him, but she stopped in midswing. "Rheumatism of the brains you got, not just of the back. What brains you got left is filled with pocus-hocus. Ulster pocus-hocus. Now, go tell Naisha before I loses me patience with you. And when you'll be returning, bring your harp with you. For once it'll be doing someone some good. Some gentle music to be easing her labor."

"Look," he said. "I made this for the babe to be cutting its teeth on when the time'll be coming." And he handed Aya a carved wooden swan about the size of a man's palm.

"Well, now, will you be looking at the likes of that," Aya said. "For once you'll be doing something what's useful with yourself. Now hurry and get Naisha."

Naisha was in the horse corrals, trying to lead a young black stallion, when MacFith stooped up. The coat of the animal was shiny as a black sun, and hard muscles and finely etched veins rippled as the animal pranced and sidestepped. The mane flowed like black waves over the high-crested neck. The sculpted ears turned at each approaching sound. It was a fine, high-tossed head with wide forehead, large eyes, and flared, quivering nostrils. The horse was skittish and pulled and shied, but Naisha held the leather halter with one fist, hard and huge as an anvil, all the while stroking and gently caressing the arched, proud neck with the other. "Easy," he kept saying. "Easy, easy," in a soft, echoing murmur that resembled the purring of a cat.

The horse was the son of Sdoirm, who was now twelve years old and getting too old for the hard, intense rides that Naisha took. Sdoirm would be pastured soon and allowed to live out his days without bridle and saddle, feeding on the lush grass and nipping lazily at the purple thistle flowers that he loved to eat. The young stallion was now three years old and ready to start his training as a riding horse. It was a work of gentle tyranny, breaking a horse to bridle and to saddle while keeping the spirit intact.

The horse walked on Naisha's right side, between him and MacFith so that the old man was hidden from Naisha's view until he turned the circle at the far side of the corral. When he saw MacFith, Naisha turned and, leading the horse, ran back to MacFith. "Well, what's the news?" he asked, and he motioned for a groom to come over. "Is it a girl or a boy? Tell me, man."

"Ain't been birthed yet. The pains is just now beginning."

"Just beginning!"

The groom ran up, and the horse started and reared, striking out at the sky with his dark hooves.

"Easy," said Naisha, as much to the groom as to the horse.

"Aya says you should be there for the birthing since you was there for the begetting. I told her that it was ill luck, but Aya won't be listening." The groom gave a bizarre, distasteful look as though he'd just tasted something very sour. MacFith changed the subject. "He'll be turning into a fine piece of horseflesh. A credit to his sire."

"Ill luck? Is it ill luck for a man to attend the birthing of his best mares? Or his cows? Then why should it be ill luck for him to attend to his wife? And why is it that it's you that Aya'll be sending here and not someone younger?"

"She's being afraid," said MacFith. "If she'd be admitting to me aches and pains, she'd be admitting to me death."

Naisha handed the halter of the stallion to the groom, but again the stallion reared and tried to pull away. "Easy. Easy! Hold him tight," Naisha said to the groom. "You'd think there was a storm coming, him skittish today as though he had a bramble stuck in his belly." Naisha looked at the sky, but it was unusually clear, with only a thin tail of cloud toward the sea. The groom took the halter. Naisha petted the horse and slipped a chunk of apple between the black velvet lips. "Hold him tight," he repeated to the groom. "And you," he said to MacFith, "—now, don't you start talking about death." He made a motion to put his arm about MacFith's shoulders but MacFith was stooped so low, that Naisha let his arm fall by his side.

"Aie, look at me. Bent over. Practically walking on me hands like I was a beast and not a man at all."

Naisha didn't know what to say, but he couldn't just keep quiet, so he said, "Surely, now, that's no way for a man like you to be talking." And this time he put his arm on MacFith's shoulders.

But MacFith gave an excruciatingly pained look and shrugged the arm off. "Surely it's the only way a man can be talking when he can no longer stand the arm of a friend 'cause the weight of it pains his bones more than he can stand. . . . Would you believe the man I once was. . . . I *detest* the man I've become."

This time Naisha remained quiet, and together he and MacFith walked toward the royal house. And then, as MacFith was walking, he clutched his heart, took one step forward, and fell into a heap on the stony ground.

"MacFith!" Naisha bent down and tried to pick him up and carry him, but MacFith stopped him.

"No! Leave me."

"You, boy!" Naisha shouted to a passing child. "Bring Aya. Don't stand there like a goose. Hurry!"

Aya came half flying, half running, her great skirts hoisted about her knees, her legs furiously churning the air.

"MacFith! You bleeding, half-wit, dimwit half-man! Get up!"

"Stop shouting, Aya, can't you see he's sick!"

"Sick, me arse! He's been in the ale again. I'll teach you to be drinking behind me back again." But she was crying as she was saying it. "MacFith, where have you hidden me foxglove leaves?"

"Aya, me darling. Heart of me heart. Soul of me soul—"

"Knock off with the soul of me soul, and get up!" She went to his head and reached her hands under his shoulders and tried to lift him. "I won't be letting you do it, MacFith. You're not going to die on me. Any man what's alive enough to hide me foxglove leaves is alive enough to be living."

" 'Tis long enough I've lived. 'Tis tired I am. Tired of not feeling nothing from night till day, and all day, except for the aching of me back, and of me knees, and of me fingers. I can't even be playing me harp no more, because of me fingers."

"Your back, your knees, your fingers! Won't you be thinking of nothing but yourself? And what about me? What about me backside, when it gets cold? Who's a-going to be snorting beside me at night?"

"Heart of me heart. Soul of me soul! But you've been a good woman." He took her hand and kissed it, held it for a moment. His eyes closed. The hand tightened, and then relaxed, and Aya's fingers slipped from it. But she grasped them back again—"MacFith!"—and held it against her cheek. "MacFith! Don't you be—" But tears choked away her words.

CHAPTER
46

They named the child Niamh, after the stories that Aya had told Deirdre as a child. Niamh was the daughter of the king of the Land of Youth. In the stories Niamh married the warrior Osian and she took him away to the land of her father, and it seemed as though he had been gone but a few days, and when he returned from across the sea and came back to Erinn, he turned instantly into a crippled old man, for he had been departed over three hundred years, and he died. But during that three hundred years not a cross word had been spoken between Osian and Niamh. Niamh, it was hoped, would have the same happy life of her namesake.

But such was not to be. Life is like playing a game of *brandub* with the gods. Men plan their lives as though they were moving the pieces around the board from square to square with care, but the gods are capricious players, and in a moment they pull away the board and spill the pieces, the king and all his men, to the floor and then the game is over, and as Naisha and Deirdre moved through their lives with Niamh, a darkness was moving toward the sun.

Niamh was a cheerful, sparkling child. "There won't be no denying of who rooted the seed what sprouted this," Aya had said when Niamh had been born. "Not with that raven head."

Several moons had changed, and Niamh was on all fours, buttocks stuck in the air, and thickly diapered with soft linen. She was chewing on the wooden swan that MacFith had carved before he died. Niamh particularly liked to chew on the head of her swan.

Deirdre picked Niamh up and kissed the dark hair. Niamh offered her saliva-covered swan's head to Deirdre, but Deirdre turned her head. Then she buried her mouth at the side of Niamh's neck and made a burst of BBBBB's, so that Niamh giggled loudly. Deirdre put her back into the cradle, and Niamh started to cry for a moment, but stopped when the saliva-covered swan caught her attention again. She bit down on the head, working at it with teeth, which were still hidden under the surface of the pink gums. She babbled and drooled. "Bee-zhoo. Ba-ba-ba-ba-ba. Bee-zhoo." Niamh stopped, then looked at Deirdre, and put the hand holding the swan out over the sides of the cradle.

"If you drop it, I won't be bending to pick it up again. It's all I'm doing. Picking up your swan."

Niamh looked at her mother with challenging eyes that were as dark as her father's, and she opened her hand and let the swan fall to the floor. She smiled at her mother.

"Niamh! Well, it can just stay there."

But Niamh started to cry, and the tears streamed down her face as though a well of sorrow had overflowed. Naisha, who was polishing his sword, came over and picked up the swan and returned it to his daughter. Instantly, the crying stopped and Niamh gave her father a smile that sparkled with tears. He picked her up and kissed her. Now she offered her swan's head to him, but he nipped playfully at the small pink fist, and she giggled like a spring brook. He put her down and she continued to babble. "Just like her mother," he said, "never does as she's told," and as he walked past Deirdre to his chair, he slapped her buttocks in play.

"Well, that's a fine thing for you to be doing, slapping my backside like I was your horse."

He grabbed her wrists and spun her about, so once more she was turned away, and reached his hands up under her skirts, lightly pinching her buttocks. "And a fine, gamy mare she is too. Gives a man a ride he'll never forget."

He pushed her down onto his chair, hoisting her skirt above her knees, and sat on her lap, making a motion with his pelvis as though he were riding horseback. He kissed her lightly and playfully, but she returned his kiss eagerly. Even after so many years together, sometimes when he kissed her, he took her breath away and made the small of her back tingle as though it was being brushed with a feather.

Her back tingled now, and her tongue searched his mouth as though this were the first time she had ever kissed him. Her excitement excited him and he kissed her harder, and holding her under the thighs, he lifted her out of the chair and sat down himself, so that now she was in his lap. He lifted his pelvis to her, and then lifted her onto his hardness so that she was deeply penetrated in one motion. A shudder of pleasure went through her. Naisha pulled her closer, and when her body was quiet again, he began to thrust up, and she rocked herself deeper against his shaft.

The first demands of her pleasure were always urgent, and she demanded them with an instant quickness, like a block of wood hewn apart with a single sharp blow of an axe. But after he indulged her urgency, he began to carve pleasure with slow attention, the way a craftsman carved shapes from a block of wood. He would work away at secret corners of her body with his phallus, until her body convulsed again and again in arcs of pleasure. He discovered different parts of her, and one day he would carve her as an eagle, and then as a deer, and then as a wildcat, and then as a dove. And each time he made love to her, she was different. Always, there was a storm in her face in her urgency, and then after, the calm tenderness of satiation.

Now as she moaned in pleasure, her head thrown back, her mouth open, his hands about her waist, bringing her closer to that moment when all tension went from her face, the baby cried out, and the mother in her instinctively responded, and she shifted, so that the pleasure was stopped, but the man in Naisha was too far gone now to accept her withdrawal, and grabbing her roughly, he forced the woman back into position, and he thrust into her violently now, trying to kill the mother in an attempt to search out the woman who had been there moments ago. And the pleasure of the moment conquered the instinct, and the baby cried again, but now Deirdre didn't hear. Her body was deaf with pleasure.

After, Naisha kissed her forehead, and her eyelids, and the side of her neck. The baby was quiet now, but the mother had returned in Deirdre, and she glanced over to the cradle. Deirdre smiled and Naisha stroked back her hair and kissed her again.

"The first time I saw you," he said, "I never thought I could love anything as much as I loved you. But I love you more now than I did then."

Niamh started crying again. She had fallen asleep momentarily in her cradle, but now was awake again. Deirdre kissed Naisha's forehead, lifted herself from him, straightened her clothes, and picked Niamh from the cradle. Holding the baby to her breast, Deirdre sat down in a rocking chair and began to sing the lullaby that Aya had sung to her when she was small.

> "Sweet babe, a golden cradle holds thee;
> Soft a snow-white fleece enfolds thee;
> Fairest flow'rs are strewn before thee;
> Sweet birds warble o'er thee.
> Sho-heen . . . sho-lo. . . ."

Naisha got up and strapped on his sword, and washed his hands and face. Niamh's hands were curled shut like sleeping flowers on Deirdre's breast. Naisha bent and kissed Deirdre's forehead, and then one small petal of his daughter's hand. He bent to the floor and picked up the carved swan and gave it to Deirdre. He smiled at her and, quietly, so as not to wake Niamh, motioned with his finger that he was going out to the stables. Deirdre nodded and continued rocking and singing.

> "Oh! Sleep my baby, free from sorrow,
> Bright thou'lt ope thine eyes tomorrow:
> Sleep while o'er thy smiling slumbers
> The gods chant happy numbers.
> Sho-heen . . . sho-lo. . . ."

CHAPTER
47

The ancients observed that at the end of summer, the full moon rises more immediately opposite to the sunset than the full moon of any other season of the year. Thus, as the sun disappears in the northwest, the full moon rises in the opposite direction, in the southeast, spreading her illuminating rays over that portion of the earth which the great luminary has abandoned. The light from the full moon allowed the harvest to continue even after the sun had set. And it was customary to dance before the full moon from evening till morning, and at the festivals of La Lughnasa, the anniversary of the moon, Naisha and Deirdre had danced, for it was the law that all couples who had conceived children must dance. The couples had danced in the direction of the moon, from right to left. Deirdre, like the other women, had worn the red cloth of the moon-blood. The men had worn the white cloths that resembled the color of the life sap that came from the man-root. The men and women were given teas made from sacred leaves collected by the Druids, which gave the dancers secret sight, and made them whirl in a frenzy, which was the ritual of the passion feast.

Husbands separated from their wives and the men would say to their spouses, "Arise and celebrate the passion feast with my brothers." And as the sun rose, the male dancers fell upon the female dancers and impregnated them, and the men and women took the ejaculation, which escaped between the thighs of the women, in their hands and held it up, offering it to the primal being of all nature, saying,

"We bring to thee this oblation
which is the embodiment of all living things.
When the life sap made molten
by the fire of great passion
falls into the mother
and mixes with her red element
the great circle of timelessness
turns again.
Thus it was and always will be."

But Deirdre cast off the advances of the other dancers, for she had loved no man except Naisha, and was not desirous of having the life sap of any other inside her.

Maeldun, the Druid, watched her as she pushed away the men who tried to cover her, and then five or six of the white-robed dancers attempted to take her at once, but Naisha came to her assistance and the redheaded one and the horse captain left the festivities of La Lughnasa before the east colored red with the rising sun. The Druid frowned in deep displeasure, and afterward he spoke to King Olum, but King Olum dismissed the concerns of Maeldun, and said that Naisha and his woman were strangers to Munster, and that the customs of strangers were often different. Maeldun said nothing, but when he turned his face from the king, the lines of displeasure in his forehead and about his mouth were deeper than before.

The sun had moved farther south, closer to the stones that scattered the horizon at Caiseal and the leaves of the oak and ash trees were turning the color of the sun, when Deirdre and Naisha rode out of the royal fort for their daily excursion. Niamh was growing and changing daily. She could crawl now and did, so quickly that Aya clutched her hand at the old withered throat and gasped. "All me life I ain't been nothing but a cooking and sweeping thing, and that little one is turning me into a crawling thing. Touching everything, she is, and putting it in her mouth, like she ain't nothing but an eating thing."

The young stallion was proving to be as good a mount as his father had been, intelligent, spirited, and swift. Naisha rode him each afternoon, schooling him, turning him on hairpins, making him slide to a sudden stop, leaping hedges and ditches, and racing the wind.

The barnacle geese and the white-fronted geese had returned from far countries to winter in Erinn, as had larks, thrushes, and marsh ducks, and the noisy honking filled the air as well as the singing of the songbirds.

They were a half-afternoon's ride from Caiseal, at a place where hawthorn bush seemingly grew out of nowhere. The white flowers that bloomed on it in spring had given way to the small red berries. Because the wind was cold, Niamh had been left in Aya's care in Deirdre and Naisha's quarters at the royal house.

It was one of those fall days when the sun shone brightly but the wind from the north sea already smelled of cold, and in the distance, dark clouds were forming on the horizon. Deirdre and Naisha dismounted by the hawthorn bush and the young stallion, who had been named Sdoirm, like his father, because of his dark, stormy color, began to nip at the hawthorn berries. Naisha scratched the horse between his ears. "You're a pig, aren't you, just like your sire."

Already the two horses' coats were growing thicker with the anticipation of colder weather. A strong gust of wind blew up, shaking the leaves of the hawthorn, and throwing Deirdre's cloak up about her face. It was a green-and-blue cloak with wide yellow and white stripes that indicated high rank. She turned against the wind, and the wind caught her hood and flung it from her head. Her fiery hair swirled about her, and Naisha caught his breath as he looked at her.

How many nights, how many mornings, and how many

days had he looked upon that face? How many times had he seen her eyes narrow in the sun? How many times had he smelled the moon on her skin? How many times had he touched her cheek where it was warmed by the sun? How many times had he brushed the hair from her face during love? How many times? And still, when he looked on her, his breath came quickly. She was as changeable and fresh as each season. Here she was, a creature of autumn, her skin vibrant as the wind itself, high colored as the ash berries. Her hair like a magnificent veil of autumn leaves, caught in the wind and tossed. He grabbed her shoulders and kissed her. She smelled of earth, and sun, and wind, and her hair whipped against his face. She returned his kiss eagerly, her cheek wind-cool against his, but her tongue hot and desirous. He wanted her now, wanted her instantly, and he pushed her brusquely up against the horse's shoulder, and pressed his hardness against her flat, hard stomach. She had softened during pregnancy as though not just her breasts, but her entire body, were flowing with mother's milk. There had been a womanly, milky softness to her, but it was gone now, and the fine-boned, muscular hardness had returned. He grasped her hips and pulled her forward. The thighs were taut against his and he felt the tightening of the buttock muscles as she leaned into him, eager to accept him. It was the hotness inside of her that surprised him. The wind was cool. Her cheeks were cool. Even her hands were cool, but there, in the center of her, she was hot and soft and wet. She had a way of tightening and loosening herself, so that he forgot the chill wind. It was hotness that surrounded him. It was as though he were, all of him, a huge, long root, buried completely in the warm, soft, hot wetness of a summer rain. He buried himself deeper in the hot wetness, wanting to drown in it. If death came, this was how he wanted to die, plunged into this woman so far that he felt he could never come out. He felt like a swimmer who had plunged off a cliff, and dived so deep that his lungs were bursting as he fought his way to break through the water's surface. And then it came, the splendid ecstasy of climax, like the moment a swimmer broke the surface of the water and breathed again. He leaned his face into her shoulder. There was always a lassitude immediately after love, when he felt as though a great white bird came swooping out of the sky and carried him away to a place of dreams, where walls, trees, grass, all were made of mist and clouds. But the feeling passed in the space of a couple of breaths, and suddenly he felt the chill again. He pulled out of her, and the chill became doubly acute against his damp member that had been so warmly and completely buried in the hot, wet center of the woman he loved. He let his tunic fall and kissed Deirdre. She touched his face, but her fingers were icy. He took them in his hands and lifted them to his mouth and repeatedly blew on them to warm them. She smiled at him, but even as she smiled at him, the look on her face changed to one of morbid fear.

He looked behind him and, for a moment, didn't see anything; but then he noticed. The world had grown dark, as though evening were falling. But it was still midafternoon. Naisha looked at the sun. The left side had grown dark as though a huge tombstone had been rolled in front of it, or as though a great invisible monster had come and were devouring it.

Deirdre uttered one word, *"Niamh,"* and before Naisha could say anything, she had grasped the reins of her horse and leapt onto its back. She dug her heels into the flanks of the horse and whipped him mercilessly in the direction of Caiseal. Naisha was behind her, but then the young stallion shied from a rock in the shape of a wolf, and he leapt sideways and took off in another direction, and it was some time before Naisha caught up with Deirdre again. She hadn't even noticed that he wasn't with her. It was as though every pore of her body screamed out Niamh's name. She could think of nothing else, except her daughter's small, smiling face, and that face was burned on her heart now. And as she rode in the direction of the sun, she could see it grow progressively dark. She flayed the horse ceaselessly, until blood was mixed in the foam that flew from the gray's dappled withers. It was a mother's desperation. She knew nothing of what the darkening sun meant. All she knew was what burned in her heart, and as she raced toward Caiseal, dodging the scattered rocks, and leaping rivulets and streams, she felt that as the sun blackened, her daughter's face was being slowly suffocated as though someone were holding a pillow over Niamh, and pushing life out of her. She heard nothing but the sound of the hooves beating against the turf. And so slow . . . nothing moved fast enough. She saw herself as though in a dream. Beating the horse, who first lifted his right foot, extended it, then slowly, slowly straightened the left leg and touched the ground with it, before lifting both back legs together and striding forward again. Nothing moved fast enough, neither her horse's legs, nor her hands. Only the blackness moving across the sun seemed to move unceasingly, inevitably smothering life from the small face. She screamed at Naisha to hurry; his horse was younger, faster. But the speed at which she was traveling took the words from her lips.

The sun blackened completely until there was nothing but a ring of pale fire around the black sun at the center. Deirdre's chest felt as though someone had ripped her heart from it. She heard nothing now but the sound of Niamh's cries.

She beat the horse again, but was she imagining things? Was the sun beginning to reappear, as though the monster who had swallowed it had allowed it to come out again, the way a magician at fairs would make an egg disappear from his palm only to bring it out again? Was this some wild game by the gods, to terrify men and women into believing that the world was being swallowed by a dragon? If only Niamh was all right. She, Deirdre, would cut off her own right hand, her own right breast, anything the gods asked of her, as long as Niamh was safe.

The sun *was* reappearing. Little by little, the way when Aya embroidered a design on a dress, it would be shapeless at first, and then little by little you could begin to see what it was, a stag, or a hound, or a circle of stars, or a crescent moon. The sun *was* reappearing. Her daughter was safe. Niamh was safe, and as soon as she reached home, Deirdre would hold her in her arms, and kiss the small fingers and the soft, silky hair. Deirdre would hold Niamh on her lap and bounce her, and sing to her, and hold her small hands and kiss them. And next spring Niamh would have her own horse, a small pony born a year ago, and the three of them would ride together. Deirdre closed her eyes and thanked the gods. The time of the black sun had passed. The yellow sun had reappeared.

CHAPTER 48

"**I**n the name of the gods, was you seeing what happened to the sun, and me so scared to death, I thought the sky was going to be falling on me head." Aya's face was ashen colored when Deirdre opened the door to her and Naisha's quarters. Deirdre didn't say a word, but went directly to her baby, and a great swell of relief flooded over her as she saw Niamh.

Niamh slept as though nothing in the world had changed. The small, pale face was at perfect rest. She lay on her stomach, her small profile turned toward Deirdre. The late-afternoon sun slanted in through a window, lightening the dark curls to the color of gold chestnuts. The wooden swan lay at the side of the cradle. The baby sensed her mother and stirred slightly. She mewed, a soft sound like a kitten, raised her head momentarily, and then turned to the other side, so that she faced the setting sun. But the brightness bothered the small eyes, even though they were closed, and Niamh stirred again. Deirdre stroked the milk-soft cheek, and bent and kissed her child. The baby's forehead was damp and smelled of the fresh baby smells of her bath, of camomile flowers and the scent of rose hip. Niamh's thumb went to her mouth, and she began to suck it, making loud, smacking sounds.

Deirdre began to cry. She lowered her face to her child's, and tears slid down her face onto Niamh's cheek. Niamh stirred again, making the small mewing sounds. Deirdre picked her up and carried her to the rocking chair. She held Niamh pressed tightly against her breast, and just rocked. She rocked back and forth for a long time. If anything had happened to Niamh . . . but she wouldn't think about that.

"Will you be looking at that little one? A regular sleeping thing, she is, and old Aya so scared." Aya clutched her hand against her throat. "And still scared, I is. There ain't no good in it, I'll be telling you. The birds so calm, you'd be thinking the world had died. I tell you. And it growing dark like that. I took Niamh, and we crawled under the bed. And she was thinking it was a game." Aya rubbed her arms, crossed them on her chest, and put her hands under her armpits, trying to warm them up. "Me so cold, no fire can be warming me up. It'll be bringing ill luck, I'll be telling you. I can feel it in me bones."

At that moment a stone came flying in through the window, and Aya ducked under the table. "See what I'll be telling you? This here earth is a-busting apart." Deirdre handed Niamh to Aya, and went to the window. Three boys were running away from the window, and all Deirdre could see was their backs and the soles of their feet, first one and then another, as they fled, their hair flying behind them. Outside the window was a dead thrush, and on the ground farther away was a slingshot, a crotched piece of wood with two leather thongs, and a pocket for throwing stones. One of the boys had dropped it as he ran. They had shot at the thrush, likely all of them had slingshots, but one of them had missed and the stone had flown into the room.

Deirdre turned to Aya. "It's nothing," she said, "just some boys."

But Deirdre was uneasy too. She wished that Naisha would come back from the stables, and for a moment thought of sending Aya to get him. But she could feel Aya's fear. Aya crawled back out from under the table and handed Niamh up to her mother. Niamh was waking now, and yawned widely, the small mouth all pinkness inside, with a speckling of white teeth. She rubbed her eyes with small pink fists. Aya crawled out farther and put one hand on the table to help lift herself. Her kneebones cracked, as though a spark had exploded in the fire. "Arrach!" she said. "These old bones is getting too old to be trying to hide them from death. Better not to be trying to hide at all. Better to let Tethra come and carry me off to Tir-na-n'Og, where I can be dancing and singing forever and ever until the very stones in this world ain't no more."

Niamh was fully awake now and began to smile and gurgle as Aya straightened. "So you'll be thinking that Aya's a funny old crow, will you now? It'll be funnier yet, when you gets to be as old as me, and you won't even be remembering what it's like to be small the same as what you is."

Deirdre picked up the swan from Niamh's cradle and handed it to her. Niamh smiled when she saw it and began to chew on it enthusiastically.

The door swung open and Deirdre turned around to greet Naisha. Instead she saw three soldiers of King Olum.

She pulled Niamh closer and instinctively reached for her sword. "What do you want?" But as she said the words, a horror came over her. Spittle rose in the back of her throat but she swallowed it. Just being silly, she told herself. Of course the soldiers had come to talk to Naisha, and she let her hand slip from her sword. "Naisha's not here," she said. "He's . . ." But something about the demeanor of the soldiers stopped her from saying the rest. Each of the soldiers held a spear and carried a shield as though preparing for battle. "He's . . . out riding. I can tell him you were looking for him."

The tallest of the three soldiers shuffled his feet. They all wore the green plaids of soldiers, with deerskin leggings and a sheepskin cloak, clasped by a gold brooch. The tallest of the three soldiers had thick jowls and a face like a ham. The other had a patch over the empty socket of his right eye. The third had scraggly, mouse-colored hair which was thin, as though dogs had been chewing on it.

It was the tallest of the three who spoke. "It's not Naisha we've come for." He looked down. And then Deirdre knew, and a wail, a mother's terror, escaped her. "No!" she cried. "NO! You're not going to—" And she drew her sword. "I'll kill each of you if you take a step closer."

"It's orders from the Druid," he said slowly. "The time of the black sun. It's a signal from Cromm Cruach. The first-born . . ." He stopped speaking. "My firstborn, too, my son!" He couldn't continue, but turned away.

"Niamh!" Deirdre shook her head with horror. "No! Not Niamh. Please! I won't let you take her."

It was the one with the scraggly hair who continued. "All the firstborns what ain't seen the first year. Animal and human. That's what the Druid said. And we's got to be hurrying. Have to be at Lough Gur at the stone circle by tonight midnight. If we ain't got the first fruits ready for sacrifice, the Bloody Crescent, Cromm Cruach hisself will be sending his frowning to the rest of us. Rivers'll be freezing, and the salmon along with 'em. And there'll be so much snow so as the earth'll be freezing. And there won't be a man what'll be planting. Not a single grain of wheat. And all of us'll be starving. So hand us over the lambkin. You and the horse-chief can be rooting the beginnings of another immediate-like. And a year from now—you won't even be remembering this one."

His spear threatening, he approached Deirdre. With her right hand Deirdre slammed her sword down on the spear, just behind the iron head, with all her might. The spearhead fell to the planked wooden floor.

The soldier stopped. To the one with the patched eye he said, "Go and be bringing some of the others," and to the one with the ham face, he sneered. "It's a fine soldier you'll be.

Wait till I'll be telling the Druid. He'll be having you tossed into the flames along with your precious *son.*"

Deirdre handed Niamh to Aya, and attacked the soldier, but it had been a long time since she'd fought and she was out of practice, slower than she used to be. His shield deflected her blow.

Aya looked at the window and, lifting up her skirts and holding Niamh, had begun to crawl out when she noticed the soldiers outside. There must have been two dozen of them. "Frog's arses!" she shouted at them. "Were you birthed from snakes, all of you, that you have no feelings?" And she closed the shutter and barred it. The room was dim now, except for a crack of light coming in through a small hole in the shutters, and she saw Deirdre struggling with the soldier. She was momentarily blinded, but when her eyes reaccustomed themselves to the light, she saw that Deirdre and the soldier were body to body, Deirdre's sword pushing uselessly away at an angle from her side. "Is that how MacFith taught you?" Aya shouted at her. "Stand back. Fight with your sword, not with your chest!"

Niamh, disturbed by the shouting and noise of swords, started to cry now. Deirdre was backed away from the soldier, and she thrust at him. He parried and, using the shaft from the spear with his other hand, knocked her across the shoulder so she dropped her sword and fell to her knees. He kicked her in the stomach so she went sprawling on the floor. The soldier rushed at Aya but she grabbed a pottery washbasin and hurled it at him. She threw wide and the basin smashed noisily but harmlessly on the floor.

"Hand over the lambkin, old woman."

"Bugger a frog's arse."

He smashed Aya across the face, and she dropped to the floor, but didn't let go of Niamh. The soldier kicked her in the

back and Aya screamed, but clung tenaciously to Niamh, rolling over on her so that her body covered Niamh's. The soldier
kicked Aya again, smashing his foot down in the middle of her
back, but Aya managed to stay on top of Niamh. The soldier
grabbed her by the hair and yanked her up by it. His sword
was at the side of his body in midswing, ready to slash through
Aya's neck, when Deirdre leaped up onto his back. She thrust
her dagger into his jugular and pulled the dagger across his
throat. His sword thrust forward into Aya's back. Between her
thighs Deirdre felt all strength go out of him, and he dropped
like an axed calf on top of Aya.

Deirdre frantically shoved him off and knelt down. Niamh
was screaming, but her screams were muffled under Aya.
Gently, Deirdre turned Aya over. She pulled Niamh to her
breast, and then lifted Aya's head into her own lap. Aya was
still, the eyes closed. Blood ran from her nostrils.

"Aya," cried Deirdre. "Aya." She bent down and kissed the
old forehead. "Aya. Aya. Wake up." Deirdre stroked the face.
In the dim light the forehead looked smooth, pale as ivory.

"Child! Child!" she choked. "What horrors are coming to
this world?" Deirdre bent her head to Aya's chest and started
to sob. Niamh was sobbing, and Aya's body began to shake
with the effort of speaking. She reached up and circled Deirdre's shoulders with her arm, and daughter, mother, and
grandmother clung to each other.

Aya spoke. "Don't weep for me." She choked again with
the effort of speaking. "I was getting too old for this world
anyway . . . me old bones . . . Tir-na-n'Og, where I'll be
singing and dancing . . . and MacFith. But take Niamh"—
she choked again—"leave now before that frog's arse of a
Druid—" A shiver went through Aya and she was still.

And in that moment, as Deirdre clutched her daughter, and
the woman who had been her mother, to her breasts, in that

moment, as her body was shaken with weeping, Deirdre was every daughter and mother who had ever wept and who ever would weep. Her sorrow was as salted as the seas, and as timeless.

CHAPTER 49

The ham-faced soldier sat quietly crying in a corner of the room. Running feet and metal sounds filled the air and another half-dozen men, all armed, came in. Deirdre turned on them, her hands bloody, her face tear stained. Her amber irises were wild, like a she-wolf's. She would fight till death.

"Deirdre! Deirdre!" came a voice from behind the soldiers.

"Naisha! They want to burn Niamh!" She called back to Naisha and, kissing Niamh, quickly put her down beside Aya. She picked up the dead man's sword and got to her feet. Metal clanged on metal and the soldiers turned to face Naisha, and Deirdre rushed at them, managing to run her sword through the back of one of them before two more turned on her. The soldiers were fighting back to back, two against her, and three against Naisha. But one of them sheathed his sword and uncurled a long whip made from bull's hide. A loud crack like a tree splitting in a lightning storm sounded, and suddenly the brown-black whip caught Deirdre's wrist, wrapping itself over and over her arm. The sword flew from her hand as the soldier dragged her toward him.

At that moment Naisha broke through and hacked down on the hand that held the whip, severing it at the wrist, so that it fell to the floor, still clutching the whip. The wrist stump began to bleed profusely. Naisha lunged at another soldier and, knocking his shield away from him, ripped open his belly.

But other soldiers came in, two of them holding a great hunting net. The soldiers threw it and Naisha and Deirdre were entangled like two trapped animals. A soldier plucked

Niamh from the floor. The carved swan fell from Niamh's
fingers to the floor and she screamed as they carried her away.

"Niamh!" screamed Deirdre. "Niamh!"

Deirdre and Naisha slashed at the net, but they couldn't get
any power with their thrusts, and the swords pierced harmlessly through the large holes. The net was heavy and cumber-
some and the more they slashed, the more entangled they
became. Naisha slashed backward, and his elbow accidentally
hit Deirdre square in the face. She fell to her knees and began
to sob helplessly. "Niamh, Niamh, Niamh," she cried. She
held her head in her hands and sobbed, her voice filling the air
and flying around it like a live thing.

CHAPTER
50

At Lough Gur, less than a day's travel in the direction of the sunset from Caiseal, the shadows from two stone circles lengthened. From the time of the ancients the shadows of the silver-gray stones in the circles had appeared in the morning like long, jagged rectangles on the grass, then shortened as the sun traveled across the sky, disappeared and then appeared on the other side of the stones, lengthening, and finally disappearing with the setting sun. "Thus it was; thus it always would be. This was the cycle of timelessness."

At the base of one of the stones a spider's web stretched tenuously into the clay and grass surrounding the stone. A fly was caught just to the right of the center of the web, and a spider was now crawling out along the web to where the fly was trapped. A little farther off in a field, a gray-brown mouse, carrying a dried bilberry in his mouth, scurried across the grass. He suddenly stopped, sat up on his haunches, sniffed the air from the direction of the sunrise, dropped to four legs, and ran even more quickly to his hole.

There were two stone circles at Lough Gur. The smaller circle was used for animal sacrifices; the larger for human ones. The larger of the circles stood a couple of hundred paces to the south of the smaller circle. The entrance to the larger circle was on the side and was marked by the two tallest stones, standing taller than full-grown men.

The diameter of the large circle was as long as twenty cows head to tail. In the center of the circle was a single standing stone, with a flat top. This stone was a slightly more than waist high. This was the altar stone.

To the north of the altar stone stood a tall stone idol, Cromm Cruach, the Bloody Crescent. He was a triple-headed god with blunt, stern features. Pure gold horns had been attached to his head. One side of his face watched the sunrise, the other side watched the sunset, and the third side followed the sun all day. It was the third side that presided over the sacrifices.

After sacrifices the blood collected was sprinkled over the spectators and poured over Cromm Cruach to ensure his continued life.

Back at Caiseal, Deirdre and Naisha had finally succeeded in escaping from the net, but by that time the soldiers had left for Lough Gur with the sacrifices. Deirdre went looking for Maeldun to plead for her child, but was told that he had gone to his secret cave and that he would be at Lough Gur at midnight. She asked the whereabouts of the cave, and was told that no one knew where it was.

Then she went to speak to King Olum. When she went into the throne room, King Olum was not sitting on his throne, but rather on the steps that led to the platform on which his throne stood. There were nine steps leading up to the throne platform. King Olum sat on the bottom one. His knees were spread apart and his hands were grasped between them. He wore a gold cloak emblazoned with green eagles. Deirdre's feet echoed in the great hall of stones.

The king looked up at her with heavy eyes. "I know why you've come," he said. "I—"

But she didn't let him finish. "King Olum," Deirdre pleaded, getting down on her knees, "I beg you. Take my life instead. But save that of my daughter."

"I cannot."

"All of the clans of Munster speak of your wisdom, your

justice. If you do this, every mother in your kingdom will curse
your name with every breath."

The king lifted his eyes to her, and then looked down again.
Deirdre continued. "How can you know what it's like to have
a child? You spend so many nights with so many women. For a
man, his life and body are always the same. It's the woman
who conceives. She carries the fruit of the night ten moons in
her body. Something grows. Something grows into her life
that never again departs from it. She is a mother. She is and
remains a mother even though her children die.

"I carried that child under my heart. And that child will
never go out of my heart, ever again. Not even"—Deirdre was
crying now—"not even when it's dead. Try and understand,
King Olum. Try and understand what it is to be a mother. I
beg you. Give me back my child."

King Olum looked at her, touched the gorget at his neck,
and dropped his hand wearily again. "Sometimes even a king
must obey laws." He looked down and shrugged as though a
tremendous pain racked his spine. "My grandson has been
taken too. There's nothing I can do. I could have ordered you
and Naisha killed because you resisted. But Naisha is valuable
to me. Him I could save. But there's nothing else—"

"But you're the king," wept Deirdre. "Please! You must be
able to do something. Everyone *must* obey you!" But it was
then that she noticed that his *brandub* board had been thrown
to the floor and the king piece smashed, and running as fast as
she could, she left the throne room.

Deirdre looked frantically for Naisha, and then she saw
him, and for a moment, when she looked, she thought he had
succeeded, but it was only her own desperation that made it
seem so, for she realized in a second moment how low his
head was hung.

They came to each other, and he reached out his hands for

her, but then dropped them, for he realized that he couldn't touch her: her every nerve was like a raw, open wound.

"There are at least fifty soldiers," he said to her. "They've taken all of the . . ." But he couldn't say the word. "They've taken them all to Lough Gur. I've tried to talk to every one of them, or threatened them. Not one of them will be bribed. They're all frightened for themselves and their own families. It is custom here that every seven years they offer up their firstborn infants in exchange for milk and corn. They pray to Cromm Cruach that he will keep evil from their lands, their cattle, and their families. Many soldiers themselves have offered up their firstborn sons and daughters in past years. The coming of the black sun only means that Cromm Cruach demands another sacrifice. They mourn and they wail, and the mothers pull their hair, but they obey."

"I won't obey! I didn't carry Niamh here where I felt her move inside of me to see her struck down by a Druid. I didn't put her mouth to my breast night after night to have her sacrificed. Let the corn freeze. Let the rivers freeze. Let the earth freeze! I'm going to Lough Gur!"

CHAPTER
51

A distance of a few hundred yards separated the entrance of the stone circle and the western edge of Lough Gur. The lake itself was serene, like a silver-and-black mirror. The light of the half-moon was reflected on it, and sometimes a small breeze lifted the waves ever so slightly so that the moon's reflection grew wavy on the water.

The soldiers had camped on the south side of the larger stone circle. They had brought the infants and the wisewomen who accompanied them, in a dozen chariots. The shadows of horses edged the camp, while small cooking fires lit the night. The smell of roasted fish was wafted on the air. There was the sound of low talking, the snorting of a horse, and the occasional crying of a baby.

Deirdre and Naisha dismounted some distance from the camp, tied their horses to a dark, leafy bush, and continued silently to the camp on foot, counting on the darkness and the brush to give them cover.

In the moonlight Deirdre could see the stone circles, and a terrifying chill came over her, as though an invisible man had wrapped his icy arms around her and pulled her to his breast. In the larger circle she could see the center altar stone, and the tall, stern silhouette of the stone statue Cromm Cruach, the dark horn crescents of his head rising to the moon. She saw the wood piled high by the dark, silhouetted statue, and the coldness spread to her legs and feet.

When they came close, Deirdre and Naisha dropped to their bellies and crawled forward to the camp. The voices were louder now, and Deirdre caught snippets of conversation, talk of horses and women, and elsewhere she heard references to Maeldun's name—"arriving shortly . . . the moon at midpoint . . ."—but she lost the rest of the words, for a baby cried, and she immediately leapt to her feet. Naisha pounced on her and pushed her back to the ground. "Not yet," he whispered.

He pulled her head against his chest, and putting his finger to his lips for her to be quiet, he pointed to a sentry who was making rounds at the edge of the camp. Naisha began to crawl toward him. The sentry's spearpoint gleamed in the moonlight, and the soldier's face was like a small moon itself. Naisha stopped crawling. The sentry looked out into the darkness. An owl cried out, and from a distant hill a lone wolf howled. In one of the fires a spark exploded, and there was a burst of laughter. The sentry turned his back to the direction from which Naisha was crawling, and fumbled with his tunic. There was the sound of urine splattering on the grass as he relieved himself.

Naisha's dark silhouette rose from a crawl to a crouch, and then a stand. And for a second the two men stood framed together, dark figures in front of a half-moon. Then both dropped to the ground. A cloud passed over the moon and the sky darkened. There was the soft sound of a struggle, but it only lasted for the time of a breath. Metal clanged softly as Naisha dragged the sentry's body back behind a shrub.

Thirty-nine soldiers had come to Lough Gur. There were thirteen changes of the moon in a year. Man lived in three times, time present, time past, time future. Thirty-nine sacrifices had to be made, so that the prosperity and justice of the time past continued through time future, through all seasons of the year. Thirty-nine soldiers had to be sprinkled with the sacrificial blood, so that the armies of King Olum could continue to be strong and put fear into the hearts of would-be invaders.

In Ulster a wisewoman was called a wisewoman because she knew how to mix medicines from herbs and roots. In Leinster, a wisewoman was any old woman who no longer lost the moon blood each month, but permanently retained it. Traveling with the soldiers was the medicine woman, as well as half a dozen wisewomen. Slightly behind the soldiers' fires the wisewomen moved in and out of several large wicker pens. They were old women, and they picked their way carefully, on the dark, rough ground, and when they bent over, their feet were far apart, and they bent down from the waist, instead of from the knees the way younger women would.

To make them calm and keep them from screaming, the infants had been given a mixture of warm wheat gruel and honey to which powders from sedative plants had been added. The wisewomen had swaddled each infant in the sacred red cloth of blood, and had crowned each small head with the sacred oak leaves.

Deirdre and Naisha now moved quietly to where the infants were. Another lone sentry moved in and out of the pens. Naisha, knowing no soldier could pass up the taste of a wild pig, made a low, snorting sound that attracted the soldier. The soldier bent down under a bush, his sword drawn, and when he lifted away the bush, Naisha daggered him square in the throat.

But the wisewomen had brought with them four geese which they planned to roast tomorrow for the midday meal. The geese sauntered about quietly on the far side of the chariots that had brought the wicker pens to Lough Gur. Previously unseen because they were on the other side of the chariots, the geese emerged just as Naisha leapt up at the second sentry and pulled him to the ground. The lead goose spied him, and sent up an alarmed honking cry that immediately brought the soldiers in a flurry.

The swords of Deirdre and Naisha were no match for the number of the soldiers, and they were quickly subdued. A large, middle-aged soldier, with a chest and belly like a warhorse, approached. He had been peering into a cooking fire, and it took his eyes a moment to focus on the intruders. He straightened his shoulders and then put both his hands under his waist as though he were lifting it up, but instead he straightened his belt. "Naisha," he said, and, looking at Deirdre, "and what is it you'll be bringing along with you?"

"The child's mother," Naisha replied.

"You'd've been wiser to leave her home."

"Would your mother have seen you go to your death without fighting for you?" Naisha asked.

"Where's my child?" asked Deirdre.

The soldier continued. "This is the third one of these I'll be doing, and I'll be telling you the truth. A man never gets used to it. Battle is one thing. I can slice a dozen men apart one after the other, and not be so much as blinking an eye. But this . . ." He shook his head. "I lost my first to this. I was younger than you. You'd think a man would harden to it. But it won't be happening. My advice to you is to be taking yourself and your woman and turning back to Caiseal. Cover your woman this night and beget another child. Leave this one to the gods."

"Please!" cried Deirdre. "Please let me have Niamh."

The soldier who had spoken looked at Naisha. "Take your wife away from here. The laws of the gods is the laws of the gods. It's the sacrifice of the few for the good of the rest."

"Take my dagger," said Deirdre. "Take it from my belt. Kill me instead." She knelt down. "I'll lay my head on a rock now. Take my blood. It's the same blood that runs in the heart of my baby."

The soldier bent down and lifted her up. He took her dagger and handed it toward Naisha. "Me own wife was the same. But she had four more. And now they're ready to be birthing ones of their own. I can't be bearing to think of evil coming to them. Take your woman home. Don't let her be watching."

"I won't let you!" Deirdre grabbed for the dagger, but the soldier pulled it back.

He continued speaking to Naisha. "Leave with your woman. What's got to be done has got to be done. But there ain't no use in paining her more than she's paining. Listen to me, man. Take her away!"

Deirdre turned on the group of soldiers. "What kind of men are you? All of you, that you allow a Druid to take your children from you? You, and you, and you. Have you no courage? Look at you. There are many of you, and one Druid. Three of you could prevent him from doing it. These are your children, and the children of your brothers and sisters. And my child."

"There's nothing to be done."

It was Naisha who spoke to the soldiers now. "Give us back our child. Come back with us to Ulster. There's a king on Ulster's throne who grows old. The land in Ulster is the finest in all of Erinn. You'll have fat cows, and your children's faces will grow round on the richness of the milk."

"It's the same sun that shines on Ulster what shines on Leinster. It's the same Cromm who'll be angered. It's the same cold what'll be killing the fruits in the trees and freezing the corn."

Then Deirdre spoke again, and Naisha looked at her, for she spoke in a voice that he didn't recognize. A remarkable calm had come over her face. It was as though a strange woman stood beside him. "Have mercy on the heart of a mother. Will you permit me to see my child one last time?

The ruffians you sent to take her, they wouldn't even allow me to give her a final embrace. Is that the way you'll send a child to the hereafter, by ripping it out of my arms without so much as a kiss?"

"It'll be paining you more to see the child now. Let it go to the gods, I'll be telling you."

"It was in pain that I birthed that child. It's in pain that I stand before you now. But I would willingly barter the pain of a thousand daggers for a chance to hold her in my arms again. Please, I beseech you."

The soldier sighed. "Let her be seeing the child, then. But not for long, for the Druid'll be coming soon enough. He'll be asking for our throats, too, if he's to know."

They led Deirdre and Naisha toward the infants. There was an eerie feeling of quiet. The half-moon was shining, as though half of it had been ripped away, devoured. But the stars shone brightly. And if they took her child from her now, what would she care about the most brilliant moonlight, or starshine? What would life be for her without Niamh? It would be looking at the cradle and seeing it empty. It would be sitting in her chair, her lap empty.

They walked so slow, these heavy-footed soldiers! And Deirdre burst out suddenly past them, and ran toward the edge of the stone circle, where she saw the wicker pens. The wise-woman looked at her with eyes full of surprise and recrimination. She rushed to each pen—six or seven swaddled babies lay in each, their small heads wound with twisted oak leaves. In the moonlight each of their small faces beckoned, but she looked only for Niamh, and rushed away to another pen. And then there was Niamh! Niamh wrapped in red swaddling clothes, Niamh wrapped round and round like a cocoon, so she couldn't even move her arms.

"Niamh, Niamh!" And she bent down and picked up Niamh, and Niamh recognized her mother and smiled at her, and Deirdre's heart broke. They would not take Niamh from her again, unless they took her from lifeless arms.

Then Naisha, still walking behind one soldier, kicked him squarely in the back, and elbowed another in the stomach. "Run, Deirdre!" he shouted. "Run!"

Men shouted and then there was the sound of sharp, clattering stones as Maeldun drove up in his chariot. Deirdre's heart pounded as she saw the gold heads and gold crescents emblazoned on his chariot, catching the firelight. Thinking of nothing now but her child, Deirdre continued to run. The soldiers were behind her. In the surprise she thought Naisha had broken away, but she wasn't sure, and she couldn't turn around to look. She was ruled completely by instinct now, like a doe running with her fawn, or like a wolf with its cub, escaping the hunter. But her feet were heavy, for it had been a long time since she had run. Sometimes she had dreamed that she was running, but her feet refused to move, or moved so very slowly, as if every step took a hundred breaths before it fell to the ground again. Somehow, she could have escaped those who followed her, but it was the two in front of her, two more sentries, two young men who had had the pleasure of women, but who had never known fatherhood, who reached out for her with their powerful young arms, and pulled her to the ground.

It was one of them who ripped Niamh from her arms one more time, and carried the child back to the stone circle.

The soldiers tied Deirdre and Naisha to the opposite wheels of a chariot. "I was telling you it would be so," said the big soldier, "and I hate to be doing this to you, but you shouldn't have come. This should keep you from interfering again." And he gave Naisha a clout to the back of the head that knocked him cold.

"Please," pleaded Deirdre. "I'll do anything you want. Anything. Anything any of the soldiers want."

"When you're dealing with the gods," said the soldier, "it don't do no good to be bartering with men."

Deirdre struggled against the ropes. They held her hands tight. The head of the wooden swan that MacFith had carved for Niamh poked out of Deirdre's pocket, and Deirdre began to pray: she prayed to Tethra not to take Niamh. To make the Druid's knife fall false. And she prayed to Aengus, god of love, to change Niamh into a bird that could fly away, and she prayed to Mam Caellach, goddess of women, to make her hands as strong as a giant to break apart the bonds. And she prayed to the spirit of Aya to help her.

The soldiers came and took the babies, one by one. She couldn't see the soldiers but heard their footsteps, the crunch of small stones and the breaking of twigs. She heard a great flaring sound, and suddenly the pile of wood stacked beside Cromm Cruach ignited. She looked at the illuminated figure of the Druid, his arms raised toward Cromm Cruach, his white robe flowing, and she screamed. She screamed so that the terrible crackling sound of the huge fire didn't hurt her ears, and so she couldn't hear the sounds of the soldiers' footsteps, and so she couldn't hear the sound of her own heartbeat. She screamed and she screamed, and tore at the rope, and she tried to kick her feet, but they, too, were tied.

And then the rope that bound her hands, it loosened, loosened enough to allow her to pull her hands free. And she loosened the ankle rope and she leapt up and ran toward the stone circle, but she hadn't taken the rope completely off her ankles, and she tripped, and fell once, and she tore away the rope and leapt up again, and ran into the stone circle.

In the blaze of the great fire she saw the altar covered with blood, and she screamed even louder. She heard the Druid's voice. ". . . the moon remembers what the sun forgets . . . corn . . . milk . . . prosperity . . ." and she saw a soldier holding up a baby for the Druid. It was— Deirdre screamed,

"NO! NO!" and in that moment she saw Niamh laid on the altar and the golden knife slash the air, and saw the blood sprinkled and saw the body of her baby cast into the roaring fire, and she threw herself after it.

But enormous arms pulled her out immediately. It was the horse-chested soldier who dragged her back. "No!" she screamed. "Let me die! Let me die!"

"No," he said, wiping the soot from her face and slapping at the sparks in her clothes. "It isn't right for you to be destroying yourself. The likes of a lovely woman such as you." He shook his head. "Let the gods have what belongs to them. Take yourself home with Naisha. Let him be holding you this night. Let him make you another child."

Deirdre was sobbing and looked away from him to the fire. On the edge of the fire the wooden swan had fallen from her pocket. A tongue of flame licked at the wing tip, then died, then caught again, and then the entire swan flared. For a moment it seemed to take flight in the fire, but it crumbled on itself in the flame.

There was nothing to pray to now. Deirdre looked at the moon and wept.

CHAPTER 52

The fingernail that had been ripped away during her struggle on the night of the sacrifices was starting to grow back. The moon of cold rains had come and gone and soon it would again be the budding season of the year.

One night, as Deirdre looked upon the empty cradle, she flew into a rage and hacked it apart with an axe, and then threw the pieces into the fire, but for the rest of the time a numbness overcame her and she moved through Caiseal as though she were a hollow woman, and time passed without Deirdre really knowing it. One day seemed as empty as the next.

But one day was always different from the day that preceded it. The sun sank lower toward the horizon as it crossed in its trajectory across the sky and then began to rise again, and one morning a servant girl told Deirdre that the buds were fat, and soon the hawthorn trees would be in bloom again. Then a bumblebee flew into her room. *If a buzzing-bee'll be entering your house, 'tis a visitor you'll be having.* Aya's words came back to her. Deirdre hadn't cried in a long time. She felt as though there were no longer tears left inside of her.

Days and nights would go by, and although she would remember Niamh and Aya, she wouldn't have the energy to cry for them. And then some small thing would bring back a memory: a spoon dropped accidentally on the floor brought back a flood of memories of Niamh, and it was as though Niamh had dropped the spoon. Or a heron's wing left standing by the chimney, and it was as though Aya herself had put it there after sweeping the floor, and the tears would well in her, and she would sit and cry, and then not cry for a long time.

Naisha's helplessness at being unable to save his daughter had been transformed into an inner fury. Always quick to temper, his anger was further ignited by copious amounts of ale. More and more, he was seen with a black bullwhip. Unless it was absolutely necessary to speak to him, his men avoided him. He was as volatile as one of the Druid's secret formulas for fire. The black bullwhip had lashed out with its savage, quick tongue a number of times across the back of the legs of men who didn't move fast enough. When Naisha's hand wasn't on the whip, it was on his sword. He challenged men for the slightest sign of what he took to be insolence, the slope of their shoulders, the waver of an eye, or the movement of a chin. Within a few weeks after Lough Gur he had killed two men.

King Olum understood the rage in men that stemmed from bereavement. He knew that time soothed the temper. Naisha had been too valuable to him, to have him put to death as he might have ordered others who broke the peace. He had sent Naisha away for a time, sent him to the coast, to Kinsale to fish for sharks with Drury, but Drury had sent back a messenger asking his "most illustrious majesty," King Olum, to reconsider asking "his most faithful servant Drury to continue to guest the chieftain of Ulster, for although the black-haired chieftain had a powerful strength and could pull in a shark that two men could not, he was a bad-tempered, immoderate, dangerous guest." Not only had the chieftain from Ulster killed a dozen sharks in the time that he had been given shelter at Kinsale, he had also killed one of Drury's best warriors. If at least the ale that the chieftain of Ulster drank in such copious amounts would incapacitate him, then he would not be such a danger, but the ale only served to make the black-haired one more quarrelsome and fierce. The king's "most faithful servant" could not afford to lose any more of his warriors.

Olum, when he heard the message, sighed loudly. If he had been at war with one of his chieftains or with one of the other kingdoms, he would have sent Naisha to the battle. But there was peace throughout Munster, and what did a king do with a man who raged inside when there was peace in the land? King Olum sighed again. "Send him back," he said.

All men lived with pain at some time in their lives. Pain was part of the timeless cycle of things, just as winter was part of the cycle of the harvest, and just as spring was part of that same cycle. The pain would pass for Naisha, but in the meantime the troops of Caiseal could not afford to be waged war upon by one of its own.

The king gave orders, and when Naisha rode back into Caiseal, a dozen men were waiting for him. When he led his horse into the stables, two men dropped a net on him from the loft, and then he was carried like a wild, fighting animal to the prison compound.

CHAPTER 53

Two strangers rode to Caiseal and were stopped at the gates. In the dim light of the half-moon the soldiers could see that one of the strangers was a tall, gaunt man with one hand. If the moon had been brighter, they would have seen that the other rider had a mouth that rose much higher on the right side than on the left one.

The tall, gaunt man announced who they were and asked to be taken to see Naisha of Ulster. Naisha was in the prison compound and with the exception of Deirdre, was not allowed any visitors unless King Olum was made aware of their presence. The two strangers were led to the king's quarters, but once there, they were told the king had retired for the night and would not see anyone until morning. The soldiers would be given lodging and food for themselves and their horses.

King Olum awoke the following morning to the cheerful lilt of larks outside his window. He sat up in bed, yawned, then stretched, and scratched the top of his head before he stretched again. He shouted for his servant, who brought him a red dressing gown emblazoned with gold eagles.

The servant told him that the captain of the guard was waiting to see him. Normally, the king didn't see anyone until after he had breakfasted, but the singing of birds had put him in a cheery mood, and he asked that the captain be sent in immediately. The captain said that two strangers were waiting to see the king about Naisha.

King Olum frowned, but when the captain told him the

name of one of the strangers, his face lit up as though the sun
had risen in it.

"Fergus, my old friend! Send him in immediately."

The king and the former king hugged each other and
slapped each other's backs and boxed each other's ears. They
complimented each other and insulted each other. They ridiculed the gray in each other's beards and the wrinkles in each
other's faces, but they noted that each still had a twinkling in
the eye, and power in the hands. But Fergus looked down
when Olum said this, for Fergus had only one hand, and then
Olum was embarrassed at having said what he had said, and a
moment of uncomfortable silence passed between them.

And then Fergus said, "Let's save regrets for winter tales.
The budding season of the year will soon be approaching. It's
time to be thinking of the future and not the past," and the
easiness returned to both of them. Fergus and Olum breakfasted together on stewed apples and bread and honey and
cranberry juice and bacon. And after breakfast the king gave
orders that Naisha and Deirdre were to be brought to him.

Naisha, too, was in a good mood. He had a sense that his
confinement was coming to a close, and he, too, instead of
looking to the past, had begun to look to the future. Three
squirrels had their nest in a birch tree outside the compound.
Naisha had begun to feed them, and each day they came and
sat on the window ledge, sitting up on their haunches and
chiding him until he fed them something. Deirdre came to
see him every day. He was ready to make peace with King
Olum's men, with the gods, and with himself.

When he walked into King Olum's throne room, he was
ready to ask his pardon for his rage and to reoffer his sword
and his statement of testament to the king. The last person in
the world he expected to see in the throne room of King Olum
was Owen of the crooked mouth.

Naisha's good mood immediately disappeared, and instinctively, although his belt was empty, he reached for his sword. But this time it was Owen who spoke first. "Stay your hand, Naisha. I come not in revenge, but in peace."

"It's true, son of my brother."

Naisha turned and saw his Uncle Fergus standing behind the throne.

"We're here to offer you forgiveness from Conor."

Fergus came down from the steps of the throne platform and embraced his nephew, and Naisha returned the embrace, and he felt tears spring to his eyes because when he saw Fergus, a flood of memories came back to him: memories from childhood, from the boy troops, and from adulthood, when he had seen Fergus time and time again, so stupored by drink that he lay like a sick animal in its own filth. How could such a man have fallen so low? And now to see Fergus again as he remembered him from his boyhood, dignified, and kingly . . . "Uncle! Fergus! Fergus!" Naisha said over and over again as he clutched him.

Deirdre entered the throne room, and all eyes were turned on her. There was a kind of passiveness to her face as though she were made of porcelain and not of flesh. She neither smiled nor frowned, her face was as expressionless as though it were sculpted. Naisha reached out his hand to her and took two steps toward her.

"I have heard much about the beauty of her," said Fergus. "Conor spoke often of her. Everything he said about her is true. She is the fairest creature ever to set foot in Erinn."

"Why have you sent for me?" Deirdre asked King Olum.

King Olum waved his hand in Fergus's direction. Fergus cleared his throat and stood tall. His eyes took on a faraway look, and he began to speak. "Many years ago, when I sat on the throne of Ulster, I held this young man on my knees. I anticipated that someday he would succeed me on the throne, for I had no son of my own since my wife had been taken by

Tethra. It is forbidden for a man to ignore his *geisa*, for if he does so, he will anger the gods. Sometimes they allow him many harvests to pass, but the gods never forget. Restitution must be made. It is the thread of fate. A corn-haired woman stumbled in front of my chariot one day as I was overseeing my cattle. She lay there without moving, her face toward the ground. And when I approached to see what her trouble was, she spoke. 'Fergus, it is *geisa* for you not to ignore the request of a corn-haired woman. I am a corn-haired woman, and I ask you to marry me and to adopt my son.' There was nothing I could do. Her name was Nessa, and I took her in marriage. Her son was approaching manhood.

"She was a woman of great desires and great thirst, and one night after I had pleasured her four, maybe five, times, she looked at my face and said, 'In all the nights that I've slept with you, I've never seen your face laugh.' I answered that a king has many responsibilities and that it is not often that he can forget them and laugh. It is children who laugh best, because it is they who have the fewest responsibilities. 'I will make you laugh,' she said. 'I will give you something that will make you feel happy like a child again.' I asked her what, but all she said was 'You must trust me.'

"You must remember that my first wife and young son were both struck by illness of the lungs and both died within days of each other. It made my heart glad to laugh again. It had been too long that I had been sad, and I wanted to be a happy man. I lost desire for the rituals of kingship. I wanted to be with Nessa, I wanted to empty one cup of ale after another. I didn't know if it was the ale or the powder she put in it, and I didn't care.

"One night I fell asleep under the coat of arms of Ulster. During the night one of the swords fell and cut off my hand." He lifted up the stump of his arm. "There were some who maintained that there had been foul play. That they had seen

Conor go from my room in the middle of the night. That I had been drugged. But none of it was true. I had no one else to blame but myself and my love of laughter. Nessa talked to me. Conor had already taken over many of the responsibilities of kingship. He would simply serve as king for one year, and then a council would reelect a new king.

"I was no longer interested in the kingship. My hand hurt, and to keep it from hurting I continued to drink ale, but in even greater quantities. Days and nights passed. All were the same to me. Moons changed, countless harvests came and went, yet I knew nothing of the seasons. Sometimes I would hear a bird sing, a lark or a thrush, and try to find out where it was singing, but I would collapse and lie there, the only thing drawing me out of my stupor being the desire for more ale.

"And what a desire it came to be. Like a fire in my guts, only to be temporarily quieted with ale. My wife died and I knew nothing of it. Her wake, her burial, all passed by me as if in a dream. Nothing mattered to me except ale.

"But a new wisewoman came under the tutelage of the old one. She came to me one night like a vision in a dream, and although I'm tall, and I was a dead, drunk weight, she somehow managed to get me to her hut. She cared for me. She wiped my head with cool cloths when the fevers came, and wrapped me in sheepskins when the shivering came. She held my head as I retched and retched. She spoke kind words while I insulted her. She tied my arm so that I wouldn't tear out my guts when the burning came, and she fed me clear soups when the burning stopped. I don't know how long I stayed with her but I can now hold my head up again like a man."

Fergus raised his one good hand. Naisha had forgotten how hairy his uncle's thumbs had been. As a small boy he had pulled the hairs beneath the knuckles. Fergus continued "You, Naisha, committed a crime against your king by stealing away the woman who was espoused to him. Like all men in middle age, for a time Conor feared for his prowess. But growing age brings with it a desire for reconciliation. You are my nephew. Conor has no sons. An old man should concern himself with making peace, not war. There are four kingdoms on this island, and news travels from kingdom to kingdom. It is as though the very gods listen in the wind and speak the news to other monarchs. He has heard of your misfortunes and his heart has been touched by them. Generosity has replaced jealousy. There is no room for small-mindedness in the sovereign of Ulster. He has promised forgiveness for all. Your lands in Ulster will be returned to you. It was he who sent me to you, and bid me hurry to return with you."

Deirdre looked at Fergus, and then at Naisha. "I had a dream last night. I dreamed that I was a white swan, but my wings were caught in a lake turned completely to ice. I don't want to return to Ulster."

It was Owen who spoke now. He looked at her hard, as though he was trying to place her. "You're very beautiful," he said, "and you carry your sorrow as though you were a queen. But you've had no home for seven years, and you, too, are older than you were when you began your journey." An old crone went by carrying the burnt ends of spent candles. She was toothless with a sunken mouth, gray, clouded eyes, and thin gray hair. Owen grabbed her, so that her basket of candles fell to the floor and scattered like white sticks. He wrenched the old woman to the floor and lifted up her skirts. "There," he said. "Is that how you want to become? Your legs covered with veins like blue worms?" He helped the old woman to her feet. "Is this what you want to look like? Toothless? Your hair is the color of fire now, but what color was your hair, old woman?"

"Eh?" The old woman held her hand to her ear in a gesture of deafness. Owen bent down and began to pick up the candles. "Too deaf to hear, too blind to see, too old to love. And all alone in a strange country. Is that how you want to be?"

"Old in Munster, or old in Ulster. It's all the same," said Deirdre.

Now Fergus spoke again. "Listen to us. You're here among strangers. Both of you. The bones of your ancestors, or your great-grandfather and my great-grandfather, lie in the burial grounds in Ulster. You will grow old here without kin. Come back to Ulster. Think of the children you will have again. They will grow up among strangers and they will know neither grandparents nor blood cousins, nor second cousins, nor see the bones of their ancestors. It is not good for man to live beyond the spirits of those who trod the earth before him. Conor has given his word. The words of kingship are sacred. He said it was pride that made him seek a young wife, but that he erred and a young wife should have a young husband. All the troops in Emain ride horseback now, just as you first did many years ago. Return to Emain. Your king welcomes you there and has made a place ready for you. Return now with us in your rightful position as chieftain and prince of Ulster."

"He is captain here," said Deirdre. "There's nothing to be gained by returning to Ulster. Conor will not forgive."

"A king's word is sacred," said Fergus. "He has promised it to both of you. That is why he sent me to you. Return now with me to your homeland. Let the laughter of your children gladden my old age. The shape of home plants itself in your loins, Naisha. You will not be truly happy until you return to Ulster."

It was Owen who spoke now, directly to Deirdre. "And you have parentage in Ulster who wait for you."

Deirdre looked at Owen, as did Naisha. "I have parentage?" she questioned. And then Naisha looked at Deirdre. For the first time in more moon changes than he could remember, he saw emotion in her face. When he was a child, in play, he would wrap a leather thong tightly about his finger. His foster mother would cuff him if she saw him do it and call him a stupid boy, but he would do it anyway when she wasn't about. The tip of the finger would grow purple and swell, and when it began to hurt, he would remove the thong, and the blood would flow back into the finger, restoring its normal pink tone. That was what was happening to Deirdre's face now. It was as though blood were flowing into it again.

"What sort of parentage?" Deirdre asked. Her amber eyes were wide.

Owen stood straighter now as he delivered his information. "Your mother," he pronounced.

"My mother!" Deirdre looked at him in disbelief, and then at Naisha.

Fergus also looked at Naisha, and then at Owen. "I was told nothing about a mother."

"You're an old man, Fergus. You were told the same time I was. But old men are given to forgetfulness."

"My mother!" Deirdre pressed the palms of her hands together and lifted them to her face. "My real mother." And Naisha saw her face turn northward toward Ulster, and saw her smile for the first time in longer than he could remember.

CHAPTER 54

Four horses stood on the slope of a hill in the rounded and rolling country looking down on Emain. The evening was advanced and cool. The budding season seemed to be delayed this year, and dark clouds were being buffeted by a heavy, threatening wind from the great sea to the north. But in another direction a daytime moon had risen pale, full and white over the green hills, and on the other side of the horizon, the late sunlight, in all shades of red and gold, shone on the royal house, so that the mighty fort shone back again as though it were also a sun. The great oak doors, polished like mirrors, were blazing in red lakes of flame. The roof of the roundhouse, painted in broad reaches of red and green and orange, glowed and sparkled in the blustery evening.

Fergus smiled when he saw the look on Naisha's face. "Welcome back to the fort where the shouts of your forefathers rang in the walls. A man can never shake the shape of these hills from his mind. Come, let's go before the storm hits. Tomorrow the sun will shine in Emain. The budding season is near, and you'll see the lambs frolic on your own homeland hills."

"It's good to look on that again," Naisha said in a low voice.

Deirdre said nothing, but it was she who advanced her horse down the slope first. She wanted to see her mother, and the others galloped down the slope toward Emain after her.

Inside the gates Naisha's eyes were everywhere, looking here and there to see if he recognized a face, a kinsman, someone he had been in the boy troops with.

"Conor has made ready the Royal Branch of his round-house," Fergus said to Naisha. "You will be housed there like his brother, or like his son."

And Deirdre's eyes, too, darted everywhere looking at every woman's face that she saw, and if she saw the backs of their heads, she craned her neck around so that she could see their faces. And every time she asked herself, "Is that her? Is that her?"

Owen said, "Take your horses to the stables. I will see to it that your lodgings have been readied for you."

"Owen," Naisha said in the same quiet voice he had used on the hillside overlooking Emain. "Thank you." He reached up to clasp Owen's forearm in the traditional friendship salutation that they had both learned in the boy troops.

Owen looked at Naisha's hand, and the hint of a smile lifted the right corner of his crooked mouth. He reached down and clasped Naisha's forearm near the elbow. The sun sank below the horizon at that moment and the colors of red deepened to purple. The calmness of sunset fell over everything for a moment. It was as though the earth and all its creatures took a breath. The sounds of evening were different from the sounds of the day. It was like changing the chords in a song; there was a moment's pause while that occurred, and then the wind picked up again, howling more shrilly than before. Naisha and Owen unclasped their gesture of friendship, and Owen rode off in the direction of the king's roundhouse, and Naisha, Deirdre, and Fergus continued on their way to the stables.

Fergus could not contain his joy. He smiled and pointed at buildings, and talked incessantly. "Remember," he said, "when you were just a youngster, a small whelp of a boy, and your father brought you into the sweathouse and you left because you said it stank. And remember when you went with us and killed your first buck, and we brought it back, and your mother. She was standing there. Right by that well. Oh, the look on her face. There never was a prouder mother than she. Aie, my lad. And remember the time that you were knocking heads with Sean, son of Adran of the strong fists? You were pretending to be two bulls. And you were down on all fours, both of you, pawing at the ground like you had hooves, and snorting and bellowing. And you came together. Collided heads, and both of you cold-cocked. Fighter, you were even then. Remember . . ." And he went on, the stories falling from his tongue one after another like apples from a tree. "Aie. I remember that like it was yestereve." And he scratched his head with his hairy thumb. "It's what happens to a man when he grows old. The memories from many harvests grow vivid in his mind. Bright like an ear of corn, ripe on the stalk. And the memories of yestereve . . . they fly away" —he opened his palm upward—"like doves loosed to the sky." He looked at his hand and then lifted his hand to his head, rubbing his forehead as though he had a headache. But then his expression lightened. "But come," he said, "there'll be time a-plenty to talk now that you have returned to Emain."

They took their horses to the stable. Naisha rubbed his knuckles across an egg-sized spot of white on Sdoirm's forehead and the horse snorted his appreciation.

Naisha looked at Deirdre and she smiled at him, and her face to him was like the splendor of the hills in flower. Oh, but she was lovely. She had never stopped being lovely to him. But the days of her mourning, she had been like a dove with a broken wing. Now once again he saw vitality return. Her back was erect and her head was high. The features of her splendid face were no longer cast down in death, but lifted upward to life. In the muted light of the stable, her fiery hair was like copper silk. The cheekbones sculpted like bronze. He pulled her to him, kissed her, and then, putting his arm around her shoulders, walked with her in the direction of the king's inner fort.

As they walked up the ramp, Deirdre saw the high wooden pole that was the man-root of Aengus, reaching skyward, looking as though it were trying to touch the full moon. She was just about to ask Naisha what the pole was, when Owen came toward them.

"Ah, there you are," Owen said, smiling. "I was wondering what was keeping you. Come," he said, "Conor has ordered your quarters readied." And they turned toward the left in the maze.

"But this isn't the way to the royal quarters," Fergus immediately said.

"No," replied Owen. "Conor sends his regrets, but you are to be housed in the Red Branch."

"The Red Branch! The Red Branch is the house of the spoils and prisoners of war!"

"Old man! Your brain grows confused again. The Red Branch has not been used for the spoils of war since . . . when I came out of the boy troops."

"Owen is right," said Naisha. "I myself slept in the Red Branch."

Fergus touched his head, as though he held invisible pieces of memory in his head, and he was trying to fit them back in.

Owen continued. "The Red Branch lodgings are the lodgings of messengers and soldiers. A private room has been readied for you there. It is not luxurious, but you will be comfortable there, I assure you."

"Common soldiers' quarters!" spit Fergus. "The Red Branch is not fit lodging for a prince of Ulster. A king's word is sacred."

"An assembly, too, is sacred. As soon as it is finished, Naisha and Deirdre will be moved to the Royal Branch. Fergus is right. Conor has given his word and given his deepest apologies. But there are many steps going up and down in the Red Branch. You're right, Fergus, it once housed prisoners and was designed to make escape difficult. But you can't expect the old chieftains, Keelta with his bad knees, or Lewy with his one foot, to walk up and down the stairs. Naisha and Deirdre are both young and strong. They could climb ten times a hundred stairs a day, and still have legs for dancing. Conor says that he was obliged to call a special assembly of his chieftains on an emergency matter of state, and the Royal Branch is full. He wasn't even certain whether you would return to Emain or not, and—"

"But he gave me his word," said Fergus, "that a suite in the Royal Branch would be readied."

"And it will be readied. The assembly will last no longer than three nights, he assured me, and then you will be moved into the Royal Branch. But believe me, the Red Branch lodgings are comfortable. I've slept there often enough myself. Conor says that you have been absent for seven years from the Royal Branch, and that three more nights will not offend the son of Usna. He says that patience flows in the veins of all the chieftains of Ulster, and that tomorrow you can take your seat in assembly with the other chieftains."

"I will speak to Conor," Fergus insisted. "A king's word is sacred. He *cannot* go back on it. It is dishonor."

But it was Deirdre who spoke. "I have been separated from my mother since birth. I have no wish now except to see her. I have slept in ditches and I have slept beside riverbanks. I've slept under the stars and in caves. I would sleep on a bed of sharp stones tonight if I knew that I could see her now. I don't care for your honor or dishonor," she said to Fergus, and turning to Owen, she said, "If you know who she is, send her to me now. Tell my mother her daughter has returned."

Owen nodded his head in a gesture of agreement.

Fergus protested, "I cannot allow the king to go back on the sacred trust of his word!" And he spun on his heel and left to speak with Conor.

"Come," said Owen. "A pleasant, sunny room has been readied for you. As soon as I've shown it to you, I'll send your mother to you."

CHAPTER 55

"Welcome, Fergus!" said King Conor. "Well done! Owen tells me that you have been successful in your mission and that Naisha and Ceantine have been brought back to their rightful place at Emain. I will deal with them shortly. Tell me, Fergus, is she as lovely as she was? My *geisa* does not allow me to see her on the day of the full moon until it rises. Oh, but that evening would come, so that I could see her again." Conor rubbed his hands against his thighs.

"She is Naisha's woman, Conor. You gave your word!"

"You have served me well, Fergus. Come, now, and have a drink of ale with your king. Put your old mind at rest."

"You promised that they would be lodged in the Royal House, under your roof, where they would be under *your* protection, and yet you put them in the Red Branch."

"Owen must have told you. The chieftains are here for an assembly."

"What sort of assembly takes place at this time of the year?"

"I have decided to have the cow counting at this time instead of later in the year. It gives me pleasure to ride out in my chariot and look upon my herds. The chieftains have brought to me their stipends of cattle earlier."

"You are king and you gave your word. A king's word is sacred, but yours tastes of treachery."

"Come now, Fergus. Is it not better to have the stipends from cow counting paid in spring when the cows carry the young in their womb? That way, when the cow gives birth, I am given two animals instead of just one young calf newly weaned from its mother. Come, now, no more talk of the assembly. It will soon be over. Let us celebrate the return of the son of Usna and—"

"He is my nephew, Conor. He came here under my protection and my honor. And your honor. You promised him safe-keeping under your roof. I will not allow that honor to be betrayed."

"Come, Fergus, a toast to the health of our young friend, and the woman he has brought with him."

"I want your word that you will not harm them. Give me testament of that!"

"Fergus! You're an old man. A kingship is like a man. It changes with the years."

"A kingship comes from the gods. A kingship is divine. A kingship does not change. Give me your testament you will not harm them."

"Fergus. You are trying my patience and my time. I have much to do."

"Give me testament, or I will return to them now and lead them out of Emain, just as I led them here."

The king sighed. For a moment his mind jumped back to when he was a young man. He had waited in the darkness for his mother to call him. He'd stood leaning, his elbows resting on the windowsill, watching the moon move across the sky. It was a crescent moon, like a huge fingernail, and it traveled so slowly across the sky. Finally she came to him. "Come," she whispered. "It is time."

He remembered the room. The polished oak walls glistening, and the low flame that burned in a corner of the room. Fergus lay sleeping under one wall and snorted in his sleep, and Conor had started, thinking that Fergus would wake. But Fergus merely moaned in his restless sleep of the drunk, and he flung out his arm so that it lay away from him, the hand lying palm up close to the wall. On the wall hung two swords crossed under the coat of arms of the Kingship of Ulster, a bull and a lion standing upright on a dragon's back, and two spears crossed between them.

"Now's the time to do it," whispered his mother. But Conor hesitated. There was a smell in the room, the sweaty smell of lust, and it nearly made him retch. "Do you want to be king or not?" His mother's voice was a whisper, but there was a menacing edge to it, like the swishing sound of a sword as it sliced the air. Her face in the dying firelight was hard as a spear blade. She took the sword from the wall, the one that crossed from the right side to the left. Conor remembered that there was a faint imprint on the wall where the sword had been hung for . . . how many generations of kings?

His mother put the sword into his hand. "Do you want to be king or not? Do you want to be king or not?" He knew her voice was soft, but somehow, in his ears, it roared like a waterfall. "Do it. Just across the wrist. One swift motion. Do it! Do it! Do it. . . . Think . . . Conor, son of Nessa the cowherd's son, or Conor, king of Ulster."

Conor drew the sword with both hands above his head. The hairy thumb twitched slightly and a shudder went through Fergus's entire arm. Conor started.

"Do it now, you fool, before he wakes! What are you waiting for? You don't have to kill him, just cut off his hand. I've drugged his ale so he won't even know! Do it *now!*"

He swung the sword, but at the last minute drew back instead of following through. The wrist was only half severed. Blood began to pour from the deep gash.

"Fool! Incompetent! You don't deserve to be anything but a cowherd! Give me the sword. If the chieftains know what a coward you are, they'll never name you king!" She grabbed the sword from him, lifted it, but Conor grabbed it back.

And he brought the sword down again. This time he com-

pleted his swing, and he nudged the severed hand away from
the wrist. Then he dropped the sword, making it look as
though it had fallen off the wall.

Now as he looked at Fergus, Conor wished that he had
slammed the sword across his neck and killed him instead of
just wounding him. "All right, Fergus," he said. "You have my
testament." Conor stood and Fergus approached him. Conor
reached and touched the shriveled, gray-haired testicles of Fergus. That's how an old man looked. Conor was repulsed and
looked away. Fergus reached under Conor's tunic and laid his
hand on Conor's heavy testicles. Conor cringed at the feel of
Fergus's hairy thumb, but he cleared his throat and spoke. "I,
Conor, King of Ulster, give testament that *I* will not harm the
son of Usna."

CHAPTER
56

The room where Owen led Naisha and Deirdre was up a flight of highly polished oak stairs. The Red Branch did not have the sumptuousness of the Royal Branch. There were no tapestries on the walls, nor were the doors sculpted with dragons or snakes eating their tails.

Owen led them down a corridor and then opened a door into a room. The curtains were drawn—they were deep-brown, heavy curtains—and it took Deirdre a moment to focus her eyes in the dim light. It was a sparsely furnished room with a low, unmade bed beside the wall, a table with a basin and a pitcher for water. There was no fire in the room, and the torches were not lit. On another small table stood a group of small figures. Deirdre went over to it, curious to see what it was—a *brandub* board.

Owen flew into a fury and began to curse and shout. "I ordered this room readied! I ordered flowers to be put in pitchers and I ordered bows from ash plants to be hung over the doors. Slave! Slave!"

A young woman with a pale, bland face came running into the room.

"Why wasn't this room made up?"

The slave protested, "I didn't know—" But Owen slapped her, knocking her to the ground before she could finish. Naisha immediately leaped at Owen, grabbing him by the tunic front.

"Naisha!" Owen sputtered. "I apologize! Unhand me, please. It's my impatience that throws me into a fury. I wanted all to be ready when you arrived so that you would be able to relax after your long journey."

Naisha released Owen, and Owen straightened his tunic. "Forgive me, Naisha, but she's a lazy good-for-nothing who never does as she's told." The slave fired a hateful, insolent look at Owen, but didn't say anything. "Now, hurry and get torches and kindling, at least, to take the chill from the room, and then make up this room in a manner fitting a chieftain of Ulster, or I'll have you whipped."

The slave ran from the room as quickly as she had entered it.

Owen rubbed his hands together and blew on them. "I truly am sorry. Coming into a cold room. You'd think the gods would finally send us spring this year. All this cold makes a man short tempered, and another storm coming tonight."

The slave came running back holding a lit torch and set three torches attached to the wall burning. The walls of the room suddenly jumped with dark shadows. Deirdre shivered with unease, but cast off the feeling. It was just the chill of the room, and would pass as soon as the fire was burning. The slave left again.

Owen spoke to Deirdre this time. "Conor tells me that he can't locate your mother. He thinks she may have gone out into the hills to gather thyme and leaves to be dried. I'll go look for her and bring her to you as soon as she returns. She can't be much longer out there, not with the weather readying for storm."

The slave came back carrying a pile of wood in her arms. She threw the sticks into the fire pit with a clatter, took a torch from the wall, and set the fire burning. Deirdre looked away from it. She could never look on fire now without thinking . . . instead, she turned to Owen. "Please tell my mother to hurry!"

Owen bowed ever so slightly, and left, closing the door behind him.

The slave scurried in and out with linen and covers and cloths to dust. Her breath came in short, quick pants.

Naisha turned to her and said, "There's time. We've been away for over seven years. There's no need to hurry so. It's not a race you're running."

"It's sorry I am, sir, but I swear on the breast of my mother, I wasn't told the room was to be readied. I woulda done it if I'da been knowing."

"Put yourself at ease. Owen has always been impatient. But he's gone now." Then he noticed the *brandub* board and said to Deirdre, "Come, love. I'll teach you how to play while we wait for your mother."

"How could I fix my mind on a game while I'm waiting to see my mother?" But she sat down on one of two chairs on either side of the table that held the board.

"A long time ago," Deirdre said, "Lewara told me a story of a prince of Erinn who fell in love with a mermaid. But she was the wife of the Manaan, king of the sea. The prince lifted her from the sea and carried her away to his fort. But Manaan grew furious and made the rivers and the oceans rise. And all of Erinn was covered by a great flood. The prince and his mermaid love found their way to Carrauntoohill, the highest mountain in Erinn. And there they played a game of *brandub* while they waited for the waters to rise and drown them."

"I know the same story," Naisha said. "The bards sing of it."

"I always thought only a mermaid, with seawater in her veins, could be so cold blooded as to play a game while waiting to die."

"*Brandub* is a favorite game of the kings and chieftains of Erinn. None of them think of themselves as being cold blooded."

"Do any of them play it while they're waiting to die?"

Naisha looked at her, his face serious. "All of us play games while we wait to die."

"I wonder what she's like. All those years I believed what Lewara told me—that she was dead. All those times she said she wished I had died with my mother."

"You mustn't think about those times now. Sad times. We mustn't think about what lies behind us now. We have to think about what lies ahead. It's not time to think about death, but about life."

"I wonder what happened to Lewara. She always said that Conor would have her killed, and MacFith and Aya, too, if anything ever happened to me."

"Aya mixed a potion—poison."

"Aya! I don't believe it. Not Aya. Not Lewara! Aya used to get angry with Lewara. But no! Not kill her. And me too. In the later years Lewara was unkind, and many times she was out of her head completely, but in the early years, she had been kind and good. I didn't like her in the end, but I never wished her dead."

"Lewara was right. The king would have ordered her killed when he discovered you gone. But before he would have ordered her killed, he would have ordered her tortured. Conor was crazy with suspicion and lust. When Aya and MacFith fled Loughadalla, they couldn't take Lewara with them. Aya knew of a leaf. It was like going to sleep and not waking up. She said she hoped Lewara would be happier in the next life than she was in this one."

"If Conor's anger was so furious, then is it not surprising he forgives us now?"

"As a man grows older, he grows weary and less lusty. Anger and jealousy trouble an old man's stomach, burn like too much bile. It is easier to have peace when one grows old than to fight, even with one's own feelings."

"Will you grow less lusty as you grow older?" she asked. But he didn't get a chance to answer, for at that moment the door to the room opened.

Naisha and Deirdre both looked. A tall woman, with gray-braided hair still colored with brown, entered the room. Naisha looked at her.

Her skin was translucent and pale, no longer the skin of a young woman, but there was a fine polished quality to it, like alabaster. She wore a cloak of rough, faded green linen, and although she was older than both Deirdre and Naisha, her carriage was straight and proud as that of any young woman in Ulster.

"Branwen," Naisha said.

"You're even handsomer than you were before, Naisha. And you!" She looked at Deirdre. "More beautiful than even a mother could have imagined."

Naisha was stunned. He looked at Deirdre and then back at Branwen, and suddenly the resemblance became obvious to him. The carriage of the head and the high, sculpted cheekbones. The hair was a different color, and Deirdre was taller and firmer muscled, but they were mother and daughter.

Branwen spoke. "You must leave this place immediately."

"We've just now—"

"If you value your life, you'll leave now."

"I can't leave now," Naisha said. "It's *geisa* for me to travel when the full moon is risen."

"You, Fergus, and Deirdre have all been tricked. The king plans to have you killed, Naisha, and to name Deirdre as his wife. Already a chamber in the Royal House is being draped with the white sheets and veils of a bridal chamber. That is why an assembly has been called—to celebrate a marriage."

"I will not marry the king," said Deirdre touching her sword.

"And a fine lot you'll be able to do about it," said her

mother, turning on her, "unless you leave immediately. I once was proud like you. I once had no notion of being the king's concubine. I once was in love with a charioteer named Falim who was as pleasing to look on as any man. I was taken by the king. I was made to crawl on my hands and knees in front of the Aengus root, and there on the forcing stone the king took me, and then I was allowed to go to the man I loved and live with him like a wife. Falim was a good man. He knew how to please a woman and I gave birth to you. But the king didn't let me keep you. A prophecy from the Druid, and they ripped you from my arms and carried you off. The wisewoman went with them. You've heard a ewe calling for a lamb that has been taken from her, or a wolf howling for her cub that's been struck down. That's how I was, crawling the hills looking for you. My breasts so bursting with milk that they were hard and burning with pain, and no babe to suckle. Time makes many things happen. It makes the milk stop flowing, and the breasts return to softness as they once were. But if time heals some things, so, too, does it worsen others, and when I was in the king's roundhouse with your father, the king looked on me again. I was your father's wife, but a king has precedence over all men in choosing his women and he claimed me for his concubine. When my husband protested, Conor took him hunting with him. Falim came back with an arrow in his chest. The king had mistaken him for a deer. The king is not a gentle man, not with his subjects, not with his women. There is no pleasure in being the king's concubine." She paused before continuing.

"One night, I overheard voices in the long house. I hid behind a curtain and there I saw the king in his nightdress talking to MacFith. They were speaking about you. 'Deirdre,' MacFith said. 'Aie, but it's a headstrong, fiery character that she'll be growing into, my Deirdre.' The king flew into a rage. 'You're not to call her Deirdre. "The Raging One." It's not a name for a king's wife.' 'But she won't be liking the name what you calls her. Ceantine.' 'It's the name I've given her. I am king, my word is law. Tell her that I'm coming again to visit her after the night of no moon. Tell her I am eager that she come to womanhood so that I may wed her. Tell her my desire for her is great. Now leave, and make certain that you're not seen by anyone.'

"I couldn't believe what my ears had told me. Deirdre. My Deirdre. My baby that had been stolen from my arms, and I thanked the gods for telling me that she was alive, but in the same breath, I cursed them. My child married to the king. I would sooner see her throat cut. The king is not like other men. He cannot take pleasure from pleasure. He must have pain with his pleasure. Not his pain—his woman's pain.

"I plotted. I cajoled. I sought him out and willingly opened my thighs to him. I let him do the things that gave him pleasure, and when they hurt me more than I could bear, I thought of you. I thought of you in a meadow somewhere, or in a forest surrounded by wild things. Feeding the deer and the squirrels. I imagined your face, how you would smile, and when I thought of those things, I didn't feel what the king did.

"I convinced him to take me with him the night of no moon. He took me with him, but only as far as Slieve-nishfinne, the hill of the white fawn. He told me he was going to see a Druid who had even greater powers than Cathbad. This Druid lived by the river and I was not allowed to see him. In a way, what he said was true. The powers of a young girl on an aging man are greater than any Druid's magic.

"It was too far from Slieve-nishfinne to the river. I could not walk there and be back in time for the king to find me there. As a concubine I was not allowed to leave Emain without the king knowing it. There had to be another way. A group of young warriors had just come back from battle in Scotland.

"There was a young warrior among Conor's troops. He was the handsomest of the group. Tall, broad shouldered, with the blackest hair of anyone I'd ever seen. He was a wanderer. It was said about him that he had traveled to the far ends of the world where dragons lived. I watched him. He didn't ride in chariots, but instead rode on top of horses. He was a great swordsman, the best in Conor's army, a fierce man, but a man with gentle hands and compassion. I had heard that he'd killed a man who had mistreated a horse.

" 'That is the man who should marry my child,' I said to myself." Branwen turned to Naisha now. "And so I began to make you notice me. A woman has ways to make a man love her, even when she belongs to another man, and I took great care to teach you to love a woman the way she needs to be loved. I told you that I had seen the magic white stag because I wanted you to find Deirdre. No man can resist the lure of the white stag, for it is said that it carries the spirit of Nemed in it. When you told me that you had seen it, I knew that you had seen Deirdre. I hoped that you would find her beautiful and that the hot desire of your manhood would make it impossible for you to resist her. I hoped that you would love her as I had taught you.

"When you left Emain in a fury that night, after the king ordered everyone in the hall to eat rats, I had no way of knowing whether you had taken Deirdre with you or not. It was only several nights later, when the king came back in a fury from Loughadalla, that I knew my prayers were answered. His bride to be had disappeared.

"There's no need to tell you any more except that I'm no longer Conor's concubine. A woman who has been a concubine cannot marry, and for a while I became a soldier's concubine and then another's, and now I'm old and finally free of

men's desires. Every night I prayed to Tethra to take Conor so
that you could return to Emain, and I could lay eyes on you
once more. All these years I've waited to see you, and now I
tell you you must go. Immediately. Both of you. Go to the
great lands across the channel. Perhaps my prayers will yet
come true, and perhaps you can someday return. Perhaps,
someday, you and I will be able to speak of those things about
which a mother and daughter talk; perhaps someday I will be
able to hold a grandchild and rock it to sleep the way I was
never able to hold you and rock you to sleep. But you must
leave now. Both of you. I've bribed the stable hands, and the
guards at the door of the Red Branch."

"I cannot go," Naisha said. "My *geis*—"

But at that moment there was a great flurry of clanging
metal and running feet in the stairway.

"Quick, this way," said Branwen. "Out the window. The
stables . . ." And she threw back the curtain from the window. It was covered with heavy bars.

"Owen masterminded this," Naisha said angrily. "He
waited until we were here, trapped in this room, to go and get
help. The coward is afraid to stand by himself to my sword.
Quick, bar the door! When I get him, I'll show him no
mercy."

"Wait!" said Branwen. "Fergus! Some of the soldiers may
follow Fergus. Fergus will not allow himself to be deceived."

Deirdre grabbed the ring off her finger. "Take this to him.
Tell him to take it to Maeve of Connacht."

Branwen grabbed for the ring, but Deirdre held it for a
moment. "All these years I've thought of you again and again.
Who were you? What did you look like? What was your tem-
perament? And now that I know you, I'm going to lose you
again, and the emptiness is even greater than before. Mother,
I . . ." And then she threw her arms around Branwen and
hugged her, and Branwen clutched back.

"You must hurry," said Naisha.

Then Branwen grabbed the ring and flew from the room, Naisha and Deirdre barring the door behind her.

"How long before they break through?" asked Deirdre.

Naisha shrugged. "I don't know. Because the Red Branch was built as a storehouse for treasures and loot, its walls and doors are the thickest of any structure at Emain." But then he noticed that Deirdre was crying. He went to her and tilted her chin up to him, and wiped aways the tears. "Eagles don't cry," he said.

"In the last few moons I've lost my daughter, my foster mother, my mother. And now I'm going to lose you. Don't tell me eagles don't cry."

"We haven't been taken yet! I'll kill any man who breaks through that door. You'll fight with me. We'll pile the bodies high enough in the doorway."

"Once," Deirdre said, "when I was small, I remember watching a butterfly settle on the sundew—you know how the plant is sticky. It was a splendid butterfly, with yellow wings and blue flecks. It hovered around the top of the sundew, around the white flowers, then floated down to the base, and landed. So softly. Can you imagine how soft a landing that must be, a butterfly on a leaf? I watched it. And its front feet stuck, and it began to flap its blue-and-yellow wings. Up and down over its body. But it was stuck to the sundew. I reached and with my fingers, as carefully as I could, I lifted the butterfly from the leaves. But two butterfly legs stuck to the sundew. They were just there, smaller than eyelashes. I dropped the butterfly into the palm of my hand, and for a moment, it just sat there. Then it flew away. But on the tip of my thumb and forefinger, there was the powder from its wings. I hadn't saved the butterfly at all, only delayed its dying. How long? A half day? A day? A day and a night? You and I are like that butterfly, Naisha. Our time has come."

"They haven't taken us yet. I'm still the best swordsman in Ulster. The walls of the Red Branch are thick, and Fergus will fly with all speed to Maeve."

"Naisha, son of Usna!" A voice called out from the other side of the door.

"Owen, why don't you go and eat a few more rats for the king?"

"You're trapped, Naisha. I've discovered the bribery of the stable guards. I'll soon have the pleasure of seeing your head on my spear."

"Come and kill me first, Owen, before you fill the air with idle words."

"I'll kill you in good time, Naisha. I owe my father a death."

Suddenly the door shook with the heavy, violent thunder of a battering ram.

"The king is willing to spare Deirdre. Come out now or you'll both die."

"You and your king have betrayed the sacred trust of hospitality."

"We have betrayed no trust. You are not being lodged under the king's roof, but under the roof of the Red Branch. It is you, Naisha, who first broke the trust. You broke the testament of allegiance to the king. And you will die under the roof of the Red Branch."

The very walls of the room vibrated, but the door held. Deirdre had no idea how long the pounding continued. She went to the window and looked out on the full moon. The clouds were being churned around, and it would appear and disappear, the cloud shapes around it threatening and frightening. The wind continued to blow, and she shivered.

"Naisha," she said, "do you remember the first time you pressed your lips against mine? It was as though my soul moved. If I think about that time, then I'm not frightened."

Naisha came close to her, put his arm around her shoulders, and led her to the bed. "All these years we've been together," he said, "and we've never married. First there was no time. My desire for you wouldn't allow it. And then it would have raised the ire of the Druids with their ritual and their ill luck. But I know the words to marry us.

"As the sun was once wed to the earth, so I wed you. May the air bless us, and the water, and the wind and the birds that sing, and may Aengus bless us and all the changes of the sun and the moon. Deirdre, I love you," he said and then he kissed her.

On the other side men continued to ram at the door, but the inside of the door was reinforced with iron. The corridor was not very wide, and the soldiers weren't able to get any momentum. The door held.

Sounds of cursing came frequently through the door and the clanging of swords and soldiers running back and forth in the corridor, trying different ways of breaking through.

Someone shouted for the ironsmith to come with his tools so that the hinges of the door might be removed, but someone shouted back, "Idiot! The doors of the Red Branch are all hinged from the inside."

Deirdre looked at the huge oak door. It was true, and she saw the forged iron hinges, four of them holding the door.

"There's water in the pitcher," Naisha said, and he smelled it. "It seems fresh enough. We'll be able to stay here until Fergus comes with Maeve's troops."

"What if he changes his mind and decides not to go?"

"Fergus? Change his mind? Decide not to go? Fergus is the most honorable man in all of Erinn."

"Then why did he give up his throne to such a tyrant?"

"You heard his story. Even honorable men are not without weakness."

They played at *brandub,* and the wandering king was captured by the other pieces.

Then Owen's voice outside the door shouted, "There's no escape. I caught Branwen with the ring. You tricked me once a long time ago with her, Naisha, but not a second time. That night, I thought you would run to her, and instead, you sought out the daughter. But your clever ruses are over. Branwen is dead."

The news fell like a stone in the pit of Deirdre's stomach. To have found her mother and lost her in the space of an evening. . . . If the gods had ever smiled on Deirdre, they had stopped these last few moons.

Owen continued. "The king sends a message. He says he is not an unreasonable man. He is willing to bargain. He says that if you send the woman out, and you agree to leave Erinn forever, he'll give you safe escort to the coast and see that you have a currach in which to leave Erinn."

"Tell the king I'll take death for a husband before I'll marry him!" shouted Deirdre.

"Surely you jest, Owen!" Naisha laughed. "Safe passage! I, too, was a fool once, but not again. Safe passage, like the welcome we were to receive here at Emain? You tricked Fergus and you tricked me, but you cannot trick the gods. Owen, you, too, are doomed as surely as I."

There was the sound of running feet, and more ramming and then silence, followed by running feet and arguing voices, and only the occasional word could be heard. ". . . hospitality . . . traitor . . . sacred."

The one voice was muted, but Owen's was loud. "Old man, you waste your time. Go back to the ale barrel." And there was laughter. Now the other voice came clear.

"You laugh at me? Fergus, who was once your king?"

"You were never king to these warriors, Fergus. These are

the youngest warriors. Still eager to prove themselves, they have known no king except Conor."

"You will all suffer the anger of the gods. Each and every one of you. You will bring their wrath down on Ulster. Ulster will fall again as she did with the curse of Macha."

"Fergus, these are an old man's ravings. Naisha is not housed in the Royal Branch, but the Red Branch. The king has not set foot in the Red Branch. No betrayal of hospitality has occurred."

"No betrayal! The king promised. Just a while ago, he gave testament to me again, that he would not harm Naisha."

"*The king* will not harm Naisha!"

"Fergus," shouted Naisha through the door.

"Naisha! My nephew! I . . . if only you knew how sorry—"

"Get away from the door, old man."

"Take your hands off me. I may no longer be king—"

"Fergus, go to Maeve!"

"Take him away. Give him a tankard of ale, and soon he'll be harmless enough again."

"Naisha—a . . ." But the old man's voice faded to nothing.

The door shook again as the ramming resumed, and then it suddenly stopped.

Owen spoke again. "The king's patience is running out. He has sent orders that the Red Branch be set on fire. Either you send the woman out now so Conor can have his rightful queen, and you leave for the coast tonight, or both of you will die in the flames."

"Tell Conor to bugger a frog's arse. Tell him I'll die before he lays his eyes on me again," Deirdre shouted.

"To see you live, or die in flames. That's no choice for me! Owen, tell Conor I'll send Deirdre—"

But Deirdre leapt up at him and covered his mouth with

her hand so he could speak no more. "Traitor! How can you say you love me and send me to Conor?"

"How can I love you and watch you die?"

"If you love me, you will kill me so that I cannot become Conor's wife. And if you won't, I will!" She grabbed for her dagger.

He twisted it out of her hands, grabbed her wrists, and held them. "My Deirdre. My fierce, passionate Deirdre. As intense in your desire for death as you once were for life." And he hugged her to him.

"Take pity on me, Naisha. Take pity on me, just as Aya and MacFith took pity on Lewara. Take your sword," she said, reaching for it, but he pulled away. She knelt down in front of him and kissed his hand.

"See this throat, Naisha? Such soft skin here. A quick thrust of your sword, and I would be forever free. Free with you. As your wife. Not the king's wife. Not just for a time, but forever. Forever young and always with you. Always loving you. As I love you now."

"Kill you!" He shook his head and lifted her so she stood. "How can I kill you? To kill you would be like killing the moon or the sun, or the dew that falls on the leaves each morning."

"But the sun rises day after day, and the moon night after night, and the dew has kissed each leaf since the beginning of time, and will kiss it for an eternity. Take me with you to Tir-na-n'Og. There'll be no unhappiness there. We'll live there on the other side of the moon, lovers forever, without sorrow.

"Remember the night I first saw the sea? There was the storm, and I felt that I was part of the storm, part of the stones, and the wind and the sea. And then you loved me, and then came the splendid calm, with the rainbow hanging from the cliffs to the sea. I wanted to stop time then. I wanted the sun to stop in the sky then, at just that place before it sank into the sea. And there was a bird flying and I wanted it to stop there. And I wanted to catch the waves of the sea, just before they crested over the rocks, when the foam was whitest. And I wanted to keep your arms wrapped around me forever. Naisha, take me with you now, and we'll be a part of everything you see around us." She went to the window and threw back the curtain. "We'll be a part of the clouds, a part of the moon, a part of the wind. We'll be together, lovers, Naisha. Always. Naisha, if you love me . . ."

"Conor is no longer a young man," Naisha said. "Make your demands on him. The way you used to make them on me. He'll die trying to keep up with you, and you'll be queen and free of him."

"Free! You talk of freedom! His body covering mine. You heard what my mother said. That's not freedom. And living without you—that's not freedom.

"How can I look upon another sunrise or moonrise without remembering the light in your eyes when you saw me each morning? How can I hear the linnet's song without thinking of your voice calling my name? How can I see a stallion mount a mare without thinking of your gentle violence? How can I look upon a single stone without thinking of how we traveled across this island, you and I, night after night? How can I look upon anything in this world without that thing being a constant reminder of you? You speak of freedom. Living without you would be like trying to fly with broken wings. Is that the kind of freedom you want me to have?

"You'll be the one who finds freedom and peace—when Owen kills you. If you love me, you'll take me with you to that place of peace. Look at me. Touch my hair. It's still red as it was the day you first saw me, and yet will you leave me alone to turn gray as Aya? Loose toothed and brittle boned, and alone, while you go into the next world?

"I've lost my child, my foster mother, and my mother, and

now I've lost you. When Conor has had his fill of me and tires of me, he'll cast me off to one of his soldiers, who, in turn, will cast me off. I'll be a hunched old woman. Will you have me the brunt of young men's jokes, while you have your peace and beauty?"

She ripped open her dress. "And these breasts, Naisha. Where you first touched your tongue, these breasts that suckled our child. Will you let them grow old and withered and let them droop low on my belly with nothing in them but a memory of life? How can you be so selfish, and still claim to love me?" She grasped his fingers in hers. "Will you touch me; touch my hair; touch my face; and still leave me alone? Naisha! . . . Naisha . . . please!" He grasped her to him and kissed her.

There was the sound of movements in the corridor, the shuffle of feet, and the *swish-swish-phlump* sound of piling wicker.

"Naisha! Son of Usna!" shouted Owen from the corridor, but Deirdre and Naisha didn't answer, and when they didn't, Owen shouted again. "You and your woman have enraged the king. Either Conor has his queen, or you prepare to die." But still there was no answer.

In the room, Deirdre and Naisha spoke in whispers. "I'm not afraid, Naisha. I think of the times you and I loved, and I'm not afraid. It's a freer thing you and I do, than if we were to loosen the bar and fight them head on. I love you, Naisha. I want to die in your arms, just as I lived in your arms. Aengus protects all lovers."

"And no one has loved better than you and I." He kissed her again, and they were taken in a tender and transcendent passion. There was the simple, sharp, explosive sound of dry wood flaming, but Deirdre and Naisha were oblivious to it. They were deaf to all sounds except the sound of each other's heart, each other's breath, each other's name.

The fire caught the heavy oak door and the resin began to crackle and flame, and soon there was nothing but a wall of flame, and when Owen, with a crooked smile on his face, tried to push through, he was driven back by the intense heat.

Outside, the wind began to howl like a wild thing, and it began to snow. It fell in thick, heavy flakes over the hills of Emain and in the bogs and on the river, and to the north at Loughadalla. The snow fell through the great barren branches of the oaks, and on the full horns of the cattle, and on the flanks of the running horses, and on the heads of the stones of Erinn.

Naisha whispered her name and the sound of his breath in her ear was like the sound of a seashell, like the rise and fall of the seas. His breath was hot and soft. His mouth traveled up her neck and the persistent touch of his lips brought tinglings again to the small of her back. And his hand was there, rubbing the small of her back where it ached from carrying her sorrow. His hands felt good, and his breath was hot, and she arched her back so that he could rub her better. He rubbed her spine and she moaned because it was as though his hands had eyes and could find the sorrow. And the touch of his fingers and his lips brought butterflies to her body, and she turned her mouth to him. His kisses were soft; his tongue, slow and searching, touched something hidden and brought it to life, and she responded. She felt the hard muscles ripple under her hand, and felt the passion. The butterflies beat in a frenzy, but now they beat with wings of flames. A sharp spark exploded and her hair caught fire. His mouth was no longer soft, but fierce and demanding. Now his fingers touched that place that needed to be touched, gentle probing fingers, spreading her, reaching in, and still he kissed her. She moved up to him, sliding her buttocks along his thighs. She had to be entered; his fingers spread her farther. She felt him slide between her thighs. Softer than a tongue, yet relentlessly hard,

something old and timeless as the first man and first woman,
something as timeless as the rain, and her tongue sought his
and she arched so he could penetrate completely. His hands
beneath her buttocks lifted her up to the hard softness. There
were gentle thrusts, each going deeper, and when he was completely in, he stopped. She could feel him throbbing inside,
and the fire rose again, and she tilted her pelvis to him. He
began to thrust again, gently, then more vigorously, and there
was a rising wave that moved through her, and she forgot her
name. She forgot where she was, who she was, and how far she
had come. She was everywhere and nowhere. She was a harp
being strummed for the first time and the last time; she was
like the white waves of the ocean breaking against the shore;
she was like a flaming star falling through the night, and when
he spilled into her, he spoke her name, "Deirdre," and she was
like the beating of swan's wings in the dawn.